A Great Deliverance

ELIZABETH GEORGE

First published in Great Britain in 1989
by Bantam Press, a division of Transworld Publishers

This edition published by permission of Hodder & Stoughton in 2014
An Hachette UK company

Hodder and Stoughton Ltd
338 Euston Road
London NW1 3BH
www.hodder.co.uk

All characters in this publication are fictitious and any resemblance to real persons, living or dead, is purely coincidental.

21, rue du Montparnasse
75283 Paris Cedex 06

HARRAP's® est une marque de Larousse SAS
www.harrap.com

ISBN 978 2 81 870326 7

About the author

Elizabeth George's first novel, *A Great Deliverance*, was honoured with[1] the Anthony and Agatha Best First Novel[2] awards[3] in America and received the Grand Prix de Littérature Policière in France. The critically acclaimed[4] *Payment in Blood* followed, and *Well-Schooled in Murder*, which was awarded[5] the prestigious German prize for international mystery fiction, the MIMI, in 1990. *A Suitable Vengeance, For the Sake of Elena, Missing Joseph, Playing for the Ashes, In the Presence of the Enemy, Deception on his Mind, In Pursuit of the Proper Sinner, A Traitor to Memory, A Place of Hiding, With No One as Witness, Careless in Red, This Body of Death* and most recently[6] *Believing the Lie* were also highly acclaimed by critics[7]. Her novels have now been adapted for television by BBC TV. Elizabeth George lives on Whidbey Island, in the state of Washington.

1. a été récompensé par
2. du meilleur premier roman
3. les prix
4. applaudi par la critique,
5. auquel a été décerné
6. tout récemment,
7. la critique

Visit her website at www.elizabethgeorgeonline.com

DIRECTION DE LA PUBLICATION : Carine Girac-Marinier

DIRECTION ÉDITORIALE : Claude Nimmo

NOTES EN MARGE : Patricia Seixas

RÉVISION DES NOTES : Marianne Mouchot

RELECTURE : Joëlle Narjollet

INFORMATIQUE ÉDITORIALE : Philippe Cazabet, Marie-Noëlle Tilliette

CONCEPTION GRAPHIQUE : Uli Meindl

MISE EN PAGES : Cynthia Savage

FABRICATION : Rebecca Dubois

Remerciements à Stephanie Carey et Marie Gabiache

Mot de l'Éditeur

Vous aimeriez lire en langue originale, mais le vocabulaire, les expressions figurées ou la syntaxe vous arrêtent parfois ?

Cette collection est faite pour vous !

Vous trouverez en effet, en note dans la marge, une traduction de certains mots et expressions qui vous permettra d'avancer facilement dans votre lecture.

Nous n'avons pas cherché à vous donner une traduction littéraire de l'ouvrage et nous sommes parfois écartés du sens littéral pour vous fournir le sens qui convient le mieux à l'histoire. Aussi les mots sont-ils traduits dans le contexte du texte original.

Les expressions figées anglaises sont, bien entendu, rendues par une expression équivalente en français.

Les allusions à des réalités culturelles du monde anglo-saxon sont expliquées également dans la marge, pour vous aider à mieux comprendre la trame de l'histoire.

Vous aurez ainsi, en regard du texte original, tout le savoir-faire d'un dictionnaire rien que pour vous et adapté à ce livre !

Notre objectif est de vous mener jusqu'au mot FIN en vous donnant les clés nécessaires à la compréhension du récit.

Laissez-vous gagner par l'angoisse, l'humour et le suspense qui règnent chez les maîtres de la littérature anglo-saxonne.

Lire en VO ? You can indeed!

For Natalie in celebration of the growth of the spirit
and the triumph of the soul

AND HE SAID, Ye have taken away my gods[1] which I made, and the priest[2] and ye are gone away; and what have I more[3]?

Judges 19:24[4]

1. Vous avez emporté mes dieux
2. le prêtre
3. que me reste-t-il
4. [Ancien Testament]

Author's note

If one can acknowledge[1] an area of the world for existing[2] and thus[3] being a source of inspiration, I would acknowledge the tremendous[4] and changing beauties of Yorkshire that so much became the heart of this book.

I am grateful to the people who have read and criticized the rough drafts[5] of all my work: Sheila Hillinger, Julie Mayer, Paul Berger, Susan Berner, Steve Mitchell, and Cathy Stephany.

I thank my parents and husband for their patience and support[6], Dr H. M. Upton for his generous input[7], and especially Deborah Schneider and Kate Miciak for their willingness to[8] take a chance on someone unknown[9].

And of course Don Martin, whose annual injunctions against[10] my addressing him in writing[11] ultimately became the spur[12] that so decisively pricked the sides of my intent[13].

1. remercier
2. d'exister
3. ainsi
4. fantastiques
5. premières épreuves
6. soutien
7. généreuse contribution
8. d'avoir bien voulu
9. parier sur une inconnue
10. qui, à force de refuser tous les ans
11. que je m'adresse à lui par écrit,
12. a fini par m'inciter
13. à sauter le pas

Coup de pouce pour vous aider à bien comprendre le début de l'histoire...

La dame du compartiment regarde de travers le père Hart qui, au mépris des bonnes manières, n'est pas fichu de se moucher et reste agrippé à son attaché-case. Il descend à Londres, à la gare de King's Cross.

Pourquoi un prêtre catholique est-il venu du fin fond du Yorkshire parler d'un meurtre à la police centrale ? Pourquoi le Yorkshire fait-il appel à New Scotland Yard ?

1

It was a solecism[1] of the very worst kind. He sneezed loudly[2], wetly[3], and quite unforgivably into the woman's face. He'd been holding it back for[4] three-quarters of an hour, fighting it off as if it were Henry Tudor's vanguard[5] at the Battle of Bosworth. But at last he'd surrendered[6]. And after the act, to make matters worse, he immediately began to snuffle[7].

The woman stared[8]. She was exactly the type whose presence always reduced him to blithering idiocy[9]. At least six feet tall, dressed in that wonderfully insouciant mismatch of clothing[10] so characteristic of the British upper classes[11], she was ageless, timeless[12], and she peered at him[13] through razor blue eyes[14], the sort that must have reduced many a parlourmaid to tears[15] forty years ago. She had to be well over sixty[16], possibly closer to eighty, but one could never tell. She sat bolt upright[17] in her seat, hands clasped in her lap[18], a finishing[19]-school posture which made no concessions towards comfort.

And she stared. First at his Roman collar[20], then at his undeniably dripping nose[21].

Do forgive, darling. A thousand apologies. Let's not allow a little faux pax like a sneeze to come between such a friendship as ours. He was always so

1. manque de savoir-vivre
2. éternua bruyamment
3. en faisant des projections
4. se retenait depuis
5. l'avant-garde
6. avait renoncé à lutter
7. à renifler
8. le dévisagea
9. au crétinisme absolu
10. tenue dépareillée
11. de l'aristocratie et de la haute bourgeoisie britannique
12. sans âge, intemporelle
13. l'observait
14. ses yeux bleus perçants
15. dû faire pleurer pas mal de femmes de chambre
16. avoir la soixantaine bien tassée
17. se tenait toute droite
18. jointes sur ses genoux
19. [enseignant les bonnes manières aux jeunes filles]
20. col de prêtre catholique
21. son nez indéniablement en train de couler

amusing when engaged in mental conversations. It was only aloud that everything became a terrible muddle[1].

He snuffled again. Again she stared. Why on earth was she travelling second class? She'd swept into the carriage[2] at Doncaster, like a creaking Salome[3] with rather more than seven veils to her ensemble[4], and for the remainder of the trip[5] she'd alternated between imbibing[6] the railway's foul-smelling tepid coffee[7] and staring at him with a disapproval that shouted Church of England[8] at every available opportunity.

And then came the sneeze. Unimpeachably correct behaviour[9] from Doncaster to London might have somehow excused his Roman Catholicism to her. But, alas, the sneeze condemned him for ever.

'I … ah … that is … if you'll excuse …' It was simply no good. His handkerchief was deep within his pocket. To reach it[10] he would have to loosen his grasp on[11] the battered[12] attaché case in his lap, and that was unthinkable. She would just have to understand. *We aren't talking about a breach of etiquette[13] here, madam. We are talking about MURDER.* Upon that thought, he snuffled with self-righteous vigour[14].

Hearing this, the woman sat even more correctly in her seat, every fibre of her body straining to project[15] disapproval. Her glance said it all.[16] It was a chronicle of her thoughts, and he could read each one: Pitiful little man. Pathetic. Not a day under seventy-five[17] and looking positively every second of it[18]. And so very much what one would expect of a Catholic priest: a face with three separate nicks[19] from a poor job at shaving[20]; a crumb[21] of morning toast embedded[22] in the corner of his mouth; shiny black suit mended at elbows and cuffs[23]; squashed hat rimmed with dust[24]. And that dreadful case in his lap! Ever since Doncaster, he had been acting as

1. terriblement embrouillé
2. avait fait son entrée dans le wagon
3. une Salomé sur le retour
4. drapée dans plus de sept voiles
5. le reste du voyage
6. avaler
7. le café tiède et puant
8. tout anglicane
9. Un comportement sans faute
10. Pour l'atteindre,
11. se résoudre à lâcher
12. tout usé
13. un manquement au protocole
14. une suffisance énergique
15. s'efforçant de manifester
16. Son regard en disait long.
17. Au moins 75 ans
18. les faisant largement
19. coupures distinctes
20. dues à un mauvais rasage
21. une miette
22. collée
23. rapiécié aux coudes et aux poignets
24. un chapeau avachi ourlé de poussière

if she'd boarded the train with the deliberate intention of snatching it from him[1] and hurling herself[2] out the window. Lord!

The woman sighed and turned away from him as if seeking salvation. But none was apparent. His nose continued to dribble[3] until the slowing of the train announced that they were finally approaching their journey's[4] end.

She stood and scourged him[5] with a final look. 'At *last* I understand what you Catholics mean by purgatory,' she hissed[6] and swept down the aisle[7] to the door.

'Oh dear,' muttered[8] Father Hart. 'Oh dear, I suppose I really *have* ...' But she was gone. The train had come to a complete halt under the vaulted ceiling[9] of the London station. It was time to do what he had come to the city to do.

He looked about[10] to make sure that he was in possession of all his belongings[11], a pointless[12] operation since he had brought nothing with him from Yorkshire save[13] the single attaché case that had as yet not left his grip. He squinted out[14] the window at the vast expanse[15] of King's Cross Station.

He had been more prepared for a station like Victoria – or at least the Victoria he remembered from his youth – with its comforting old brick walls, its stalls[16] and buskers[17], these last always staying one step ahead[18] of the Metropolitan Police. But King's Cross was something altogether[19] different: long stretches of tiled floor[20], seductive advertisements[21] hanging from the ceiling, newsagents, tobacconists[22], hamburger shops. And all the people – many more than he had expected – in queues for tickets, gobbling down hurried snacks[23] as they raced for trains, arguing[24], laughing, and kissing goodbye. Every race, every colour. It was all so different. He wasn't sure he could bear[25] the noise and confusion[26].

1. le lui arracher
2. de se jeter
3. à couler
4. du voyage
5. le fustigea
6. persifla-t-elle
7. s'engouffra dans le couloir
8. marmonna
9. la voûte
10. regarda autour de lui
11. toutes ses affaires
12. inutile
13. à part
14. jeta un œil par
15. l'immensité
16. étals
17. chanteurs de rue
18. avec une longueur d'avance
19. de complètement
20. de longues étendues de sol carrelé
21. publicités
22. des marchands de journaux, des bureaux de tabac
23. avalant des en-cas à toute allure
24. tout en se disputant
25. de pouvoir supporter
26. la pagaille

'Getting out, Father, or planning to stop t' night[1]?'

Startled, Father Hart looked up into the ruddy[2] face of the porter who had helped him find his seat earlier that morning upon the train's departure from[3] York. It was a pleasant North Country face with the winds of the moors[4] etched upon it[5] in a hundred separate blood vessels that rode and broke[6] near the surface of his skin.

His eyes were flinty blue[7], quick and perceptive[8]. And Father Hart felt them like a touch as they slid[9] in a friendly but querying[10] movement from his face to the attaché case. Tightening his fingers round the handle[11], he stiffened his body[12], hoping for resolution and getting an excruciating[13] cramp in his left foot instead. He moaned[14] as the pain balled hotly to its zenith[15].

The porter spoke anxiously. 'Maybe you oughtn't be travellin' alone. Sure you don't need no help, like?[16]'

He did, of course he did. But no one could help. He couldn't help himself.

'No, no. I'm off this very moment.[17] And you've been more than kind. My seat, you know. The initial confusion.'

The porter waved his words away[18]. 'Don't mind that. There's lots of folks[19] don't realize them tickets means reserved[20]. No harm done[21], was there?'

'No. I suppose ...' Father Hart drew in a quick, sustaining breath[22]. Down the aisle, out the door, find the Tube[23], he told himself. None of that could be as insurmountable as it seemed. He shuffled towards the exit.[24] His case, clutched two-handed[25] upon his stomach, bounced with each step.

Behind him, the porter spoke. ' 'Ere, Father, the door's a bit much. I'll see to 't.[26]'

He allowed the man space to get past him in the aisle. Already two surly-looking[27] railway cleaners were squeezing in the rear door, rubbish sacks over

1. vous avez l'intention de rester pour la nuit
2. rougeaud
3. lorsque le train avait quitté
4. la lande
5. gravés dessus
6. vaisseaux sanguins allant se briser
7. d'un bleu intense
8. observateurs
9. passaient
10. interrogateur
11. Serrant fort la poignée
12. se raidit
13. terrible
14. gémit
15. atteignait son paroxysme
16. N'auriez pas besoin d'aide, des fois ?
17. Je m'en vais tout de suite.
18. balaya tout ça d'un geste
19. gens
20. que ces billets réservent la place
21. Y a pas de mal
22. prit une profonde inspiration
23. métro
24. Il se dirigea vers la sortie d'un pas traînant
25. qu'il tenait serré à deux mains
26. Je m'en occupe.
27. à l'air revêche

their shoulders, ready to prepare the train for its return trip to York. They were Pakistani and, although they spoke English, Father Hart found that he couldn't understand a single word beneath the obfuscation of their accents[1].

The realization filled him with dread.[2] What was he doing here in the nation's capital where the inhabitants[3] were foreigners[4] who looked at him with cloudy, hostile eyes[5] and immigrant faces? What paltry good could he hope to do?[6] What silliness was this? *Who* would ever believe—?

'Need some help, Father?'

Father Hart finally moved decisively. 'No. Fine. Simply fine.'

He negotiated the steps[7], felt the concrete platform[8] beneath his feet, heard the calling of pigeons high in the vaulted ceiling of the station. He began to make his distracted way down[9] the platform towards the exit and Euston Road.

Behind him again he heard the porter. 'Someone meeting you[10]? Know where you're going? Where you off to now?'

The priest straightened his shoulders[11]. He waved a goodbye. 'Scotland Yard,' he replied firmly.

St Pancras Station, directly across the street from[12] King's Cross, was such an architectural antithesis of the latter[13] that Father Hart stood for several moments simply staring at its neo-Gothic magnificence. The clamour of traffic[14] in Euston Road and the malodorous belching[15] of two diesel-fuelled lorries[16] at the pavement's edge[17] faded into insignificance. He was a bit of an architecture buff[18], and this particular building was architecture gone wild[19].

'Good heavens, that's wonderful,' he murmured, tilting his head[20] to have a better view of the railway station's peaks and valleys. 'A bit of a cleaning and she'd be a regular[21] palace.' He looked about

1. un traître mot avec cet accent déroutant
2. Ce constat le terrifia.
3. habitants
4. des étrangers
5. un regard triste et hostile
6. Ça servirait un tant soit peu, ce qu'il allait faire ?
7. s'engagea dans l'escalier
8. quai en béton
9. à parcourir, distrait
10. vient vous chercher
11. redressa les épaules
12. juste en face de
13. de cette dernière
14. bruit de la circulation
15. les gaz malodorants
16. camions diesel
17. au bord du trottoir
18. féru d'architecture
19. débridée
20. inclinant la tête
21. véritable

absently, as if he would stop the next passer-by[1] and give a discourse on the evils[2] that generations of coal fires[3] had wrought upon[4] the old building. 'Now, I wonder who ...'

The two-note siren of a police van howled[5] suddenly down Caledonian Road, shrieking through[6] the intersection on to Euston Road. It brought the priest back to reality. He shook himself mentally, part in irritation but another, greater part in fear. His mind was wandering daily[7] now. And that signalled the end, didn't it? He swallowed a gagging lump of terror[8] and sought new determination. His eyes fell upon the scream of a headline[9] across the morning paper[10] propped up[11] on a nearby newsstand[12]. He stepped towards it curiously. RIPPER[13] STRIKES AT VAUXHALL STATION!

Ripper! He shrank from the words[14], cast a look about, and then gave himself over to one quick paragraph from the story, skimming it[15] rapidly lest a closer perusal[16] betray[17] an interest in morbidity unseemly in a man of the cloth[18]. Words, not sentences, caught his sight. *Slashed*[19] *... semi-nude bodies ... arteries ... severed*[20] *... victims male ...*

He shivered[21]. His fingers went to his throat and he considered its true vulnerability. Even a Roman collar was no certain protection from the knife of a killer. It would seek. It would plunge.[22]

The thought was shattering[23]. He staggered back[24] from the newsstand, and mercifully saw the Underground sign a mere thirty feet away[25]. It jogged his memory[26].

He groped in his pocket for[27] a map of the city's Underground system and spent a moment painstakingly perusing its crinkled[28] surface. 'The Circle Line to St James's Park,' he told himself. And then again with more authority, 'The Circle Line to St James's Park. The Circle Line to St James's Park.'

1. le premier passant venu
2. les maux
3. de feux au charbon
4. avaient infligés au
5. se mit à mugir
6. hurlant en traversant
7. Il avait tous les jour des absences
8. tenta de surmonter un accès de terreur
9. sur un gros titre tapageur
10. journal
11. bien visible
12. [le présentoir d'un] kiosque
13. L'Éventreur
14. Devant ce titre, il eut un mouvement de recul
15. le parcourant
16. au cas où un regard plus attentif
17. trahirait
18. inconvenant chez un homme d'Église
19. Tailladés
20. tranchées
21. frissonna
22. Il chercherait. Il s'enfoncerait.
23. bouleversante
24. s'écarta en titubant
25. à moins de 10 m
26. lui rafraîchit la mémoire
27. chercha dans sa poche
28. froissée

Like a Gregorian chant, he repeated the sentence as he descended the stairs. He maintained its metre and rhythm[1] up to the ticket window and did not cease until he had placed himself squarely on the train. There he glanced at the other occupants of the car[2], found two elderly ladies watching him with unveiled avidity[3], and ducked his head[4]. 'So confusing,' he explained, trying out a timid smile of friendship. 'One gets so turned about.[5]'

'All *kinds* is what I'm tellin' you, Pammy,' the younger of the two women declared to her companion. She shot a look[6] of practised, chilling contempt[7] at the cleric[8]. 'Disguised as *anything*, I hear[9].' Keeping her watery eyes on the confused priest, she dragged her withered[10] friend to her feet, clung to the poles[11] near the door, and urged her out[12] loudly at the very next stop.

Father Hart watched their departure with resignation. No blaming them[13], he thought. One couldn't trust. Not ever. Not really. And that's what he'd come to London to say: that it wasn't the truth. It only looked like the truth. A body, a girl, and a bloody axe[14]. But it wasn't the truth. He *had* to convince them, and ... Oh Lord, he had so little talent for this. But God was on his side. He held on to[15] that thought. *What I'm doing is right, what I'm doing is right, what I'm doing is right.* Replacing the other, this new chant took him right to the doors of New Scotland Yard.

'So damned if we don't have[16] another Kerridge-Nies confrontation on our hands[17],' Superintendent Malcolm Webberly concluded. He paused to light[18] a thick cigar that immediately permeated[19] the air with a nasty pall of smoke[20].

'Christ in heaven[21], Malcolm, open a window if you insist on smoking that thing,' his companion replied. As chief superintendent[22], Sir David Hillier

1. continua à la scander
2. la rame
3. une âpreté non déguisée
4. rentra la tête dans les épaules
5. On peut être vite déboussolé.
6. lança un regard
7. d'un mépris glacial étudié
8. prêtre
9. il paraît
10. toute rabougrie
11. s'accrocha aux barres
12. la pressa de sortir
13. Impossible de leur en vouloir
14. une hache ensanglantée
15. se raccrocha à
16. Ça ne m'étonnerait pas qu'on ait
17. sur les bras
18. allumer
19. imprégna
20. d'un voile de fumée désagréable
21. Pour l'amour du Ciel
22. commissaire principal

was Webberly's superior, but he liked to let his men run their individual divisions in their own way[1]. He himself would never dream of launching[2] such an olfactory assault so shortly[3] before an interview, but Malcolm's ways were not his own and they had never been proven ineffectual[4]. He moved his chair to escape the worst of the fumes[5] and let his eyes take in the worst of the office.

Hillier wondered how Malcolm ever managed[6] his department as efficiently[7] as he did, given his bent[8] for chaos. Files[9] and photographs and reports and books covered every surface. There were empty coffee cups and overfull ashtrays[10] and even a pair of ancient running shoes high on a shelf. Just as Webberly intended[11], the room looked and smelt like the disordered digs[12] of an undergraduate[13]: cramped, friendly, and fusty[14]. Only an unmade bed was missing. It was the sort of place that made gathering, lingering, and talking easy[15], that bred[16] camaraderie among men who had to work as a team. Clever Malcolm, Hillier thought. Five or six times shrewder[17] than his ordinary, stoop-shouldered, overplump looks would indicate[18].

Webberly pushed himself away from his desk and played about with[19] the window, grunting and straining with the latch[20] before finally forcing it open. 'Sorry, David. I always forget.' He sat back down at his desk, surveyed its litter[21] with a melancholy gaze, and said, 'What I didn't need was this right now.' He ran one hand back through his sparse[22] hair. Ginger once[23], it was now mostly grey.

'Trouble at home?' Hillier asked carefully, eyes fixed on his gold signet ring[24]. It was a difficult question for both of them since he and Webberly were married to sisters, a fact that most of the Yard knew nothing about, of which the two men themselves rarely spoke.

1. diriger leurs services à leur façon
2. Lui-même n'aurait jamais lancé
3. si peu de temps
4. n'avaient jamais manqué d'efficacité
5. aux pires émanations
6. pouvait bien diriger
7. efficacement
8. vu son penchant
9. Des dossiers
10. des cendriers débordants
11. Exactement comme le voulait Webberly
12. la piaule mal rangée
13. étudiant
14. encombrée, accueillante et sentant le renfermé
15. où on avait envie de rester à plusieurs à discuter
16. qui suscitait
17. plus malin
18. que ne le laissait présager son air banal, voûté et enrobé
19. bricola
20. grognant en s'acharnant sur le loquet
21. en parcourut le désordre
22. rares
23. Naguère roux
24. chevalière

Their relationship was one of those quirks of fate[1] in which two men find themselves locked together[2] in a number of ways which are generally better not discussed between them. Hillier's career had mirrored his marriage. Both were successful, deeply satisfying. His wife was perfection: a rock of devotion[3], an intellectual companion, a loving mother, a sexual delight. He admitted that she was the very centre of his existence, that his three children were merely tangential objects[4], pleasant and diverting, but nothing at all of real importance compared to Laura. He turned to her – his first thought in the morning, his last thought at night – for virtually every need in his life. And she met each one.[5]

For Webberly it was different: a career that was, like the man, plodding along[6], one not brilliant but cautious, filled with countless[7] successes for which he rarely took credit[8], for Webberly simply was not the political animal he needed to be to succeed at the Yard. Thus, no knighthood[9] loomed seductively on his professional horizon[10], and this was what had put the enormous strain[11] upon the Webberly marriage.

Knowing that her younger sister was *Lady* Hillier clawed at the fabric[12] of Frances Webberly's life. It had turned her from a shy but complacent[13] middle-class housewife[14] to a social climber of the pushiest kind[15]. Dinner parties, cocktail parties, dreary[16] buffets which they could ill afford[17] were given for people in whom they had no interest, all of them part of what Frances perceived as her husband's climb to the top[18]. And to them all the Hilliers faithfully[19] went, Laura out of sad loyalty to[20] a sister with whom she no longer lovingly communicated and Hillier himself to protect Webberly as best he could from the piercingly cruel comments[21] Frances often made publicly about her husband's

1. lien de parenté était un de ces caprices du destin
2. par lequel deux hommes se retrouvent liés
3. le dévouement personnifié
4. étaient secondaires
5. les comblait tous
6. comme lui, avançait bon an mal an
7. innombrables
8. dont on lui attribuait rarement le mérite
9. aucun anoblissement
10. ne pointait à l'horizon de sa carrière
11. pression
12. minait
13. satisfaite
14. femme au foyer
15. en arriviste des plus agressives
16. ennuyeux
17. qu'ils ne pouvaient se permettre
18. la progression de son mari vers les hautes sphères
19. fidèlement
20. affligée mais loyale envers
21. des commentaires cinglants que

lacklustre[1] career. Lady Macbeth incarnate[2], Hillier thought with a shudder.

'No, not there,' Webberly was responding. 'It's merely[3] that I thought I'd got Nies and Kerridge sorted out years ago. To have a confrontation crop up again[4] between them is disconcerting.'

How typical of Malcolm to take responsibility for the foibles[5] of others, Hillier thought. 'Refresh my memory on their last fray[6],' he said. 'It was a Yorkshire situation, wasn't it? Gypsies[7] involved in a murder?'

Webberly nodded[8]. 'Nies heads up[9] the Richmond police.' He sighed heavily[10], forgetting for a moment to blow the smoke[11] from his cigar towards the open window. Hillier strained not to cough[12]. Webberly loosened his tie a fraction[13] and absently fingered the frayed collar[14] of his white shirt. 'An old gypsy woman was killed up there three years ago. Nies runs a tight[15] CID[16]. His men are meticulous, accurate to the last detail[17]. They conducted an investigation and arrested the old crone's[18] son-in-law. It was an apparent dispute over the ownership of a garnet necklace[19].'

'Garnets? Were they stolen?'

Webberly shook his head, tapping his cigar against a dented tin ashtray[20] on his desk. The action dislodged debris from previous cigars, which drifted like dust to mingle[21] with papers and manila folders[22]. 'No. The necklace had been given to them by Edmund Hanston-Smith.'

Hillier sat forward in his chair. 'Hanston-Smith?'

'Yes, you're remembering it now, aren't you? But that case was after all this. The man arrested for the old woman's murder – Romaniv, I think his name was – had a wife. About twenty-five years old and beautiful in the way only those women can be: dark, olive-skinned[23], exotic.'

1. terne
2. Une vraie lady Macbeth
3. juste
4. une nouvelle bisbille
5. des faiblesses des autres
6. leur dernier accrochage
7. Des Roms
8. acquiesça de la tête
9. dirige
10. soupira profondément
11. de rejeter la fumée
12. eut du mal à ne pas tousser
13. desserra un peu sa cravate
14. toucha distraitement le col usé
15. dirige d'une main de fer
16. sa police judiciaire
17. d'une précision scrupuleuse
18. de la vieille
19. collier en grenats
20. cendrier en fer-blanc cabossé
21. qui se soulevèrent en poussière, se mêlant
22. aux chemises kraft
23. la peau mate

'More than a bit enticing[1] to a man like Hanston-Smith?'

'In truth.[2] She got him to believe[3] that Romaniv was innocent. It took a few weeks – Romaniv hadn't come up before the assizes yet[4]. She convinced Hanston-Smith that the case needed to be reopened. She swore that they were only being persecuted because of their gypsy blood, that Romaniv had been with her the entire night in question.'

'I imagine her charms made that easy to believe.'

Webberly's mouth quirked[5]. He stubbed out[6] the tip of his cigar in the ashtray and clasped his freckled hands over his stomach. They effectively hid the stain on his waistcoat[7].

'From the later testimony[8] of Hanston-Smith's valet, the good Mrs Romaniv had no trouble keeping even a man of sixty-two more than busy for one entire night. You'll recall[9] that Hanston-Smith was a man of some considerable[10] political influence and wealth[11]. It was no difficult matter for him to convince the Yorkshire constabulary[12] to become involved. So Reuben Kerridge – he's still Yorkshire's chief constable[13] in spite of all that happened – ordered Nies' investigation reopened. And, to make matters worse[14], he ordered Romaniv released[15].'

'How did Nies react?'

'Kerridge is his superior officer[16], after all. What could he do? Nies was wild with anger[17], but he released Romaniv and ordered his men to begin again.'

'It would seem that releasing Romaniv, while making his wife happy, would bring a premature end to Hanston-Smith's joy,' Hillier noted[18].

'Well, of course, Mrs Romaniv felt duty-bound[19] to thank Hanston-Smith in the manner to which he'd become so accustomed[20]. She slept with him one last time – wore the poor bloke out[21] until the wee hours of the morning[22], if I have the story straight

1. Plus que séduisante
2. En effet.
3. lui a fait croire
4. pas encore comparu aux assises
5. se fit narquoise
6. écrasa
7. parvenaient à cacher la tache sur son gilet
8. témoignage ultérieur
9. Rappelez-vous
10. disposant de pas mal
11. richesse
12. police
13. chef régional de la police
14. pour ne rien arranger
15. que Romaniv soit libéré
16. supérieur hiérarchique
17. vert de rage
18. remarqua
19. s'est crue obligée
20. à laquelle il avait pris goût
21. épuisa le pauvre bougre
22. jusqu'au petit matin

– and then let[1] Romaniv into the house.' Webberly looked up at a sharp knock on the door[2]. 'The rest, as they say, is a bit of bloody history[3]. The pair murdered Hanston-Smith, took everything they could carry, got to Scarborough, and were out of the country before dawn[4].'

'And Nies' reaction?'

'Demanded Kerridge's immediate resignation[5].' The knock sounded again.[6] Webberly ignored it. 'He didn't get it, however. But Nies' mouth has been watering like the devil for it ever since[7].'

'And here we are back with them again, you say.'

A third knock, much more insistent. Webberly called entrance to Bertie Edwards, the Met's[8] head of forensics[9], who entered the room in his usual brisk manner[10], scribbling on his clipboard[11] and speaking to it at the same time. To Edwards, the clipboard was as human as most men's secretaries.

'Severe contusion on the right temple[12],' he was announcing happily, 'followed by the main laceration to the carotid artery. No identification, no money, stripped down to the underclothes[13]. It's the Railway Ripper, all right.[14]' He finished writing with a flourish[15].

Hillier surveyed the little man with profound distaste[16]. 'Christ, these Fleet Street[17] appellations. We're going to be haunted[18] by Whitechapel[19] till the end of time.'

'Is this the Waterloo corpse[20]?' Webberly asked.

Edwards glanced at Hillier, his face an open book in which he considered whether he should argue the merits of nameless killers being dubbed something[21] – anything – for the sake of public awareness[22]. He apparently rejected that line of communication, for he wiped at his forehead[23] with the sleeve of his lab coat[24] and turned to his immediate superior.

1. fit entrer
2. leva les yeux au coup sec frappé à la porte
3. un peu sanglant
4. l'aube
5. démission
6. On frappa à nouveau.
7. l'attend toujours avec impatience
8. de la police londonienne
9. le chef de la police scientifique
10. de son pas vif habituel
11. tout en griffonnant sur son bloc-notes
12. tempe
13. ne portant plus que ses sous-vêtements
14. C'est bien l'Éventreur du Rail.
15. dans un grand geste
16. répugnance
17. que donnent les journalistes
18. hantés
19. [quartier où sévissait Jack l'Éventreur]
20. cadavre
21. d'affubler les tueurs anonymes de surnoms
22. pour sensibiliser le public
23. s'essuya le front
24. la manche de sa blouse de labo

'Waterloo.' He nodded. 'Number eleven. We've not quite finished Vauxhall yet. Both are typical of the Ripper victims we've seen. Transient types.[1] Broken nails. Dirty. Badly cut hair. Body lice[2] as well. King's Cross is still the only one out of sync[3], and that's the bloody devil after all these weeks. No ID[4]. No missing-person's call[5] on him yet. I can't make it out[6].' He scratched his head with the end of his pen. 'Want the Waterloo snap[7]? I've brought it.'

Webberly waved towards the wall on which were already posted the photographs of the twelve recent murder victims, all of them killed in an identical manner in or near London railway stations. Thirteen murders now in just over five weeks. The papers were screaming for[8] an arrest. As if he were oblivious to this, Edwards whistled airily[9] between his teeth and rooted[10] on Webberly's desk for a drawing-pin[11]. He carried the latest[12] victim to the wall.

'Not a bad shot.[13]' He stepped back to admire his work. 'Sewed him up quite nice.[14]'

'Jesus!' Hillier exploded. 'You're a ghoul[15], man! At least have the decency to remove that filthy coat[16] when you come here! Have you no sense at all?[17] We've women on these floors!'

Edwards wore the guise of patient attention[18], but his eyes flicked over the chief superintendent and lingered longest on the fleshy neck[19] that hung over his collar and on the thick hair that Hillier liked to have called leonine. Edwards shrugged[20] at Webberly in mutual understanding. 'Quite the gent, he is[21],' he commented before leaving the room.

'Sack him![22]' Hillier shouted as the door shut behind the pathologist[23].

Webberly laughed. 'Have a sherry[24], David,' he said. 'It's in the cabinet[25] behind you. We none of us ought to be here on a Saturday.'

1. Vagabonds.
2. Des parasites partout
3. qui ne colle pas avec les autres
4. de papiers d'identité
5. d'avis de recherche
6. ne comprends pas
7. cliché
8. réclamaient à cor et à cri
9. sifflotait gaiement
10. fouilla
11. une punaise
12. toute dernière
13. Pas mal, cette photo.
14. Vraiment bien recousu.
15. d'une morbidité dégoûtante
16. d'ôter cette blouse répugnante
17. Vous n'avez donc aucun discernement ?
18. fit mine d'écouter patiemment
19. sur le cou adipeux
20. haussa les épaules
21. Un vrai gentleman
22. Virez-le !
23. médecin légiste
24. xérès
25. placard

Two sherries considerably palliated[1] Hillier's irritation with the pathologist. He was standing before Webberly's display wall[2], staring morosely at the thirteen photographs.

'This is one hell of a mess[3],' he noted sourly[4]. 'Victoria, King's Cross, Waterloo, Liverpool, Blackfriars, Paddington. God *damn* it, man, why can't he at least be alphabetical[5]!'

'Maniacs[6] often lack that little organizational touch,' Webberly responded placidly.

'Five of these victims don't even have *names*, for God's sake,' Hillier complained.

'ID is always removed, so are money and clothes. If there's no missing-person report filed[7], we start with prints[8].

You know how long something like that takes, David. We're doing our best[9].'

Hillier turned round. The one thing he knew for a certainty[10] was that Malcolm would always do his absolute best and would quietly remain in the background[11] when the kudos was given[12]. 'Sorry. Was I frothing?[13]'

'A bit.'

'As usual. So this new Nies-Kerridge squabble[14]? What's it all about?'

Webberly glanced at his watch[15]. 'Another Yorkshire murder being disputed[16], no less. They're sending someone down with the data[17]. A priest.'

'A *priest*? Christ – what kind of case is this?'

Webberly shrugged. 'Evidently he's the only third party[18] that Nies and Kerridge could agree upon to bring us the information.'

'Why's that?'

'Seems he found the body.'

1. calmèrent
2. l'affichage mural de
3. un vrai bordel
4. amèrement
5. respecter l'ordre alphabétique
6. Les fous
7. Si personne n'a déclaré la disparition
8. par les empreintes
9. de notre mieux
10. S'il était sûr d'une chose,
11. resterait tranquillement dans l'ombre
12. à l'heure des lauriers
13. J'écumais ?
14. querelle
15. consulta sa montre
16. contesté
17. avec les éléments
18. la seule tierce personne

2

Hillier walked to the office window. Afternoon sunlight shafted across his face[1], detailing lines[2] that spoke of too many late nights[3], highlighting puffy pink flesh[4] that spoke of too much rich[5] food and port[6]. 'By God, this is irregular. Has Kerridge gone quite mad?'

'Nies has certainly been claiming that[7] for years.'

'But to have the first person on the scene ... and not even a member of the force[8]! What can the man be thinking?[9]'

'That a priest is the only person they both can trust[10].' Webberly glanced at his watch again. 'He should be here within the hour[11], in fact. That's why I asked you to come down.'

'To hear this priest's story? That's certainly not your style.'

Webberly shook his head slowly. He had come to the tricky part[12]. 'Not to hear the story. Actually,[13] to hear the plan.'

'I'm intrigued.' Hillier went to pour himself[14] another sherry and held the bottle towards[15] his friend, who shook his head. He returned to his seat and crossed one leg over the other, careful not to destroy the razor crease[16] in his beautifully tailored trousers[17]. 'The plan?' he prompted[18].

1. lui éclaira le visage
2. pointant des rides
3. qui trahissaient des nuits trop courtes
4. en soulignant des chairs roses bouffies
5. grasse
6. d'apéritifs
7. le prétend
8. policier
9. Mais à quoi pense-t-il donc ?
10. en qui tous deux aient confiance
11. d'ici une heure
12. le moment délicat
13. En fait,
14. se verser
15. proposa d'un geste la bouteille à
16. le pli parfait
17. de son impeccable pantalon sur mesure
18. souffla-t-il

Webberly poked at a stack of files[1] on his desk. 'I'd like Lynley on this.'

Hillier cocked an eyebrow[2]. 'Lynley and Nies for a second go-round[3]? Haven't we had trouble enough in that quarter[4], Malcolm? Besides, Lynley's not on rota[5] this weekend.'

'That can be dealt with.[6]' Webberly hesitated. He watched the other man. 'You're letting me hang here[7], David,' he said at last.

Hillier smiled. 'Forgive me. I was waiting to see how you were going to ask for her.'

'Damn you,' Webberly cursed softly[8]. 'You know me too well by half[9].'

'Let's say I know you're too fair[10] for your own good. Let me advise you on this[11], Malcolm. Leave Havers where you put her.'

Webberly winced[12] and swiped at a nonexistent fly[13]. 'It grates[14] on my conscience.'

'Don't be a bloody fool. Don't be worse than that – don't be a sentimental fool. Barbara Havers proved herself[15] incapable of getting along[16] with a single DI[17] for her entire tenure[18] in CID. She's been back in uniform[19] these past eight months and doing a better job there. Leave her.'

'I didn't try her with Lynley.'

'You didn't try her with the Prince of Wales[20] either! It's not your responsibility to keep moving detective sergeants[21] around until they find a little niche[22] in which they can grow old happily[23]. It's your responsibility to see that[24] the flaming job gets done[25]. And *no* job got done with Havers on it. Admit it!'

'I think she's learned from the experience.'

'Learned what? That being a truculent pigheaded little bitch[26] is not likely to advance her up the ranks[27]?'

1. tapota une pile de dossiers
2. leva un sourcil
3. manche
4. de ce côté-là
5. de service
6. On peut arranger ça.
7. Tu me laisses tourner autour du pot, là
8. jura doucement
9. trop bien
10. que tu te soucies trop d'équité
11. Un conseil
12. fit une grimace
13. chassa une mouche imaginaire
14. Cela pèse
15. s'est révélée
16. s'entendre
17. officier de police judiciaire [detective inspector]
18. pendant toute son affectation
19. Elle a repris l'uniforme
20. le prince de Galles
21. les agents de police judiciaire
22. un bon petit poste
23. vieillir paisiblement
24. de veiller à ce que
25. le fichu boulot soit fait
26. petite tête de mule
27. la faire monter en grade

Webberly let Hillier's words scathe the air between them[1]. 'Well,' he said finally, 'that was always the problem, wasn't it?'

Hillier recognized the sound of defeat in his friend's voice. That was indeed the problem: advancing through theranks. God, what an ignorant thing to say. 'Forgive me, Malcolm.' He quickly finished his sherry, an act that gave him something to do other than look at his brother-in-law's face. 'You deserve[2] my job. We both know it, don' t we?'

'Don't be absurd.'

But Hillier stood. 'I'll put a call out for[3] Havers.'

Detective Sergeant Barbara Havers tugged the door of the super's office shut[4], walked stiffly past his secretary, and made her way into[5] the corridor. She was white with rage.

God! God, how dare they[6]! She pushed her way past a clerk[7], not bothering to stop[8] when the folders he was carrying slipped from his grasp and scattered[9]. She marched right through them. Who did they think they were dealing with[10]? Did they think she was so stupid she couldn't see the ploy[11]? God damn them! God *damn* them!

She blinked[12], telling herself that there would be no tears, that she would not cry, that she would not react. The sign LADIES[13] appeared miraculously in front of her and she ducked inside[14]. No one was present. Here, it was cool. Had it really been so hot in Webberly's office? Or had it been her outrage[15]? She fumbled at her tie, jerked it loose[16], and stumbled over to the basin[17]. The cold water gushed out of the tap[18] beneath her fumbling fingers, sending a spray on to her uniform skirt and across her white blouse. That did it.[19] She looked at herself in the mirror and burst into tears[20].

1. ne réagit pas aux cinglantes paroles d'Hellier
2. mériterais
3. convoquer
4. referma bien la porte du bureau du chef
5. gagna
6. comment osent-ils
7. bouscula un employé
8. sans s'arrêter
9. lui échappèrent des mains et s'éparpillèrent
10. avoir affaire
11. la ruse
12. ferma les yeux une seconde
13. toilettes pour dames
14. s'y réfugia
15. colère
16. desserra sa cravate comme elle put
17. tituba jusqu'au lavabo
18. jaillit du robinet
19. C'en fut trop.
20. éclata en sanglots

'You cow[1],' she sneered[2]. 'You stupid, ugly cow!' She was not a woman easily given to tears[3], so they were hot and bitter, tasting strange and feeling stranger as they coursed down her cheeks, making unattractive rivulets[4] across what was an extremely plain, extremely pug-like[5] face.

'You're a real sight[6], Barbara,' she upbraided[7] her reflection[8]. 'You're an absolute vision!' Sobbing, she twisted away[9] from the basin, resting[10] her head against the cool tile[11] of the wall.

At thirty years old, Barbara Havers was a decidedly unattractive woman[12], but a woman who appeared to be doing everything possible to make herself so. Fine, shiny hair the colour of pinewood[13] might have been suitably styled[14] for the shape[15] of her face. But instead she wore it cut bluntly[16] at an unforgivable length[17] just below her ears as if a too-small bowl had been placed upon her head for a model. She used no make-up[18]. Heavy, unplucked eyebrows[19] drew attention to the smallness of her eyes rather than to their fine intelligence. A thin mouth, never heightened[20] in any way by colour, was pressed permanently into a disapproving frown[21]. The entire effect was that of a woman stubby, sturdy[22], and entirely unapproachable.

So they've given you the golden boy, she thought. What a treat for you[23], Barb! After eight miserable[24] months, they bring you back from the street 'for another chance' – and all the while it's Lynley!

'I will not,' she muttered.' I will *not* do it! I will not work with that sodding little fop[25]!'

She pushed herself away from the wall and returned to the basin. She ran cold water into it carefully this time, bending to bathe[26] her hot face and scrub away[27] the incriminating sign[28] of her tears.

'I'd like to give you another opportunity in CID,' Webberly had said. He'd been fingering a letter-opener[29] on his desk, but she'd noticed the Ripper

1. Pauvre conne
2. lança-t-elle, méprisante
3. qui pleure
4. des ruisselets disgracieux
5. sans aucun charme, avec un air de bouledogue
6. Tu fais peine à voir
7. tança
8. image
9. En pleurs, elle se détourna
10. posant
11. le carrelage frais
12. n'était vraiment pas une femme séduisante
13. bois de pin
14. auraient pu être coupés
15. pour mieux convenir à la forme
16. grossièrement
17. d'une longueur qui ne pardonnait pas
18. maquillage
19. Des sourcils fournis, pas épilés
20. rehaussée
21. moue
22. courtaude, trapue
23. Quelle bonne surprise
24. horribles
25. ce sale petit dandy
26. baigner
27. effacer
28. trace révélatrice
29. tripotait un coupe-papier

photos on the walls and her heart had soared[1]. To be on the Ripper! *Oh God, yes! When do I start? Is it with MacPherson?*

'It's a peculiar case[2] involving a girl up in Yorkshire.' *Oh, so it's not the Ripper. But, still, it's a case. A girl, you say? Of course I can help. Is it Stewart, then? He's an old hand[3] in Yorkshire. We'd work well together. I know we would.*

'In fact, I'm expecting to receive the information in about three-quarters of an hour. I'll need you here then – if you're interested, that is[4].' *If I'm interested! Three-quarters of an hour gives me time to change[5]. Have a bite to eat.[6] Get back here. Then be on the late train[7] to York. Will we meet up there? Shall I see about a car?*

'I'll need you to pop round[8] to Chelsea before then, I'm afraid.'

The conversation ground to a sudden halt[9]. 'To Chelsea, sir?' What on earth had Chelsea to do with all this?

'Yes,' Webberly said easily, dropping the letter-opener on to the general clutter[10] on his desk. 'You'll be working with Inspector Lynley, and unfortunately we've got to pull him out[11] of the St James wedding in Chelsea.' He glanced at his watch. 'The wedding was at eleven, so no doubt they're well into the reception by now[12]. We've been trying to raise him on the phone[13], but apparently it's been left off the hook[14].' He looked up in time to see the shock on her face. 'Something wrong[15], Sergeant?'

'Inspector Lynley?' She saw it all at once[16], the reason they needed her, the reason why no one else would really quite do[17].

'Yes, Lynley. Is there a problem?'

'No, no problem at all.' And then, as an afterthought[18], 'Sir.'

Webberly's shrewd eyes evaluated her response. 'Good. I'm glad to hear it. There's a lot you might

1. bondi
2. une étrange affaire
3. quelqu'un d'expérience
4. bien sûr
5. de me changer
6. De manger un morceau.
7. le dernier train
8. Il faut que vous fassiez un saut
9. tomba
10. au beau milieu du fouillis
11. l'arracher
12. que la réception bat son plein à l'heure qu'il est
13. de le joindre par téléphone
14. il est décroché
15. ne va pas
16. D'un coup, elle comprit
17. ne conviendrait vraiment
18. comme après réflexion

learn from working with Lynley.' Still the eyes watched, gauging[1] her reaction. 'Try to be back here as fast as you can.' He gave his attention back to the papers on his desk. She was dismissed[2].

Barbara looked at herself in the mirror and fumbled in the pocket of her skirt for a comb[3]. Lynley. She tugged the plastic through her hair mercilessly, dragging it against her scalp[4], abrading[5] the skin, welcoming the pain. *Lynley!* It was only too obvious why they'd brought her back out of uniform. They wanted Lynley on the case. But they needed a woman as well. And every person in Victoria Street knew that there wasn't a female[6] in CID who was safe near Lynley. He'd slept his way through[7] department and division, leaving a trail of the discarded[8] behind him. He had the reputation of a racehorse put out to stud[9] and, from all the tales told[10], the endurance as well. She angrily shoved the comb back into her pocket.

So, how does it feel, she demanded of her reflection, to be the one lucky woman whose virtue is quite secure in the presence of the almighty[11] Lynley? No wandering hands[12] while our Barb's in the car! No confidential dinners to 'go over our notes[13]'. No invitations to Cornwall to 'think the case out[14]'. No fear here, Barb. God knows that you're safe with Lynley. In her five years working in the same division with the man, she was certain he'd managed to avoid so much as saying her name, let alone having a single second's foul contact with her. As if a grammar-school[15] background and a working-class[16] accent were social diseases[17] that might infect him if he were not scrupulously careful to keep himself clear of them[18].

She left the room and stalked down[19] the corridor towards the lift. Was there *anyone* in all of New Scotland Yard whom she hated more than she hated Lynley? He was a miraculous combination of every

1. jaugeant
2. congédiée
3. à la recherche d'un peigne
4. en raclant le cuir chevelu
5. éraflant
6. femme
7. Il avait couché avec tout le monde dans
8. laissant un sillage d'anciennes conquêtes
9. d'un ancien cheval de course qui fait des saillies
10. ragots
11. tout-puissant
12. Pas de mains baladeuses
13. bosser le dossier
14. travailler à tête reposée
15. d'école secondaire d'excellence
16. populaire
17. des maladies
18. éviter le contact
19. parcourut d'un pas raide

single thing that she thoroughly[1] despised: educated at Eton[2], a first[3] in history at Oxford, a public-school voice[4], and a bloody family tree[5] that had its roots somewhere just this side of[6] the Battle of Hastings. Upper class. Bright[7]. And so damnably charming that she couldn't understand why every criminal in the city simply didn't surrender[8] to accommodate him[9].

His whole reason for working at the Yard was a joke, a flaming little myth[10] that she didn't believe for a moment. He wanted to be useful, to make a contribution. He preferred a career in London to life on the estate[11]. What a ruddy good laugh![12]

The lift doors opened and she punched furiously for the[13] garage. And hadn't his career been convenient and sweet, purchased lock, stock, and barrel[14] with the family funds? He bought his way right into his current position[15] and he'd be a Commissioner[16] before he was through[17]. God knew inheriting that precious title[18] hadn't hurt his chances for success one bit[19]. He'd gone from sergeant to inspector in record time straight away. Everyone knew why.

She headed for her car, a rusty[20] Mini in the far corner of the garage. How nice to be rich, to be titled[21] like Lynley, to work only for a lark[22], and then to swing home to the Belgravia townhouse or, better yet, fly to the Cornish[23] estate. With butlers and maids[24] and cooks and valets[25].

And think of it, Barb: picture yourself in the presence of such greatness[26]*. What shall you do? Shall you swoon*[27] *or vomit first?*

She flung her handbag into the rear[28] seat of the Mini, slammed the door, and started the car with a sputter and a roar[29]. The wheels squealed on the pavement as she ascended the ramp, nodded

1. totalement
2. [prestigieuse école privée]
3. mention très bien
4. une façon de parler très smart
5. un putain d'arbre généalogique
6. remontant presque à
7. Intelligent
8. ne se rendait pas
9. pour lui être agréable
10. fichue légende
11. que rester sur ses terres
12. Cette bonne blague !
13. appuya rageusement sur le bouton du
14. intégralement achetée
15. grade actuel
16. préfet de police
17. la retraite
18. qu'hériter de ce titre à la noix
19. ne lui avait pas nuit
20. rouillée
21. d'avoir un titre de noblesse
22. pour le plaisir
23. de Cornouailles
24. des majordomes et des femmes de chambre
25. des cuisiniers et des valets
26. grandeur
27. t'évanouir
28. arrière
29. qui crachota puis vrombit

brusquely towards the officer on guard in the kiosk, and headed for the street.

The light weekend traffic made getting from Victoria Street to the Embankment a manoeuvre of a few minutes only, and, once there, the mild breeze[1] of the October afternoon cooled her temper[2], calmed her nerves, and coaxed her into forgetting[3] her indignation. It was a pleasant drive, really, to the St James house.

Barbara liked Simon Allcourt-St James, had liked him from the first time she had met him ten years ago when she was a nervous twenty-year-old probationary police constable[4] all too aware of being a woman in a closely guarded man's world[5] where women police were still called Wopsies[6] after a few drinks. And she'd been called worse than that – she knew it. Damn them all to hell.[7] To them[8], any woman who aspired to[9] CID was a bona-fide freak[10] and made to feel that way[11]. But to St James, two years her senior[12], she had been an acceptable colleague, even a friend.

St James was now an independent forensic scientist[13], but he had begun his career at the Yard. By his twenty-fourth birthday, he was the very best of the scene-of-crime men, quick, observant, intuitive. He could have gone in any direction: investigations, pathology, administration, anywhere. But it had all ended one night eight years ago on a drive[14] with Lynley, a wild junket[15] through the back roads[16] of Surrey. They had both been drunk – St James was always prompt to admit this fact[17]. But everyone knew that it was Lynley who had been driving that night, Lynley who had lost control on a curve[18], Lynley who had walked away without a scratch[19] while his childhood friend[20], St James, had emerged a cripple[21]. And, although he could have continued his career at the Yard, St James had instead retired to a family house in Chelsea, where for the next

1. la douce brise
2. apaisa son humeur
3. lui fit oublier
4. agent de police stagiaire
5. un monde exclusivement masculin
6. fliquettes
7. Qu'ils aillent tous au diable.
8. Pour eux
9. souhaitant intégrer
10. forcément sinoque
11. on le lui faisait bien sentir
12. plus âgé qu'elle
13. expert légiste
14. en voiture
15. lors d'une folle escapade
16. sur les petites routes
17. l'admettait volontiers
18. dans un virage
19. s'en était sorti sans une égratignure
20. ami d'enfance
21. était devenu handicapé

four years he had lived like a recluse[1]. Score that[2] to old Lynley, she thought sourly[3].

She couldn't believe that St James had actually maintained his friendship[4] with the man. But he had, and something, some sort of quirky[5] situation, had cemented their relationship nearly five years ago and had brought St James back into the field where he belonged[6]. Score *that*, she thought reluctantly[7], to Lynley as well.

She pulled[8] the Mini into an available space in Lawrence Street and walked back along Lordship Place towards Cheyne Row[9]. Not far from the river, it was an area of the city where elaborate white plaster[10] and woodwork[11] decorated deep umber[12] brick buildings and black paint restored the wrought iron[13] at windows and balconies. In keeping with[14] the village that Chelsea once had been, the streets were narrow, metamorphosed into bright autumn tunnels by sycamores and elms[15]. St James' house stood on a corner, and as she passed by[16] the high brick wall that fenced in[17] the garden, Barbara heard the sounds of the party in progress[18]. A voice was raised in a toast[19]. Shouts of approval followed applause. An old oak[20] door in the wall was closed, but that was just as well[21]. Dressed as she was, she hardly wanted[22] to burst into the festivities[23] as if she were making an arrest.

She rounded the corner[24] to find the front door of the tall, old house open to the late-afternoon sun. The sound of laughter floated towards her, the pure tones of silver and china[25], the popping of champagne[26], and somewhere in the garden the music of violin and flute. There were flowers everywhere, right out on to the front steps where the balustrades were twined with[27] white and pink roses that filled the air with a heady[28] perfume. Even the balconies above held potted convolvuluses that tumbled

1. en ermite
2. Et tout ça grâce
3. avec amertume
4. ait pu rester ami
5. bizarre
6. dans son domaine de prédilection
7. à contrecœur
8. gara
9. rue
10. des stucs sophistiqués
11. des boiseries
12. ocre brun foncé
13. fer forgé
14. S'accordant bien avec
15. les sycomores et les ormes
16. longeait
17. entourait
18. la réception en cours
19. s'éleva pour porter un toast
20. en chêne
21. tant mieux
22. préférait éviter
23. de débouler en pleines réjouissances
24. tourna à l'angle
25. le tintement pur de l'argenterie et de la porcelaine
26. le champagne qu'on débouchait
27. étaient ornées de guirlandes de
28. entêtant

trumpet-shaped flowers[1] in a riot of colours[2] over the edge.

Barbara drew in a breath[3] and mounted the steps. There was no point to knocking, for although several guests near the door gave her inquisitive glances[4] as she hesitated outside in her ill-fitting[5] uniform, they strolled back towards the garden without speaking to her, and it soon became apparent that if she wanted to find Lynley she would have to barge right into[6] the wedding reception to do so. The thought made her more than a little bit ill.

She was about to retreat cravenly[7] to her car to retrieve[8] an old mackintosh[9] that would at least cover up her clothes – too tight in the hips[10] and straining the material at shoulder and neck[11] – when the sounds of footsteps[12] and laughter close by directed her attention to the stairway in the hall. A woman was descending, calling over her shoulder[13] to someone who remained on the floor above.

'Just the two of us are going. You must come as well and we'll make a party of it[14], Sid.' She turned, saw Barbara, and stopped where she was, one hand on the banister[15]. It was very nearly a pose, for she was the kind of woman who could manage to make yards of haphazardly arranged[16] teal-coloured silk[17] look like the very latest word[18] in haute couture. She was not particularly tall, but very slender[19], with a fall[20] of chestnut[21] hair framing[22] a perfect oval face. From the dozens of times she had been to fetch[23] Lynley from the Yard, Barbara recognized her at once. She was Lynley's longest-running mistress[24] and St James' lab assistant, Lady Helen Clyde. Lady Helen completed her descent and crossed the hall to the door. So confident[25], Barbara noted, so completely self-possessed[26].

'I've the most dreadful feeling that you've come for Tommy,' she said immediately, extending her hand. 'Hello. I'm Helen Clyde.'

1. des liserons en pot, leurs fleurs en trompette cascadant
2. dans une profusion de couleurs
3. prit une goulée d'air
4. des regards curieux
5. mal ajusté
6. faire irruption dans
7. lâchement battre en retraite
8. pour y prendre
9. imperméable
10. trop serré aux hanches
11. trop juste au niveau du cou
12. un bruit de pas
13. s'adressant par-dessus son épaule
14. comme ça on s'amusera plus à trois
15. la rampe
16. drapés au hasard
17. soie bleu canard
18. du dernier chic
19. mince
20. cascade
21. châtains
22. encadrant
23. était venue chercher
24. la conquête la plus ancienne et toujours actuelle
25. Si sûre d'elle
26. avec une telle maîtrise de soi

Barbara introduced herself, surprised at the firmness of the woman's grip[1]. Her hands were thin, very cool to the touch. 'He's wanted[2] at the Yard.'

'Poor man. How miserable. How damnably unfair.[3]' Lady Helen spoke more to herself than to the other woman, for she suddenly shot Barbara an apologetic smile[4]. 'But it's not your fault, is it? Come, he's just this way.'

Without waiting for a reply, she moved down the hallway to the garden door, giving Barbara no choice but to follow. However, at her first glimpse of the cluster[5] of linen-covered tables[6] at which fashionably clad[7] guests chatted and laughed, Barbara stepped quickly back[8] into the dimly lit[9] hall. Her fingers wandered up to her neck.

Lady Helen paused, her dark eyes reflective[10]. 'Shall I search Tommy out for you[11]?' she offered with another quick smile. 'It's a crush[12] out there, isn't it?'

'Thank you,' Barbara replied stiffly[13] and watched her walk across the lawn[14] to a group standing in merry conversation[15] round a tall man who managed to look as if somehow he'd been born wearing morning dress[16].

Lady Helen touched his arm and said a few words. The man looked towards the house, revealing a face that bore the unmistakable stamp[17] of aristocracy. It was a Greek sculpture sort of face, unaccountably[18] timeless. He brushed his blond hair back from his forehead, placed his champagne glass on a table nearby, and, after exchanging a quip[19] with one of his friends, came towards the house with Lady Helen at his side.

From the safety of the shadows, Barbara watched Lynley's approach. His movements were graceful, fluid, like a cat's. He was the handsomest man she had ever seen. She loathed him.[20]

1. poignée de main
2. On le demande
3. Comme c'est injuste.
4. un sourire navré
5. dès qu'elle aperçut le groupe
6. tables recouvertes de nappes
7. habillés à la mode
8. se retrancha vite
9. peu éclairé
10. songeurs
11. vous chercher Tommy
12. la cohue
13. sèchement
14. pelouse
15. en pleine conversation joyeuse
16. il avait toujours porté une queue-de-pie
17. la marque indéniable
18. inexplicablement
19. une plaisanterie
20. Elle le détestait.

1. de service
2. comprit le sous-entendu
3. avec douceur
4. une bouffée de colère
5. Enfer et damnation
6. vers
7. Ça concerne l'Éventreur ?
8. une affaire
9. autant que je sache
10. Un peu de piquant dans le dossier
11. une nana
12. les détails
13. primordiaux
14. mensurations
15. la demoiselle qu'il serait ravi de sauver du péril
16. tant pis pour notre projet
17. que nous n'y pouvons rien
18. Les androgynes faisant fureur
19. plus ou moins une plaisanterie

'Sergeant Havers.' He nodded when they joined her. 'I'm not on call[1] this weekend.' Barbara read the implication clearly[2]: *You're interrupting me, Havers.*

'Webberly sent me, sir. Ring him if you like.' She didn't look at him directly as she replied but, rather, focused her eyes somewhere just over his left shoulder.

'But surely he *knows* that today's the wedding, Tommy,' Lady Helen protested mildly[3].

Lynley let out his breath in a puff of anger[4]. 'Damn and blast[5], of course he knows.' He glanced out at[6] the lawn, then sharply back to Barbara. 'Is this Ripper business?[7] I'd been told that John Stewart would join MacPherson.'

'It's business[8] in the North as far as I know[9]. Some girl's involved.' Barbara thought he'd appreciate that piece of information. Some spice to the case[10], just the way he liked it: a tart[11] for dessert. She waited for him to demand the particulars[12] that, no doubt, were first and foremost[13] on his mind: age, marital status, and measurements[14] of the damsel whose distress he was only too willing to alleviate[15].

His eyes narrowed. 'In the North?'

Lady Helen laughed regretfully. 'Well, there go our plans[16] to go dancing tonight, Tommy darling, and I was just persuading Sidney to come as well.'

'I suppose it can't be helped[17],' Lynley replied. But he moved abruptly from the shadows into the light, and both the tightness of the movement and the play of a repressed reaction on his face told Barbara how irritated he really was.

Lady Helen evidently saw this as well, for she spoke again cheerfully. 'Of course, Sid and I *could* easily go dancing alone. With androgyny the rage[18], no doubt one of us might be taken for a man no matter how we dress. Or there's Jeffrey Cusick. We could telephone him.' It was somehow a personal joke[19] between them and it had its desired effect, for Lynley relaxed into a smile. He followed it with a dry chuckle[1].

'Cusick? My God, these *are* desperate times[2].'

'Oh, you may laugh,' Lady Helen replied and did so herself, 'but he took us to Royal Ascot[3] when you were far too busily engaged in[4] some blood-thirsty murder watch[5] at St Pancras Station. Cambridge men, you see, have all sorts of fine qualities.'

Lynley laughed outright[6]. 'Among which is the tendency to look like a penguin when formally dressed[7].'

'You dreadful creature!' Lady Helen gave her attention to Barbara. 'May I at least offer you some lovely crab salad before you drag Tommy back to the Yard? Years ago, I was served the most terrifying egg sandwich there. If the food's not improved[8], this may be your last chance to eat well today.'

Barbara glanced at her watch. She sensed an undercurrent of urgency[9] in[10] Lynley and knew quite well that he wanted her to accept the invitation so that he'd have a few more minutes with his friends before being called back to duty. She wasn't about to accommodate him[11]. 'There's a meeting in twenty minutes, I'm afraid.'

Lady Helen sighed. 'Well, that's hardly enough time[12] to do it the justice it deserves[13]. Shall I wait for you, Tommy, or shall I phone Jeffrey?'

'Don't do that,' Lynley responded. 'Your father would never forgive you[14] for putting your future into the hands of Cambridge.'

She smiled. 'Very well. If you're off, then, let me fetch the bride and groom[15] to bid you farewell[16].'

His face altered swiftly[17]. 'No. Helen. I … just make[18] my excuses.'

A look passed between them[19], something said without being said[20]. 'You must see them, Tommy,' Lady Helen murmured. There was another pause, a

1. d'un ricanement

2. les temps sont rudes en effet

3. [course hippique – événement très mondain]

4. bien trop pris par

5. une planque sur un meurtre sanglant

6. franchement

7. ils sont en tenue de soirée

8. ne s'est pas améliorée

9. une insistance muette

10. de la part de

11. lui faire ce plaisir

12. ce n'est pas assez

13. pour la savourer

14. ne te pardonnerait jamais

15. je vais chercher les mariés

16. pour qu'ils te disent au revoir

17. changea brièvement

18. transmets-leur

19. Ils échangèrent un regard

20. un échange muet

compromise being sought. 'I'll tell them you're waiting in the study.' She left quickly, giving Lynley no chance to respond.

He uttered[1] something inaudible under his breath[2], following Lady Helen with his eyes as she wove back through[3] the crowd. 'Have you brought a car?' he asked Barbara suddenly and started down the hall, away from the celebration.

Nonplussed[4], she followed. 'A Mini. You're not exactly dressed for its splendour.'

'I'll adjust[5], I'm sure. Chameleon-like.[6] What colour is it?'

She was puzzled by the query[7], an ill-concealed[8] attempt to make conversation as they walked to the front of the house. 'Mostly rust[9], I'm afraid.'

'My favourite.' He held open a door and motioned her into[10] a darkroom.

'I'll just wait in the car, sir. I've left it—'

'Stay here, Sergeant.' It was a command[11].

Reluctantly, she preceded him. The curtains had been drawn; the only light came from the door which they had opened. But Barbara could see it was a man's room, richly panelled in dark oak[12] and filled with shelves of books[13], well-used furniture, and an atmosphere redolent of[14] comfortable old leather[15] and the fragrance of Scotch[16].

Lynley gravitated absently[17] to a wall that was covered with framed photographs[18] and stood there quietly, his eyes on a portrait that was central to the display[19]. It had been taken in a cemetery, and the man who was its subject bent to[20] touch the inscription on a tombstone whose carving[21] had long since been obliterated[22] by time. The skilful composition[23] of the piece[24] directed the viewer's eyes[25] not to the awkward leg brace[26] that distorted the man's posture but to the piercing interest that lit his gaunt face[27]. Studying the picture, Lynley seemed to have forgotten her presence.

1. marmonna
2. dans sa barbe
3. retraversait
4. Perplexe
5. Je m'adapterai
6. Tel le caméléon.
7. La question l'intrigua
8. évidente
9. rouille
10. lui fit signe d'entrer dans
11. un ordre
12. aux riches boiseries en chêne sombre
13. de rayonnages de livres
14. sentant
15. le vieux cuir
16. le whisky
17. se dirigea distraitement
18. photographies encadrées
19. placé au centre
20. se penchait pour
21. sur une pierre tombale dont la gravure
22. effacée
23. La composition maîtrisée
24. l'œuvre
25. orientait le regard du spectateur
26. l'embarrassante prothèse orthopédique
27. qui illuminait son visage hâve

The moment, Barbara decided, was probably as good as any to give him the news.

'I'm off the street[1],' she announced bluntly[2]. 'That's why I've come, if you're wondering.'

He turned slowly towards her. 'Back in CID?' he asked. 'Good for you, Barbara.'

'But not for you.'

'What do you mean?'

'Well, someone's got to tell you, since Webberly obviously hasn't. Congratulations: you're stuck with me[3].' She waited to see his look of surprise. When it was evident that none was forthcoming[4], she pushed on[5]. 'Of course, it's damned awkward[6] having me assigned to you[7] – don't think I don't know it. I can't figure out[8] *what* Webberly wants.' She was stumbling on[9], barely hearing her own words, uncertain whether she was trying to forestall[10] or provoke his inevitable reaction: the sharp[11] explosion of anger, the movement to the telephone to demand an explanation, or, worse, the icy[12] politeness that would last until[13] he got the superintendent behind closed doors[14].' All that I can think is that there's no one else available or that I've got some sort of wonderful latent[15] talent that only Webberly knows of. Or maybe it's a bit of a practical joke[16].' She laughed, a little too loudly.

'Or perhaps you're the best for the job[17],' Lynley finished. 'What do you know about the case?'

'I … nothing. Only that—'

'Tommy?' They swung around[18] at the sound of the voice, the single word spoken as if on a breath[19]. The bride[20] stood in the doorway, a spray[21] of flowers in one hand and others tucked[22] into the tumble of coppery[23] hair that fell round her shoulders and down her back. Backlit[24] from the hallway, she looked in her ivory dress as if she were surrounded entirely by a cloud, a Titian creation come to life[25]. 'Helen tells me you're leaving …?'

1. Je ne vais plus faire de patrouilles
2. sans prévenir
3. vous allez m'avoir sur le dos
4. qu'il n'en serait rien
5. insista
6. vraiment fâcheux
7. que je vous aie été affectée
8. Je ne vois pas
9. insistait péniblement
10. d'anticiper sur
11. brutale
12. glaciale
13. durerait le temps
14. qu'il prenne le chef à part
15. caché
16. juste une bonne blague
17. la plus qualifiée
18. se retournèrent
19. dans un souffle
20. La mariée
21. une gerbe
22. piquées
23. cuivrés
24. Éclairée de dos
25. un tableau vivant de Titien

Lynley appeared to have nothing to say. He felt[1] in his pockets, brought out a gold cigarette case[2], opened it, and then snapped it shut[3] with a flash of annoyance[4]. During this operation, the bride watched him, the flowers in her hand trembling momentarily.

'It's the Yard, Deb,' Lynley finally answered. 'I have to go.'

She watched him without speaking, fingering a pendant[5] she wore at her throat. Not until he met her eyes did she reply. 'What a disappointment for everyone. It's not an emergency, I hope. Simon told me last night that you might be reassigned[6] to the Ripper case.'

'No. Just a meeting.'

'Ah.' She looked as if she might say something more – indeed, she began to do so – but instead she turned to Barbara with a friendly smile. 'I'm Deborah St James.'

Lynley rubbed his forehead[7]. 'Lord, I *am* sorry[8].' Mechanically,[9] he completed the introduction[10]. 'Where's Simon?'

'He was right behind me, but I think Dad caught him. He's absolutely terrified to let us off on our own[11], certain I'll never take care of Simon well enough.' Her laughter bubbled up.[12] 'Perhaps I should have considered the problems of marrying a man my father is so inordinately fond of[13]. "The electrodes," he keeps lecturing me[14]. "You mustn't forget to see to[15] his leg every morning." I think he's told me that ten times today.'

'I imagine it was all you could do to keep him from going on the honeymoon[16] as well.'

'Well, of course, they've not been apart[17] for more than a day since …' She stopped suddenly, awkwardly[18]. Their eyes met. She bit the inside of her lip and an ugly flush stained her cheeks[19].

1. fouilla
2. étui à cigarettes
3. le referma d'un coup sec
4. l'air contrarié
5. pendentif
6. réaffecté
7. passa la main sur son front
8. je suis vraiment désolé
9. L'air absent,
10. acheva les présentations
11. de nous lâcher
12. Son rire s'éleva.
13. apprécie autant
14. me serine
15. t'occuper de
16. lune de miel
17. ils ne se sont pas quittés
18. gênée
19. une rougeur fâcheuse marqua ses joues

There was an immediate, anxious silence between them, the kind in which the most telling[1] sort of communication exists[2] in body language and tension in the air. It was finally – mercifully[3], Barbara decided – broken by the sound of slow, painfully uneven footsteps[4] in the hall, awkward harbinger of[5] Deborah's husband.

'I see that you've come to capture[6] Tommy.' St James paused in the doorway but continued to speak quietly, as was his habit, to direct attention away from his disability[7] and put others at ease[8] in his presence. 'That's a strange twist on tradition[9], Barbara. Time was when[10] the brides were kidnapped, not the best man[11].'

He was, Barbara decided, very much Hephaestus[12] to[13] Lynley's Apollo[14]. Aside from[15] his eyes, the satin blue of a highland[16] sky, and his hands, the sensitive tools of an artist, Simon Allcourt-St James was singularly unattractive. His hair was dark, unruly with curls[17], and haphazardly[18] cut in a way that did nothing to make it manageable[19]. His face was a combination of aquilinity and angles[20], harsh in repose[21], forbidding[22] in anger, yet vibrant with good nature[23] when softened by his smile. He was sapling thin[24], but not sapling sturdy[25], a man who had known too much pain and sorrow[26] at far too young an age.

Barbara smiled as he joined them, her first genuine[27] smile of the entire afternoon. 'But even best men are generally not kidnapped to New Scotland Yard. How are you, Simon?'

'Fine. Or so my father-in-law continues to tell me. Lucky as well. It seems he saw it all[28] from the beginning. He knew it directly the day of her birth. You've been introduced to Deborah?'

'Only just now.[29]'

'And we can keep you no longer?'

1. des plus éloquentes
2. se matérialise
3. par bonheur
4. des pas douloureusement irréguliers
5. signe qu'arrivait
6. enlever
7. pour détourner l'attention de son handicap
8. à l'aise
9. une drôle d'entorse aux traditions
10. Il fut un temps où
11. le témoin
12. Héphaïstos [dieu estropié et difforme]
13. comparé à
14. Apollon [le plus beau des dieux grecs]
15. Mis à part
16. d'Écosse
17. avec des boucles indomptables
18. n'importe comment
19. les rendre dociles
20. un tout aquilin et anguleux
21. dur au repos
22. menaçant
23. de bienveillance
24. mince comme un if
25. sans la résistance de l'if
26. de chagrin
27. vrai
28. qu'il avait tout prévu
29. À l'instant.

1. nous convoque à une réunion
2. dans peu de temps
3. au cas où
4. dit-il en fin de compte
5. Bizarre,
6. avec regret
7. Je ferais n'importe quoi
8. de débauché
9. qu'elle avait surgi
10. J'avais un discours tout prêt
11. une pluie de gypsophiles
12. Spirituelles
13. nulle pour
14. Vraiment pas dans mes cordes.
15. teckel
16. dans sa gueule
17. sac brodé de perles
18. chaussés de satin
19. l'offrande serait appréciée
20. Il remua la queue
21. d'une façon des plus amicales
22. l'objet dérobé

'Webberly's called a meeting[1],' Lynley put in. 'You know how that is.'

'How I do. Then, we won't ask you to stay. We're off ourselves in a very little while[2]. Helen has the address if anything should come up[3].'

'Don't give a thought to that.' Lynley paused as if he were not quite sure what to do next. 'My warmest congratulations, St James,' he settled on saying[4].

'Thank you,' the other man replied. He nodded to Barbara, touched his bride's shoulder lightly, and left the room.

How odd,[5] Barbara thought. They didn't even shake hands.

'Will you go to the Yard dressed like that?' Deborah asked Lynley.

He looked at his clothes ruefully[6]. 'Anything[7] to keep up my reputation as a rake[8].' They laughed together. It was a warm communication that died as suddenly as it had risen[9]. From it grew yet another little silence.

'Well,' Lynley began.

'I'd a speech all planned[10],' Deborah said quickly, looking down at her flowers. They trembled once again in her hand and a shower of baby's breath[11] fell to the floor. She raised her head. 'Something … it was just the kind of thing Helen might say. Talk about my childhood, Dad, this house. You know the sort of thing. Witty[12] and clever. But I'm absolutely pathetic at[13] that sort of thing. Quite out of my depth.[14] A hopeless incompetent.' She looked down again to see that a very small dachschund[15] had come into the study and carried in its jaws[16] a woman's sequined handbag[17]. The dog placed the bag at Deborah's satin-shod[18] feet, supremely confident that the offering had merit[19]. A tail wagged[20] in the friendliest fashion[21]. 'Oh, no! *Peach!*' Laughing, Deborah bent to retrieve the purloined article[22], but when she straightened, her green eyes glittered with tears[1]. 'Thank you, Tommy. For everything. Really. For it all.'

'The best[2], Deb,' he said lightly in reply. He went to her, hugged her quickly to him[3], and brushed a kiss against her hair[4].

And it came to Barbara[5], as she stood there watching, that for some reason St James had left the two of them together precisely so that Lynley could do just that.

1. brillaient de larmes

2. Tous mes vœux

3. la serra brièvement contre lui

4. effleura ses cheveux d'un baiser

5. Barbara comprit

3

The body had no head. That single, grisly detail[1] was the most prominent feature[2] of the police photographs that were being passed[3] among the three CID officers gathered at the circular table[4] in the Scotland Yard office.

Father Hart looked nervously from one face to the next, and he fingered the tiny silver rosary[5] in his pocket. It had been blessed[6] by Pius XII[7] in 1952. Not an individual audience, of course. One could never hope for that.[8] But certainly that trembling, numinous[9] hand making the sign of the cross[10] over two thousand reverential pilgrims[11] counted for a powerful sort of something[12]. Eyes closed, he'd held the rosary high above his head as if somehow[13] that would allow the Pope's blessing[14] to strike it more potently[15].

He was well on his way into the third decade[16] of the sorrowful mysteries[17] when the tall, blond man spoke.

' "What a blow was there given[18]," ' he murmured, and Father Hart looked his way.

Was he a policeman? Father Hart couldn't understand why the man was dressed so formally[19], but now, upon hearing[20] the words, he looked at him hopefully. 'Ah, Shakespeare[21]. Yes. Just the very thing[22] somehow.' The big man with the awful cig-

1. Ce simple détail, atroce
2. l'élément le plus frappant
3. circulaient
4. réunis autour de la table ronde
5. petit chapelet en argent
6. béni
7. Pie XII
8. Ce ne serait pas imaginable.
9. sainte
10. signe de croix
11. pèlerins recueillis
12. c'était bien quelque chose de puissant
13. d'une façon ou d'une autre
14. à la bénédiction du pape
15. de l'atteindre avec plus de force
16. allait entamer la troisième dizaine [sur son chapelet]
17. mystères douloureux
18. « Quel coup il a donné là ! »
19. en tenue de soirée
20. en entendant
21. [dans la Tempête]
22. C'est tout à fait ça

ar looked at him blankly[1]. Father Hart cleared his throat[2] and watched them continue to scrutinize the pictures.

He'd been with them for nearly a quarter of an hour and in that time barely[3] a word had been exchanged. A cigar had been lit by the older man, the woman had twice bitten off[4] something she'd intended to say, and nothing more had occurred until that line[5] from Shakespeare.

The woman tapped her fingers restlessly[6] on the top of the table. *She* at least was some sort of police person. Father Hart knew that by the uniform she wore. But she seemed so entirely unpleasant[7] with her tiny, shifting[8] eyes and her grim[9] little mouth. She would never do[10]. Not what he needed. Not what Roberta needed. What should he say?

The horrid photographs continued to be passed among them. Father Hart did not need to see them. He knew far too well[11] what they captured[12]. He'd been there first, and it was all so unspeakably engraved[13] on his mind. William Teys sprawled out on his side[14] – all six feet four of him[15] – in a ghastly[16], quasi-foetal position, right arm extended as if he'd been reaching for[17] something, left arm curled into[18] his stomach, knees drawn up halfway to his chest, and where the head had been … there was simply nothing. Like Cloten[19] himself. But no Imogen there to awaken in horror[20] by his side. Just Roberta. And those terrifying words: 'I did it. I'm not sorry.'

The head had rolled into a mound of sodden hay[21] in a corner of the stall[22]. And when he'd seen it … Oh God, the stealthy eyes of a barn rat[23] glittered[24] in the cavity – quite small, of course – but the quivering grey snout[25] was brilliant with blood and the tiny paws[26] dug! *Our Father, who art in heaven*[27] *… Our Father, who art in heaven … Oh, there's more, there's more and I can't remember it now!*

1. impassible
2. se racla la gorge
3. à peine
4. avait contenu à deux reprises
5. ce vers
6. impatiemment
7. si désagréable
8. fuyants
9. dure
10. ne conviendrait pas
11. ne savait que trop
12. ce qu'elles avaient immortalisé
13. gravé
14. gisant sur le côté
15. de tout son mètre quatre-vingt-quinze
16. effrayante
17. comme s'il avait voulu atteindre
18. replié sur
19. [personnage décapité dans Cymbeline, de Shakespeare]
20. pour s'éveiller, horrifiée
21. un tas de foin trempé
22. la stalle
23. les yeux furtifs d'un rat de grange
24. étincelaient
25. le museau gris frétillant
26. pattes
27. qui êtes aux cieux

'Father Hart.' The blond man in the morning coat had removed his reading spectacles[1] and had taken from his pocket a gold cigarette case. 'Do you smoke?'

'I … yes, thank you.' The priest snatched quickly at[2] the case so that the others might not see how his hand trembled. The man passed the case to the woman, who shook her head sharply in refusal[3]. A silver lighter[4] was produced. It all took a few moments, blessed time to allow him to gather together his fragmented thoughts[5].

The blond man relaxed in his chair and studied a long line of photographs that had been posted[6] on one of the walls of the office. 'Why did you go to the farm that day, Father Hart?' he asked quietly, his eyes moving from one picture to the next.

Father Hart squinted myopically[7] across the room. Were those pictures of suspects? he wondered hopefully. Had Scotland Yard seen fit[8] to begin pursuing this malevolent beast[9] already? He couldn't tell[10], wasn't even certain from this distance that the photographs were of people at all[11].

'It was Sunday,' he replied as if that would somehow say everything.

The blond man turned his head at that[12]. Surprisingly, his eyes were an engaging brown[13]. 'Were you in the habit[14] of going to Teys' farm on Sundays? For dinner or something?'

'Oh … I … excuse me, I thought the report, you see …' This would never do. Father Hart sucked eagerly at the[15] cigarette. He looked at his fingers. The nicotine stains[16] climbed past every joint[17]. No wonder[18] he'd been offered one. He shouldn't have forgotten his own, should have bought a packet back at King's Cross. But there was so very much then. … He puffed hungrily at the[19] tobacco.

'Father Hart?' the older man said. He was obviously the blond's superior. They'd all been intro-

1. lunettes
2. prit vivement
3. refusa sèchement de la tête
4. briquet
5. pour mettre de l'ordre dans ses pensées
6. affichées
7. plissa ses yeux myopes
8. jugé utile
9. cette bête malveillante
10. n'aurait su le dire
11. représentaient même des gens
12. à ces mots
13. d'un agréable marron
14. Aviez-vous l'habitude
15. pompa avec force sur sa
16. taches
17. atteignaient la deuxième phalange
18. Pas étonnant
19. Avec avidité, il tira une bouffée de

duced but he'd stupidly forgotten their names. The woman's he knew: Havers. Sergeant, by her garments[1]. But the other two had slipped his mind[2]. He gazed at their grave faces in mounting panic[3].

'I'm sorry. You asked ...?'

'Did you go to Teys' farm every Sunday?'

Father Hart made a determined effort[4] to think clearly, chronologically, systematically for once[5]. His fingers sought the rosary in his pocket. The cross dug into his thumb[6]. He could feel the tiny corpus stretched out in agony[7]. *Oh Lord, to die that way.* 'No,' he answered in a rush[8]. 'William is ... was our precentor[9]. Such a wonderful basso profundo[10]. He could make the church ring with sound[11] and I ...' Father Hart took a ragged breath[12] to put himself back on the track[13]. 'He'd not come to Mass[14] that morning, nor had Roberta[15]. I was concerned[16]. The Teys never miss Mass. So I went to the farm.'

The cigar smoker squinted at him through the pungent[17] smoke. 'Do you do that for all your parishioners? Must certainly keep them in line[18] if you do.'

Father Hart had smoked his cigarette down to[19] the filter. There was nothing for it but to stub it out[20]. The blond man did the same although his was not half-smoked[21]. He brought out the case and offered another. Again the silver lighter appeared; the flame caught, produced the smoke that seared his throat[22], soothed[23] his nerves, numbed his lungs[24].

'Well, it was mostly because Olivia was concerned.'

A glance at the report. 'Olivia Odell?'

Father Hart nodded eagerly[25]. 'She and William Teys, you see, had just become engaged[26]. The announcement was to be made at a small tea that afternoon. She'd rung him several times after Mass but got nothing. So she came to me.'

'Why didn't she go out there herself?'

1. vu sa tenue
2. lui échappaient
3. avec une angoisse grandissante
4. s'efforça
5. pour une fois
6. s'enfonça dans son pouce
7. le petit corps étiré dans son martyre
8. précipitamment
9. chef de chœur de la paroisse
10. voix de basse
11. résonner toute l'église
12. inspiration rauque
13. pour reprendre le fil
14. la messe
15. Roberta non plus
16. inquiet
17. âcre
18. Cela doit les discipliner
19. jusqu'au
20. qu'à l'écraser
21. n'était qu'à moitié consumée
22. lui brûlait la gorge
23. calmait
24. engourdissait ses poumons
25. hocha vivement la tête
26. venaient de se fiancer

'She wanted to, of course. But there was Bridie and the duck. He'd got lost somehow, the usual family crisis, and she couldn't be settled down[1] until he was recovered.'

The three others glanced at one another warily[2]. The priest reddened[3]. How *absurd* it all sounded! He plunged on. 'You see, Bridie is Olivia's little girl. She has a pet duck.

Well, not really a pet[4], not in the actual sense[5].' How could he explain all of it to them, all the twists and turns[6] of their village life? Even the predominantly Catholic persuasion of[7] the villagers was odd in an English village.

The blond man spoke, kindly. 'So while Olivia and Bridie were looking for the duck, you went out to the farm.'

'That's so exactly right. Thank you.' Father Hart smiled gratefully[8].

'Tell us what happened when you arrived.'

'I went to the house first, but no one was there. The door wasn't locked[9], and I remember thinking that was strange. William always locked everything tight as a drum[10] if he went out. He was peculiar that way[11]. Insisted I do the same with the church if I wasn't about[12]. Even when the choir practised[13] on Wednesdays, he never once left until every person was gone and I'd seen to the doors[14]. That's the way he was.'

'I imagine his unlocked house gave you a bit of a turn[15],' the blond man said.

'It did, really. Even at one o'clock in the afternoon. So, when I couldn't raise anyone with a knock' – he looked at them all apologetically – 'I suppose I walked right in[16].'

'Anything peculiar[17] inside?'

'Nothing at all. It was perfectly clean, as it always was. There was, however …' His eyes shifted to the window. How to explain?

1. ne pouvait se calmer
2. avec méfiance
3. rougit
4. animal de compagnie
5. au sens où on l'entend d'habitude
6. les spécificités
7. Même la majorité de catholiques chez
8. avec reconnaissance
9. fermée à clef
10. à double tour
11. maniaque avec ça
12. quand je n'y étais pas
13. lorsque la chorale répétait
14. que j'aie bien fermé les portes
15. vous a fait un choc
16. que je suis carrément entré
17. de bizarre

'Yes?'

'The candles had burned down.[1]'

'Have they no electricity?'

Father Hart looked at them earnestly[2]. 'These are votive candles[3]. They were always lit. Always. Twenty-four hours a day.'

'For a shrine[4], you mean?'

'Yes, that's exactly what it is. A shrine,' he agreed immediately and hurried on. 'When I saw that, I knew at once[5] something was wrong. Neither William nor Roberta would ever have let the candles go out[6]. So I went through the house. And from there, out to the barn.'

'And there ...?'

What was there really left to report? The chilling tranquillity[7] had told him at once. Outside, in the near pasture[8], the bleating of sheep[9] and the cry of birds spoke of sanity and peace[10]. But in the barn, the absolute quiet was the core of diablerie[11]. Even from the door, the rich cloying[12] smell of pooled blood[13] had reached him, over the mixed odours of manure[14] and grain and rotting hay[15]. It had drawn him forward with seductive, unavoidable hands[16].

Roberta had been sitting on an overturned pail[17] in one of the stalls[18], a big girl born of her father's stock[19], used to the labour of a farm. She was motionless[20], staring not at the headless monstrosity that lay at her feet but at the opposite wall and at the cracks that mapped its surface[21].

'Roberta?' he had called urgently. He felt sickness rising[22] from stomach to throat and his bowels loosening[23].

There was no response, not a breath, not a movement. Just the sight of her broad back, her sturdy legs curled beneath her, the axe[24] at her side. And then, over her shoulder, he'd seen the body clearly for the first time.

'I did it. I'm not sorry.' The only thing she'd said.

1. Les bougies s'étaient consumées.
2. gravement
3. des cierges
4. un autel
5. J'ai su tout de suite
6. s'éteindre
7. Le calme impressionnant
8. pré
9. bêlement des moutons
10. évoquaient la normalité et la paix
11. était la marque du diable
12. forte et écœurante
13. de la mare de sang
14. masquant les effluves de fumier
15. de foin pourrissant
16. d'une irrésistible attirance
17. un seau retourné
18. stalles
19. tenant de son père
20. immobile
21. les fissures qui le zébraient
22. avait senti la nausée monter
23. ses intestins se relâcher
24. hache

Father Hart squeezed his eyes shut[1] against the memory[2]. 'I went at once to the house and rang Gabriel.'

For a moment Lynley believed that the priest was talking about the archangel himself[3]. The odd little man did seem a bit in touch with other worlds[4] as he sat there painfully struggling through[5] his story.

'Gabriel?' Webberly asked incredulously[6]. Lynley could tell[7] that the super's patience was wearing thin[8]. He fingered through the report for some indication of the name and found it quickly enough.

'Gabriel Langston. Village constable[9],' he said. 'And I take it[10], Father, that Constable Langston phoned the Richmond police at once?'

The priest nodded. He looked warily at Lynley's cigarette case and the other man opened it and offered another round[11]. Havers refused and the priest was about to do so as well until Lynley took one himself. His throat felt raw[12], but he knew they'd never get to the end of the story unless the cleric was supplied with nicotine, and it appeared that he needed a companion in his vice[13]. Lynley swallowed uncomfortably, longed for a[14] whisky, lit up again, and let the cigarette burn itself to nothing[15] in the ashtray.

'Police came down from Richmond. It was all very quick. It was … they took Roberta.'

'Well, what could you expect? She admitted to the crime.[16]' Havers had spoken. She'd risen from her seat and wandered to the window. Her voice clearly informed them that in her opinion they were wasting[17] their time with this foolish old man[18], that they ought to be barrelling[19] towards the North at this very moment.

'Lots of people admit to crimes,' Webberly said, motioning her back to her seat[20]. 'I've had twenty-five confessions to the Ripper killings so far.'

1. ferma les yeux avec force
2. pour se protéger du souvenir
3. l'archange en personne
4. en contact avec d'autres mondes
5. à dévider
6. incrédule
7. voyait bien
8. le chef allait perdre patience
9. Le policier du village
10. je suppose
11. en offrit à nouveau
12. Il avait la gorge irritée
13. qu'il lui fallait un compagnon de débauche
14. eut des envies de
15. se consumer intégralement
16. Elle a reconnu avoir commis le crime.
17. perdaient
18. ce vieil idiot
19. qu'ils devraient être en train de foncer
20. en l'invitant à se rasseoir

'I just wanted to point out[1]—'

'That can come later.'

'Roberta didn't kill her father,' the priest went on as if the other two had not spoken. 'It's just not possible.'

'But family crimes happen,' Lynley said gently.

'Not when there's whiskers[2].'

To the priest's bizarre comment[3] – so obviously logical[4] and satisfactory to himself[5] – no one made a response. No one spoke at all or looked particularly at anyone else. There was a lengthy, unendurable[6] pause in the proceedings[7], broken by Webberly, who pushed away[8] from the table. '*Jesus*,' he muttered. 'I'm terribly sorry, but …' He stalked to a cabinet in a corner of the room and pulled out three bottles. 'Whisky, sherry, or brandy[9]?' he asked the others.

Lynley sent a prayer of thanksgiving to[10] Bacchus. 'Whisky,' he replied.

'Havers?'

'Nothing for me,' she said primly[11]. 'I'm on duty.[12]'

'Yes, of course. Father, what'll it be?'

'Oh, a sherry would be only too—'

'Sherry it is.[13]' Webberly tossed back[14] a small, neat whisky[15] before pouring again[16] and returning to the table.

They all stared meditatively[17] into their glasses, as if each wondered who'd be the first to ask the question[18]. Lynley finally did so, his throat newly soothed[19] by the fragrant[20] single malt[21]. 'Ah … whiskers?' he prompted.

Father Hart looked down at the papers spread out[22] on the table. 'Isn't it in the report?' he asked plaintively. 'About the dog?'

'Yes, it does mention the dog[23].'

'That was Whiskers,' the priest explained, and sanity was restored.

1. souligner
2. une barbe
3. remarque
4. à l'évidence si logique
5. pour lui
6. péniblement longue
7. déroulement de l'entretien
8. s'écarta
9. un cognac
10. rendit grâces à
11. d'un ton guindé
12. Je suis en service.
13. D'accord pour le xérès.
14. s'avala
15. un petit whisky sec
16. de s'en resservir un
17. d'un air méditatif
18. qui poserait la question en premier
19. apaisée
20. odorant
21. [whisky de qualité, produit dans une seule distillerie]
22. étalés
23. il y est bien question du chien

There was collective relief.[1] 'It was dead in the stall with Teys,' Lynley noted aloud.

'Yes, don't you see? That's why we all of us know Roberta's innocent. Aside from the fact that she was devoted to[2] her father, there's Whiskers to consider. She would *never* hurt Whiskers.' Father Hart eagerly sought out[3] the words to explain. 'He was a farm dog, part of the family since Roberta was five. He was retired[4], of course, a bit blind[5], but one just doesn't put down dogs like that[6]. Everyone in the village knew Whiskers. He was a bit of a pet to all of us. He'd wander down of an afternoon[7] to Nigel Parrish's house on the common[8], have a bit of a lie in the sun[9] whilst[10] Nigel played the organ[11] – he's our organist at church, you see. Or sometimes he'd have his tea[12] at Olivia's.'

'Got on[13] with the duck, did he?' Webberly asked, straight-faced[14].

'Oh, famously[15]!' Father Hart beamed[16]. 'Whiskers got on with us all. And when Roberta was out and about[17], he followed her everywhere. That's why, when they took Roberta, I had to do something. And here I am.'

'Yes, indeed, here you are,' Webberly concluded. 'You've been more than helpful[18], Father. I believe Inspector Lynley and Sergeant Havers have all that they need for now[19].' He got to his feet and opened the door of his office. 'Harriman?'

The Morse-like[20] tapping of word-processor keys[21] stopped. A chair scraped[22] on the floor. Webberly's secretary popped into the room.

Dorothea Harriman bore a modest resemblance[23] to the Princess of Wales, which she emphasized[24] to a disconcerting degree by tinting[25] her sculptured hair the approximate shade of sunlight on wheat[26] and refusing to wear her spectacles in the presence of anyone likely to comment upon the Spencerian shape[27] of her nose and chin. She was eager to

1. Le soulagement fut général.
2. adorait
3. s'évertua à trouver
4. à la retraite
5. aveugle
6. on n'abat pas un chien comme ça
7. les après-midi
8. terrain communal
9. pour s'étendre un peu au soleil
10. pendant que
11. de l'orgue
12. il prenait un goûter
13. Il s'entendait bien
14. gardant un air sérieux
15. à merveille
16. dit avec un sourire radieux
17. sortait
18. d'une aide précieuse
19. pour le moment
20. semblable à du morse
21. le bruit des touches du clavier
22. crissa
23. ressemblait légèrement
24. qu'elle accentuait
25. en teignant
26. d'une teinte proche du blé doré
27. ligne très lady Di

advance[1], swept up in her 'c'reer,' as she monosyllabically called it. She was intelligent enough to make a success of her job and would most likely do so, especially if she could bring herself to renounce her distracting manner of dress[2], which everyone referred to as Parody Princess. Today she was wearing what looked like a drop-waisted[3] pink ball gown[4] that had been shortened[5] for everyday wear[6]. It was utterly hideous.

'Yes, Superintendent?' she asked. In spite of threats[7] and imprecations, Harriman insisted upon calling every employee at the Yard by his or her full title.

Webberly turned to the priest. 'Are you staying in London, Father, or returning to Yorkshire?'

'I'm on the late train back.[8] Confessions were this afternoon, you see, and as I wasn't there I *did* promise to have them until eleven tonight.'

'Of course.' Webberly nodded. 'Call a cab[9] for Father Hart,' he told Harriman.

'Oh, but I haven't enough—'

Webberly held up a restraining hand. 'It's on the Yard[10], Father.'

On the Yard. The priest mouthed the words[11], coloured with pleasure[12] at the implication of brotherhood[13] and acceptance behind them[14]. He allowed[15] the superintendent's secretary to shepherd him from[16] the room.

'What do you drink when you *do* drink, Sergeant Havers?' Webberly asked when Father Hart had gone.

'Tonic water, sir,' she replied.

'Right,' he muttered and opened the door again. 'Harriman,' he barked[17], 'find a bottle of Schweppes for Sergeant Havers. ... Don't pretend[18] you haven't the slightest idea[19] where to get one. Just *get* one.'

1. monter en grade
2. à son look déconcertant
3. à taille basse
4. robe de soirée
5. raccourcie
6. pour être portée tous les jours
7. Malgré les menaces
8. Je rentre par le dernier train.
9. taxi
10. aux frais de Scotland Yard
11. répéta ces mots en silence
12. rose de plaisir
13. à l'idée de la fraternité
14. qu'ils recélaient
15. laissa
16. l'escorter hors de
17. aboya-t-il
18. Ne faites pas comme si
19. vous ne saviez pas

He slammed the door, went to the cabinet, and brought out the bottle of whisky.

Lynley rubbed his forehead and pressed tightly at his temples[1]. 'God, what a headache[2],' he murmured. 'Has either of you any aspirin?'

'I have,' Havers replied crisply[3] and rooted through her handbag for[4] a small tin. She tossed it across[5] the table to him. 'Take as many as you like, Inspector.'

Webberly regarded them both thoughtfully[6]. He wondered, not for the first time, if this partnership of two such antipodal personalities[7] had even the ghost[8] of a chance for success. Havers was like a hedgehog[9], curling herself into a protective ball of thistle[10] at the least provocation. Yet underneath that prickly exterior of hers was a fine, probing[11] mind. What was left to question was[12] whether Thomas Lynley was the right combination of patience and congeniality[13] to encourage that mind to overcome[14] the wrangling of the termagant personality[15] that had made it impossible for[16] Havers to work in successful partnership with anyone else.

'Sorry to take you out of the wedding, Lynley, but there was no other way. This is the second run-in[17] Nies and Kerridge have had up North. The first one was a disaster: Nies was right all along, and crisis ensued[18]. I thought' – he fingered the rim[19] of his glass and chose his words carefully – 'that your presence might serve to remind[20] Nies that he can sometimes be wrong[21].'

Webberly watched carefully for a reaction from the younger man – a stiffening[22] of muscles, a movement of the head, a flicker behind the eyelids[23]. But there was nothing to betray him. It was no particular secret among his superior officers at the Yard that Lynley's single run-in with Nies nearly five years before in Richmond had resulted in his own arrest. And, however premature and ultimate-

1. appuya sur ses tempes
2. quelle migraine
3. d'un ton brusque
4. repêcha au fond de son sac
5. la lança à l'autre bout de
6. l'air pensif
7. des personnalités aussi opposées
8. ne serait-ce que l'ombre
9. hérisson
10. se roulant en une boule de piquants protectrice
11. pénétrant
12. Restait à savoir
13. de sympathie
14. à surmonter
15. la hargne
16. avait empêché
17. prise de bec
18. une crise en a résulté
19. le bord
20. contribuerait peut-être à rappeler à
21. avoir tort
22. une contraction
23. un éclair dans le regard

ly spurious[1] that arrest had been, it was the only black mark[2] on an otherwise admirable record of service[3], a denigration that Lynley would have to live with[4] for the rest of his career.

'It's fine, sir,' Lynley replied easily. 'I understand.'

A knock on the door announced Miss Harriman's successful quest for the[5] Schweppes, which she placed triumphantly on the table in front of Sergeant Havers. She glanced at the clock. Its hands were nearing six.

'As this isn't a regularly scheduled workday[6], Superintendent,' she began, 'I thought I might—'

'Yes, yes, go on home[7].' Webberly waved[8].

'Oh, no, it isn't that at all,' Harriman said sweetly[9]. 'But I think in Regulation[10] Sixty-five-A regarding compensatory time[11] ...'

'Take Monday and I'll break your arm, Harriman,' Webberly said with equivalent sweetness. 'Not in the middle of this Ripper business.'

'Wouldn't think of it[12], sir. Shall I just put it on the slate[13]? Regulation Sixty-five-C indicates that—'

'Put it *anywhere*, Harriman.'

She smiled understandingly[14] at him. 'Absolutely, Superintendent.' The door closed behind her.

'Did that vixen wink at you[15] as she left the room, Lynley?' Webberly demanded.

'I didn't notice, sir.'

It was half-past eight when they began gathering together the papers from the table in Webberly's office. Darkness had fallen and the fluorescent lighting[16] did nothing to hide the room's genial air of disarray[17]. If anything, it was worse[18] now than it had been before, with the additional[19] files from the North spread out on the table and an acrid cirrus[20] of cigarette and cigar smoke that, in conjunction with the mixed scents[21] of whisky and sherry,

1. finalement sans fondement
2. la seule tache
3. dans des états de service par ailleurs admirables
4. devrait assumer
5. que Miss Harriman avait trouvé du
6. un jour habituellement travaillé
7. rentrez chez vous
8. autorisa d'un geste
9. d'une voix doucereuse
10. le règlement
11. les heures de récupération
12. Naturellement
13. le porter à mon crédit d'heures
14. avec bienveillance
15. Cette diablesse vous a-t-elle fait un clin d'oeil
16. l'éclairage au néon
17. le joyeux désordre de la pièce
18. C'était même pire
19. supplémentaires
20. un nuage âcre
21. joint aux odeurs

produced the effect of being in a rather down-at-heel[1] gentlemen's club.

Barbara noticed the deep lines of exhaustion that were drawn on Lynley's face and judged that the aspirin had done him little good[2]. He had gone to the wall of Ripper photographs and was inspecting them, moving from one to the next. As she watched, he lifted a hand to one of them – it was the King's Cross victim, she noted needlessly[3] – and traced a finger along[4] the crude incision[5] that the Ripper's knife had made.

' "Death closes all[6]," ' he murmured. 'He's black and white, flesh with no resilience[7]. Who could ever recognize a living man from this?'

'Or from this, for that matter[8],' Webberly responded. He brusquely gestured to the photographs that Father Hart had brought.

Lynley rejoined them. He stood near Barbara but was, she well knew, oblivious of her. She watched the expressions pass quickly across his face as he sorted through the photographs one last time: revulsion, disbelief, pity[9]. His features[10] were so easy to read that she wondered how he ever managed to conduct a successful investigation[11] without giving everything away to[12] a suspect. But he did it all the time. She knew his record of success[13], the string of follow-up convictions[14]. He was the golden boy in more ways than one[15].

'We'll head up there[16] in the morning, then,' he said to the superintendent. He picked up a manila envelope and tucked all the materials inside[17].

Webberly was examining a railway timetable[18] which he had unearthed from the jumble[19] on his desk. 'Take the eight forty-five.'

Lynley groaned. 'Have a bit of mercy[20], sir. I'd like at least the next ten hours to get rid of this migraine.'

1. un peu miteux
2. n'avait guère agi
3. inutilement
4. suivit du doigt
5. l'incision grossière
6. [citation de Tennyson]
7. de la chair sans consistance
8. d'ailleurs
9. de l'incrédulité, de la pitié
10. Ses traits
11. de mener à bien une enquête
12. sans trahir ses émotions devant
13. tableau d'honneur
14. la kyrielle de condamnations qui avaient pu s'ensuivre
15. à plus d'un titre
16. On partira là-bas
17. glissa tous les documents dedans
18. un horaire des trains
19. extrait du fouillis
20. pitié

'Then, the nine-thirty. And no later than that.' Webberly glanced round his office one last time as he shrugged into[1] a tweed overcoat[2]. Like his other clothing, it was becoming threadbare in spots[3], and a small patch[4] was worked poorly into[5] the left lapel[6] where, no doubt, cigar ash[7] had done its worst[8]. 'Report in on Tuesday[9],' he said as he left.

The superintendent's absence seemed to rejuvenate Lynley at once, Barbara noted, for he moved with amazing alacrity of spirit[10] to the telephone the moment[11] the man was gone. He dialled a number, tapped his fingers rhythmically against the desk top, and peered at the face[12] of the clock. After nearly a minute, his face lit with a smile[13].

'You *did* wait, old duck[14],' he said into the phone. 'Have you broken it off[15] with Jeffrey Cusick at last? … Ha! I knew it, Helen. I've told you repeatedly[16] that a barrister[17] can't possibly make you happy. Did the reception end well? … He *did*? Oh Lord, what a scene that must have been. Has Andrew ever cried in his life? … Poor St James. Was he absolutely slain with mortification[18]? … Well, it's the champagne does it, you know. Did Sidney recover?[19] … Yes, well, she did look for a while as if she'd get a bit maudlin[20] at the end. She's never made a secret of it[21] that Simon's her favourite brother. … Of course dancing's still on[22]. We promised ourselves, didn't we? … Can you give me, say, an hour or so? … Hmm, *what* was that? … Helen! My God, what a naughty little girl!' He laughed and dropped the phone back on to its cradle[23]. 'Still here, Sergeant?' he asked when he turned from the desk.

'You've no car, sir,' she replied stonily[24]. 'I thought I'd wait to see if you needed a ride home[25].'

'That's awfully good[26] of you, but we've all been kept here long enough for one evening, and I'm sure you've far better things to do[27] on a Saturday night

1. en enfilant
2. pardessus
3. il s'élimait par endroits
4. une pièce de tissu
5. rapiéçait
6. le revers gauche
7. cendre
8. sévi
9. Faites-moi un rapport mardi
10. empressement
11. dès que
12. regarda le cadran
13. s'éclaira d'un sourire
14. ma vieille
15. rompu
16. mille fois
17. avocat
18. mort de honte
19. Est-ce que Sidney s'est remise ?
20. comme si elle allait verser une larme
21. Elle n'a jamais caché
22. qu'on peut encore aller danser
23. reposa le combiné sur son support
24. froidement
25. s'il fallait que je vous ramène
26. très gentil à vous
27. bien mieux à faire

than see me home. I'll take a cab.' He bent over Webberly's desk for a moment, writing quickly on a piece of paper. 'This is my address,' he said, handing it to her. 'Be there at seven tomorrow morning, will you?[1] That should give us some time to make more sense of all this[2] before we head to Yorkshire. Good evening, then.' He left the room.

Barbara looked down at the paper in her hand, at the handwriting which even in a hurry still managed to be an elegant scrawl[3]. She studied it for more than a minute before she ripped it into tiny pieces[4] and tossed them into the rubbish[5]. She knew quite well[6] where Thomas Lynley lived.

The guilt began[7] on the Uxbridge Road. It always did. Tonight it was worse when she saw that the travel agency[8] was closed, preventing her from gathering the material[9] on Greece as she'd promised. Empress Tours. Where had they ever come up with[10] a name like that for such a grubby[11] little shop where people sat behind plastic-topped[12] desks that were painted to look as if they were wood? She slowed the car, peering through the dirty wind-screen[13] to look for signs of life. The owners[14] lived above the shop. Perhaps if she banged on[15] the door a bit, she could rouse them[16]. No, it was too ridiculous. Mum was no more going to Greece than to the moon; she'd just have to wait for the brochures a bit longer.

Still, she'd passed at least a dozen agencies in the city today. Why hadn't she stopped? What else[17] did Mum have to live for[18] but[19] those silly little dreams? Overcome with[20] the need to compensate in some way for her failure[21], Barbara pulled the car over in front of Patel's Grocery[22], a ramshackle affair[23] of green paint, rusting shelves, and precariously stacked crates[24] from which emanated that peculiar blend of odours[25] that comes from vegetables not quite as fresh as they ought to be. Patel was

1. s'il vous plaît.
2. d'y voir un peu plus clair
3. un élégant gribouillage
4. avant de le déchirer en mille morceaux
5. de les jeter à la poubelle
6. parfaitement
7. Le sentiment de culpabilité survint
8. agence de voyages
9. documentation
10. D'où sortaient-ils
11. aussi sordide
12. recouverts de plastique
13. pare-brise
14. propriétaires
15. cognait à
16. attirer leur attention
17. À quoi d'autre
18. se raccrocher
19. à part
20. Accablée par
21. son manquement
22. épicerie
23. une boutique délabrée
24. des cageots en équilibre instable
25. cette étrange odeur composite

still open, at least. Leave it to him[1] never to miss a chance to make ten pence.

'Barbara!' He greeted her from inside the shop as she bent over the boxed fall fruit[2] on the pavement outside. Mostly apples. A few late[3] peaches shipped in from[4] Spain. 'Whassa doin' out so late?[5]'

He couldn't imagine her having a date[6], of course. No one could. She couldn't herself. 'Had to work late, Mr Patel,' she replied. 'How much for the peaches?'

'Eighty-five a pound, but for you, Pretty Face, we say eighty.'

She picked out[7] six. He weighed them[8], wrapped them[9], and handed them over. 'I was seeing your father today.'

She looked up quickly and caught the guard dropping over Mr Patel's dark face[10] like a mask when he saw her expression. 'Was he behaving himself?[11]' she asked casually, shouldering[12] her handbag.

'My goodness, yes. He *always* behaves!' Mr Patel took her money, counted it twice carefully, and dropped it into his register[13]. 'You take care now, Barbara. Men see a nice girl like you and—'

'Yes, I'll take care,' Barbara interrupted. She tossed the peaches on to the front seat of the car. *Nice girl like you, Barb. You take care. Keep those legs crossed.*[14] *Virtue like yours is definitely easy to lose, and a woman fallen*[15] *is fallen for ever.* She laughed bitterly, jerked the car into gear[16], and pulled out on to the road.

In Acton there were two potential areas of residence, simply called by inhabitants[17] the right and wrong streets. It was as if a dividing line split[18] the suburb arbitrarily, condemning one set of residents while it elevated others[19].

In the right streets of Acton, pristine[20] brick houses boasted woodwork[21] which always sparkled[22] admirably in the morning sun in a multiplicity of

1. On pouvait compter sur lui
2. cageots de fruits [issus d'arbres fruitiers]
3. tardives
4. importées d'
5. Vous faites quoi dehors à c't'heure-ci ?
6. un rendez-vous galant
7. en choisit
8. les pesa
9. les emballa
10. vit le visage de M. Patel se refermer
11. Il a été sage ?
12. en remettant à l'épaule
13. sa caisse-enregistreuse
14. Reste les jambes bien croisées.
15. une femme déchue
16. démarra brutalement
17. les habitants
18. une ligne de démarcation divisait
19. tout en mettant les autres à l'honneur
20. d'impeccables
21. étalaient leurs boiseries
22. reluisaient

1. des jardinières suspendues
2. des trottoirs propres
3. ornait les toits à pignon
4. de dômes en
5. ormes
6. se promenaient
7. de querelle
8. ni de combats de rue
9. absolue
10. voguait paisiblement
11. à moins d'une rue de là
12. qu'il y avait de l'animation du mauvais côté d'Acton
13. était descendue
14. avait mis en pagaille
15. un peu délingué
16. ne se donnait du mal avec
17. sombraient tristement
18. fleuris autrefois
19. totalement
20. laissés à l'abandon
21. à des jeux bruyants
22. pour que cesse le tapage
23. ébranlait
24. disjointes
25. qui s'infiltrait par les toits
26. il n'y avait plus d'espoir
27. Il n'y avait ni jardin ni clôture devant
28. une parcelle dure comme du béton

colours. Roses grew in abundance there. Fuchsias flourished in hanging pots[1]. Children played games on unlittered pavements[2] and in patchwork gardens. Snow kissed gabled roofs[3] in peaks of[4] meringue in the winter, while in summer tall elms[5] made green tunnels through which families strolled[6] in the perfumed evening light. There was never an argument[7] in the right streets of Acton, never loud music, the smell of cooking fish, or fists raised in a fight[8]. It was sheer[9] perfection, the single ocean on which every family's boat of dreams sailed placidly forward[10]. But things were much different as close as a single street away[11].

People liked to say that the wrong streets of Acton got the heat of the day[12] and that's why things were so different there. It was as if an enormous hand had swept down[13] from the sky and jumbled up[14] houses and avenues and people so that everything was always just a bit out of sorts[15]. No one worked quite so hard on[16] appearances: houses sagged moodily into decay[17]. Gardens once planted[18] were soon ignored, then forgotten altogether[19] and left to fend for themselves[20]. Children played noisily on the dirty pavements, disruptive games[21] that frequently brought mothers to doorways, shrieking for peace from the din[22]. The winter wind spat through[23] poorly sealed[24] windows and summer brought rain that leaked through the roofs[25]. People in the wrong streets didn't think much about being anywhere else, for to think of being elsewhere was to think of hope. And hope was dead[26] in the wrong part of Acton.

Barbara drove there now, turning the Mini in on a street lined with cars that were rusting like her own. Neither garden nor fence fronted[27] her own house but, rather, a pavement-hard patch of dirt[28] on which she parked her little car.

Next door, Mrs Gustafson was watching BBC1. Since she was nearly deaf[1], the entire neighbourhood was nightly regaled[2] with the doings of[3] her favourite television heroes. Across the street, the Kirbys were engaging in their usual pre-intercourse argument[4] while their four children ignored them as best they could by throwing dirt clods[5] at an indifferent cat that watched from a nearby first-floor window-sill[6].

Barbara sighed, groped for her front-door key, and went into her house. It was chicken and peas[7]. She could smell it at once, like a gust of foul breath[8].

'That you, lovey?' her mother's voice called. 'Bit late, aren't you, dear? Out with some friends?'

What a laugh! 'Working, Mum. I'm back on CID.'

Her mother shuffled to the door of the sitting-room. Like Barbara, she was short, but terribly thin, as if a long illness had ravaged her body and taken it sinew by sinew[9] on a march towards the grave[10]. 'CID?' she asked, her voice growing querulous[11]. 'Oh, must you, Barbara? You know how I feel about that, my lovey.' As she spoke, she raised a skeletal hand to her thin hair in a characteristic nervous gesture. Her overlarge eyes were puffy and rimmed with red[12], as if she had spent the day weeping[13].

'Brought you some peaches,' Barbara responded, gesturing with the bag. 'The travel agent was closed, I'm afraid. I even banged on the door to get them down from above, but they must've gone out.'

Diverted[14] from the thought of CID, Mrs Havers' face changed, lighting with a dusty glow[15]. She caught at the fabric[16] of her shabby housedress[17] and held it bunched[18] in one hand, as if containing excitement. 'Oh, that doesn't matter at all. *Wait* till you see. Go in the kitchen and I'll be right there. Your dinner's still warm.'

1. presque sourde
2. tout le voisinage profitait chaque soir
3. de ce qui arrivait à
4. rituelle scène de ménage avant ébats
5. des mottes de terre
6. rebord de fenêtre
7. poulet aux petits pois
8. une bouffée de mauvaise haleine
9. sapé ses forces
10. pour la mener vers sa tombe
11. geignarde
12. bouffis et ourlés de rouge
13. à pleurer
14. Distraite
15. d'une lueur cendrée
16. agrippa le tissu
17. sa robe d'intérieur usée
18. serré

Barbara walked past the sitting-room, wincing at the chatter[1] of the television and the fusty smell[2] of a chamber too long kept closed. The kitchen, fetid with the odour of[3] tough broiled chicken[4] and anaemic peas, was little better. She looked gloomily at the plate on the table, touched her finger[5] to the withered flesh of the fowl[6]. It was stone cold[7], as slippery and puckered[8] as something kept preserved in formaldehyde[9] for forensic examination. Fat had congealed[10] round its edges, and a single rancid dab of butter[11] had failed to melt[12] on peas that looked as if they had had their last warming in a former decade[13].

Wonderful, she thought. Could the 'lovely crab salad' have even come close to[14] this epicurean splendour? She looked for the daily paper[15] and found it, as always, on the seat of one of the wobbly[16] kitchen chairs. She grabbed the front section, opened it to the middle, and deposited her dinner on the smiling face of the Duchess of Kent.

'Lovey, you've not thrown away[17] your nice dinner!'

Damn! Barbara turned to see her mother's stricken[18] face, lips working in rejection, lines drawn in deep grooves[19] down to her chin[20], pale blue eyes filled with tears. She clutched[21] an artificial leather[22] album to her bony chest[23].

'Caught me[24], Mum.' Barbara forced a smile, putting an arm round the woman's bird-like[25] shoulders and leading her to the table. 'I had a bite[26] at the Yard, so I wasn't hungry. Should I have saved it for you or Dad?'

Mrs Havers blinked quickly. The relief on her face was pathetic. 'I … I suppose not. No, of course not. We wouldn't want chicken and peas two nights in a row[27], would we?' She laughed gently and laid[28] her album on the table. 'Dad got me Greece,' she announced.

1. se crispant au vacarme
2. à l'odeur de renfermé
3. empestant
4. le poulet trop grillé
5. tâta du doigt
6. la volaille desséchée
7. gelé
8. aussi glissante et fripée
9. conservé dans le formol
10. Le gras avait figé
11. une seule noix de beurre rance
12. n'avait pas fondu
13. dix ans auparavant
14. espérer rivaliser avec
15. journal du jour
16. bancales
17. jeté
18. atterré
19. un faisceau de rides
20. jusqu'au menton
21. étreignait
22. en faux cuir
23. contre sa poitrine osseuse
24. Tu me prends la main dans le sac
25. trop frêles
26. mangé un morceau
27. deux soirs de suite
28. posa

'Did he?' *So that's what he was doing out of the cage.* 'All by himself?[1]' Barbara asked casually.

Her mother looked away[2], fingering the edges of her album, picking nervously at[3] the artificial gold leaf[4]. She gave a sudden movement, a quick, brilliant smile, and pulled out a chair. 'Sit here, lovey, let me show you how we went.'

The album was opened. Previous trips[5] through Italy, France, Turkey – now, there[6] was a bizarre one – and Peru were flipped through[7] quickly until they arrived at the newest section[8], devoted[9] to Greece.

'Now, here's the hotel we stayed at in Corfu. Do you see how it's just right there on the bay? We could have gone down to Kanoni to a newer one, but I liked the view, didn't you, lovey?'

Barbara's eyes smarted.[10] She refused to submit. *How long will it take? Will it never end?*

'You've not answered me, Barbara.' Her mother's voice quivered with anxiety[11]. 'I did work so hard on the trip all today. Having the view was better than the new hotel in Kanoni, wasn't it, lovey?'

'Much better, Mum.' Barbara forced the words out[12] and got to her feet[13]. 'I've got a case tomorrow. Can we do Greece later?' Would she understand?

'What sort of case?'

'It's a ... bit of a problem with a family in Yorkshire. I'll be gone[14] a few days. Can you manage, do you think, or shall I ask Mrs Gustafson to come and stay?' Wonderful thought, the deaf leading the mad[15].

'Mrs Gustafson?' Her mother closed the album and drew herself stiffly upright[16]. 'I think not, my lovey. Dad and I can manage on our own[17]. We always have, you know. Except that short time when Tony ...'

The room was unbearably, stiflingly hot.[18] Oh God, Barbara thought, just a wisp of air[19]. Just this

1. Tout seul ?
2. détourna le regard
3. tiraillant nerveusement
4. feuille d'or
5. De précédents voyages
6. en voilà un qui
7. furent passés
8. la partie la plus récente
9. consacrée
10. Les larmes vinrent aux yeux de Barbara.
11. trembla d'inquiétude
12. parvint à articuler
13. se leva
14. Je serai absente
15. les sourds en charge des fous
16. se redressa
17. on peut se débrouiller seuls
18. La chaleur de la pièce était intenable, étouffante.
19. une bouffée d'air

once. For a moment. She went to the back door, which led out to the weed-choked[1] garden.

'Where're you going?' her mother asked quickly, that familiar note of hysteria creeping into her voice[2]. 'There's nothing out there! You mustn't go outside after dark!'

Barbara picked up the discarded chicken dinner[3]. 'Rubbish[4], Mum. I won't be a moment. You can wait by[5] the door and see I'm all right.'

'But I.... By the door?'

'If you like.'

'No, I mustn't be by the door. We'll leave it open just a bit, though. You can shout if you need me.'

'That sounds the plan[6], Mum.' She picked up the package and went hurriedly out[7] into the night.

A few minutes. She breathed the cool air, listened to the familiar neighbourhood sounds, and felt in her pocket for[8] a crumpled[9] packet of Players. She shook one out[10], lit it, and gazed up at the sky.

What had started the seductive descent into madness[11]? It was Tony, of course. Bright, freckle-faced imp.[12] Fresh spring air in the constant darkness of winter. *Watchme, watchme, Barbie! I can do anything!* Chemistry sets[13] and rugger balls[14]. Cricket on the common and tag[15] in the afternoon. And horribly, stupidly chasing a ball[16] right on to the Uxbridge Road.

But he didn't die from that. Just a stay in hospital. A persistent fever, a peculiar rash[17]. And a lingering, etiolating kiss[18] from leukaemia[19]. The wonderful, delicious irony of it all: go in with a broken leg, come out with leukaemia.

It had taken him four agonizing years to die. Four years for them to make this descent into madness.

'Lovey?' The voice was tremulous.

'Right here, Mum. Just looking at the sky.' Barbara crushed[20] her cigarette out on the rock-hard ground[21] and walked back inside.

1. asphyxié par les mauvaises herbes
2. perceptible dans son ton
3. le dîner qu'elle avait jeté
4. Je vais aux poubelles
5. près de
6. Faisons comme ça
7. sortit précipitamment
8. chercha dans sa poche
9. froissé
10. en fit sortir une
11. cette descente insidieuse dans la folie
12. Ce lutin malin, avec ses taches de rousseur.
13. Les coffrets de chimiste
14. les ballons de rugby
15. jouer à chat
16. courant bêtement après un ballon
17. une étrange rougeur
18. la longue étreinte anémiante
19. la leucémie
20. écrasa
21. le sol dur comme de la pierre

4

Deborah St James braked the car to a halt[1] on a breath of laughter[2] and turned to her husband. 'Simon, have you never been told you're quite the world's worst navigator[3]?'

He smiled and closed the road atlas[4]. 'Never once.[5] But have a heart[6]. Consider the fog.[7]'

She looked through the windscreen at the large, dark building that loomed[8] in front of them. 'Poor excuse for not being able to[9] read a road map, if you ask me. Are we at the right place? It doesn't look as if a soul's waited up for us[10].'

'I shouldn't be surprised. I told them we'd arrive at nine and now it's …' He peered at his watch in the weak interior light of the car. 'Good God, it's half-past eleven.' She heard the laughter in his voice. 'Are you for it[11], my love? Shall we spend our wedding night[12] in the car?'

'Teenagers grappling hotly[13] in the back seat, do you mean?' She tossed her long hair back with a shake of her head. 'Hmm, it is a thought[14]. But I'm afraid in that case you should have hired[15] something larger than an Escort. No, Simon, there's nothing for it, I'm afraid, but[16] banging on the doors and rousing someone. But *you* shall make all our excuses.' She stepped out into the chilly night air, taking a moment to study the building before her.

1. stoppa la voiture
2. prise de rire
3. copilote
4. la carte routière
5. Jamais.
6. un peu d'indulgence
7. Regarde ce brouillard.
8. se dressait
9. Un peu court, pour expliquer qu'on ne sait pas
10. On dirait que plus personne ne nous attend
11. Qu'en dis-tu
12. nuit de noce
13. Comme des ados qui se pelotent
14. c'est une idée
15. aurais dû louer
16. désolée, il va falloir

It was a pre-Elizabethan[1] structure by initial design[2], but one which had undergone a number of Jacobean changes[3] that added to its air of rakish whimsicality[4]. Mullioned[5] windows winked[6] in the moonlight that filtered through the wispy[7] fog which had settled on the moors[8] and was now drifting down into the dales[9]. Walls were covered with Virginia creeper[10], its leaves burning the old stone to rich russet[11]. Chimneys germinated upon[12] the roof in a helter-skelter pattern[13] of capricious warts[14] against the night sky. There was a contumacy[15] about the building that denied the very existence of the twentieth century, and this quality spread to the grounds[16] that surrounded it.

Here enormous English oaks[17] stretched out their branches over lawns where statuary[18], encircled by flowers, interrupted the flow of the land[19]. Pathways meandered into[20] the woods beyond the house with a beckoning siren charm[21]. In the absolute stillness[22], the play of water from a fountain nearby and the cry of a lamb[23] from a distant farm were the only auditory concomitants[24] to the whisper of the breeze that soughed through[25] the night. They might have been Richard and Anne[26], home to Middleham[27] at last.

Deborah turned back to the car. Her husband had opened his door and was watching her, waiting in his usual patient fashion for her photographer's reaction to the beauty of the place. 'It's wonderful,' she said. 'Thank you, my love.'

He lifted his braced[28] left leg from the car, dropped it with a thump[29] on to the drive, and extended his hand. With a practised movement[30], Deborah helped him to his feet. 'I feel as if we've been going round in circles for hours,' St James remarked, stretching.

1. [donc avant 1558]
2. à l'origine
3. subi des changements sous Jacques Ier [début XVIIe s.]
4. fantasque et désinvolte
5. à meneaux
6. scintillaient
7. épars
8. sur la lande
9. descendait dans les vallons
10. de vigne vierge
11. d'un somptueux brun roux
12. hérissaient
13. en débandade
14. comme des verrues capricieuses
15. une insubordination
16. au parc
17. chênes
18. des statues
19. émaillaient le terrain
20. Des sentiers serpentaient vers
21. un charme de sirène
22. calme
23. agneau
24. contributions sonores
25. au chuchotement de la brise de
26. [Richard III et sa femme]
27. [château du Yorkshire]
28. appareillée
29. bruit sourd
30. D'un geste expérimenté

'That's because we *have*,' she teased[1]. ' "Just two hours from the station, Deborah. A *wonderful* drive." '

He laughed softly. 'Well, it was, love. Admit it.'

'Absolutely. The third time I saw Rievaulx Abbey, I was positively enchanted.' She glanced at the forbidding[2] oak door before them. 'Shall we try it, then?'

They crunched across the gravel drive[3] to the dark recess[4] into which the door was set. A pitted wooden bench[5] was tipped drunkenly[6] against the wall next to it, and two enormous urns stood on either side. With the perversity of plants, one urn held a burgeoning beauty of flowers[7] while the other was home to[8] a withering colony of geraniums[9] whose dried leaves fluttered[10] raspingly[11] to the ground as Deborah and her husband passed.

St James applied some considerable strength to the large brass fixture[12] that hung in the centre of the door. Silence greeted its fading echoes. 'There's a bell as well,' Deborah noticed. 'Have a go with that.'

The ringing far back in the deepest reaches[13] of the house immediately roused what sounded like an entire pack of hounds[14] into furious howling[15]. 'Well, that's certainly done it,' St James laughed.

'Dammit[16], Casper! Jason! S'only the bell, you devils!' Pitched very much like a man's[17] but with the unmistakable cadence of a country woman born and bred[18], a raucous[19] voice shouted brisk reprovals[20] behind the door. 'Down with you![21] Out! Get back t' the kitchen.' A pause, followed by some desperate scuffling[22]. 'No, blast you! Out in the back! Why[23], you blackguard fiends[24]! Give me my slips[25]! Damn your eyes!' With that, a bolt shrieked back[26] from the inside of the door, which was pulled briskly open. A barefooted[27] woman hopped back and forth[28] on the icy stones of the entry, her frizzy grey hair flying about her shoulders in bursts of

1. dit-elle, pour le taquiner
2. imposante
3. prirent l'allée de gravier
4. renfoncement
5. Un banc en bois vermoulu
6. complètement de travers
7. de belles fleurs bourgeonnantes
8. abritait
9. des géraniums étiolés
10. voletèrent
11. en bruissant
12. le gros heurtoir en bronze
13. profondeurs
14. toute une meute de chiens
15. aboiements
16. Bon sang
17. Avec un timbre très masculin
18. de pure souche
19. rauque
20. de sèches réprimandes
21. Au pied !
22. piétinement
23. Non mais
24. bande de vauriens
25. pantoufles
26. un verrou s'ouvrit en grinçant
27. pieds nus
28. dansait d'un pied sur l'autre

electricity. 'Mr Allcourt-St James,' she said without preamble. 'Come in with you both. Damn!' She removed the woollen shawl[1] she had thrown about her shoulders and dropped it to the floor, where it immediately became a rug[2] for her feet. She tugged the edges of a voluminous crimson dressing-gown[3] more closely round her and, the moment the others entered, energetically slammed home[4] the door.

'There, that's better, thank God.' She laughed, a bellow[5] both ungoverned and unrefined[6]. 'Pardon me. I'm generally not so awfully Emily Brontë. Did you get lost?'

'Extensively[7],' St James admitted. 'This is my wife, Deborah, Mrs Burton-Thomas,' he added.

'You must be frozen solid[8],' their hostess noted. 'Well, we'll take care of that soon enough[9]. Let's get out of here and into the oak hall[10]. I've a nice fire there. Danny!' she shouted over her left shoulder. Then, 'Come, it's just this way. Danny!'

They followed her through the old stone-flagged[11] room. White-walled, dark-beamed[12], it was bone-chillingly cold[13], with recessed windows uncovered by curtains, a single black refectory[14] table in the centre of the floor, and a large unlit fireplace[15] sinking deep[16] into the far wall. Above it hung an assortment of firearms[17] and oddly peaked[18] military helmets[19]. Mrs Burton-Thomas nodded as St James and Deborah gave their attention to these.

'Oh, yes, Cromwell's Roundheads[20] were here,' she said. 'They had a nice bite out[21] of Keldale Hall for a stretch of ten months in the Civil War. Sixteen forty-four[22],' she added darkly, as if expecting them to commit to memory[23] the year of infamy in the history of the Burton-Thomas clan. 'But we rid ourselves of them just as soon as we could. Blackguard devils, the lot!'

She led them through the shadows of a darkened dining-room and from there to a long, richly

1. châle en laine
2. un tapis
3. peignoir
4. claqua
5. beuglement
6. incontrôlé et peu raffiné
7. Largement
8. gelés
9. sans attendre
10. le salon en chêne
11. aux dalles de pierre
12. avec ses poutres sombres
13. il y faisait froid à se glacer jusqu'aux os
14. de réfectoire
15. cheminée sans feu
16. profondément encastrée
17. une collection d'armes à feu
18. aux pointes curieuses
19. casques
20. les Têtes rondes [faction puritaine, partisans du Parlement]
21. Ils ont profité
22. 1644
23. à ce qu'ils gardent en mémoire

panelled[1] chamber where scarlet curtains[2] were drawn across embrasured windows and a coal fire roared in the grate[3]. 'Well, Lord, where's she got herself to[4]?' Mrs Burton-Thomas muttered and went to the door through which they'd just come. 'Danny!' That brought a responding running of footsteps, and a tousle-haired[5] girl of about nineteen appeared in the doorway.

'Sorry!' the newcomer laughed. 'Got your slips, though.' She tossed these to the woman, who caught them deftly[6]. 'Chewed a bit here and there[7], I'm afraid.'

'Thanks, pet[8]. Will you fetch some brandy for our guests? That dreadful Watson man finished off a good third of a decanter[9] before he staggered off to bed[10] tonight. It's gone dry and there's more in the cellar[11]. Will you see to it?[12]'

As the girl went to do so, Mrs Burton-Thomas examined her slippers, frowning at a hole newly chewed in one heel[13]. She muttered beneath her breath[14], put the slippers back on her feet, and replaced[15] the shawl – which she had been using as a sort of earth-bound flying carpet[16] in their progress through the house – on her shoulders.

'Please do sit down. Didn't want to light the fire in your room till you arrived, so we'll have a bit of a chat[17] whilst it heats up[18]. Bloody cold for October, isn't it? Early winter, they say.'

The cellar was obviously closer than the word itself implied, for within moments[19] young Danny returned with a fresh[20] bottle of brandy. She opened and decanted it[21] at a Hepplewhite[22] table which stood[23] under a portrait of some glowering, hawk-featured[24] Burton-Thomas ancestor, then returned to them with a tray[25] on which three brandy glasses and a decanter sparkled[26].

'Shall I see to the room, Aunty[27]?' she asked.

1. aux somptueuses boiseries
2. des rideaux écarlates
3. rugissait dans l'âtre
4. où est-elle passée
5. ébouriffée
6. avec agilité
7. Quelque peu mâchouillées
8. mon chou
9. au moins un tiers de carafe
10. d'aller se coucher en titubant
11. à la cave
12. Tu t'en occupes ?
13. talon
14. marmonna dans sa barbe
15. remit
16. tapis volant posé
17. causer
18. le temps qu'il chauffe
19. car en quelques instants
20. nouvelle
21. le décanta
22. [ébéniste de renom, XVIIIe s.]
23. placée
24. au regard noir et aux traits de faucon
25. plateau
26. étincelaient
27. tatie

1. les bagages
2. s'ils mettent le nez dehors
3. pourquoi tout ce vacarme
4. généreux
5. ce n'est pas ça qui manque, ici
6. à gorge déployée
7. Je suis haute en couleur
8. joyeusement
9. Faites le coup de la vieille excentrique
10. vous serez dans tous les guides touristiques
11. L'allure
12. confirmait
13. déclaration
14. look seigneurial
15. larges
16. aisance indifférente
17. les meubles inestimables
18. paysan
19. chevilles
20. vieillissante
21. enfoncés au-dessus de pommettes
22. saillantes
23. crochu
24. ombrer
25. toute sa lèvre supérieure
26. vous n'avez pas faim
27. lorgnant
28. l'horloge [de parquet]
29. Vous voyez le genre.

'Please. Get Eddie for the luggage[1]. And *do* apologize to that American couple if they're wandering about[2] wondering what all the uproar is[3], will you?' Mrs Burton-Thomas poured three healthy[4] drinks as the girl left the room once again. 'Ah, but they came here for atmosphere and, by God, I can dish it up in spades[5]!' She laughed uproariously[6] and threw down her drink in a single gulp. 'I cultivate colour[7],' Mrs Burton-Thomas admitted gleefully[8], pouring herself another. 'Give them a bit of the old eccentric[9], and you'll make every guidebook[10] from Frommer to Ronay.'

The woman's appearance[11] served as complete verification of[12] this last statement[13]. She was a combination of stately home[14] and gothic horror: imposingly tall, with a man's broad[15] shoulders, she moved with a loose-limbed indifference[16] to the priceless furniture[17] with which the room was filled. She had the hands of a labourer[18], the ankles[19] of a dancer, and the face of an ageing[20] Valkyrie. Her eyes were blue, deep-sunken above cheekbones[21] jutting across her face[22]. She had a hook-shaped[23] nose that with the passage of years had grown more pronounced, so that now in the uncertain light of the room it seemed to be casting a shadow[24] upon her entire upper lip[25]. She looked about sixty-five years old, but age to Mrs Burton-Thomas was obviously a very relative matter.

'Well' – she was looking them over – 'hungry at all[26]? You did miss dinner by about' – a glance cast towards[27] the grandfather clock[28] ticking sonorously against a far wall – 'two hours.'

'Hungry, my love?' St James asked Deborah. His eyes, Deborah saw, were alive with amusement.

'Ah ... no, not a bit.' She turned to Mrs Burton-Thomas. 'You've others staying here, then?'

'Just one American couple. You'll see them at breakfast. You know the sort.[29] Polyester and showy[1] gold chains. God-awful diamond ring on the man's little finger. Kept me howlingly entertained[2] last night with a discourse on dentistry. Wanted me to have my teeth sealed[3], it seems. The very latest thing[4].' Mrs Burton-Thomas shuddered and downed another drink. 'Bit Egyptian-sounding. Something for posterity, you know. Or was it to prevent cavities[5]?' She shrugged with grand indifference. 'Haven't the slightest.[6] What *is* this fixation[7] Americans all have with their teeth, I ask you? All straight and shiny.[8] Well, God! Crooked teeth[9] give a face a bit of *dash*[10], I say.' She poked ineffectually at[11] the fire, sent a shower of sparks[12] out on to the rug, then stamped on these[13] with terrific energy. 'Well, delighted *you're* here, is all I can say. Not that Grandpapa isn't still doing flip-flops in the grave[14] at my opening the place up to the tourist trade[15]. But it was that or the bleeding National Trust[16].' She winked at them over the rim of her glass. 'And pardon me for saying so, but this sort of life is ever so roaringly more amusing[17].'

There was a clearing of the throat[18] from the direction of the doorway, where a boy stood awkwardly in plaid flannel[19] pyjamas, an antique smoking jacket several sizes too large belted clumsily[20] round his slender waist[21]. It gave his appearance an anachronistic panache. He carried a pair of crutches[22] in his hands.

'What is it, Eddie?' Mrs Burton-Thomas asked impatiently. 'You've done the luggage[23], haven't you?'

'These're in the boot[24], Aunty,' he responded. 'Shall I do 'em as well?'

'Of course, you ninny[25]!' He turned and scurried from her sight[26]. She shook her head darkly[27]. 'I'm a martyr to my family. An absolute religious martyr. Well, come now, little ones[28], let me show you to[29] your room. You must be dropping with[30] fatigue. No, no, bring the brandy with you.'

1. tape-à-l'œil
2. M'a fait hurler de rire
3. que je fasse faire un plombage
4. Du dernier cri
5. pour éviter les caries
6. Aucune idée.
7. manie
8. Bien droites et éclatantes.
9. Les dents de travers
10. un peu d'allure
11. tisonna inutilement
12. une gerbe d'étincelles
13. les piétina
14. de se retourner dans sa tombe
15. aux touristes
16. ou se faire bouffer par les Monuments historiques
17. follement plus amusante
18. un raclement de gorge
19. de flanelle écossaise
20. nouée maladroitement
21. taille
22. béquilles
23. Tu t'es occupé des bagages
24. coffre de la voiture
25. idiot
26. détala
27. l'air sombre
28. mes petits
29. vous conduire à
30. tomber de

1. menait aux étages
2. enveloppés dans la pénombre
3. Escalier seigneurial
4. ces belles choses
5. tapisseries flamandes
6. Il faut vraiment que je les déplace.
7. ouvrit grand
8. Tout le confort moderne.
9. claquant
10. de façon réconfortante
11. Un tas de charbon
12. dans la cheminée
13. séduisants
14. peintes par Gainsborough
15. [la pièce] les enveloppait
16. de siècles d'hospitalité et d'élégance
17. des abat-jour roses
18. lustrait l'acajou
19. lit à baldaquin
20. Une imposante armoire projetait son ombre
21. coiffeuse
22. une collection de diffuseurs en cristal
23. en argent
24. aux pieds galbés [style XVIIIe s.]
25. une composition de lys
26. le bord cannelé

They followed her back through the dining-room to the stone hall and from there through another doorway that took them to the stairway. Polished, uncarpeted oak stairs led to the upper regions[1] of the house, swathed in deep shadows[2]. 'Baronial stairway[3],' Mrs Burton-Thomas informed them, slapping her hand on its thick wood railing. 'Don't even *make* these dandies[4] any more. Come, it's just this way.'

In the upper hall, she led them down a dimly lit corridor in which ancestral portraits battled with three Flemish tapestries[5]. Mrs Burton-Thomas nodded moodily towards the latter. 'Simply must move them.[6] God knows they've been hanging there since 1822, but no one could ever convince Great-Grandmamma that these things look better from a bit of a distance. Tradition. You understand. I battle it everywhere. Here we are, little ones.' She threw open[7] a door. 'I shall leave you here. All the mod cons.[8] But you'll find them, no doubt.' With that she was gone, dressing-gown flapping[9] round her ankles, slippers slapping comfortingly[10] upon the floor.

A tumble of coals[11] upon the hearth[12] welcomed them into the bedroom. It was, Deborah thought as she entered, the most beautiful room she had ever seen. Oak-panelled, with the beguiling[13] faces of two Gainsborough[14] women smiling down from either end, it embraced them[15] with centuries-old welcome and grace[16]. Small table lamps with rose shades[17] put forth a diffused radiance that burnished the mahogany[18] of the enormous four-poster[19]. A looming wardrobe cast an elongated shadow[20] against one wall, and a dressing-table[21] held an array of crystal atomizers[22] and silver-backed[23] brushes. At one of the windows stood a cabriole-legged[24] table on which an arrangement of lilies[25] had been placed. Deborah walked to this and touched her fingers to the fluted edge[26] of one ivory flower.

'There's a card,' she said, pulled it off and read it. Her eyes filled with tears. She turned to her husband. He had gone to the hearth and lowered himself into an overstuffed chair[1] that sat to one side of it. He was watching her as he so often did, with that familiar reserve, the only communication coming from his eyes. 'Thank you, Simon,' she whispered. She tucked the card back into the flowers, swallowed[2] an emotion she couldn't define, and forced herself to speak lightly[3]. 'How did you ever find this place?'

'Do you like it?' he asked in answer.

'You couldn't possibly have chosen anything more wonderful. And you know it, don't you?'

He didn't reply. A knock at the door, and he looked at her, a smile dancing round the corners of his mouth, his expression plainly saying[4]: *What's next?*[5] 'Come in,' he called.

It was the girl, Danny, a pile of blankets in her arms. 'Sorry. Forgot these. There's an eiderdown[6] already, but Aunty thinks the world's as cold as herself.' She walked into the room with an air of friendly proprietorship[7]. 'Eddie get your things in?' she asked, opening the wardrobe and plopping[8] the blankets unceremoniously[9] inside. 'He's just a bit thick[10], you know. Got to excuse him.' She studied herself in the wavy[11] mirror on the inside of the wardrobe door, fingered a few wandering hairs just a bit more out of place than they'd been before, and caught them watching her. 'Now, you'd best beware[12] of the baby's cry[13],' she pronounced solemnly. It was as if she'd spoken exactly on cue[14]. The hounds would surely howl next.

'The baby's cry? Have the Americans a child with them?' Deborah asked.

Danny's dark eyes widened[15]. She looked from woman to man. 'You don't know? Has no one ever told you?'

1. un fauteuil rembourré
2. ravala
3. d'un air détaché
4. signifiant clairement
5. Quoi encore ?
6. édredon
7. avec l'aisance de quelqu'un qui est chez lui
8. en fourrant
9. sans façon
10. bêta
11. ondulé
12. prenez garde
13. aux pleurs du bébé
14. au bon moment
15. s'écarquillèrent

Deborah saw from the girl's behaviour that they were soon to be enlightened[1], for Danny wiped her hands prefatorily[2] down the sides of her dress, glanced from one end of the room to the other for[3] unwanted listeners[4], and walked to the window. In spite of the cold, she unfastened the latch[5] and swung it open. 'Has no one told you about *that*?' she asked dramatically[6], gesturing out into the night.

There was nothing for it but to see what 'that' was. Deborah and St James joined Danny at the window, where, in the distance[7], the skeletal walls[8] of a ruined building[9] rose through[10] the fog.

'Keldale Abbey,' Danny intoned[11] and settled right in next[12] to the fire for a confidential chat. 'That's where the cry of the baby comes from, not from here.'

St James pulled the window closed, drew across the heavy curtains, and led Deborah back to the fire. She curled up[13] on the floor next to his chair, warming herself, allowing the fire to tingle against her skin[14].

'A ghost baby[15], I take it?' she said to Danny.

'An absolute one that I heard myself. You'll hear it as well. Wait and see.[16]'

'Ghosts always have legends attached[17],' St James noted.

Glad you asked, Danny's posture replied as she wriggled back into her chair[18]. 'As does this,' she said solemnly. 'Keldale was Royalist, you know, during the war.' She spoke as though the late seventeenth century were only a week removed[19]. 'Loyal t' the last man of 'em t' the King[20]. The village of Keldale, down the road a mile[21]. You've seen it?'

St James chuckled[22]. 'We should have, but I'm afraid we came in from a … different direction.'

'The scenic route[23],' Deborah added.

Danny chose to ignore the diversion. 'Well,' she went on, 'was towards the end of t' war. And old

1. n'allaient pas tarder à savoir
2. en signe préliminaire
3. pour s'assurer qu'il n'y avait pas
4. de témoins indésirables
5. défit le loquet
6. théâtralement
7. au loin
8. les murs lugubres
9. un bâtiment en ruine
10. se dressaient dans
11. entonna
12. s'installa tout près
13. se pelotonna
14. laissant le feu lui picoter la peau
15. Un bébé fantôme
16. Vous verrez.
17. qui vont avec
18. se recalait dans le fauteuil
19. ne remontait qu'à la semaine précédente
20. Fidèles au roi jusqu'au dernier
21. à env. 1,5 km d'ici
22. eut un rire
23. La route touristique

blackguard devil[1] Cromwell' – obviously Danny had learned her history at her aunty's knee[2] – 'got word[3] that the Lords o' the North were planning an uprising[4]. So he swept through the dales one last, grand time, taking manor houses, ruining[5] castles, destroying Royalist villages. Keldale's well hidden.'

'So we discovered,' St James put in.

The girl nodded earnestly. 'But days in advance the village got word that the murd'rous[6] Roundheads were coming. 'Twasn't the *village* that old Cromwell wanted, but the villagers themselves, all o' them that was loyal t' King[7] Charlie[8].'

'To kill them, of course,' Deborah prompted as the girl paused in her story to catch her breath[9].

'T' kill every last one!' she declared. 'When word came[10] that Cromwell was looking for the Kel, the village got a plan together[11]. They'd move every stick, every stitch[12], every soul t' the grounds o' the abbey[13]. So when the Roundheads arrived, there'd be Keldale, all right, but not a soul in her[14].'

'Rather an ambitious plan,' St James remarked.

'An' it worked!' Danny replied proudly. Her pretty eyes danced above rosy cheeks, but she lowered her voice. ' 'Cept[15] for the baby!' She inched forward[16] in her chair; obviously they had reached the climax of the tale[17]. 'The Roundheads arrived. 'Twas just[18] as the villagers hoped. 'Twas deserted, and silent with a heavy fog. And throughout all[19] the village, not a soul, not a stitch, not a living creature[20]. And then' – Danny's swift[21] glance made certain her audience was with her[22] – 'a baby began t' cry in the abbey where all the villagers were. Ah God!' She clutched her lovely bosom.[23] 'The terror! For they'd escaped Cromwell only t' be betrayed by a babe[24]! The mother hushed the baby by offering her breast[25]. But 'twas no good. The wee baby[26] cried and cried. They were desperate in terror that the dogs from the village would begin t' howl with

1. cette canaille de
2. c'était sa tante qui lui avait appris l'histoire de l'Angleterre
3. eut vent
4. projetaient de se soulever
5. détruisant
6. sanguinaires
7. tous ceux qui étaient fidèles au roi
8. [Charles Ier]
9. pour reprendre son souffle
10. Quand ils ont su
11. a concocté un plan
12. Ils déplaceraient tout ce qu'ils pourraient
13. sur le domaine de l'abbaye
14. sans âme qui vive
15. Sauf
16. s'avança
17. atteint le point fort du récit
18. Tout était
19. dans tout
20. rien ni personne
21. rapide
22. qu'elle tenait son auditoire
23. Elle étreignit sa jolie poitrine.
24. pour finalement être trahis par un bébé
25. a tenté de le faire taire en le mettant au sein
26. tout petit

the noise and Cromwell would find them. So they hushed the poor child. An' they smothered it[1]!'

'Good heavens!' Deborah murmured. She edged closer[2] to her husband's chair. 'Just the sort of story one longs[3] to hear on a wedding night, isn't it?'

'Ah, but you *must* know.' Danny's expression was fervent. 'For the sound of the babe is terrible luck[4] 'less you know what t' do[5].'

'Wear garlic?[6]' St James asked. 'Sleep with a crucifix clutched in one's hand?'

Deborah punched him lightly[7] on the knee. 'I want to know. I insist upon knowing. Shall I have my life blighted[8] because I've married a cynic? Tell me what to do, Danny, should I hear[9] the baby.'

Gravely, Danny nodded. ' 'Tis always a' night when the baby cries from the abbey grounds. You must sleep on your right side[10], your husband on his left. An' you must hold on t' one another close[11] till the wailing[12] stops.'

'That's interesting,' St James acknowledged[13]. 'Sort of an animated amulet.[14] May we hope that this baby cries often?'

'Not terrible often. But I …' She swallowed and suddenly they saw that this was no amusing legend for love-struck honeymooners[15], for to her the fear and the story were real. 'But I heard i' myself some three years back! 'Tis not something I'll soon forget!' She got to her feet. 'You'll remember what t' do? You'll not forget?'

'We'll not forget,' Deborah reassured the girl as she vanished[16] from the room.

They were quiet at her departure[17]. Deborah rested[18] her head against St James' knee. His long, thin fingers moved gently through her hair, smoothing the curly mass back from her face[19]. She looked up at him.

'I'm afraid, Simon. I didn't think I would be, not once this last year, but I am.' She saw in his eyes

1. l'ont étouffé
2. se rapprocha
3. qu'on a envie
4. porte malheur
5. sauf si on sait quoi faire
6. Avoir de l'ail sur soi ?
7. lui donna un petit coup
8. ma vie gâchée
9. si j'entends
10. sur votre côté droit
11. vous serrer l'un contre l'autre
12. les vagissements
13. reconnut
14. Une amulette animée, en quelque sorte.
15. pour amoureux en voyage de noces
16. alors qu'elle disparaissait
17. après son départ
18. posa
19. lui enlevant les boucles de devant les yeux

that he understood. Of *course* he did. Had she ever truly doubted that he would?

'So am I,' he replied. 'Every moment today[1] I felt just a little bit mad with terror[2]. I never wanted to lose myself[3], not to you, not to anyone[4] in fact. But there it is. It happened.' He smiled. 'You invaded my heart with a little Cromwellian force of your own[5] that I couldn't resist, Deborah, and I find now that, rather than lose myself, the true terror is that I might somehow lose you.' He touched the pendant he'd given her that morning, nestling in the hollow[6] of her throat. It was a small gold swan[7], so long[8] between them a symbol of commitment[9]: choosing once, choosing for life[10]. His eyes moved from it back to her own[11]. 'Don't be afraid,' he whispered[12] gently.

'Make love to me, then.'

'With great pleasure.'

Jimmy Havers had little pig's eyes that darted round the room[13] when he was nervous. He might feel[14] as if he were putting on[15] the bravura performance of a lifetime[16], lying his way grandly out[17] of everything from an accusation of petty larceny[18] to being caught *in flagrante delicto*[19], but the reality was that his eyes betrayed him every time, as they were doing now.

'Didn't know if you'd be home in time to get your mum the Greece stuff, so Jim went out himself, girl.' It was his habit to speak of himself in the third person. It allowed him to evade responsibility for virtually[20] any unpleasantness that cropped up[21] in his life. Like this one now. *No, I didn't go to the turf accountant*[22]. *Didn't pick up snuff*[23], *either. If it was done at all, was Jimmy that done it, not me.*

Barbara watched her father's eyes dance their way round the sitting-room. God, what a grim little death pit it was: a ten-by-fifteen-foot room whose

1. Aujourd'hui, à chaque instant
2. fou de terreur
3. m'éprendre à ce point
4. ni de quiconque
5. à toi
6. niché dans le creux
7. cygne
8. depuis si longtemps
9. d'engagement
10. pour toute la vie
11. pour revenir aux siens
12. murmura-t-il
13. qui lançaient des regards partout
14. croyait peut-être
15. jouer
16. le rôle le plus courageux de sa vie
17. en mentant ouvertement pour se défendre
18. vol simple
19. en flagrant délit
20. presque
21. survenant
22. bookmaker
23. Suis pas allé chercher du tabac à priser

windows were permanently sealed shut by years of filth and grime[1], crammed with that wonderful three-piece suite[2] so essential to delicate living, but this one a creation that had billed itself as[3] 'artificial horsehair[4]' thirty-five years ago when even real horsehair was a hideous concept of comfort. The walls were papered[5] with a maddening design[6] of interlocking rose-buds[7] that simpered their way to the ceiling[8]. Racing[9] magazines overflowed[10] from tables on to the floor and argued there with the fifteen simulated-leather[11] albums that assiduously documented[12] every inch, every mile of her mother's breakdown[13]. And through it all[14] Tony smiled and smiled and smiled.

A corner of the room held his shrine.[15] The last picture of him before his illness – a distorted, unfocused little boy kicking a football into a temporary goal net[16] set up in a garden that had once leapt with[17] flowers – was enlarged to beyond life-size proportions[18]. On either side, suitably framed in mock oak[19], hung every school report he had ever done, every note of praise[20] from every teacher he'd had, and – God, have mercy on us all – given pride of place[21], the certificate of his death[22]. Beneath this, an arrangement of plastic flowers did obeisance[23], a rather dusty obeisance considering the state of the room itself.

The television blared[24], as it always did, from the opposite corner, placed there 'so Tony can watch it as well'. His favourite shows[25] still played regularly to him, frozen in time, as if nothing had happened, as if nothing had changed. While the windows and doors were closed and locked, chained and barred to hold out[26] the truth of that August afternoon and the Uxbridge Road.

Barbara strode across[27] the room and switched off the set[28].

1. de crasse
2. canapé et deux fauteuils
3. s'était vantée d'être en
4. crin de cheval
5. tapissés
6. un motif exaspérant
7. boutons de rose entrelacés
8. minaudaient jusqu'au plafond
9. de course
10. débordaient
11. en faux cuir
12. montraient dans le détail
13. la dépression
14. au milieu de tout ça,
15. L'autel à sa mémoire était dans un coin.
16. cage de but
17. jadis plein de
18. démesurément agrandi
19. bien encadrés en simili chêne
20. commentaire élogieux
21. trônant au centre
22. son certificat de décès
23. se prosternait
24. beuglait
25. émissions
26. pour empêcher d'entrer
27. traversa à grands pas
28. le poste

'Hey, girl, Jim was watching that!' her father protested.

She faced him. My God, he was a pig. When was the last time he'd had a bath? She could smell him from here – the sweat; the body oils that collected in his hair[1], on his neck, behind the creases of his ears[2]; the unwashed clothing.

'Mr Patel told me you were by[3],' she said, sitting down on the horrible couch[4]. It prickled against her skin.[5]

The eyes flicked around. From the dead television to the plastic flowers to the obscene roses scaling[6] the wall. 'Jim went to Patel's sure.' He nodded.

He grinned[7] at his daughter. His teeth were badly stained[8], and along the gumline[9] Barbara saw the liquid building[10] within his mouth. The coffee tin was by his chair, inexpertly[11] hidden by a racing form[12]. She knew he wanted her to look away for a moment so that he'd have time to do his business[13] without getting caught. She refused to play along.

'Spit it out[14], Dad,' she said patiently. 'There's no use swallowing it[15] and making yourself sick, is there?' Barbara watched her father's body sag in relief[16] as he reached for the tin and spat the snuff-induced[17] brown slime[18] from his mouth.

He wiped himself off with a stained handkerchief, coughed into it heavily[19], and adjusted the tubes that fed[20] the oxygen into his nose. Mournfully[21], he looked at his daughter for tenderness and found none. So his eyes quickly shifted and began their slither[22] round the room.

Barbara watched him thoughtfully[23]. Why wouldn't he die? she wondered. He'd spent the last ten years decaying by degrees; why not one big jump into black oblivion[24]? He'd like that. No more gasping for breath[25], no more emphysema. No more need for snuff to soothe his addiction[26]. Just emptiness, nothingness, nothing at all.

1. le gras de ses cheveux
2. les plis de ses oreilles
3. que tu étais passé
4. canapé
5. Il piquait.
6. qui escaladaient
7. sourit
8. affreusement tachées
9. le long des gencives
10. s'accumuler
11. mal
12. feuille de pari
13. cracher son truc
14. Crache-le
15. Inutile de l'avaler
16. se détendre, soulagé
17. de sa chique
18. jet gluant
19. toussa violemment dedans
20. amenaient
21. L'air triste
22. commencèrent à divaguer
23. pensivement
24. dans le néant de l'oubli
25. Plus besoin de chercher sa respiration
26. pour calmer son manque

'You'll get cancer, Dad,' she said. 'You know that, don't you?'

' 'Ey, Jim's OK, Barb. Don't you worry, girl.'

'Can't you think of Mum? What would happen if you had to go into hospital again?' *Like Tony.* It hung unspoken in the air.[1] 'Shall I speak to Mr Patel? I don't want to have to do that, but I shall, you know, if you persist in this business with snuff.'

'Patel gave Jim the idea in the first place,' her father protested. His voice was a whine[2]. 'After you told him to cut off Jim's fags[3].'

'You know I did that for your own good. You can't smoke round an oxygen tank[4]. The doctors told you that.'

'But Patel said snuff was OK for Jim.'

'Mr Patel is *not* a doctor. Now, give me the snuff.' She held out her hand for it.

'But Jim wants—'

'No argument[5], Dad. Give me the snuff.'

He swallowed. Twice. Hard.[6] His eyes darted here and there. 'Got to have something, Barbie,' he whimpered[7].

She winced at the name. Only Tony had called her that. On her father's lips it was a malediction. None the less, she moved to him, put her hand on his shoulder, and forced herself to touch his unwashed hair. 'Dad, try to understand. It's Mum we have to consider.[8] Without you, she would never survive. So we've got to keep you healthy and fit[9]. Don't you see? Mum … loves you so much.'

Was there a glimmer[10] there at that? Did they still see each other in this little hell they so richly deserved[11], or was the fog too thick?

He gave a choked sob.[12] A dirty hand went into his pocket and the small round tin was produced[13]. 'Jim don't mean no harm[14], Barbie,' he said as he handed the tin[15] to his daughter. His eyes slid from her face to the shrine, to the plastic flowers in their

1. Inutile de le préciser pour en être conscients.
2. plaintive
3. de plus vendre de clopes à Jim
4. près d'une bouteille d'oxygène
5. Discute pas
6. Difficilement.
7. gémit-il
8. Nous devons penser à Maman.
9. en bonne santé
10. une lueur
11. ce petit enfer qu'ils méritaient tant
12. Il étouffa un sanglot.
13. apparut
14. Jim veut pas faire de mal
15. en tendant la boîte

plastic vases beneath it[1]. She went to them at once, dumped out the flowers[2], and confiscated the additional three tins[3] of snuff hidden there.

'I'll speak to Mr Patel in the morning,' she said coldly and walked out of the room.

Of *course* it would be Eaton Terrace. Eaton Place was simply too, too Belgravia[4], and Lynley would never stoop to[5] ostentation. Besides, this was just the city townhouse[6]. Howenstow – the Cornish estate[7] – was where the Lynleys really hung their hats[8].

Barbara stood looking at the elegant white building. How enchantingly[9] clean everything was in Belgravia, she thought. How upper-class chic. It was the only area in the city where people would consent to live in converted stables[10] and boast about it to[11] all their friends!

We're in Belgravia now. Did we mention it? Oh, do stop by for tea! It's nothing much.[12] *Just three hundred thousand pounds, but we like to think of it as such an investment. Five rooms. With the sweetest little cobblestone*[13] *street that you've ever seen. Do say you'll be here at half-past four. You'll recognize the place. I've planted begonias in* every *window-box.*

Barbara mounted[14] the spotless marble steps[15] and, with a scornful shake of her head[16], noted the small Asherton coat of arms[17] beneath the brass light fixture[18]. *Armigerous*[19], *Lynley! No converted stable for you.*

She lifted her hand to press the bell but stopped herself[20] and turned to survey the street. Since yesterday there had been no time to consider her position. Her initial meeting with Webberly, fetching Lynley from the wedding, and the subsequent meeting[21] at Scotland Yard with the peculiar little priest had all followed so swiftly[22] that there had been no moment in which she could sort out[23] her feel-

1. au-dessous
2. renversa les fleurs
3. les trois autres boîtes
4. [quartier chic de Londres]
5. ne tomberait jamais dans
6. sa maison de ville
7. domaine en Cornouailles
8. vivaient réellement
9. admirablement
10. des étables rénovées
11. à s'en vanter auprès de
12. Rien de grandiose.
13. pavée
14. gravit
15. les marches en marbre immaculé
16. en secouant la tête dédaigneusement
17. blason
18. l'applique en bronze
19. [qui porte un emblème héraldique]
20. s'arrêta net
21. la réunion qui avait suivi
22. tout s'était enchaîné si rapidement
23. d'y voir clair dans

ings and devise[1] a strategy for surviving this new apprenticeship[2].

True, Lynley had not been as appalled at the assignment[3] as she had thought he would be, certainly not as appalled and outraged as she herself had been. But, then, his mind had been occupied with other matters: the wedding of his friend and, no doubt, his late-night assignation[4] with Lady Helen Clyde. Now, with some time to reflect upon it[5], he would surely allow her to feel[6] the full brunt[7] of his irritation at being saddled with[8] such a pariah as herself.

So what to do? Here it was at last, the opportunity she had been waiting for – hoping for, praying for – the chance to prove herself[9] in CID once and for all[10]. It was the chance to make up for the arguments[11], the slips of the tongue[12], the impetuous decisions, the foolish mistakes of the past ten years.

'There's a lot you might learn from working with Lynley.' Webberly's words returned to her, and she knotted her brow[13]. *What* could she possibly learn from Lynley? The right wine to order with dinner, a few dance steps[14], how to dazzle a roomful of people[15] with engaging[16] conversation? What could she learn from Lynley?

Nothing, of course. But she knew too well that he represented her only chance of being reassigned to CID. So, as she stood on his fine doorstep[17], she considered thoughtfully her best approach to getting along[18] with the man.

It would have to be complete co-operation, she decided. She would offer no suggestions, would agree with every thought he had, with every statement he made.

Survive, she told herself, and turned and pressed the bell.

She had been expecting a buxom[19], uniformed, pert little maid[20] to answer her ring, so she was sur-

1. mettre au point
2. apprentissage
3. aussi horrifié par son affectation
4. rendez-vous
5. en prenant le temps d'y penser
6. lui ferait certainement sentir
7. tout le poids
8. à l'idée qu'on lui ait collé
9. de faire ses preuves
10. une bonne fois pour toutes
11. de se racheter pour les disputes
12. les lapsus
13. plissa le front
14. pas de danse
15. éblouir tout un auditoire
16. aimable
17. sur son élégant perron
18. à la meilleure façon de s'entendre
19. à la poitrine plantureuse
20. une jolie petite bonne

prised. For Lynley himself opened the door, a piece of toast in one hand, slippers on his feet, and his reading spectacles perched on the end of his aristocratic nose.

'Ah, Havers,' he said, looking over them at her, 'you're early. Excellent.'

He led the way to the back of the house and into an airy morning-room[1], fresh with white wainscoting[2], pale-green walls, and an unusually restrained[3] Adams[4] ceiling. French doors[5] at one end were bare[6] to allow a view of[7] a late-blooming garden[8], and breakfast was laid out[9] in silver serving dishes[10] along an ornate walnut sideboard[11]. The room smelt invitingly of[12] warm bread and bacon, and in answer to the odour Barbara felt her stomach rumble hollowly[13]. She pressed her arm against it and tried not to think of her own morning's fare[14] of a single overboiled egg[15] and toast. The dining table was laid for two, a number that momentarily surprised Barbara until she remembered Lynley's evening rendezvous with Lady Helen Clyde. Her ladyship was no doubt at this moment still in his bed, unused to rising before half-past ten.

'Do help yourself.[16]' Lynley motioned absently towards[17] the sideboard with his fork and gathered up a few sheets of the police report that lay in haphazard fashion[18] among the china[19]. 'There isn't a person I know who can't think better while eating. But avoid the kippers[20]. They seem a bit off[21].'

'No, thank you,' she replied politely. 'I've eaten, sir.'

'Not even a sausage? They, at least, are remarkably good. Do you find that the butchers are finally having a whack at[22] putting more pork than meal[23] into sausages these days? It's refreshing, to say the least. Nearly five decades after the Second World War and we're finally coming off rationing[24].' He picked up a teapot[25]. Like everything else on the table, it was

1. petit salon clair et spacieux
2. lambris blancs
3. sobre
4. [architectes et décorateurs du XVIIIe s.]
5. Des portes-fenêtres
6. sans rideaux
7. pour garder la vue sur
8. un jardin à la floraison tardive
9. servi
10. des plats en argent
11. buffet en noyer sculpté
12. sentait bon
13. gronder sourdement
14. son propre petit déjeuner
15. composé d'un seul œuf dur trop cuit
16. Je vous en prie, servez-vous.
17. désigna distraitement
18. qui traînait
19. porcelaine
20. harengs fumés
21. n'ont plus l'air bons
22. essayent enfin de
23. farine
24. enfin sortis du rationnement
25. une théière

antique bone china, no doubt part of the man's family history. 'What about something to drink? I have to warn you, I'm addicted to Lapsang Souchong tea. Helen claims that it tastes like dirty socks.'

'I ... I could do with a cuppa[1]. Thank you, sir.'

'Good,' he declared. 'Have some and tell me what you think.'

She was adding a lump[2] of sugar to the brew[3] when the front bell rang again. Footsteps came running up a stairway in the back. 'I'll get it[4], my lord,' a woman's voice called. It was a Cornish accent. 'Sorry about the last time. The baby and all.'

'It's the croup[5], Nancy,' Lynley murmured to himself. 'Take the poor child to the doctor.'

The sound of a woman's voice floated down the hall. *'Breakfast?'* A lighthearted laugh.[6] 'What a propitious arrival I've effected[7], Nancy. He'll never believe it's purely coincidental.' Upon her last sentence Lady Helen breezed[8] into the room and paralysed Barbara into a moment of breath-catching[9], ice-sheathed[10] despair.

They were wearing identical suits[11]. But while Lady Helen's had obviously been cut by the designer himself to fit her figure[12], Barbara's own was off-the-rack[13], a through-the-looking-glass chain-store copy[14] with rucked seams[15] and altered hemline[16] to prove it. Only the differing colours might possibly save her from complete humiliation, she thought. She grasped her teacup but lacked the will[17] to lift it to her lips.

Lady Helen paused only fractionally[18] at the sight of the policewoman. 'I'm in a mess[19],' she said frankly. 'Thank God you're here as well, Sergeant, for I've a terrible feeling it'll take three heads to see me clear[20] of the muddle I've made for myself[21].' That said, she deposited a large shopping bag on the nearest chair and went directly to the sideboard,

1. prendrais bien une tasse
2. morceau
3. l'infusion
4. J'y vais
5. C'est le croup
6. Un rire enjoué.
7. J'arrive fort à propos
8. entra en coup de vent
9. à couper le souffle
10. glacé
11. ensembles
12. fait sur mesure par le créateur lui-même
13. du prêt-à-porter
14. une copie sommaire de grand magasin
15. aux finitions approximatives
16. un ourlet refait
17. fut incapable
18. à peine un quart de seconde
19. dans le pétrin
20. pour que j'y voie clair
21. la pagaille que j'ai fichue

where she began browsing through[1] the covered dishes as if food alone were sufficient to see her through her dilemma[2].

'Muddle?' Lynley asked. He glanced at Barbara. 'How do you like the Lapsang?'

Her lips felt stiff.[3] 'It's very nice, sir.'

'*Not* that awful tea again!' Lady Helen groaned. 'Really, Tommy. You're a man without mercy[4].'

'Had I known you were coming, I'd hardly have been so remiss as to serve it[5] twice in one week,' Lynley replied pointedly[6].

Unoffended[7], she laughed. 'Isn't he piqued, Sergeant?[8] From the way he talks[9], you'd think I was here every morning, eating him out of house and home[10].'

'There *is* yesterday, Helen.'

'You vicious man.' She turned her attention back to the sideboard. 'These kippers smell appalling[11]. Did Nancy bring them up in her suitcase?' She joined them at the table with a plate piled high with a gastronomic argument[12] of eggs and mushrooms, grilled tomatoes and bacon. 'What's she doing here, by the way? Why isn't she at Howenstow? Where's Denton this morning?'

Lynley sipped his tea, his eyes on the report on the table before him. 'As I'll be out of town, I've given Denton the next few days off[13],' he replied absently. 'No need for him to come with me.'

A crisp piece of bacon halted in mid-air[14]. Lady Helen stared. 'You're joking[15], of course. Tell me you're joking, darling.'

'I'm perfectly capable of getting along[16] without my valet. I'm not totally incompetent, Helen.'

'But that's not what I mean!' Lady Helen drank a mouthful[17] of the Lapsang Souchong, grimaced at the taste[18], and set down the cup. 'It's Caroline. She's gone off on holiday for this entire week. You don't think … Tommy, if she's run off[19] with Den-

1. à parcourir
2. pour résoudre son dilemme
3. Du mal à remuer les lèvres.
4. sans pitié
5. J'aurais veillé à ne pas en servir
6. avec insistance
7. Sans se vexer
8. Mais c'est qu'il le prend mal, hein, sergent !
9. À l'entendre
10. à lui manger la laine sur le dos
11. terriblement mauvais
12. où s'empilaient en une tour gastronomique
13. congé pour quelques jours
14. s'arrêta en route
15. Vous plaisantez
16. me débrouiller
17. but une gorgée
18. eut un rictus de dégoût
19. si elle s'est enfuie

ton, I'll be absolutely lost. No' – this as he was about to speak – 'I know what you're going to say. They have every right to their personal lives. I agree completely. But we simply must come to some sort of compromise[1] over this – you and I – because if they get married and live with you—'

'Then, you and I shall get married as well,' Lynley replied placidly. 'And we'll be as happy as hedgehogs[2], the four of us[3].'

'You think it's amusing, don't you? But just look at me. One morning without Caroline in the flat[4] and I'm a complete disaster. Surely you don't think this is an ensemble that she would approve of?'

Lynley regarded the ensemble in question. Barbara didn't need to do so. The vision of Lady Helen was branded into her mind[5]: a smartly tailored burgundy[6] suit, silk blouse[7], and a mauve scarf[8] that cascaded down to a trim waist[9].

'What's wrong with it?' Lynley asked. 'It looks fine to me. In fact, considering the hour' – he glanced at his pocket watch – 'I'd say you're almost too sartorially splendid[10].'

Lady Helen turned to Barbara in exasperation. 'Isn't that every bit just like a man, Sergeant? I end up this morning looking like an overripe strawberry[11] and he murmurs "looks fine to me" and buries his nose[12] in a murder file.'

'Far better that than assist you with your clothing for the next few days.' Lynley nodded at the ignored[13] shopping bag that had toppled over[14] and now spilled a few assorted pieces of material[15] on to the floor. 'Is that why you've come?'

Lady Helen pulled the bag towards her. 'I only wish it were that simple,' she sighed. 'But it's worse by far[16] than the Denton-Caroline affair – we've not finished with that, by the way[17] – and I'm at a total loss. I've mixed up Simon's bullet holes[18].'

1. nous devons vraiment trouver un compromis
2. heureux comme tout
3. tous les quatre
4. appartement
5. gravée dans son esprit
6. bordeaux
7. un chemisier en soie
8. un foulard mauve
9. une taille fine
10. trop élégante
11. une fraise trop mûre
12. se plonge
13. abandonné
14. s'était renversé
15. répandait des bouts de tissu
16. bien pire
17. au fait
18. impacts de balles

Barbara was beginning to feel as if she'd walked into something designed[1] by Wilde[2]. Surely at any moment Lane[3] would enter stage left[4] with the cucumber sandwiches.

'Simon's bullet holes?' Lynley, more accustomed to Lady Helen's pirouettes of thought, was patient.

'You *know*. We were working on the patterns of blood-splattering[5] based on trajectory, angle, and calibre. You remember that, don't you?'

'The piece to be presented next month?'

'The very one.[6] Simon had left it all organized[7] for me in the lab. I was supposed to run off[8] the preliminary set of data[9], attach them to the cloth[10], and set up the lab[11] for the final study. But I—'

'Mixed up[12] the cloths,' Lynley finished. 'St James *will* go on about that[13], Helen. What do you propose to do?'

She looked forlornly down[14] at the samples[15] that she had dumped unceremoniously[16] on to the floor. 'Of course, I'm not hopelessly ignorant[17] in the matter. After four years in the laboratory, at least I recognize the twenty-two calibre[18] and can easily find the forty-five and the shot-gun[19]. But as to the others … and, even worse, as to which blood pattern[20] goes with each trajectory …'

'It's a muddle,' Lynley finished.

'In a word,' she agreed. 'So I thought I'd pop by[21] this morning to see if perhaps we could sort it all out[22].'

Lynley leaned down and fingered his way through[23] the pile of material. 'Can't be done[24], old duck. Sorry, but you've hours of work here and we've a train to catch[25].'

'Then, whatever shall I say to Simon? He's been working on this for ages.'

Lynley pondered the question. 'There's one thing …'

'What?'

1. croyait assister à une pièce
2. d'Oscar Wilde
3. [le valet, dans De l'importance d'être constant]
4. côté cour
5. sur l'aspect caractéristique des éclaboussures de sang
6. Exactement.
7. tout laissé bien en ordre
8. Je devais imprimer
9. ensemble de données
10. à la toile
11. préparer le labo
12. Mélangé
13. ne va pas apprécier
14. baissa un regard désespéré
15. sur les échantillons
16. avait fichus
17. totalement ignare
18. calibre 22
19. le fusil de chasse
20. éclaboussure caractéristique
21. faire un saut ici
22. si on ne pourrait pas tout remettre en ordre
23. feuilleta
24. Impossible
25. un train à prendre

'Professor Abrams at Chelsea Institute. Do you know him?' When she shook her head, he went on. 'He and Simon both have testified as expert witnesses[1]. They did in the Melton case only last year. They know each other. Perhaps he'd help. I could phone him for you before I leave.'

'*Would* you, Tommy? I'd be so grateful. I'd do anything for you.'

He lifted an eyebrow. 'Surely not the thing to say to a man over breakfast.'

She laughed engagingly. 'Even the dishes![2] I'd even give up[3] Caroline if it came to that[4].'

'And Jeffrey Cusick?'

'Even Jeffrey. Poor man. Traded for[5] bullet holes without a second thought[6].'

'All right, then. I'll see to it as soon as we've finished our breakfast. I take it that we *may* now finish our breakfast?'

'Oh, yes, of course.' She dug happily[7] into her plate while Lynley put on his spectacles and looked at his papers once more. 'What kind of case is it that has you two rushing off[8] so early in the morning?' Lady Helen asked Barbara, pouring herself a second cup of tea, to which she added sugar and milk with a liberal hand[9].

'A decapitation.'

'That sounds particularly grim.[10] Are you travelling far?'

'Up to Yorkshire.'

The teacup was suspended[11] and then lowered carefully to the saucer[12] beneath. Lady Helen's eyes moved to Lynley, regarding him for a moment[13] before she spoke. 'Where in Yorkshire, Tommy?' she asked impassively.

Lynley read a few lines. 'A place called … here it is, Keldale. Do you know it?'

There was a minute pause. Lady Helen considered the question[14]. Her eyes were on her tea and,

1. témoigné comme experts judiciaires
2. Même la vaisselle !
3. Je renoncerais même à
4. s'il le fallait
5. Échangé contre
6. sans remords
7. plongea allègrement la fourchette
8. est-ce donc pour que vous deviez filer
9. en ayant la main lourde
10. Ça a l'air bien sinistre.
11. resta en suspens
12. sur la soucoupe
13. l'observant un instant
14. réfléchit à la question

although her face was without expression[1], a pulse began to beat in the vein[2] at her throat. She looked up but the smile she offered[3] did not touch her eyes. 'Keldale? Not at all.'

1. ne montrait rien
2. une veine se mit à battre
3. le sourire qu'elle afficha

5

Lynley tossed down[1] his newspaper and considered Barbara Havers. There was no need to do so surreptitiously[2], for she was bent over the glaucous-hued[3] Formica train table[4] between them, perusing[5] the Keldale murder report. He gave momentary, idle consideration[6] to the depths to which British Rail was sinking[7] with its current colour scheme[8] designed to take maximum wear[9] with minimum upkeep[10], but then his thoughts returned to the officer opposite him.

He knew about Havers. Everyone did. She'd failed miserably through her first tenure in[11] CID, swiftly alienating[12] MacPherson, Stewart, and Hale, three of the easiest[13] DIs with whom one could ever hope to work. MacPherson especially, with his rolling Highland humour[14] and his paternal approach, should have been a mentor *extraordinaire* for someone like Havers. The man was a virtual teddy bear[15]. Had *any* DS[16] ever failed to work successfully at his side? Only Havers.

Lynley remembered the day of Webberly's decision to put her back in uniform. Everyone had known it was coming[17], of course. It had been coming for months. But no one had been quite prepared[18] for the woman's reaction.

1. laissa tomber
2. en douce
3. verdâtre
4. tablette en Formica
5. en train de lire
6. considéra un instant
7. ce qu'était prêt à faire British Rail
8. son jeu de couleurs actuel
9. pour supporter l'usure maximum
10. un minimum d'entretien
11. lors de son premier passage à
12. se mettant à dos
13. des plus faciles à vivre
14. sa bonne humeur d'Écossais
15. incroyablement facile à vivre
16. [detective sergeant]
17. que ça allait arriver
18. ne s'attendait

'If I was lah-dee-dah Eton[1], you'd be keeping me,' she'd shouted in Webberly's office in a broken voice loud enough for the entire floor[2] to hear. 'If I'd a cheque-book large enough[3] and a title on my name[4] and a willingness to screw everything in sight[5] – woman, man, child, or animal – I'd be quite good enough[6] for your precious department!'

At the mention of Eton, three heads had swivelled[7] in Lynley's direction. By the end of the diatribe, a quick cessation of workday noise[8] indicated to him that every person within range of vision[9] was looking his way. He'd been standing at a cabinet[10], rooting about for the file[11] on that miserable little worm[12] Harry Nelson but found that his fingers had suddenly become clumsy[13]. Of course, he really didn't need the file. Not exactly at the moment. Indeed, he couldn't stand there for ever[14]; he had to turn, to go back to his desk.

He made himself do it[15], made himself say quite lightly, 'Good Lord, I always draw the line at animals[16],' and made himself walk casually across the room.

Nervous, uncomfortable laughter greeted[17] his remark. Then Webberly's door slammed and Havers stormed wildly down the corridor. Her mouth was twisted with rage[18], her face blotched[19] and mottled with[20] tears that she wiped off savagely with the sleeve of her coat. Lynley felt the entire force of her hatred wash over him[21] as her eyes met his and her lips curled in contempt[22]. It was like being struck by an illness for which there was no cure[23].

A moment later, MacPherson lumbered[24] by his desk, tossed down[25] the file on Harry Nelson, and said, 'Ye're a class act, laddie[26],' in his amiable rumble[27]. But, still, it had taken at least ten minutes for his hands to stop shaking so that he could dial the phone for Helen.

'Lunch, old duck?' he had asked her.

1. Si j'étais une snob sortie d'Eton
2. étage
3. un carnet de chèques assez gros
4. un nom aristocratique
5. prête à me taper tout ce qui bouge
6. je ferais l'affaire
7. s'étaient tournées
8. les bruits de bureau soudain absents
9. dans son champ de vision
10. devant un placard
11. où il cherchait le dossier
12. ce petit salopard de
13. maladroits
14. éternellement
15. Il se força à le faire
16. je me suis toujours interdit les animaux
17. avait accueilli
18. déformée par la rage
19. bouffi
20. couvert de
21. déferler sur lui
22. formaient un rictus dédaigneux
23. incurable
24. était passé d'un pas lourd
25. sur lequel il avait jeté
26. t'as de la classe, mon gars
27. de son aimable voix rocailleuse

She could tell. She could hear it at once. 'Absolutely, Tommy. Simon's been forcing me all morning to look at the most hideous hair samples imaginable – did you know that scalp actually comes off[1] when you pull out someone's hair, darling? – and somehow lunch seems just the very thing[2]. Shall we say the Connaught?'

Blessed Helen.[3] God, what a wonderful anchor[4] she'd been in his life this past year! Lynley pushed the thought from his mind and returned to his study of Havers. She reminded him just a bit of a turtle[5]. Especially this morning when Helen had come into the room. The poor wretch[6] had absolutely frozen[7], muttered less than ten words, and retreated right into her shell[8]. What bizarre behaviour! As if she had something to fear from Helen! He felt in his pockets for his cigarette case and lighter.

Sergeant Havers glanced up at his movement, then returned to her report, her face impassive. She doesn't smoke or drink, Lynley thought and smiled wryly[9]. *Well, get used to it*[10]*, Sergeant. I'm not at all a man who neglects his vices*[11]*. Not in the past year, at least.*

He'd never quite been able to comprehend the woman's remarkable antipathy towards him. There was, if one thought about it, the entire ridiculous subject of class[12] – and God knows he'd taken a fair share of ribbing[13] once his colleagues discovered he'd inherited a title. Yet after a week or two of their mocking bows and fanfares[14] whenever he entered a room[15], the title had simply ceased to be an issue[16] at all. But not for Havers, who seemed to hear the orotund[17] words *Eighth Earl*[18] *of Asherton* booming out[19] every time he walked anywhere near her, something he'd scrupulously avoided doing since she'd been returned to uniform.

He sighed. And here they were now together. What was it exactly that Webberly had in mind in

1. le cuir chevelu se détache réellement
2. exactement ce qu'il me faut
3. Bénie soit Helen.
4. quel soutien admirable
5. une tortue
6. pauvre fille
7. s'était figée
8. retranchée vite fait dans sa carapace
9. il eut un sourire ironique
10. il va falloir vous habituer
11. qui renonce à ses vices
12. cette ridicule histoire de classe sociale
13. sa part de taquineries
14. leurs courbettes moqueuses et leurs quolibets
15. dès qu'il entrait quelque part
16. cessé d'être un problème
17. pompeux
18. comte
19. résonner

establishing this grotesque alliance of theirs? The super was by far[1] the most intelligent man he'd ever run across[2] at the Yard, so this quixotic little partnership[3] hadn't come out of nowhere[4]. He looked out of the rain-splattered[5] window. *If I can only determine which one of us is Sancho Panza, we'll get on famously*[6]. He laughed.

Sergeant Havers looked up curiously but said nothing. Lynley smiled. 'Just looking for windmills[7],' he told her.

They were drinking the railway's Styrofoam coffee[8] from its Styrofoam cups[9] when Sergeant Havers tentatively brought up[10] the question of the axe.

'No prints on it at all,' she observed.

'It does seem odd, doesn't it?' Lynley replied. He winced at the taste of the liquid and shoved the cup aside[11]. 'Kill your dog, kill your father, sit there waiting for the police to arrive, but wipe the axe handle[12] clean of your fingerprints[13]? It doesn't follow.[14]'

'Why do you think she killed the dog, Inspector?'

'To silence it.[15]'

'I suppose so,' she agreed reluctantly.

Lynley saw that she wanted to say something more. 'What do *you* think?'

'I … It's nothing. You're probably quite right, sir.'

'But you have another idea. Let's hear it.' Havers was eyeing him warily[16]. 'Sergeant?' he prompted.

She cleared her throat. 'I was only thinking that she really[17] wouldn't need to silence it. I mean[18]… it was *her* dog. Why would it bark at her[19]? I could be wrong, but it seems that it would bark at an intruder[20] and an intruder would want to silence it.'

Lynley studied the tips of his steepled fingers[21]. ' "The curious incident of the dog in the night-time," ' he murmured. 'It *would* bark at a girl it knew if she were killing her father,' he argued.

1. Le chef était de loin
2. qu'il ait jamais rencontré
3. ce petit binôme à la Don Quichotte-Sancho Panza
4. ne tombait pas du ciel
5. éclaboussée de pluie
6. on va bien s'entendre
7. Je cherchais juste des moulins à vent
8. café à emporter
9. gobelets en polystyrène
10. hésitante, souleva
11. repoussa le gobelet
12. vous essuyez le manche de la hache
13. pour effacer vos empreintes
14. Ce n'est pas logique.
15. Pour le faire taire.
16. le regardait avec méfiance
17. en fait
18. Comment dire
19. lui aboierait-il dessus
20. en voyant quelqu'un qui se serait introduit
21. les extrémités de ses mains, jointes en triangle

'But … I was thinking, sir.' Havers nervously pushed her clipped[1] hair behind her ears, a gesture that made her more unattractive than ever. 'Doesn't it look[2] as if the dog was killed first?' She leafed through the papers[3] that she had replaced in the folder and took out one of the photographs. 'Teys' body has collapsed[4] right over the dog.'

Lynley examined the picture. 'Yes, of course. But she could have arranged it.'

Havers' sharp little eyes widened in surprise[5]. 'I don't think she could, sir. Not really.'

'Why not?'

'Teys was six feet four inches tall[6].' She clumsily pulled out more of the report. 'He weighed[7] … here it is, fourteen and a half stone[8]. I can't see this Roberta slinging round[9] fourteen and a half stone of dead weight[10] just to arrange[11] a crime scene. Especially if she intended to confess[12] immediately after. It doesn't seem possible. Besides, the body had no head, so you'd think there'd be[13] a bit of blood on the walls if she'd slung it about. But there wasn't.'

'Score a point for you[14], Sergeant,' Lynley said, pulling his reading spectacles out of his pocket. 'I think I agree. Here, let me have a look at that.' She handed him the entire file. 'Time of death was put at[15] between ten and midnight,' he said, more to himself than to her. 'Had chicken and peas for dinner. Something wrong, Sergeant?'

'Nothing, sir. Someone walked over my grave.[16]'

A charming expression. 'Ah.' He read on.[17] 'And barbiturates[18] in the blood.' He looked up, his brow furrowed[19], and stared sightlessly[20] at Sergeant Havers over the top of his spectacles[21]. 'Somehow[22] one never thinks of a man like that needing sleeping pills[23]. There he is, putting in a hard day's work on a farm[24], out in that wonderful fresh air of the dales. He eats a hearty dinner[25] and just drops off

1. mal coupés
2. Ne dirait-on pas
3. fureta dans les papiers
4. s'est écroulé
5. de surprise
6. mesurait 1,95 m
7. Il pesait
8. 92 kg
9. remuer
10. un poids mort de 92 kg
11. maquiller
12. d'avouer
13. il devrait bien y avoir
14. Un point pour vous
15. L'heure de la mort a été établie
16. [se dit lorsqu'on est pris d'un frisson inexpliqué]
17. Il reprit sa lecture.
18. des barbituriques
19. le front plissé
20. fixa sans la voir
21. par-dessus ses lunettes
22. C'est curieux,
23. ait besoin de somnifères
24. faisant de rudes journées à la ferme
25. fait un dîner copieux

to sleep by the fire[1]. Bucolic bliss.[2] So why sleeping pills?'

'It looks as if he'd only just taken them.'

'Obviously. One hardly expects him to have somnambulated his way out[3] to the barn.'

She froze at once at his tone, retreated back into her shell. 'I only meant—'

'Excuse me,' Lynley interrupted quickly. 'I was joking. I do sometimes. It relieves[4] the tension. You'll have to try to get used to it.'

'Of course, sir,' she replied with deliberate courtesy[5].

The man accosted them as they walked over the pedestrian bridge[6] towards the exit[7]. He was extremely thin, anaemic-looking, obviously someone who was victim to at least[8] a thousand different kinds of stomach problems that were the bane of his existence[9]. Even as he approached them, he popped a tablet[10] into his mouth and began chewing upon it[11] with furious determination.

'Superintendent Nies,' Lynley remarked affably. 'Have you come all the way from Richmond to meet us? That's quite a drive for you.'

'Sixty bloody miles[12], so let's get it straight right from the top[13], Inspector,' Nies snapped[14]. He'd stopped dead[15] in front of them, blocking their way[16] to the stairs that would lead them down to the departures platform[17] and out of the station. 'I don't want you here. This is Kerridge's goddamned game[18] and I've *nothing* to do with it. You want anything, you get it from Newby Wiske, not from Richmond. Is that perfectly clear? I don't want to see you. I don't want to hear from you. If you've come up here with a personal vendetta in mind[19], Inspector, then just shove it up your arse[20] right now. Got it? I've no time for poncy schoolboys[21] itching for a pretty scratch of revenge[22].'

1. s'endort au coin du feu
2. Un vrai bonheur champêtre.
3. Il n'est certes pas sorti en dormant
4. Cela pemet de relâcher
5. une politesse appuyée
6. passerelle piétonne
7. la sortie
8. souffrait d'au moins
9. lui pourrissaient la vie
10. glissa un cachet
11. et se mit à le mâcher
12. 96 km, putain
13. que ce soit bien clair, dès maintenant
14. dit d'un ton sec
15. s'était arrêté net
16. leur bloquant le passage
17. le quai des départs
18. Kerridge qui l'a voulu
19. une vendetta personnelle en tête
20. vous pouvez vous la mettre au cul
21. Je n'ai que faire de collégiens péteux
22. qui rêvent de vengeance

There was a moment of silence. Watching Nies' dyspeptic[1] face, Barbara wondered if anyone ever spoke to Lord Asherton in such a colourful[2] manner on his Cornish estate.

'Sergeant Havers,' Lynley said mildly[3], 'I don't believe you've ever been introduced to Chief Superintendent Nies of the Richmond police force.'

She had never seen a man driven to a loss so swiftly[4], done with an impeccable show of manners[5]. 'Nice to meet you, sir,' she said dutifully[6].

'Damn you to hell[7], Lynley,' Nies snarled[8]. 'Just stay out of my way.' With that, he turned on his heel[9] and pushed his way through the crowd[10] towards the exit.

'Nicely done, Sergeant.' Lynley's voice was serene. His eyes searched through the swarm of humanity[11] in the terminal. It was nearly noon, and the usual bustle[12] of York's station was intensified by the lunch hour as people took the opportunity to purchase tickets, to argue car-hire prices[13] with the station agents, to meet loved ones[14] who had timed arrivals[15] to fit into the schedules[16] of a working world[17]. Lynley found the person he was looking for, said, 'Ah, I see Denton up ahead,' and raised his hand in acknowledgement to a young man who was approaching them.

Denton had just come out of the cafeteria, caught in the midst of a meal[18]. He was chewing, swallowing, and wiping his mouth with a paper napkin[19] as he dodged through the crowd[20]. He additionally managed to comb[21] his thick dark hair neatly, straighten his tie[22], and give a quick glance at his shoes, all before reaching them.

'Good trip, my lord?' he asked, handing Lynley a set of keys. 'The car's just outside.' He smiled pleasantly, but Barbara saw that he avoided Lynley's eyes.

Lynley gazed at his valet critically. 'Caroline,' he said.

1. mécontent
2. grossière
3. avec douceur
4. comme on pouvait vite décontenancer quelqu'un
5. tout en gardant des manières irréprochables
6. scrupuleusement
7. Allez au diable
8. grogna
9. tourna les talons
10. se fraya un chemin dans la foule
11. la nuée d'êtres humains
12. l'effervescence habituelle
13. contester le prix d'une location de voiture
14. aller chercher des êtres chers
15. programmé leur arrivée
16. de façon compatible avec l'emploi du temps
17. gens qui travaillent
18. surpris au beau milieu de son repas
19. serviette en papier
20. tandis qu'il zigzaguait à travers la foule
21. à peigner
22. à bien réajuster sa cravate

Denton's round, grey eyes grew immediately rounder. 'Caroline, my lord?' he repeated innocently. His cherubic[1] face became, if possible, even more cherubic. He flicked a nervous glance[2] back in the direction from which he'd just come.

'Don't "Caroline, my lord?" me.[3] We've a few things to straighten up[4] here before you go off on this holiday of yours. This is Sergeant Havers, by the way.'

Denton gulped[5] and nodded quickly at Barbara. 'Pleased[6], Sergeant,' he said and turned his eyes back to Lynley. 'My lord?'

'Stop being so obsequious. You don't do it at home and in public it makes my skin positively crawl with embarrassment[7].' Impatient, Lynley shifted his black overnight case from one hand to the other.

'Sorry.' Denton sighed and dropped the pose[8]. 'Caroline's in the cafeteria. I've a cottage lined up[9] in Robin Hood's Bay.'

'What a romantic you are,' Lynley observed drily. 'Spare me[10] the details. Just tell her to phone Lady Helen and reassure her you're not off to Gretna Green[11]. Will you do that, Denton?'

The young man grinned. 'Will do. In a tick.[12]'

'Thank you.' Lynley reached into his pocket and from his wallet extracted a credit card. He handed it to the man. 'Don't get any ideas,' he warned[13]. 'I want *only* the car on this. Is that clear?'

'Absolutely,' Denton replied crisply. He glanced over his shoulder to the cafeteria, where a pretty young woman had come outside and was watching them. She was as fashionably dressed and as fashionably coiffured as[14] Lady Helen Clyde herself always was. Practically her clone if it came down to it, Barbara thought sourly[15] and wondered if it was a requirement[16] of the job: hand-maiden[17] to the youngest daughter of an earl, just like someone stepping out of the nineteenth century[18]. The only real difference between Caroline and her lady-

1. angélique
2. jeta un regard nerveux
3. Inutile de faire l'ingénu.
4. à régler
5. déglutit
6. Enchanté
7. Cela me gêne tant que j'en ai la chair de poule
8. redevint naturel
9. J'ai réservé un cottage
10. Épargnez-moi
11. que vous n'êtes pas partis vous marier en douce
12. En moins de deux
13. dit-il en avertissement
14. était aussi élégamment vêtue et coiffée que
15. avec aigreur
16. une condition préalable
17. bonne
18. débarquant du dix-neuvième siècle

ship was a minor lack of self-assurance[1] evidenced by Caroline's grip upon her handbag: a two-fisted clinging to the handles[2] as if it were to be used as a defensive weapon.

Denton spoke. 'Shall I be off, then?'

'Be off,' Lynley responded, and added as the man scurried back in the direction he had come, 'Take some care[3], will you?'

'Not a fear[4], my lord. Not a fear,' was the swift reply.

Lynley watched him disappear into the crowd, the young woman on his arm. He turned to Barbara. 'I think that's the last interruption,' he said. 'Let's be on our way.[5]'

With that, he led her out on to Station Road and directly up to a sleek silver Bentley[6].

'I – have – got – the – *poop*[7],' Hank Watson said confidentially[8] from the next table. 'The – straight – certified – verified[9] – *poop*!' Satisfied that he had the undivided attention[10] of the others in the dining-room, he went on. 'About the baby-in-the-abbey story. JoJo-bean and I[11] had the straight certified from Angelina this morning.'

St James looked at his wife. 'More coffee, Deborah?' he asked politely. When she demurred[12], he poured some for himself and gave his attention back to the other couple.

Hank and JoJo Watson hadn't wasted much time becoming elbow-rubbing intimates[13] of the only other guests[14] at Keldale Hall. Mrs Burton-Thomas had seen to that by seating them at adjoining[15] tables in the hall's immense dining-room. She hadn't bothered[16] with introductions[17]. She knew quite well there would be no need. The beautiful bolection mouldings[18] of the room's panelled walls[19], the Sheraton[20] sideboard, and the William[21] and Mary[22] chairs became entirely lost to the American

1. un léger manque de confiance en soi
2. ses deux poings agrippaient les anses
3. Faites attention à vous
4. N'ayez crainte
5. Mettons-nous en route.
6. élégante Bentley couleur argent
7. scoop
8. sur le ton de la confidence
9. garanti strictement authentique
10. Content d'avoir toute l'attention
11. Ma JoJo et moi
12. Devant son refus
13. à faire ami-ami
14. clients
15. voisines
16. n'avait pas pris la peine
17. de les présenter
18. corniches
19. boiseries murales
20. [ébéniste anglais, fin XVIIIe s.]
21. Guillaume d'Orange
22. Mary II [fin XVIIe s.]

couple's interest[1] once St James and Deborah entered the room.

'Hank, hon[2], maybe they don't want to hear about the baby in the abbey.' JoJo fingered her gold chain from which were hanging[3] a veritable excrescence of trinkets[4]. #1 *Mom*[5], *Applepie* and *Sugarbean*[6] danced alongside a Mercedes-Benz symbol, a diminutive spoon[7], and a minuscule Eiffel Tower.

'Hellsapoppin they don't![8]' was Hank's riposte. 'You just *ask* them, Bean.'

JoJo rolled her eyes in apology[9] at the other couple. 'Hank's charmed with[10] England. Just really charmed,' she explained.

'Love it.' Hank nodded. 'If I could just get some toast that's h-o-t, the place'd be perfect. Why in heck d'you people[11] eat your toast cold?'

'I've always thought it was a cultural deficiency[12],' St James responded.

Hank brayed appreciatively[13], his mouth open wide to display a row of startlingly white teeth[14]. 'Cultural deficiency! That's good! That's real good! Hear that, Bean? Cultural deficiency!' Hank always repeated any remark that made him laugh. Somehow, it gave him a certain authorship over it[15]. 'Now, back to[16] the abbey.' He was also not easily diverted.

'Hank,' his wife murmured. She was a bit like a rabbit, exophthalmic[17], with a little upturned nose[18] that continually twitched and flexed[19] on her face as if she were not quite used to the air she breathed[20].

'Loosen up[21], Bean,' her husband urged. 'These people here are the salt – of – the – earth[22].'

'I think I *will* have more coffee, Simon,' Deborah said.

Her husband poured, met her eyes, and said, 'Milk, dear?'

'Yes, please.'

1. perdirent tout intérêt aux yeux du couple américain
2. chéri [abrév. de « honey »]
3. d'où pendaient
4. un amas de breloques
5. Meilleure Maman
6. [surnom affectueux]
7. cuillère miniature
8. Mon œil
9. pour l'excuser
10. est sous le charme de
11. Pourquoi diable, vous autres
12. une défaillance culturelle
13. eut un gros rire approbateur
14. une rangée de dents d'une blancheur surprenante
15. il s'en appropriait ainsi la paternité
16. Bon, pour en revenir à
17. avec des yeux globuleux
18. nez retroussé
19. qui remuait constamment
20. qu'elle respirait
21. Relax
22. la crème de la crème

'H-o-t milk for the coffee!' Hank remarked, seeing a new avenue in which to[1] demonstrate his considerable verbal flexibility. 'Now, that's something else I just haven't got used to. Hey! Here's Angelina now!'

The said young girl[2] – obviously by her physical resemblance to Danny yet another member of the curiouser and curiouser[3] Burton-Thomas clan – was carrying a large tray into the dining-room with intense concentration. She was not as pretty as Danny: a plump little red hen of a girl[4] whose scrubbed[5] cheeks and rough[6] hands made her look as if she'd be more at home[7] on a farm than attempting to be part of her family's eccentric establishment. She bobbed a nervous good morning[8], avoiding their eyes, and awkwardly distributed[9] breakfast, gnawing[10] her bottom lip miserably[11] as she did so.

'Shy little thing[12],' Hank observed loudly, squashing[13] a square of toast into the centre of his fried[14] egg. 'But she gave us the true poop last night after dinner. Now, you've heard about that baby, right?'

Deborah and St James looked at each other, deciding which one of them would take up the conversational ball[15]. It was tossed to[16] Deborah. 'Yes, indeed we did,' she replied. 'Crying from the abbey. Danny told us about it just after we arrived.'

'Ha! Bet she did,' Hank said obscurely[17], and then, to make sure his meaning was clear[18], added, 'Nice little piece.[19] You know. Likes the attention.[20]'

'Hank ...,' his wife murmured into her porridge. Her hair was very short, strawberry blonde[21], and the tips of her ears[22], showing through it, had become quite red.

'JoJo-bean, these people are not d-u-m[23],' Hank replied. 'They know the score[24].' He waved a fork at[25] the other two. A piece of sausage was poised perilously on the prongs[26]. 'You gotta excuse the Bean,' he explained. 'You'd think living in Laguna Beach'd

1. occasion de
2. La jeune fille en question
3. de plus en plus fêlé [digne d'Alice au pays des merveilles]
4. petite rousse dodue
5. lustrées
6. abîmées
7. plus à sa place
8. les salua d'un mouvement nerveux
9. leur servit gauchement
10. mordillant
11. l'air malheureux
12. Timide, la petite
13. écrasant
14. sur le plat
15. assurerait la conversation
16. Cela tomba sur
17. énigmatiquement
18. de bien se faire comprendre
19. Mignonne.
20. Aime bien se faire remarquer.
21. blond vénitien
22. le bout de ses oreilles
23. idiots
24. savent à quoi s'en tenir
25. agita sa fourchette vers
26. en équilibre instable sur les dents

make a swinger outa her[1], wouldn't you? You familiar with Laguna Beach, California?' No pause for an answer. 'It is the finest place in the world to live – no offence to you here, of course. JoJo-bean and I've lived there for – how long is it now, Pretty Face? Twenty-two years? – and she still blushes[2], I tell you, when she sees two queers getting personal[3]! "JoJo," I tell her, "there – is – no – use getting hot and bothered[4] about queers." ' He lowered his voice. 'We got them coming out our verified *ears*[5] in Laguna,' he confided.

St James could not bring himself[6] to look at Deborah. 'I beg your pardon?[7]' he asked, unsure if he had correctly heard the unusual gymnastic pun[8].

'*Queers*, man! Faggots[9]! Ho-mo-sex-shuls. By the certified, verified millions in Laguna! They all want to live there! Now, as to the abbey.' Hank paused to slurp gustily at[10] his coffee. 'Seems the real story is that Danny and her you-know-what used to meet at the abbey on a regular basis[11]. You know what I mean. For a little clutch-and-feel.[12] And on the night in question some three years back[13] they've just decided it's time to consecrate the relationship[14]. You follow me?'

'Completely,' St James replied. He studiously avoided Deborah's eyes.

'Now, Danny, see, is a little leery of this[15]. After all, being a virgin on the wedding night's a *puh-retty*[16] big item to let go of[17], don't you agree? 'Specially in this neck of the woods[18]. And if little Danny lets this fella have his way[19]... well, there's no backward road[20], is there?' He awaited St James' response.

'I should imagine not.'

Hank nodded sagely. 'So, as her sister Angelina tells it—'

'She was there?' St James asked incredulously.

1. l'aurait décoincée
2. rougit encore
3. deux homos se montrer de la tendresse
4. de te mettre dans tous tes états
5. On en a des tonnes, je vous jure
6. ne put se résoudre
7. Je vous demande pardon ?
8. l'image scabreuse [avec jeu de mots douteux sur « coming out »]
9. Des pédés
10. pour aspirer bruyamment
11. régulièrement
12. Pour se faire des petits câlins
13. il y a de ça 3 ans
14. de consommer leur union
15. est un peu méfiante
16. [façon de prononcer « pretty »]
17. ne se sacrifie pas à la légère
18. dans ce coin paumé
19. cède à ce gars
20. impossible de revenir en arrière

Hank spent a moment guffawing[1] at the thought, banging his spoon with tympanic delight[2] on the top of the table. 'You're a card, fella![3]' He directed his attention to Deborah. 'He always like this?'

'Always,' she replied promptly.

'That's great! Well, back to the abbey.'

Of course, Deborah and St James' exchanged looks replied.

'So here's this fella with Danny.' Hank painted[4] the scene in the air with his knife and fork. 'The gun is loaded[5] and the trigger cocked[6]. When all of a sudden comes this baby wailing fit to beat the band[7]! Can you see it? Huh, *can* you?'

'In detail,' St James replied.

'Well, these two hear that baby and think it's the worda God himself[8]. They get outa that abbey so fast that you'd think the devil was chasing them[9]. And *that*[10], my friends, put an end to *that*[11].'

'To the baby crying, do you mean?' Deborah asked. 'Oh, Simon, I was hoping we'd hear it to-night. Or perhaps even this afternoon. Warding off evil[12] turned out to be so much more rewarding[13] than I expected it to be.'

Minx[14], his look said.

'*Not* to the crying baby,' Hank instructed. 'To the you-know-what between Danny and whoever he was. Who the hell was he, anyway[15], Bean?'

'A weird name.[16] Ezra somebody.'

Hank nodded. 'Well, anyway[17], Danny comes back to the Hall here with a case of the who-ha's[18] that just won't quit[19]. Wants to confess her sins[20] and go right to the Lord[21]. So they call the local priest in. It is ex-or-cism time![22]'

'For the abbey, the hall, or Danny?' St James enquired.

'All *three*, fella! So this priest comes rushing down and does the bit with the holy water[23], goes on to the abbey, *and*— He stopped completely, his face

1. à s'esclaffer
2. comme sur une timbale musicale
3. Vous êtes impayable, vieux
4. traça
5. Le pistolet est chargé
6. la détente est armée
7. ces pleurs de bébé à réveiller un mort
8. c'est la parole de Dieu en personne
9. qu'ils avaient le diable aux trousses
10. alors là
11. ça a été la fin de tout
12. Tenir le mal à distance
13. tellement plus satisfaisant
14. Friponne
15. Bon sang, c'était qui, déjà
16. Un drôle de nom.
17. quoi qu'il en soit
18. une frousse d'enfer
19. qui ne la lâche pas
20. ses péchés
21. s'en remettre à Dieu
22. On exorcise !
23. fait son truc avec l'eau bénite

lit with joy, his eyes alive with delight[1]: a master storyteller[2] with the audience tearing and clawing[3] to hear every last[4] syllable.

'More coffee, Deborah?'

'Thank you, no.'

'And what do you *think*?' Hank demanded.

St James considered the question. He felt his wife's foot nudge[5] his good leg. 'What?' he dutifully responded.

'Damn if there wasn't a real baby there.[6] A newborn[7] with the cord[8] still attached. Couldn't be more than a couple hours old.[9] Deader'n a door knocker[10] by the time the old priest got there. Exposure, they say.[11]'

'How dreadful.' Deborah's face paled. 'What a horrible thing!'

Hank nodded solemnly. 'You're talking horrible, just think of poor Ezra! Bet he couldn't you-know-what for another two years!'

'Whose baby was it?'

Hank shrugged. He turned his attention to his now-cold[12] breakfast. Clearly, the juicier elements[13] of the story were the only ones that he had pursued[14].

'No one knows,' JoJo answered. 'They buried it[15] in the churchyard[16] in the village. With the funniest epitaph on the poor little grave. I can't recall it[17], offhand[18]. You'll have to go see it.'

'They're newlyweds[19], Bean,' Hank put in with a broad wink[20] at St James. 'I bet they got plenty m-o-r-e on their minds than traipsing through graveyards[21].'

Obviously, Lynley favoured the Russians. They'd begun with Rachmaninov, moved to Rimsky-Korsakov, and were now slam-banging their way through[22] the cannonades of the '1812' Overture[23].

1. pétillants de délectation
2. un narrateur hors pair
3. dont l'auditoire se serait damné pour
4. la moindre
5. lui tapoter
6. Figurez-vous qu'il y avait un vrai bébé.
7. nouveau-né
8. cordon ombilical
9. Sûrement né depuis à peine 2 heures.
10. Mort de chez mort,
11. Hypothermie, il paraît.
12. qui avait refroidi
13. la partie la plus croustillante
14. l'avait intéressé
15. On l'a enterré
16. cimetière
17. Ça ne me revient pas
18. là tout de suite
19. de jeunes mariés
20. un gros clin d'œil
21. crapahuter dans les cimetières
22. progressaient dans les percussions
23. [de Tchaïkovski]

'There. Did you notice it?' he asked her, once the music had crashed to its finale. 'One of the cymbalists was just a counter-beat behind[1]. But it's my only bone of contention[2] with that particular recording[3] of "1812".' He flipped the stereo off.

Barbara noticed for the first time that he wore absolutely no jewellery – no crested signet ring[4], no expensive wrist-watch to flash gold richly[5] when it caught the light. For some reason, that fact was as distracting to her[6] as an unsightly display[7] of opulent ornamentation would have been.

'I didn't catch it.[8] Sorry. I don't know a lot about music.' Did he really expect her – with her background[9] – to be able to converse with him about classical music?

'I don't know much about it either,' he admitted ingenuously[10]. 'I just listen to it a great deal. I'm afraid I'm one of those ignoramuses[11] who say, "I don't know a thing about it, but I know what I like".'

She listened to his words with surprise. The man had a first in history, an Oxford education. Why in the world[12] would he ever apply the word *ignoramus* to himself? Unless, of course, it was designed to put her at ease with a liberal dose[13] of charm, something he was capable of doing quite well. It was effortless for him[14], as easy as breathing.

'I must have developed my liking for it[15] during the very last part[16] of my father's illness. It was always playing in the house when I could get away[17] to see him.' He paused, removed the tape[18], and the silence in the car became every bit as loud[19] as the music had been, but far more disconcerting. It was some moments before he spoke again and, when he did, it was to pick up the thread of his original thought[20]. 'He simply wasted away to nothing[21]. So much pain.' He cleared his throat. 'My mother wouldn't consider[22] putting him into hospital. Even towards the end when it would have been so much

1. avait un petit temps de retard
2. mon seul reproche
3. à cet enregistrement
4. pas de chevalière avec armoiries
5. lançant des reflets d'or
6. pour elle aussi dérangeant
7. qu'un étalage déplacé
8. Je n'ai pas remarqué.
9. vu son milieu
10. avec candeur
11. ignares
12. Pourquoi diable
13. une bonne dose
14. Cela ne lui coûtait rien
15. développer ce goût
16. la toute dernière phase
17. quand je pouvais m'échapper
18. retira la cassette
19. aussi assourdissant
20. pour reprendre le fil de sa première pensée
21. a dépéri irrémédiablement
22. ne voulait en aucun cas

easier on her, she wouldn't hear of it. She sat with him hour after hour, day and night, and watched him die by degrees. I think it was music that kept them both sane[1] those last weeks.' He kept his eyes on the road. 'She held his hand and listened to Tchaikovsky. In the end he couldn't even speak. I've always liked to think the music did his speaking for him[2].'

It was suddenly crucial to stop the direction the conversation was taking. Barbara gripped the stiff edges[3] of the folded roadmap with dry, hot fingers and searched for another subject.

'You know that bloke Nies[4], don't you?' It blurted out badly[5], all too obviously an ill-concealed attempt[6] to digress[7]. She shot a wary look at him[8].

His eyes narrowed, but otherwise he gave no immediate reaction to the question. One hand merely dropped from the steering wheel[9]. For a moment, Barbara thought, ridiculously, that he intended to use it to silence her, but he simply chose another tape at random[10] and slid it into the stereo. He did not, however, turn the unit on. She stared out at the passing countryside[11], mortified.

'I'm surprised you don't know about it,' he finally said.

'Know about what?'

He looked at her then. He appeared to be trying to read her face for[12] insolence or sarcasm or perhaps a need to wound[13]. Apparently satisfied with what he saw, he returned his eyes to the road.

'Just about five years ago, my brother-in-law[14], Edward Davenport, was murdered in his home north of Richmond. Superintendent Nies saw fit to arrest me[15]. It wasn't a long ordeal[16], just a matter of a few days. But quite long enough.' A glance at her again, a self-deprecatory[17] smile. 'You've not heard that story, Sergeant? It's nasty enough to make good cocktail-party gossip[18].'

1. qui les a empêchés de devenir fous
2. parlait à sa place
3. agrippa le bord rigide
4. ce Nies
5. Cela lui était sorti, maladroitement
6. une tentative flagrante
7. de s'écarter du sujet
8. lui lança un regard méfiant
9. se borna à lâcher le volant
10. au hasard
11. à la campagne, qui défilait
12. lire sur son visage des traces d'
13. une volonté de blesser
14. beau-frère
15. a jugé utile de m'arrêter
16. L'épreuve n'a pas duré longtemps
17. d'autodérision
18. faire jaser dans les cocktails

1. sans rien voir,
2. que la bifurcation
3. passablement ébranlée
4. le panorama
5. continuer de discuter
6. s'y laissait aller
7. rythme effréné
8. crasse
9. la saisit complètement
10. nuances
11. le patchwork
12. des étendues de lande
13. plongeait dans les vallons
14. impeccables
15. grimpait et virait
16. la bruyère et les ajoncs
17. la seule forme de vie, c'était les moutons
18. allaient et venaient en liberté
19. sans l'entrave des antiques murets en pierre sèche
20. bornaient le terrain de
21. congénères
22. de chaque fissure, de chaque haie
23. cerfeuil sauvage
24. silène
25. vesce
26. digitale
27. menaient un troupeau de moutons dodus
28. berger

'I … no … no, I'd not heard it. And, anyway, I don't go to cocktail parties.' She turned blindly[1] to the window. 'I should guess the turn-off[2] is near. Perhaps three miles,' she said uselessly.

She was shaken to the core[3]. She could not have said why, did not want to think about it, and forced herself to study the scenery[4], refusing to be caught up in any further conversation[5] with the man. Concentration on the land became imperative, and as she gave herself over to it[6] the country began its process of seduction upon her, for she was so used to the frenetic pace[7] of London and the desperate grime[8] of her neighbourhood in Acton that Yorkshire came as a bit of a shock[9].

The countryside was a thousand different shades[10] of green, from the patchwork quilts[11] of the cultivated land to the desolation of the open moors[12]. The road dipped through dales[13] where forests protected spotless[14] villages and then climbed switchbacked curves[15] to take them again up to the open land where the North Sea wind blew unforgivingly across heather and furze[16]. Here, the only life belonged to the sheep[17]. They wandered free and unfenced[18], unfettered by the ancient drystone walls[19] that constructed boundaries for[20] their fellows[21] in the dales below.

There were contradictions everywhere. In the cultivated areas, life burgeoned from every cranny and hedgerow[22], a thick vegetation that in another season would produce the mixed beauties of cow parsley[23], campion[24], vetch[25], and foxglove[26]. It was an area where traffic was delayed while two dogs expertly herded a flock of plump sheep[27] across pasture, down hillside, and along the road for a two-mile stroll into the centre of a village, directed only by the whistling of the shepherd[28] who followed, his fate and the fate of the animals he owned left to the skill of the running dogs. And then suddenly the plants, villages, magnificent oaks, elms, and chestnuts[1] – this truly insubstantial pageant[2] – faded to nothing[3] in the glory of the moors.

Here, the cerulean[4] sky exploded with clouds. It swept down to meet the rough, unconquered land. Earth and air: there was nothing else, save the sapient presence[5] of the black-faced[6] sheep, stalwart denizens[7] of this lonely place.

'It's beautiful, isn't it?' Lynley asked after some minutes. 'In spite of everything that's happened to me here, I still love Yorkshire. I think it's the loneliness here. The complete desolation.'

Again Barbara resisted the confidence, the implicit message behind the words that here was a man who could understand. 'It's very nice, sir. Not like anything I've ever seen.[8] I think this is our turn[9].'

The road to Keldale switched back and forth[10], taking them to the deepest section of the dale. Moments after the turn, the woods closed in on them. Trees arched[11] over the road, ferns grew thickly[12] at its sides[13]. They came to the village the way that Cromwell had come[14], and they found it as he had: deserted.

* * *

The ringing[15] of St Catherine's church bells[16] told them immediately why there was no sign of life in the village. Upon the cessation of[17] what Lynley was beginning to believe was surely Sayers' nine tailors[18], the church doors opened and the ancient building spewed forth[19] its tiny congregation.

'At last,' he murmured. He stood leaning against the car, thoughtfully surveying the village. He'd parked in front of Keldale Lodge, a trim little hostelry[20], heavily hung with ivy[21] and multipaned[22] windows, from which he had a sweeping view in four directions. Taking it in, he concluded that there

1. châtaigniers
2. somptueux spectacle
3. se désintégra
4. d'azur
5. hormis la sage présence
6. à tête noire
7. hôtes vaillants
8. Différent de tout ce que j'ai pu voir jusqu'ici.
9. c'est là qu'il faut tourner
10. tournicotait
11. formaient des arches
12. les fougères poussaient dru
13. au bord de celle-ci
14. du même côté que Cromwell
15. Le son
16. cloches
17. Dès que cessa
18. les cloches d'un roman policier de Dorothy L. Sayers
19. recracha
20. une petite auberge proprette
21. la façade couverte de lierre
22. aux multiples carreaux

couldn't possibly have been a more unlikely spot[1] on earth for a murder.

To the north was the narrow high street[2], flanked by[3] grey stone buildings with tiled roofs[4] and white woodwork containing the requisite elements for comfortable village life: a shoebox-sized[5] post office; a nondescript[6] greengrocer's[7]; a shop advertising Lyons cakes on a rusty yellow sign[8] and looking like the purveyor[9] of everything from motor oil[10] to baby food; a Wesleyan chapel wedged[11] with delightful incongruity between Sarah's Tea Room and Sinji's Beauty Shoppe[12]: 'Pretty Curls Make Lovely Girls'. The pavement on either side of the street was raised only slightly off the road[13], and water pooled in front of doorways[14] from the morning's rainfall[15]. But the sky was clear now, and the air was so fresh that Lynley could taste its purity.

To the west, a road called Bishop Furthing led off towards farmland[16], enclosed on either side by the ubiquitous[17] drystone walls of the district. On its corner stood a tree-shaded[18] cottage with a front door only steps from the street[19]. It had an enclosed garden to one side from which the excited yelping of small dogs burst forth[20] at regular intervals, as if someone were playing with them rough and tumble[21]. The building itself was labelled as inconspicuously[22] as possible with the single word POLICE, blue letters on a white sign that stuck out from a window. Home of the archangel Gabriel, Lynley concluded, suppressing a smile.

To the south, two roads veered off from[23] an overgrown two-bench common: Keldale Abbey Road, ostensibly leading to the same, and over the humped bridge[24] that spanned[25] the lazy movement of the River Kel, Church Street, with St Catherine's built on a hillock[26] on the corner. It, too, was surrounded by a low stone wall, and embedded into this[27] was a First World War memorial plaque,

1. un lieu aussi improbable
2. l'étroite rue principale
3. bordée de
4. aux toits de tuiles
5. riquiqui
6. ordinaire
7. un marchand de fruits et légumes
8. une enseigne jaune rouillée
9. semblant fournir
10. de l'huile de moteur
11. coincée
12. institut de beauté
13. à peine plus haut que la chaussée
14. formait des flaques devant les portes
15. averse
16. partait vers les terres agricoles
17. omniprésents
18. ombragé
19. à deux pas
20. s'élevaient
21. chahutait avec eux
22. discrètement
23. partaient d'
24. pont en arc
25. enjambait
26. une butte
27. au centre

the sombre commonality[1] of every village in the nation.

To the east was the road down which they had wended their way[2] to this bit of Yorkshire heaven. It had been deserted earlier, but now the bent form[3] of a woman trudged up the incline[4], a scarf tucked into her black coat. Shod in heavy brogues[5] and dazzling blue ankle-socks[6], she carried a mesh bag[7] over one arm. It dangled there limply[8], empty. On a Sunday afternoon, there was little hope of filling it with foodstuffs[9] purchased at the grocer's, for everything was locked up tight and, even if it were not, she was heading in the wrong direction to be making a purchase[10]: out of the village, back up towards the moors. A farmer's wife, perhaps, having made some delivery.

The village was surrounded by woods, by the upward slope of meadow[11], by the feeling of absolute security and peace. Once St Catherine's bells ceased ringing, the birds took up[12], tittering from rooftops[13] and trees. Somewhere, a fire had been lit and wood-smoke, just the ghost of its fragrance[14], was like a whisper in the air[15]. It was hard to believe that three weeks past[16], a mile out of town, a man had been decapitated by his only daughter.

'Inspector Lynley? I hope I haven't kept you waiting long. I always lock up during church since there's no one else to watch the place[17]. I'm Stepha Odell. I own the lodge[18].'

At the sound of the voice, Lynley turned from his inspection of the village, but at the sight of her his polite introduction[19] died on his lips.

A tall, shapely[20] woman – perhaps forty years old – stood before him. She was dressed for church in grey linen[21], a well-cut dress[22] with a white collar. The rest of her was black: shoes, belt[23], handbag, and hat. Except for her hair, which was coppery red[24] and fell to her shoulders. She was stunning[25].

1. morne trait commun
2. ils s'étaient acheminés
3. la silhouette courbée
4. montait péniblement la pente
5. Chaussée de gros souliers
6. de socquettes bleu vif
7. filet à provisions
8. Il se balançait mollement
9. aliments
10. pour faire une emplette
11. la pente ascendante des prairies
12. prirent le relais
13. ricanant sur les toits
14. de vagues effluves
15. un chuchotement dans l'air
16. trois semaines plus tôt
17. pour surveiller les lieux
18. ce relais
19. sa phrase polie de présentation
20. bien faite
21. lin
22. robe de bonne coupe
23. ceinture
24. cuivrés
25. éblouissante

He found his voice. 'Thomas Lynley,' he said idiotically. 'This is Sergeant Havers.'

'Do come in.' Stepha Odell's voice was warm and pleasant. 'I've your rooms ready. You'll find us a quiet inn[1] at this time of year.'

There was a chill[2] in the building they entered, an atmosphere produced by thick walls and stone floors. These were covered with a faded Axminster[3] carpet. She led them into a tiny reception area[4], moving with a swift, unconscious grace[5], and produced an oversized register[6] for them to sign. 'You've been told I only do breakfast, haven't you?' she asked earnestly, as if satisfying hunger[7] were the uppermost[8] thing on his mind at this moment.

Do I look that desperate?[9] 'We'll manage, Mrs Odell,' Lynley said. *Tricky move, old boy*[10]. *Transparent as hell*[11]. Havers stood mute at his side[12], her face without expression.

'Miss,' their hostess replied. 'Stepha really. You can get meals at the Dove and Whistle[13] in St Chad's Lane or at the Holy Grail[14]. Or, if you want something special, there's Keldale Hall.'

'The Holy Grail?'

She smiled. 'The pub across[15] from St Catherine's.'

'That name must certainly propitiate the abstinent gods[16].'

'At least it does[17] Father Hart. But he's been known[18] to tip a pint or two[19] in an evening there. Shall I show you your rooms?'

Without waiting for an answer, she led them up the crooked stairs[20], displaying, Lynley noted, a remarkably pretty pair of ankles above which rose[21] an even prettier pair of legs. 'You'll find us glad to have you in the village, Inspector,' she stated[22] as she opened the door to the first room and then with a gesture of her hand indicated the room next door[23] with the unspoken message that it was up to them to decide who stayed where.

1. un hôtel paisible
2. Il faisait froid
3. [manufacture anglaise]
4. accueil
5. avec une grâce rapide et naturelle
6. un énorme registre
7. comme si satisfaire son appétit
8. primordial
9. Ai-je l'air si désespéré ?
10. Risqué, mon vieux.
11. comme tout
12. se tenait, muette, à ses côtés
13. au pub [Colombe et Sifflet]
14. au Saint Graal
15. en face
16. apaiser les dieux de l'abstinence
17. cela apaise bien
18. il n'est pas contre
19. avaler une ou deux bières
20. l'escalier de guingois
21. chevilles surmontées d'
22. déclara-t-elle
23. la chambre voisine

'That's helpful. I'm glad to hear it.'

'We've none of us anything against Gabriel, you see. But he's not been a popular man round here since they carted[1] Roberta off to the asylum[2].'

1. qu'ils ont emmené
2. à l'asile psychiatrique

6

Lynley was positively white with rage, but there was not the slightest indication of that emotion[1] in his voice. Barbara watched his performance on the telephone with grudging admiration[2]. A virtuoso, she admitted.

'The name of the admitting psychiatrist[3]? … There wasn't one? What a fascinating procedure. Then, upon whose authority. … When exactly did you expect me to stumble upon this information[4], Superintendent, since you've conveniently left it out of[5] the report? … No, you've got things backwards[6], I'm afraid. You don't move a suspect to an institution without formal paperwork[7]. … It's unfortunate that your police matron[8] is on holiday, but you find a replacement. You don't move a nineteen-year-old girl into a mental hospital for the simple reason that she refuses to speak to anyone.'

Barbara wondered if he would allow himself to explode, if he would show even a crack[9] in that well-tailored[10] Savile Row[11] armour[12] of his.

'I'm afraid that bathing daily[13] is not the pre-eminent indication of unshakable sanity[14], either. … Don't pull rank on me[15], Superintendent. If this is any indication of[16] the manner in which you've handled this case[17], there's no wonder to me[18] that Kerridge is after your skin[19]. … Who's her solicitor[20]? …

1. n'en laissait rien paraître
2. admirative malgré elle
3. du psychiatre qui l'a fait interner
4. pensiez-vous que j'allais l'apprendre
5. comme par hasard, vous ne le mentionnez pas dans
6. à l'envers
7. sans paperasse administrative
8. [femme agent de police]
9. ne serait-ce qu'une faille
10. bien coupée
11. venant des meilleurs tailleurs de Londres
12. armure
13. se laver tous les jours
14. d'une santé mentale intacte
15. N'usez pas de votre grade avec moi
16. Si cela illustre
17. dont vous avez géré ce dossier
18. je ne suis pas étonné
19. veuille votre peau
20. avocat

Shouldn't you be getting her one yourself, then? … Don't tell me what you have no intention of doing. I've been brought in on this case[1] and henceforth[2] it shall be conducted correctly. Am I being quite clear? Now, please listen carefully. You have exactly two hours to get everything to me in Keldale: every warrant[3], every paper[4], every deposition, every note that was taken[5] by every officer on this case. Do you understand? Two hours … Webberly. W-e-b-b-e-r-l-y. Phone him, then, and have done with it[6].'

Stone-faced[7], Lynley handed the telephone back to Stepha Odell.

She replaced it behind the reception counter and ran a finger along the receiver[8] several times before looking up[9]. 'Should I have said nothing?' she asked, a trace of anxiety in her voice. 'I don't want to cause trouble between you and your superiors.'

Lynley flipped open his pocket watch[10] and checked the time. 'Nies is not my superior. And, yes, you should have told me. Thank you for doing so. You saved me a needless trip[11] to Richmond that no doubt Nies was longing to force me to make.'

Stepha didn't pretend to understand. Instead, she gestured vaguely to[12] a door on their right. 'I … May I offer you a drink, Inspector? You as well, Sergeant? We've got a real ale[13] that, as Nigel Parrish is fond of saying, "sets you to rights[14]". Come this way.'

She led them into a typical English country-inn lounge[15], whose air was heavy with the scent of a recent fire. The room had been cleverly designed[16] with enough home-like qualities[17] to keep residents comfortable while maintaining a formal enough atmosphere to keep villagers out. There were a variety of plump, chintz-covered couches[18] and chairs decorated with *petit-point* pillows[19]; tables spread out in no particular arrangement were maple[20], well used and ringed on their tops[21] where too many glasses had been placed on the wood without pro-

1. J'ai été sollicité sur ce dossier
2. dorénavant
3. mandat
4. document
5. toute note rédigée
6. qu'on en finisse
7. Impassible
8. passa le doigt sur le combiné
9. de lever les yeux
10. ouvrit sa montre de gousset
11. un déplacement inutile
12. désigna vaguement
13. une bière traditionnelle
14. vous remet d'aplomb
15. salon d'auberge campagnarde
16. conçue intelligemment
17. de touches accueillantes
18. de canapés rebondis, recouverts de chintz
19. de coussins brodés au petit point
20. en érable
21. le dessus maculé de traces de verres

tection; the carpet was a floral design, patchy with darker colours[1] in some sections where furniture had recently been moved; suitably tedious prints[2] hung on the walls: riding to hounds[3], a day at Newmarket, a view of the village. But behind the bar at the far side[4] of the room and over the fireplace were two watercolours[5] that displayed a distinctive talent[6] and remarkable taste. Both were views of a ruined abbey.

Lynley wandered to one of these as Stepha worked behind the bar. 'This is lovely,' he remarked. 'A local artist?'

'A young man named Ezra Farmington does them,' she replied. 'They're of our abbey. Those two are how he paid for his board[7] here one autumn. He lives in the village permanently now.'

Barbara watched the redheaded woman deftly work the taps[8] and scoop the foam[9] from the churning brew[10] that was developing a life of its own in the glass. Stepha laughed in a breathless, charming way[11] when the foam slipped over the side[12] and on to her hand, and she unconsciously raised her fingers to her lips to lick the residue[13]. Barbara idly wondered how long it would take Lynley to get her into bed[14].

'Sergeant?' Stepha asked. 'An ale for you as well?'

'Tonic water, if you have it,' Barbara replied. She looked out the window. On the common, the old priest who had been to see them in London was having an anxious conversation with another man. From the gesturing[15] and pointing at the silver Bentley, the news[16] of their arrival was apparently the topic of[17] the village. A woman crossed from the bridge to join them. She was wispy-looking[18], an effect produced by a dress too gauzy[19] for the season and by baby-fine hair[20] which the smallest air current ruffled[21]. She rubbed her arms for warmth[22], and, rather than joining in the conversation of the

1. tacheté de couleurs plus sombres
2. des lithographies ternes
3. chasse à courre [avec la meute]
4. tout au bout
5. aquarelles
6. montrant un réel talent
7. ont servi à payer sa pension
8. actionner avec dextérité les pompes [à bière]
9. retirer la mousse
10. liquide tourbillonnant
11. eut un petit rire charmant
12. déborda
13. pour en lécher les résidus
14. coucher avec elle
15. D'après leurs gesticulations
16. la nouvelle
17. l'info du jour dans
18. paraissait toute menue
19. trop fine
20. des cheveux fins de bébé
21. que le moindre courant d'air ébouriffait
22. se frottait les bras pour se réchauffer

two men, she merely listened[1] as if waiting for one or the other of them to walk off[2]. In a moment, the priest said a few final[3] words and meandered back towards[4] the church. The other two remained standing together. Their conversation went in fits and starts[5], with the man saying something with a quick look at[6] the woman and then away[7] and the woman replying briefly. There were long silences in which the woman looked at the bank of the river[8] next to the common and the man focused[9] his attention on the lodge – or perhaps the car in front of it. Someone was significantly interested in[10] the arrival of the police, Barbara decided.

'A tonic water and an ale,' Stepha was saying as she placed both glasses on the bar. 'It's a home brew[11], my father's recipe[12]. We call it Odell's. You must tell me what you think of it, Inspector.'

It was a rich brown liquid shot through with gold[13]. 'Has a bit of a kick[14], doesn't it?' Lynley said when he tasted it. 'Are you sure you won't have one, Havers?'

'Just the tonic water, thank you, sir.'

He joined her at the couch in front of which he had earlier spilled out[15] the contents of the report on the Teys murder and had icily flipped through[16] every paper looking for the explanation of Roberta Teys' placement in Barnstingham Mental Asylum. There had been none. That had set him off[17] on the telephone[18] to Richmond. Now he began to go through the paperwork again, stacking things in categorical fashion[19]. From the bar, Stepha Odell watched them with friendly interest, sipping an ale that she'd poured for herself[20].

'We've got the original warrants, the forensics report[21], the signed depositions, the photographs.' Lynley fingered the materials as he named them. He looked up at Barbara. 'No keys to the farmhouse.[22] *Damn* the man.'

1. se contentait d'écouter
2. s'en aille
3. pour conclure
4. reprit tranquillement le chemin de
5. se déroulait par à-coups
6. en la regardant furtivement
7. puis en détournant son regard
8. la berge de la rivière
9. concentrait
10. s'intéressait beaucoup à
11. Elle est brassée ici
12. recette
13. strié d'or
14. de la vigueur
15. il avait étalé, auparavant
16. épluché, l'air glacial
17. C'était ce qui avait déclenché
18. son appel téléphonique
19. en faisant des piles par catégorie
20. qu'elle s'était servie
21. les rapports du médecin légiste
22. Il n'y a pas les clefs de la ferme.

'Richard has a set of those[1] if you need them,' Stepha said quickly, as if hoping to make up for her remark about Roberta that had set Lynley off on a collision course[2] with the Richmond police in the first place. 'Richard Gibson. He was … is William Teys' nephew. He lives in the council cottages[3] in St Chad's Lane. It's just off the high street.'

Lynley looked up. 'How does he come to have[4] keys to the farmhouse?'

'Having arrested[5] Roberta … well, I suppose they just gave them to Richard. He's to inherit it[6] anyway once the estate's all settled[7],' she added. 'In William's will[8]. I suppose he's seeing to the place[9] in the meantime. Someone must.'

'He's to inherit? How was Roberta treated in the will?'

Stepha gave the bar a thoughtful sweep[10] with a cloth[11]. 'It was fixed[12] between Richard and William that the farm would go to Richard. It was a sensible arrangement[13]. He works there with William. … Worked there,' she corrected herself, 'ever since he returned to Keldale two years ago. Once they got over their row[14] about Roberta, it all worked out to everyone's advantage. William had someone to help him, Richard had a job and a future, and Roberta had a place to live for life[15].'

'Sergeant.' Lynley nodded at her notebook[16], which was lying unused[17] next to her tonic water. 'If you would, please. …'

Stepha flushed[18] as she saw Barbara reach for her pen[19]. 'Is this an interview[20], then?' she asked, flashing an anxious smile[21]. 'I don't know how much I can help you, Inspector.'

'Tell us about the row and Roberta.'

She came round the bar and joined them, pulling a comfortable, cushioned chair[22] to the other side of the table. She sat down, tucking her legs to

1. en a un trousseau
2. en conflit
3. les logements sociaux
4. Comment se fait-il qu'il ait
5. Puisqu'ils avaient arrêté
6. C'est lui qui doit en hériter
7. quand la succession sera réglée
8. testament
9. qu'il s'occupe de la ferme
10. essuya le bar pensivement
11. un linge
12. Il avait été établi
13. un accord raisonnable
14. Après leur dispute et leur réconciliation
15. à vie
16. d'un signe de tête, indiqua le carnet
17. dont elle ne se servait pas
18. rougit
19. attraper son stylo
20. interrogatoire
21. en lançant un sourire inquiet
22. siège bien rembourré

one side, and glanced at the stack of photographs in front of her. She looked away quickly.

'I'll tell you what I can, but it isn't much. Olivia's the one who can tell you more.'

'Olivia Odell … your …'

'Sister-in-law. My brother Paul's widow[1].' Stepha placed her glass of ale on the table and used the same movement to cover[2] the photographs with a pile of forensic reports. 'If you don't mind …'

'Sorry,' Lynley said quickly. 'We get so used to looking at horrors like that that we become immune[3].' He replaced it all in the folder. 'Why did they have a row about Roberta?'

'Olivia told me later – she was with them at the Dove and Whistle when it happened – that it was all due to the way Roberta looks[4].' She fingered her glass, made a pattern of lace[5] on the moisture[6] of its surface. 'Richard's from Keldale, you see, but he'd been gone a good few years[7] trying his luck with barley[8] in the fens[9]. He'd married down there, had two children as well. When the farming didn't work out[10], he returned to the Kel.' She smiled at them. 'They say that the Kel never lets one go easily, and that was the case for Richard. He was gone for eight or nine years and, when he returned, he was quite a bit shocked to see the change in Roberta.'

'You said it was all due to the way she looks?'

'She didn't always look as she does now. She was always a big girl[11], of course, even at eight when Richard left. But she was never …' Stepha hesitated, clearly searching delicately for the right word[12], for a euphemism that would be factual[13] at the same time as it was non-committal[14].

'Obese,' Barbara finished. *Like a cow.*

'Yes,' Stepha went on gratefully[15]. 'Richard had always been great friends[16] with Roberta, for all he's twelve years her senior[17]. And to come back and find his cousin so sadly deteriorated[18] – physical-

1. La veuve
2. et en profita pour masquer
3. que cela ne nous fait plus rien
4. entièrement dû à l'apparence de Roberta
5. traça une dentelle
6. buée
7. longtemps
8. tenter sa chance dans l'orge
9. la région des anciens marais [à l'est de l'Angleterre]
10. n'a pas marché
11. un peu forte
12. le mot qui convenait
13. basé sur les faits
14. neutre
15. avec reconnaissance
16. s'était toujours très bien entendu
17. même s'il a 12 ans de plus qu'elle
18. en si piteux état

ly I mean, she was much the same otherwise[1] – was a terrible shock to him. He blamed[2] William for ignoring the girl[3]. Said she had done it to herself to try to get his attention. William raged at that.[4] Olivia said she'd never seen him so angry. Poor man, there'd been problems enough in his life without an accusation like that from his own nephew. But they got it sorted out[5]. Richard apologized the very next day[6]. William wouldn't take Roberta to a doctor – he wouldn't bend that far[7] – but Olivia found a diet[8] for the girl, and from that time on all went well.'

'Until three weeks ago,' Lynley observed.

'If you choose to believe that Roberta killed her father, then, yes, it all went well until three weeks back. But I don't believe she killed him. Not for one *blessed* moment.[9]'

Lynley looked surprised at the force behind her words. 'Why not?'

'Because aside from[10] Richard – who heaven knows has enough trouble just dealing with that family of his own[11] – William was all that Roberta had. Besides her reading and dreams, there was only her father.'

'She'd no friends her own age? No other girls nearby on the farms[12] or in the village?'

Stepha shook her head. 'She kept to herself.[13] When she wasn't working on the farm with her father, mostly she read[14]. She was here every day for the *Guardian*, in fact, for years on end[15]. They never did take a paper[16] on the farm, so she'd come every afternoon once everyone'd seen it and we'd let her take it home with her. I think she'd read every book of her mother's in the house, all of Marsha Fitzalan's, and the newspaper was the only thing left for her. We've no lending library[17], you see.' She frowned down at the glass in her hands.[18] 'She stopped looking at the paper a few years back,

1. pour le reste, elle n'avait pas beaucoup changé
2. a reproché à
3. de l'avoir négligée
4. Cela a mis William en rage.
5. ils se sont expliqués et ça s'est arrangé
6. le lendemain même
7. n'avait pas l'intention d'aller jusque-là
8. un régime
9. Pas une seconde.
10. à part
11. à s'occuper de sa propre famille
12. des fermes voisines
13. Elle recherchait la solitude.
14. la plupart du temps, elle lisait
15. des années durant
16. Ils n'ont jamais acheté un journal
17. bibliothèque de prêt
18. Sourcils froncés, elle baissa le nez dans son verre.

though[1]. When my brother died. I couldn't help thinking....[2]' Her grey-blue eyes darkened[3]. 'That perhaps Roberta was in love with Paul. After he died four years ago, we saw nothing of the girl for quite some time[4]. And she never came again to ask for the *Guardian*.'

If a village as small as Keldale could even have an undesirable area out of which residents aspired to escape[5], St Chad's Lane would have been that spot[6]. It was more like an alley than a street, an unpaved thoroughfare[7] to nowhere[8], having the one distinction of a pub[9] on the corner. This was the Dove and Whistle, its doors and woodwork painted a blinding shade of purple[10], itself looking very much as if it wished it could have had the good fortune to be settled somewhere – anywhere – else[11].

Richard Gibson and his brood[12] lived in the last attached[13] house in this lane, a pinched[14] stone building with chipped window sashes[15] and a front door that had once been painted royal blue[16] but now was fading to a decided grey[17]. This stood open[18] to the late afternoon, mindless[19] of the rapidly dropping temperature in the dale, and from within the confines[20] of the tiny house came the noise of a family quarrelling passionately.

'God damn you, *do* something with him, then. He's your son as well. Jesus Christ! You'd think he was a miraculous little version of virgin birth[21] from all the interest you take in his upbringing[22]!' It was a woman speaking, a shrieking that sounded as if at any moment it would choose hysteria or cachinnation[23] as a second line of attack.

A man's voice rumbled in answer, indistinguishable in the general uproar[24].

'Oh, it *will* be better, then? That's a fine laugh, Dick. When you've the whole bleeding farm to use as an excuse? Just like last night! You couldn't wait

1. il y a pourtant plusieurs années
2. Je n'ai pu m'empêcher de penser...
3. s'assombrirent
4. pendant longtemps
5. dont les habitants auraient voulu partir
6. c'était bien St Chad's Lane
7. une artère non goudronnée
8. ne menant nulle part
9. avec un pub pour seul trait distinctif
10. en violet criard
11. situé n'importe où, mais ailleurs
12. sa progéniture
13. mitoyenne
14. fatigué
15. des cadres de fenêtres abîmés
16. bleu roi
17. avait nettement viré au gris
18. Cette dernière était grande ouverte
19. indifférente
20. du fond
21. d'immaculée conception
22. son éducation
23. le rire convulsif
24. noyée dans le vacarme

to get there, could you? So don't tell me about the farm! We'll *never* see you then when you've five hundred acres to hide in[1]!'

Lynley rapped[2] sharply with the rust-grimed[3] knocker on the open door, and the scene froze before them[4].

With a plate on his knee, obviously attempting to eat some sort of utterly unappetizing[5] afternoon meal, a man sat on a sagging[6] couch in a cramped[7] sitting-room while in front of him a woman stood, her arm upraised[8], a hairbrush in her hand. Both stared at the unexpected visitors.

'You've caught us[9] at our very best moment. It was straight to bed next[10],' Richard Gibson said.

The Gibsons were a portrait of contrasts[11]: the man was enormous, nearly six and a half feet[12], with black hair, swarthy skin[13], and sardonic brown eyes. He was bull-necked[14], with the thick limbs of a labourer[15]. His wife, on the other hand, was a scrap of a blonde[16], sharp-featured[17] and, at the moment, white to the lips with[18] rage. But there was an electricity in the air between them that gave credence to[19] what the man had said. Here was a relationship where every argument and discussion was merely a skirmish[20] before the major battle[21] of who would be master between the sheets[22]. And the answer to that, judging from what Lynley and Havers could see before them, was clearly a toss-up[23].

Shooting a final, smouldering look[24] at her husband that spoke of desire as much as of rage, Madeline Gibson left the room, slamming the kitchen door behind her. The big man chuckled when she was gone.

'Eight stone of tiger[25],' he commented, getting to his feet. 'One hell of a woman.' He extended a large paw.[26] 'Richard Gibson,' he said genially[27]. 'You must be Scotland Yard.' When Lynley had made

1. 200 ha où te cacher
2. frappa
3. incrusté de rouille
4. se figea sous leurs yeux
5. vraiment peu appétissant
6. avachi
7. exigu
8. un bras en l'air
9. Vous nous surprenez
10. L'étape suivante, c'était le lit
11. formaient un tableau contrasté
12. 1,98 m
13. la peau basanée
14. avait un cou de taureau
15. les membres massifs d'un paysan
16. un petit bout de blonde
17. aux traits anguleux
18. totalement blême de
19. rendait crédible
20. n'était qu'une escarmouche
21. la grande bataille
22. au lit
23. se jouait visblement à pile ou face
24. dernier regard de braise
25. Une tigresse de 50 kilos
26. Il leur tendit sa grande patte.
27. cordialement

the introductions, Gibson went on. 'Sundays are always the worst round here[1].' He jerked his head[2] towards the kitchen from which a steady wailing indicated the state of the relationship between mother and what sounded like fourteen children. 'Roberta used to help out[3]. But we're without her now. Of course, you know that. That's why you've come.' He hospitably indicated two antiquated chairs[4] that were belching stuffing[5] on to the floor. Lynley and Havers picked their way across the room to them[6], avoiding broken toys[7], scattered newspapers, and at least three plates of half-consumed food[8] that lay on the bare[9] floor. Somewhere, a glass of milk had been left too long in the room, for its sour smell[10] overcame even the other odours of poorly cooked[11] food and plumbing gone bad[12].

'You've inherited the farm, Mr Gibson,' Lynley began. 'Will you move there soon?'

'It can't be soon enough for me.[13] I'm not sure my marriage can survive another month of this place.' Gibson toed his plate away[14] from the couch. A scrawny[15] cat slid out[16] of nowhere, sniffed[17] at the dried bread and pungent[18] sardines, and rejected the offering[19] by attempting to bury it. Gibson watched the animal, his face amused.

'You've lived here several years, haven't you?'

'Two to be exact. Two years, four months, and two days, to be even more precise. I could probably get it down to the hours as well, but you get the idea.'

'I couldn't help overhearing[20] the fact that your wife doesn't seem to be enthusiastic about the Teys farm.'

Gibson laughed. 'You're well bred[21], Inspector Lynley. I like that sort of thing when the police come calling[22].' He ran his hands through his thick hair, looked at the floor beneath his feet, and found a bottle of ale that, in the general confusion, had

1. le pire, ici
2. Il fit un geste brusque de la tête
3. donnait un coup de main
4. fauteuils antédiluviens
5. dont le rembourrage s'échappait de partout
6. traversèrent avec précaution pour les atteindre
7. en évitant les jouets cassés
8. de restes de nourriture
9. sans tapis
10. son odeur aigre
11. mal cuisinée
12. de canalisations défaillantes
13. Pour moi, le plus tôt sera le mieux.
14. écarta du pied son assiette
15. efflanqué
16. surgit
17. renifla
18. âcres
19. l'offrande
20. Je n'ai pu m'empêcher d'entendre
21. bien élevé
22. nous rend visite

become positioned precariously[1] against the side of the couch. He picked it up and drained it[2] before going on, wiping his mouth on the back of his hand. It was the gesture of a man used to taking his meals out in the fields. 'No. Madeline wants the fens again. She wants the open spaces, the water and the sky. But I can't give that to her. So I've got to give her what I can.' Gibson's eyes flicked over Sergeant Havers, who kept her head bent over her notebook.

'Sound like the words[3] of a man who would kill his uncle, don't they?' he asked pleasantly.

Hank finally caught up with them[4] in the novices' room[5]. St James looked up from kissing his wife – her skin smelt intoxicatingly[6] of lilies, her fingers moved silkily[7] through his hair, her murmured 'my love'[8] against his mouth fired his blood[9] – and there was the American, grinning wickedly[10] down at them from his perch[11] on the wall of the day room[12].

'Cotcha.[13]' Hank winked.

St James contemplated murder[14]. Deborah gasped in surprise[15]. Hank hopped down, unbidden[16], to join them. 'Hey, Bean,' he shouted. 'Found the lovebirds[17] in here.'

JoJo Watson appeared only moments later, struggling through the doorway in the ruined abbey, teetering dangerously on high heels[18]. Round her neck, as a complement to the chains and trinkets, hung an Instamatic camera.

'Taking some shots[19],' Hank said in explanation, nodding towards the camera. 'A few minutes more and we'd've had a few sweet ones-a you[20]!' He snorted with laughter, slapping St James affectionately on the shoulder. 'Don't blame you a bit, fella! If she belonged to me, I couldn't keep my mitts off her[21].' He gave brief attention to his wife. 'Dammit, Bean, be careful, woman! Break your neck in this place.[22]' He

1. s'était logée périlleusement
2. l'éclusa
3. On dirait les paroles
4. finit par les dénicher
5. la salle des novices
6. l'odeur enivrante
7. doucement
8. le « mon amour » qu'elle murmura
9. l'excita violemment
10. souriant avec malice
11. de son perchoir
12. la salle commune
13. Je vous tiens.
14. eut envie de le tuer
15. sursauta
16. sauta à terre, sans y être invité
17. les tourtereaux
18. chancelant sur ses talons hauts
19. On prend des photos
20. quelques photos tendres de vous
21. je voudrais toujours la peloter
22. Casse-gueule, ici.

turned back to the other two and noticed Deborah's equipment – camera-case, tripod[1], discarded lenses[2]. 'Hey, you taking shots, too? Got sidetracked[3], huh? That's honeymooners for you. Come on down here, Bean. Join the party.'

'Back from Richmond so soon?' St James finally managed to ask with strangled courtesy. Deborah, he noted, was surreptitiously[4] trying to straighten her clothes. Her eyes met his, full of laughter and mischief[5], alive with desire[6]. What in God's name were the Americans doing here *now*?

'Well,' Hank admitted as JoJo reached them at last[7], 'I gotta tell you[8], fella, Richmond wasn't quite everything[9] that you promised it'd be. Not that we didn't get a bang outa the drive.[10] Whatsay, JoJo-bean? Didn't we love it?'

'Hank loves driving on the wrong side of the road,' JoJo explained. Her nose twitched. Her eyes caught the exchange of looks between the two younger people. 'Hank, why don't we take a nice long walk[11] towards Bishop Furthing Road? Wouldn't that be a sweet way to end the afternoon?' She put her bejewelled[12] hand on her husband's arm, attempting to draw him out[13] on to the abbey grounds[14].

'Hellsapoppin, no,' Hank answered pleasantly. 'I have done e-n-u-f-f walking[15] on this trip to last me a lifetime[16].' He cocked his head at St James shrewdly[17]. 'That was some m-a-p[18] you gave us, fella! If the Bean here wasn't so fast at reading road signs[19], we'd be in Edinburgh by now.' He pronounced it Ed-in-berg. 'Well, there's no harm done[20], is there? We got here in time to show you the death hole itself[21].'

There was nothing for it but to go along.[22] 'Death hole?' Deborah enquired. She had knelt[23] and was replacing[24] her equipment – forgotten for a few moments in the lovely blue of Simon's eyes – in its case.

1. le sac de l'appareil photo, le trépied
2. les objectifs non utilisés
3. Vous avez été distraits
4. discrètement
5. d'espièglerie
6. frémissants de désir
7. les rejoignait enfin
8. Faut que je te dise
9. n'était pas vraiment à la hauteur
10. C'est pas qu'on n'ait pas aimé le trajet.
11. promenade
12. couverte de bijoux
13. en tentant de l'attirer
14. le terrain de l'abbaye
15. assez marché
16. pour tenir jusqu'à la fin de mes jours
17. l'air sagace
18. C'est une sacrée carte, que
19. les panneaux de signalisation
20. Y a pas de mal
21. le fameux trou de la mort
22. Il fallut bien les suivre.
23. s'était agenouillée
24. remettait

'The baby, remember?' Hank said patiently. 'Although considering what you two's up to in here[1], I can see the baby story didn't exactly scare the livin' hell outa you[2], did it?' He winked lasciviously[3].

'Ah, the baby,' St James responded. He picked up Deborah's case.

'Now I got your interest!' Hank approved. 'I could tell at first you mighta been a little peeved[4] at me popping in on you[5] like that. But now I got you[6], I can tell.'

'Yes, indeed,' Deborah responded, but her thoughts were elsewhere. Curious, how it had all happened in a moment. She loved him, had loved him from her childhood. But in a dizzying lightning-bolt moment of time[7] she'd realized that it had changed somehow, becoming quite different between them from what it had been before. He'd all of a sudden become not that gentle Simon whose tender presence had filled her heart with joy but a whip-bodied lover[8] whose very look aroused her[9]. Good heavens, Deborah, you've become quite silly with lust[10], she thought.

St James heard his wife's bubble of laughter[11]. 'Deborah?' he asked.

Hank nudged him in the ribs[12] with a knowing elbow[13]. 'Don't worry about the bride,' he confided. 'They're all shy at first.' He strutted on[14] ahead like Stanley with Livingstone in sight[15], pointing out areas of interest to his wife with a 'Catch that[16], Bean. Get it in the lens![17]'

'Sorry, my love,' St James murmured as they followed the progress of the other two through the ruined day-room, across court and warming-house[18] and into the cloister[19]. 'I thought I had him taken care of[20] until midnight at least. Five minutes more and I'm afraid he would have caught me getting you into some truly serious trouble[21].'

1. ce que vous alliez faire, ici
2. ne vous a pas trop fichu la frousse
3. lubrique
4. que vous étiez un peu en rogne
5. que je vous tombe dessus
6. Je vous tiens
7. en un éclair étourdissant
8. un amant au corps sec
9. dont la seule vue l'excitait
10. obsédée
11. petit rire
12. lui donna un coup dans les côtes
13. coude
14. continua à se pavaner
15. Stanley apercevant Livingstone [explorateurs ; le 1er était parti à la recherche du 2nd, dont on était sans nouvelles]
16. Chope ça
17. Prends une photo de ça !
18. le chauffoir
19. le cloître
20. qu'on en serait débarrassé
21. dans un bel embarras

'What a thought!' she laughed. 'Oh, Simon, what if he had![1] He would have shouted, "Get it in the lens, Bean!" and our love life might have been destroyed for ever!' Her eyes danced and sparkled[2]. Her hair gleamed brightly[3] in the afternoon sun, blowing about[4] her throat and shoulders carelessly.

St James drew in a sharp breath. It was like a pain. 'I don't think so,' he said evenly[5].

The death hole was in what remained of the vestry[6]. This was no more than a narrow roofless hallway[7], overgrown with grass[8] and wild flowers, just beyond the south transept of the ancient church. Here, a series of four arched recesses[9] lined the wall, and it was to these that Hank pointed with ghoulish drama[10].

'In one-a *them*,' he announced. 'Get it in the lens, Bean.' He tromped through the grass[11] and posed toothily[12]. 'Seems this was the place where the monks kept their church duds[13]. Sorta a cupboard or something. And on the night in question, the baby was plopped[14] right in and left to die. Pretty sickening[15] when you think about it, huh?' He bounced back[16] to their sides. 'Just the right size for a kid, though,' he added thoughtfully. 'Like a whad daya-call-it[17]? Sacrificial offering.[18]'

'I'm not sure the Cistercian monks[19] were in that line of business[20],' St James commented. 'And human sacrifices have been out of fashion[21] for a good number of years.'

'Well, whaddaya think[22], then? Whose baby was it?'

'I couldn't even begin to guess[23],' St James replied, knowing full well[24] the theory was forthcoming[25].

'Then, lemme tell you how it happened, because the Bean and I figgered it out[26] the first day. Didn't we, Bean?' A wait for the woman to nod her head

1. et alors !
2. pétillaient
3. scintillaient
4. flottant autour
5. posément
6. sacristie
7. un étroit couloir à ciel ouvert
8. envahi d'herbes hautes
9. quatre alcôves voûtées
10. avec une emphase macabre
11. traversa, en écrasant l'herbe
12. prit une pose souriante
13. leurs fringues d'église
14. déposé
15. c'est vraiment répugnant
16. revint en quelques bonds
17. comment ça s'appelle
18. Un sacrifice rituel.
19. que les moines cisterciens
20. s'adonnaient à ce genre de chose
21. ne se pratiquent plus
22. à votre avis
23. Je n'en ai pas la moindre idée
24. parfaitement
25. qu'il allait leur sortir sa théorie
26. on l'a imaginé

1. les pavés disjoints
2. par un trou
3. sentier
4. s'esclaffa
5. n'y avez pas réfléchi à fond
6. [surnom affectueux]
7. de lapin
8. en silence, l'air contrit
9. poursuivit son époux
10. on n'avait pas tout bien saisi
11. caravanes
12. au bord de la route
13. un de leurs bébés
14. adorent
15. pas cet enfant
16. sans se démonter
17. voilà l'histoire
18. prêts à sauter le pas
19. à pas de loup
20. une vieille bique
21. « Abandonné dans un fossé »
22. balaya d'un haussement d'épaules
23. [aux sorcières de Macbeth]
24. comme une vulgaire poussière

loyally. 'Come on over here. Lemme show you two love-birds a thing or two.'

Hank led them through the south transept, across the uneven paving[1] of the presbytery, and out on to the abbey grounds through a gap[2] in the wall. 'There you have it!' He pointed triumphantly to a narrow track[3] that led to the north through the woods.

'I see indeed,' St James replied.

'Got it figgered out too?'

'Ah, no.'

Hank hooted[4]. 'Sure you don't. That's 'cause you haven't thought it through[5] like me 'n' the Bean have, right, Sugar-plum[6]?' Sugarplum nodded mournfully, moving her bunny[7] eyes from St James to Deborah in silent contrition[8]. 'Gypsies!' her spouse went on[9]. 'OK, OK, I admit it. Bean and I didn't get the full handle on this[10] till we saw them today. You know who I mean. Those trailers[11] parked on the side-a the road[12]. Well, we figgered out that there musta been some-a the same here that night. It had to be a baby-a theirs[13].'

'I understand gypsies are inordinately fond of[14] their children,' St James noted drily.

'Well, not-a this kid[15], anyway,' Hank replied, undeterred[16]. 'So get the pitcher here[17], fella. Danny and Ezra are over there somewhere' – he waved vaguely in the direction from which they had come – 'getting ready for the plunge[18], you know? And tippy-toeing[19] along this path comes some old crone[20] with a kid.'

'Old crone?'

'Well, sure, don't you see it?'

' "Ditch-delivered[21]", no doubt,' St James said.

'Ditch-who?' Hank shrugged off[22] the literary allusion[23] like lint[24] from his coat. 'The old crone looks around, right and left' – Hank demonstrated – 'and slips into the abbey. Looks around for a deposit box[1] and bingo[2], Bob's-yer-uncle[3].'

'It certainly is an interesting theory,' Deborah put in. 'But I always feel just a bit sorry for the gypsies. They seem to get blamed for everything, don't they?'

'*That*, little bride, brings me right on up to theory number two.'

JoJo-bean blinked her apologies[4].

Gembler Farm was in excellent condition[5], a fact unsurprising since Richard Gibson had continued to work it[6] throughout the three weeks since his uncle's death. Opening the well-oiled gates[7] that hung between two stone posts[8], Lynley and Havers entered and surveyed it.

It would be quite an inheritance[9]. To their left stood the farmhouse[10], an old building constructed from the common brown bricks[11] of the district[12], with freshly painted white woodwork and frail clematis[13] conscientiously trimmed and trellised[14] over windows and door. It was set back[15] from Gembler Road, and a well-tended[16] garden, fenced[17] to keep out the sheep, separated the two. Next to the house was a low out-building[18], and, forming another side to the quadrangle that comprised the yard, the barn loomed[19] to their right.

Like the house, it was constructed of brick with a heavy tiled roof[20]. It was two floors high, with gaping windows[21] on the second floor through which the tops of ladders could be seen[22]. Dutch doors were used[23] on the ground level[24] of the barn, for this was a building for tools[25] and animals only. Vehicles would be kept in the outbuilding to the far side of the house.

They walked across the well-swept yard[26], and Lynley inserted a key into the rusting lock that hung[27] on the barn door. It swung noiselessly open.

1. une consigne où laisser le bébé
2. hop
3. le tour est joué
4. l'excusa d'une mimique
5. état
6. d'y travailler la terre
7. les grilles bien graissées
8. piliers
9. un bel héritage
10. le corps de ferme
11. en briques brunes ordinaires
12. de la région
13. de fragiles clématites
14. taillées et grimpant sur un treillis
15. en retrait
16. bien tenu
17. avec palissade
18. dépendance
19. la grange se dressait
20. un lourd toit de tuiles
21. des fenêtres béantes
22. on distinguait le haut des échelles
23. Il y avait des portes à deux vantaux
24. rez-de-chaussée
25. l'outillage
26. la cour bien balayée
27. le cadenas rouillé suspendu

Inside, it was eerily[1] still[2], dim[3], musty[4], and over-cold, too much the place where a man had met a violent end.

'Quiet,' Havers observed. She hesitated at the door while Lynley entered.

'Hmm,' he responded from the third stall. 'Expect that's due to the sheep.'

'Sir?'

He looked up at her from where he had squatted[5] on the pockmarked[6] stone floor. She was quite pale. 'Sheep, Sergeant,' he said. 'They're in the upper meadow, remember? That's why it's so quiet. Have a look here, will you?' Seeing that she was reluctant to approach[7], he added, 'You were right.'

She came forward at that[8] and passed her eyes over the stall. At the far end was heaped a mouldy pile of hay[9]. To the centre was a not over-large[10] pool of dried blood – brown, not red. There was nothing else.

'Right, sir?' Havers asked.

'Dead on the button[11], if you'll pardon the expression. Not a drop[12] of blood on the walls. I don't think we had any body-slinging[13] here. No crime-scene arrangement done after the fact. Nice thinking[14], Havers.' He looked up in time to see the surprise on her face.

She reddened in confusion. 'Thank you, sir.'

He stood up and directed his attention back to the stall. The over-turned bucket upon which Roberta had been sitting when the priest found her was still in its place. The hay into which the head had rolled remained untouched. The pool of dried blood had scraping marks[15] from the forensic team[16] and the axe was gone, but otherwise everything remained as it had been originally photographed. Except for the bodies. *The bodies.* Good God. Feeling like the fool[17] Nies intended him to be[18], Lynley gaped numbly at[19] the outer edge of the stain where

1. de façon inquiétante
2. calme
3. sombre
4. ça sentait le renfermé
5. s'était accroupi
6. grêlé
7. hésitait à s'approcher
8. s'avança aussitôt
9. du foin moisi était entassé
10. pas trop grande
11. En plein dans le mille
12. Pas une goutte
13. qu'on ait déplacé le corps
14. Belle analyse
15. les marques de prélèvement
16. laissées par l'équipe médico-légale
17. Se sentant aussi idiot que
18. l'avait prévu
19. regarda, hébété

a heelprint[1] matted[2] several black and white hairs[3] into the coagulated blood. He swung to[4] Havers.

'The *dog*,' he said.

'Inspector?'

'Havers, what in God's name did Nies do with the dog?'

Her eyes went to the same heelprint, saw the same hairs. 'It was in the report, wasn't it?'

'It *wasn't*,' he replied with a muttered curse[5] and knew that he was going to have to drag every scrap of information out of[6] Nies as if he were a surgeon[7] probing for shrapnel[8]. It would be absolute hell. 'Let's look at the house,' he said grimly.

They entered as the family would, through an enclosed porch-like[9] hallway in which old coats and mackintoshes hung on pegs[10] and workboots stood beneath a single-plank bench[11] along the wall. The house had gone unheated[12] for three weeks, so the air was tomb-like[13]. A car rumbled past[14] on Gembler Road, but the sound was muffled[15] and distant.

The hall took them immediately into the kitchen. It was a large room, with a red linoleum floor, dark ash cabinets[16], and brilliantly white appliances[17] that looked as if they were still polished[18] daily. Nothing whatsoever was out of place[19]. Not a dish was out of a single cupboard[20]; not a crumb lay[21] on a single worktop[22]; not a stain marred[23] the surface of the white cast-iron sink[24]. In the centre of the room stood a work-table of unpainted pine[25], its top scarred[26] with the slashings[27] of thousands of knives cutting thousands of vegetables, with the discoloration of generations of cooking.

'No wonder Gibson is eager for the place[28],' Lynley remarked as he looked it over. 'Certainly a far cry from[29] St Chad's Lane.'

'Did you believe him, sir?' Havers asked.

Lynley paused in his inspection of the cupboards. 'That he was in bed with his wife when Teys was

1. une empreinte de talon
2. avait agglutiné
3. poils
4. se retourna vivement vers
5. en jurant dans sa barbe
6. soutirer la moindre bribe d'information à
7. chirurgien
8. cherchant les éclats d'obus
9. au plafond formant une voûte
10. étaient suspendus à des patères
11. banc
12. n'était plus chauffée
13. si bien qu'il y régnait une fraîcheur de caveau
14. passa dans un grondement
15. étouffé
16. des placards en frêne
17. de l'électroménager blanc rutilant
18. astiqués
19. qui ne soit à sa place
20. du moindre placard
21. pas une miette
22. plan de travail
23. pas une tache ne gâtait
24. l'évier en fonte
25. en pin brut
26. balafré
27. entailles
28. soit pressé d'être ici
29. rien à voir avec

killed? Considering the nature of their relationship, it's a credible alibi, wouldn't you say?'

'I … suppose so, sir.'

He glanced at her. 'But you don't believe it.'

'It's only that … well, she looked like she was lying[1]. Like she was angry with him as well. Or maybe angry with us.'

Lynley considered Havers' statement. Madeline Gibson had indeed spoken to them grudgingly[2], spitting the words out[3] with barely a glance[4] of corroboration at her husband. For his part, the farmer had smoked stolidly[5] during her recitation, a blank expression of disinterest[6] on his face but, unmistakably[7], a lurking touch[8] of amusement behind his dark eyes. 'There's something not quite right there, I'll agree. Let's go through here.'

They went through a heavy[9] door into the dining-room, where a mahogany[10] table was covered with clean, cream-coloured lace[11]. On it, yellow roses in a vase had long since died, weeping petals[12] on to the fret of the cloth[13]. A matching[14] sideboard stood to one side with a silver epergne[15] placed in its exact centre, as if someone with a measuring tool[16] had made certain it was equidistant from each end. A china cabinet[17] held a beautiful collection of dishes obviously unused by the inhabitants of the house. They were antique Belleek[18] pieces, each one stacked or tilted or turned[19] in some way to display it best[20]. As in the kitchen, nothing was out of place. Save for the flowers, they might have been wandering through a museum.

It was across the hall from the dining-room, however, where they first found signs of the life of the house. For here in the sitting room the Teys had kept[21] their shrine.

Havers preceded Lynley into the room, but at the sight she cried out involuntarily, and stepped back quickly, one arm raised as if to ward off a blow[22].

1. on aurait dit qu'elle mentait
2. à contrecœur
3. en crachant ses mots
4. à peine un regard
5. flegmatique
6. l'air absent et indifférent
7. indéniablement
8. une vague lueur
9. massive
10. en acajou
11. dentelle blanc cassé
12. et perdaient leurs pétales
13. le motif ajouré du tissu
14. assorti
15. un centre-de-table en argent
16. un instrument de mesure
17. Une vitrine à porcelaines
18. [fabrique de porcelaines d'Irlande du Nord]
19. empilée, inclinée ou tournée
20. pour la mettre en valeur
21. avaient installé
22. comme pour éviter un coup

'Something wrong, Sergeant?' Lynley inspected the room to see what had startled her, observing nothing but furniture and a collection of photographs in one corner.

'Excuse me. I think …' She produced an unnatural grimace to pass for a smile[1]. 'Sorry, sir. I … think I must be hungry or something. A little lightheaded.[2] I'm fine.' She walked to the corner of the room in which the photographs hung, before which the candles rested, underneath which the flowers died. 'This must be the mother,' she said. 'Quite a tribute.[3]'

Lynley joined her at a three-cornered table[4] that backed into the wall[5]. 'Beautiful girl[6],' he replied softly, studying the pictures. 'She really wasn't much more than that, was she? Look at the wedding picture[7]. She looks as if she were ten years old! Such a little creature.[8]'

It was unspoken between them.[9] How had she produced[10] a cow like Roberta?

'Don't you think it's a bit …?' Havers paused and he glanced at her. She clasped her hands stiffly behind her[11]. 'I mean, if he was planning to marry Olivia, sir.'

Lynley set down what was obviously the final portrait of the woman. She looked about twenty-four: a fresh, smiling face; golden freckles[12] sprinkled across the bridge of her nose[13]; long, gleaming[14] blonde hair tied back and curled[15]. Beguiling.[16] He stepped back from the collection.

'It's as if Teys established a new religion in the corner of this room,' he said. 'Macabre, wouldn't you agree?'

'I …' She tore her eyes from the picture. 'Yes, sir.'

Lynley turned his attention to the rest of the room. Everyday living[17] had gone on in it. There was a comfortably worn[18] couch, several chairs, a rack holding[19] numerous magazines, a television

1. simulacre d'un sourire
2. J'ai un peu la tête qui tourne.
3. Un bel hommage.
4. une table d'angle
5. collée au mur
6. jeune fille
7. photo de mariage
8. Si menue.
9. Ils ne formulèrent pas leur pensée.
10. Comment avait-elle pu engendrer
11. se tint raide, les mains dans le dos
12. des taches de rousseur dorées
13. l'arête de son nez
14. brillants
15. bouclés
16. Charmante.
17. La vie de tous les jours
18. bon vieux
19. un porte-revue contenant

set, and a woman's escritoire[1]. Lynley opened this. Neatly stacked stationery[2], a tin of postage stamps, three unpaid bills[3]. He glanced at them: a chemist's receipt[4] for Teys' sleeping pills, the electricity, the telephone. He looked at the last, but there was nothing of interest. No long-distance calls.[5] Everything neat and clean.

Beyond the sitting-room was a small library-office[6] and they opened the door to this, looked at each other in surprise, and walked into the room. Three of the four walls had shelves that climbed to the ceiling[7], and every shelf was littered with[8] books. Books stacked. Books piled. Books falling loosely[9] to one side. Books standing up at rigid attention[10]. Books everywhere.

'But Stepha Odell said—'

'That there was no lending library so Roberta came for the newspaper,' Lynley finished. 'She'd read all of her own books – how was *that* possible? – and all of Marsha Fitzalan's[11]. Who, by the way, is Marsha Fitzalan?'

'Schoolteacher[12],' Havers responded. 'She lives in St Chad's Lane. Next door to the Gibsons.'

'Thank you,' Lynley murmured, inspecting the shelves[13]. He put on his spectacles. 'Hmm. A bit of everything. But heavily into the Brontës[14], weren't they?'

Havers joined him. 'Austen,' she read, 'Dickens, bit of Lawrence. They went in for the classics[15].' She pulled down *Pride and Prejudice*[16] and opened it. *Tessa's!* was scrawled childishly across the flyleaf[17]. This same declaration was in Dickens and Shakespeare, two Oxford anthologies, and all the Brontës.

Lynley moved to a book stand[18] that was fixed underneath the room's only window. It was the kind used for large dictionaries, but on its top rested[19] an immense illuminated[20] Bible. He ran his fingers down the page at which the book was open. ' "I am

1. secrétaire
2. Des piles soignées de papier à lettres
3. factures à payer
4. un reçu de la pharmacie
5. Pas d'appels longue distance
6. bureau-bibliothèque
7. des étagères allant jusqu'au plafond
8. encombrée de
9. penchant
10. bien droits
11. tous ceux de Marsha Fitzalan
12. L'institutrice
13. en examinant les rayonnages
14. énormément de Brontë
15. privilégiaient les classiques
16. prit sur l'étagère Orgueil et préjugés [de Jane Austen]
17. page de garde
18. un lutrin
19. dessus était posée
20. enluminée

Joseph your brother, whom ye sold into Egypt," ' he read. ' "Now therefore be not grieved[1], nor angry with yourselves[2], that ye sold me hither[3]. For God did send me before you[4] to preserve life. For these two years hath the famine been[5] in the land: and yet there are five years, in the which there shall neither be earing nor harvest[6]. And God sent me before you to preserve you a posterity in the earth, and to save your lives by a great deliverance[7]." ' He looked up at Havers.

'I'll never understand why he forgave[8] his brothers,' she said. 'After what they'd done to him, they deserved[9] to die.'

The bitterness[10] behind her words burned[11]. He closed the book slowly, marking the place with a scrap of paper[12] from the desk. 'But he had something they needed.'

'Food,' she scoffed[13].

He removed his spectacles. 'I don't think it had anything at all to do with food. Not really,' he noted. 'What's above stairs?[14]'

The second floor[15] of the house was simple: four bedrooms, lavatory[16], bathroom, all opening off[17] a central, square landing[18] illuminated by a skylight[19] of opaque glass. An obvious modernization to the house, this last architectural feature[20] gave the effect of being in a greenhouse[21]. Not altogether unpleasant, but unusual on a farm.

The room on their right appeared to be a guestroom[22]. A neatly made[23], pink-counterpaned[24] bed, a rather smallish affair[25] considering the size of the house's occupants, stood against one wall on a rug printed with a design of roses and ferns. It was obviously quite old, and the once brilliant reds and greens were muted now[26], bleeding one into the other[27] in a soothing rust[28]. The walls were hung[29] with paper on which tiny flowers – daisies and

1. Aussi, ne te lamente pas
2. envers toi-même
3. ici
4. m'a fait venir à toi
5. la famine a régné
6. ni épi, ni récolte
7. par un immense salut
8. il a pardonné à
9. méritaient
10. L'amertume
11. était âpre
12. marquant la page avec un bout de papier
13. persifla-t-elle
14. Qu'y a-t-il à l'étage ?
15. [premier étage]
16. des toilettes
17. donnant sur
18. palier
19. puits de lumière
20. détail
21. d'être dans une serre
22. chambre d'amis
23. soigneusement bordé
24. avec un dessus-de-lit rose
25. plutôt petit
26. avaient pâli
27. se confondant
28. en un ton rouille apaisant
29. étaient tapissés

marigolds[1] – sprinkled down[2]. On the bedside-table a small lamp stood upon a circle of lace. The chest of drawers held nothing[3], as did the wardrobe.

'Reminds me of a room in an inn,' Lynley remarked.

Barbara noted the view from the window: an uninteresting panorama of the barn and the yard. 'Looks as if no one's ever used it.'

Lynley was examining the counterpane across the bed. He pulled it back to reveal a badly stained mattress[4] and a yellowing pillow[5]. 'No guests expected here. Odd to leave a bed unmade, wouldn't you say?'

'Not at all. Why put sheets on it if it's never going to be used?'

'Except that—'

'Look, shall I go on to the next room, Inspector?' Barbara asked impatiently. The house was oppressing her.

Lynley glanced up at the tone of her voice. He drew the counterpane back over the bed exactly as it had been placed before and sat on the edge[6]. 'What is it[7], Barbara?' he asked.

'Nothing,' she replied, but she heard the edge of panic[8] in her voice. 'I'd just like to get on with it. This room obviously hasn't been used in years[9]. Why examine every inch[10] of it like Sherlock Holmes, as if the murderer were going to pop out of the floorboards[11]?'

He didn't reply at once, so the shrillness of her voice[12] seemed to linger[13] in the room long after she had spoken. 'What's wrong?' he repeated. 'May I help?' His eyes were on her, dark with their concern[14], so infinitely kind. It would indeed be easy—

'There's nothing wrong!' she exploded. 'I just don't want to have to follow you around like a spaniel[15]. I don't know what you expect of me. I feel like an idiot. I've a *brain*[16], goddammit! Give me something to do!'

1. des pâquerettes et des soucis
2. dégringolaient
3. La commode était vide
4. un matelas constellé de taches
5. un oreiller jauni
6. sur le bord
7. Qu'est-ce qui ne va pas
8. la panique
9. depuis des années
10. centimètre
11. surgir de dessous le parquet
12. son ton perçant
13. retentir encore
14. sombres d'inquiétude
15. comme un toutou
16. cerveau

He got to his feet, his eyes still on her. 'Why don't you go across the landing and deal with[1] the next room?' he suggested.

She opened her mouth to say more, decided against it[2], and left him, pausing for a moment in the greenish[3] light of the landing. She could hear her own breathing, harsh and loud[4], and knew he must be able to hear it as well.

That damnable[5] shrine! The farm itself was bad enough with its ghastly lifelessness[6], but the shrine had completely unnerved her[7]. It had been set up in the very finest corner[8] of the room. With a view of the garden, Barbara thought weakly. Tony has the telly and she has the damn garden!

What had Lynley called it? A religion. Yes, sweet Jesus! A temple to[9] Tony! She compelled her breathing to return to[10] normal, crossed the landing, and went into the next room.

That's torn it[11], Barb, she told herself. What happened to agreement, to obedience, to co-operation? How will you feel back in uniform[12] next week?

She looked about furiously, her lips quivering in disgust[13]. Well, who bloody well cared?[14] After all, it was a preordained failure[15]. Had she really expected this to be a success?

She crossed the room to the window and fumbled with the latch[16]. What had he said? *What's wrong? May I help?* The insanity[17] was that for just a moment she had actually thought about talking to him, about telling him everything there was to tell. But, of course, it was unthinkable. No one could help, least of all[18] Lynley.

She unlocked the window, threw it open to feel the fresh air on her burning cheeks, then turned back, determined to do her job.

This was Roberta's room, neat like the other, but with a lived-in air about it[19]. A large four-poster was covered by a quilt, a patchwork affair[20] with

1. vous occuper de
2. se ravisa
3. verdâtre
4. rauque et sonore
5. Saleté de
6. cette torpeur effrayante
7. l'avait salement ébranlée
8. dans le plus joli coin
9. à la mémoire de
10. se força à reprendre une respiration
11. Tu as tout gâché
12. quand tu remettras ton uniforme
13. tremblant de dégoût
14. Bon, et alors ?
15. un échec annoncé
16. agita le loquet
17. Ce qui était fou
18. encore moins
19. on voyait que quelqu'un y vivait
20. un couvre-lit en patchwork

a bright, cheerful design of[1] sun, clouds, and rainbow[2] on a sapphire background sky[3]. Clothes hung in the wardrobe. Sturdy[4] shoes – work shoes, walking shoes, slippers – were lined beneath them[5]. A dressing-table with a wavy cheval glass[6] stood[7] by a chest of drawers on which a framed photograph lay[8], face down[9], as if it had toppled over[10]. Barbara glanced at it curiously. Mother, father, and a newborn Roberta in the father's arms. But the picture itself, slightly distended, was crowded into its frame[11] as if it didn't quite fit. She turned the frame in her hands and prised off the backing[12].

She was correct in her guess.[13] The photograph *had* been too large for the purchased frame, so it had been folded back[14]. Unfolded, the picture was very much different, for to the left of the father, hands clasped behind her, stood the mirror image[15] of the baby's mother, a smaller version, certainly, but undoubtedly the offspring[16] of Tessa Teys.

Barbara was about to call out to[17] Lynley when he came to the door, a photograph album in his hands. He paused as if trying to decide how to get their relationship back in order[18].

'I've found the strangest thing, Sergeant,' he said.

'As have I[19],' she replied, as determined as he to forget her outburst[20]. They exchanged their items[21].

'Yours explains mine, I dare say[22],' Lynley remarked.

She gave curious attention to[23] the open pages of the album. It was a pictorial family record[24], the kind that documents weddings and births[25], Christmas, Easter, and birthdays. But every picture that had more than one child in it had been cut up[26] in some way, oddly defaced[27], so that pictures had central slices missing[28] or wedges cut into them[29], and the size of the family was systematically reduced in every one. The effect was chilling.

'A sister of Tessa's, I'd say,' Lynley observed.

1. un motif gai et éclatant représentant
2. un arc-en-ciel
3. dans un ciel couleur saphir
4. robustes
5. alignées dessous
6. une psyché ondulée
7. était posée
8. reposait un cadre de photo
9. retourné à plat
10. s'était renversé
11. gondolait dans son cadre
12. retira la fermeture côté dos
13. Elle avait deviné juste.
14. repliée
15. portrait craché
16. un enfant
17. appeler
18. comment remettre leur relation sur les rails
19. Moi aussi
20. son éclat
21. leurs articles
22. je crois
23. regarda avec curiosité
24. un album photo familial
25. qui illustre les mariages et les naissances
26. découpée
27. curieusement endommagée
28. des parties centrales manquantes
29. des morceaux découpés

'Perhaps her first child,' Barbara offered.

'Surely she's too old to be a first child unless Tessa produced her when she was a child herself.' He set the frame down, slipped the photograph into his pocket, and turned his attention to the drawers. 'Ah,' he said, 'at least we know why Roberta was so anxious for[1] the *Guardian*. She's lined the drawers with it.[2] And ... Havers, look at this.' From the bottom[3] drawer, beneath a pile of worn jerseys[4], he pulled something which had been placed face down, hidden. 'The mystery girl once again.'

Barbara looked at the photograph he handed to her. It was the same girl, but older this time, a teenager[5]. She and Roberta were standing in the snow[6] in St Catherine's churchyard, both grinning at the camera[7]. The older girl had her hands on Roberta's shoulders, pulling her back against her[8]. She had bent over[9] – although certainly not far, for Roberta was nearly as tall as she – and had pressed her cheek[10] to the other girl's. Her dark gold hair touched Roberta's brown curls. In front of them, with Roberta's hand clutched into his fur[11], was a border collie[12] who looked very much as if he were grinning as well. Whiskers.

'Roberta doesn't look half bad there[13],' Barbara said, handing the picture to Lynley. 'Big, but not fat.'

'Then, this must have been taken some time before Gibson left. Remember what Stepha said? She'd not been fat then, not until Richard had gone.' He pocketed[14] the additional photograph and looked round the room. 'Anything else?' he asked.

'Clothes in the wardrobe. Nothing much of interest.' As he had done in the other room, she drew back the quilt from the bed. Unlike the other[15], however, this bed was made, and its fresh, laundered linen[16] gave off the scent of[17] jasmine. But underneath it, as if the jasmine were incense subtly burning[18] to hide the odour of cannabis, was the

1. tenait tant à avoir
2. Elle en a tapissé ses tiroirs.
3. du bas
4. vieux pulls
5. à l'adolescence
6. debout dans la neige
7. souriant pour la photo
8. l'attirant vers elle
9. s'était penchée en avant
10. appuyé sa joue
11. agrippant sa fourrure
12. un chien de berger écossais
13. n'est pas si moche là-dessus
14. empocha
15. Contrairement à l'autre
16. les draps récemment lavés
17. sentaient
18. était de l'encens brûlant subtilement

cloying smell[1] of something else. Barbara looked at Lynley. 'Do you—?'

'Absolutely,' he replied. 'Help me pull off the mattress.'

She did so, covering her mouth and nose when the stench[2] filled the room and they saw what lay beneath[3] the old mattress. The boxspring covering[4] had been cut away in the far corner of the bed, and resting within[5] was a storehouse of food[6]. Rotting fruit, bread grey with mould[7], biscuits and candy[8], pastries half-eaten[9], bags of crisps[10].

'Oh, Jesus,' Barbara murmured. It was more prayer than exclamation and, in spite of the catalogue of gruesome sights[11] she had seen as a member of the force[12], her stomach heaved uneasily[13] and she backed away[14]. 'Sorry,' she gasped with a shaky[15] laugh. 'Bit of a surprise.'

Lynley dropped the mattress back into place. His face was expressionless. 'It's sabotage[16],' he said to himself.

'Sir?[17]'

'Stepha said something about a diet.'

As Barbara had done before, Lynley walked to the window. Evening was drawing on[18], and in a fading patch of the dying light he withdrew the photographs from his coat pocket and examined them. He stood motionless, perhaps in the hope that an uninterrupted, undisturbed[19] study of the two girls would tell him[20] who killed William Teys and why, and what a storehouse of rotting food had to do with anything. Watching him, Barbara was struck by how a trick of light[21] falling across hair, cheek, and brow made him look vastly younger[22] than his thirty-two years. And yet nothing altered or obscured the man's intelligence or the wit behind his eyes[23], not even the shadows. The only noise in the room was his breathing, steady and calm, very sure.

1. perçait l'odeur écœurante
2. lorsque la puanteur
3. ce que recelait
4. Le revêtement du sommier
5. à l'intérieur
6. un garde-manger
7. Des fruits pourris, du pain gris de moisi
8. des bonbons
9. des gâteaux entamés
10. chips
11. série de visions d'horreur
12. en tant que policière
13. eut un haut-le-cœur
14. recula
15. incertain
16. C'est du sabotage
17. Pardon ?
18. Le soir tombait
19. sans être interrompu, ni dérangé
20. lui révélerait
21. un effet de lumière
22. beaucoup plus jeune
23. l'esprit dans son regard

He turned, found her watching him, and began to speak.

She stopped him. '*Well*,' she said forcefully[1], pushing her hair behind her ears in a pugnacious[2] gesture, 'see anything else in the other rooms?'

'Just a box of old keys in the wardrobe and a veritable museum of Tessa,' he replied. 'Clothing, photographs, locks of hair[3]. Among Teys' own things[4], of course.' He replaced the photographs in his pocket. 'I wonder if Olivia Odell knew what she was in for[5].'

They had walked[6] the three-quarters of a mile[7] from the village down Gembler Road to the Teys farm. As they returned, Lynley began to wish that he had driven his car. It was not so much concern that darkness had fallen[8] but a longing for[9] music to distract him. Without it[10], he found himself glancing[11] at the woman walking wordlessly at his side[12], and he reluctantly considered[13] what he had heard about her.

'One angry vairgin[14],' MacPherson had said. 'What she needs is a faer toss i' the hay[15].' Then he had roared with laughter and lifted his pint in his big, bear's grasp[16]. 'But no' *me*, laddies[17]. I'll not test *those* waters.[18] I leave that plaisure to a young'r man!'

But MacPherson was wrong, Lynley thought. There was no question of angry virginity here. It was something else.

This wasn't Havers' first murder investigation, so he could not understand her reaction to the farm: her initial reluctance[19] to enter the barn, her strange behaviour[20] in the sitting-room, her inexplicable outburst upstairs.

For the second time he wondered what on earth Webberly had in mind in creating their partnership, but he found he was too weary[21] to attempt an explanation.

1. énergiquement
2. agressif
3. des mèches de cheveux
4. les effets personnels
5. ce qui l'attendait
6. parcouru à pied
7. les 1200 m
8. pas tant l'inquiétude de voir le soir tomber
9. une envie de
10. En l'absence de celle-ci
11. se prit à jeter des regards obliques
12. en silence à ses côtés
13. repensa malgré lui
14. Une pucelle aigrie
15. de se faire culbuter une bonne fois dans le foin
16. de sa grosse poigne d'ours
17. les mecs
18. Je ne vais pas m'aventurer sur ce terrain-là.
19. sa réticence, au départ
20. comportement
21. trop fatigué

The lights of the Dove and Whistle came in sight[1] upon the final curve[2] of the road. 'Let's get something to eat,' he said.

'Roast chicken[3],' the proprietor announced. 'It's our Sunday-night dinner. Get you some up quick[4] if you have a seat in the lounge.'

The Dove and Whistle was doing a brisk evening's business[5]. In the public bar, which had fallen into stillness[6] upon their entrance, a pall[7] of cigarette smoke hung like a heavy rain cloud[8] over the room. Farmers gathered in conversation in a corner, their mud-encrusted[9] boots placed on rungs of ladder-backed chairs[10], two younger men played a boisterous game of darts[11] near a door marked TOILETS, while a group of middle-aged women compared the Sunday-evening remnants[12] of Saturday's crimps and curls[13], courtesy of Sinji's Beauty Shoppe. The bar itself was surrounded by patrons[14], most of whom were joking with the girl who worked the taps behind it.

She was clearly the village anomaly. Jet-black[15] hair rose out of her scalp in spikes[16], her eyes were heavily outlined in purple[17], and her clothes were night-time-in-Soho explicit[18]: short black leather skirt, white plunging[19] blouse, black lace stockings[20] with holes held together by safety pins[21], black-laced shoes of the sort that grandmothers wear. Each of her ears – pierced[22] four times – wore the dubious decoration of a line of stud earrings[23], except for the bottom right hole, which sported a feather[24] dangling to her shoulder.

'Fancies herself[25] a rock singer,' the publican[26] said, following their glance. 'She's m' daughter, but I try not to let the word out often[27].' He thumped a pint of ale[28] on the wobbly table in front of Lynley, gave a tonic water to Barbara, and grinned. 'Hannah!' he shouted back into the public bar. 'Stop

1. apparurent
2. au dernier virage
3. Poulet rôti
4. Je vous en sers rapidement
5. était bondé, ce soir-là
6. où tout s'était tu
7. un voile
8. planait comme un gros nuage de pluie
9. incrustées de boue
10. sur les barreaux au dos des chaises
11. jouaient bruyamment aux fléchettes
12. ce qui restait
13. de crans et de boucles
14. clients
15. d'un noir de jais
16. formaient des épis
17. fardés de violet
18. du style pour sortir en boîte
19. décolleté
20. des collants
21. des épingles à nourrice
22. percées
23. d'une rangée de clous
24. arborait une plume
25. Elle se prend pour
26. patron du bar
27. je ne le dis pas trop
28. un demi

making a spectacle of yourself, girl! Y're driving every man present insane with lust[1]!' He winked at them wickedly.

'Oh, Dad!' She laughed. The others did as well.

'Tell him off[2], Hannah!' somebody called. And another, 'What's the poor bloke ever known about style?'

'Style, is it?' the publican called back cheerfully. 'She's a cheap one[3] to dress, all right. But she's running through my fortune[4] buying gunk[5] for her hair.'

'How d'you keep them spikes up, Han?'

'Got scared in the abbey, I'd say.'

'Heard the baby howl, did you, Han?'

Laughter. A playful swing[6] at the speaker. The statement made: *See, we're all friends here.* Barbara wondered if they'd rehearsed[7] the whole thing.

She and Lynley were the only occupants of the lounge, and once the door closed behind the publican she longed for the noise of the public bar again, but Lynley was speaking.

'She must have been a compulsive eater[8].'

'Who murdered her father because he put her on a diet[9]?' It slipped out before Barbara could stop herself. Sarcasm was rich[10] in her voice.

'Who obviously did a lot of eating in secret,' Lynley went on. His own voice was unperturbed.

'Well, it doesn't look that way to me,' she argued. She was pushing him[11], and she knew it. It was defensive and stupid. But she couldn't help it[12].

'What does it look like to you?'

'That food's been forgotten. Who knows how long it's been there?'

'I think we can agree that it's been there three weeks and that any food that's left out for three weeks is likely to spoil[13].'

'All right, I'll accept that,' Barbara said. 'But not the compulsive eating.'

1. fou de désir
2. Gronde-le
3. Elle coûte pas cher
4. elle me ruine
5. des gels dégueulasses
6. geste cordial
7. répété
8. boulimique
9. parce qu'il l'avait mise au régime
10. Il y avait beaucoup de sarcasme
11. Elle le provoquait
12. c'était plus fort qu'elle
13. a des chances de se gâter

'Why not?'

'Because you can't *prove* it, dammit!'

He ticked off[1] items on his fingers. 'We have two rotting apples, three black bananas, something that at one time might have been a ripe pear[2], a loaf of bread[3], sixteen biscuits, three half-eaten pastries, and three bags of crisps. Now, you tell me what we have here[4], Sergeant.'

'I've no idea,' she replied.

'Then, if you've no idea, perhaps you'll consider mine[5].' He paused. 'Barbara ...'

She knew at once from his tone[6] that she had to stop him. He couldn't, he wouldn't understand. 'I'm sorry, Inspector,' she said swiftly[7]. 'I got spooked[8] at the farm and I ... I've jumped all over you[9] for it ever since. I ... I'm sorry.'

He appeared to be taken aback[10]. 'All right. Let's start again, shall we?'

The publican approached and plopped two plates down on to the table. 'Chicken and peas,' he announced proudly.

Barbara got up and stumbled from the room[11].

1. Il lista
2. une poire mûre
3. un pain
4. Alors dites-moi ce que c'est
5. peut-être pourriez-vous écouter les miennes
6. à son ton
7. vivement
8. J'ai eu un peu les jetons
9. j'ai été agressive avec vous
10. surpris
11. sortit précipitamment

7

'No! Ezra, stop! I can't!'

With a deliberately unstifled curse[1], Ezra Farmington lifted himself off[2] the struggling[3] girl beneath him, swung to the edge of the bed, and sat there, fighting for breath[4] and composure[5], his entire body – but most particularly, he noticed sardonically, his head – throbbing[6]. He lowered this to this hands, burying his fingers in honey-coloured hair. Now she would cry, he thought. 'All right, all *right*!' he said and added savagely, 'I'm not a rapist[7], for God's sake!'

She did begin to cry at that[8], a fist at her mouth, dry hot sobs[9] erupting from deep within her. He reached for the lamp. 'No!' Her voice stopped him.

'Danny,' he said, trying to speak calmly but aware that he was forcing words out[10] between clenched teeth[11]. He couldn't look at her.

'I'm sorry!' she wept.

It was all too familiar. It couldn't go on. 'This is ridiculous, you know.' He reached for his watch, saw from the luminous dial[12] that it was nearly eight, and put it on. He began to dress.

At that, the crying increased[13]. A hand reached for[14] him, touched his naked back[15]. He flinched.[16] The sobbing continued. He picked up the rest of his clothes, left the room, went into the lavatory, and,

1. Laissant volontairement échapper un juron
2. se souleva de
3. qui se débattait
4. reprenant sa respiration
5. son calme
6. lui faisait des élancements
7. violeur
8. à ces mots
9. de violents sanglots sans larmes
10. les paroles sortaient avec peine
11. de ses dents serrées
12. cadran
13. les pleurs s'intensifièrent
14. se tendit vers
15. dos nu
16. Il frémit.

after dressing, stared morosely at his reflection in the dusky[1] mirror while his watch ticked away[2] five minutes.

When he returned, the weeping[3] had stopped. She still lay on the bed, her ivory body shimmering in the moonlight[4], and stared at the ceiling. Her hair was darkness; the rest of her was light[5]. His artist's eyes travelled the length of her[6]: the curve of cheek, the fullness of breast[7], the swelling of hip[8], the softness of thigh[9]. An objective study in black and white, translated quickly to canvas[10]. It was an exercise he often engaged in[11], one which dissociated mind from body, something he most particularly wanted to do right now. His eyes fell on the curling triangle of darkness[12]. Objectivity shot out the window[13].

'For God's sake, get dressed,' he snapped. 'Am I supposed to stand here staring at you as retribution[14]?'

'You know why 'tis,' she whispered. She made no other move. 'You know why.'

'That I do,' he replied. He stayed across the room by the lavatory door. It was safer there. A few feet closer and he'd be on her again[15], and there'd be no stopping it. He felt his jaw tighten[16], felt every muscle coil with a life of its own[17]. 'You don't lose a chance to remind me.'

Danny sat up, swung on him. 'Why should I?' she shouted. 'You know wha' you did!'

'Be quiet! Do you want Fitzalan to report back[18] to your aunt? Have *some* sense[19], won't you?'

'Why should I? When did *you*?'

'If you won't let it go, then what's the point, Danny? Why see me at all?'

'You c'n ask *that*? Even now? When everyone knows?'

He crossed his arms in front of him, steeling himself to the sight of her[20]. Her hair was tangled[21] round her shoulders; her lips were parted[22]; her

1. mat
2. égrenait
3. les pleurs
4. luisant au clair de lune
5. ensuite, elle n'était que lumière
6. la parcoururent
7. la rondeur de sa poitrine
8. et de ses hanches
9. ses cuisses
10. vite couchée sur la toile
11. auquel il se livrait souvent
12. le triangle sombre et bouclé
13. se volatilisa
14. en punition
15. il se jetterait à nouveau sur elle
16. sa mâchoire se serrer
17. se contracter tout seul
18. aille tout raconter
19. Sois raisonnable
20. s'armant contre le spectacle qu'elle offrait
21. emmêlés
22. entrouvertes

cheeks were wet with tears, glistening in the dull light[1]. Her breasts ... He forced his eyes to remain on her face.

'You know what happened. We've been over it[2] a thousand times. Going over it a thousand times more won't change the past. If you can't let it go[3], then we've got to stop seeing each other.'

More tears welled up[4] and spilled down[5] her cheeks. He hated to see her cry. It made him want to cross the room and crush her[6] in his arms, but what was the use? It would only begin again and end in disaster.

'No.' She was still crying, but her voice was low. She hung her head[7]. 'I don' want that.'

'Then, what *do* you want? I need to know because I know very well what *I* want, Danny, and if we both don't want the same thing, then there's really no use, is there?' He was struggling to summon up control[8] but what little he had[9] was vanishing[10] quickly. He thought he might actually cry with frustration.

'I want you[11],' she whispered.

Oh God, that cuts it[12]*. That really does.* 'You don't want that,' he replied miserably. 'Because even if you did, and even if you had me, at every juncture[13] you'd throw the past in my face. And I can't bear that, Danny. I've had *enough*.' To his horror, his voice caught[14] on the last word.

Her head flew up.[15] 'I'm sorry,' she whispered. She slipped off the bed[16] and came across the room, her body sculpted by moonlight. He looked away. Her smooth fingers found their way to his cheek[17], across it, into his hair. 'I never do think o' your pain[18],' she said. 'Only my own. I'm so *sorry*, Ezra.'

He drove his gaze[19] to the wall, the ceiling, the square of night sky beyond the window. If he met her eyes[20], he knew he was lost.

1. brillant dans la lumière blême
2. On en a parlé
3. Si tu n'arrives pas à le surmonter
4. affluèrent
5. ruisselèrent sur
6. la serrer très fort
7. baissa la tête
8. retrouver la maîtrise de lui-même
9. le peu qu'il avait
10. se volatilisait
11. J'ai envie de toi
12. c'est le pompon
13. à chaque occasion
14. s'étrangla
15. Elle releva vivement la tête.
16. se glissa au bas du lit
17. touchèrent sa joue
18. à ta souffrance
19. se força à regarder
20. S'il croisait son regard

'Ezra?' Her voice was like a caress in the darkness. She smoothed back his hair, took a step closer.

He could smell her musky fragrance[1], feel the tips[2] of her breasts sear his chest[3]. Her hand dropped to his shoulder and pulled him closer. 'Don't you think', she continued, 'we both have t' forgive[4]?'

It was finally too much. There was nowhere else to look. His last sane thought was: *Better lost than alone.*

Nigel Parrish waited until they returned from the lounge to the public bar. He was still sitting in his usual corner, taking his time about nursing a Courvoisier[5], when they finished their meal.

He regarded them with the kind of interest he usually reserved for the village inhabitants, quite as if they were going to be around for the next few years. They were certainly worth[6] the time and consideration, he decided, for they were so deliciously bizarre a couple.

The man's dressed absolutely to kill[7], Nigel thought and chuckled inwardly at his tasteless pun[8]. Charcoal suit[9], hand-tailored and fairly shrieking[10] Savile Row, gold pocket-watch looped across waistcoat[11], Burberry tossed casually[12] on to the back of a chair – why is it that people with the money to buy Burberry always toss them about without a second thought[13]? – shoes polished to a sombre, unscuffed shine[14]. *This* was Scotland Yard?

Somehow the woman was more what he had in mind[15]. She was short and dumpy[16], sort of a walking rubbish-bin type[17]. She wore a wrinkled, stained suit that fitted her badly[18]. Entirely the wrong colour for her as well, Nigel noted. *Baby blue's a lovely colour, but not on you, dumpling*[19]. Her blouse was yellow and did distressing things to her sallow complexion[20], not to mention the fact that it was very badly tucked in[21] all around. And the shoes! Sensi-

1. parfum de musc
2. le bout
3. lui brûler la poitrine
4. tous les deux, nous devons pardonner
5. en faisant durer son cognac
6. Ils méritaient bien
7. Ce mec est super fringué à mort
8. mauvais jeu de mots
9. Costume anthracite
10. fait main, forcément de
11. dont la chaîne pendait sur son gilet
12. négligemment jeté
13. sans réfléchir
14. un éclat sombre, sans éraflure
15. correspondait plus à son idée
16. petite et boulotte
17. un peu boudin sur pattes
18. qui ne lui allait pas
19. bouboule
20. teint cireux
21. mal rentré

ble brogues[1] were what one would expect of the police and indeed she wore them. But with blue tights to match the suit[2]? Lord, what a vision[3] the poor woman was. He clucked his disapproval[4] and got to his feet.

He sauntered over to[5] the table they had chosen near the door. 'Scotland Yard?' he began chattily[6], without introduction. 'Has anyone told you about Ezra?'

As he lifted his head to look at the newcomer[7] Lynley's first thought was, *No, but I should guess you're about to.* A man stood there, brandy glass in hand, obviously waiting for an invitation to sit[8]. When Sergeant Havers automatically opened her notebook, he considered himself[9] a member of their party[10] and pulled out a chair.

'Nigel Parrish,' he introduced himself.

The organist, Lynley recalled[11]. He guessed that the man was somewhere in his forties[12], and he was blessed with features[13] that middle age enhanced[14]. Thinning[15] brown hair, touched by grey at the temples[16], was combed neatly off an intelligent brow[17]; a firm, straight nose gave Parrish's face distinction; a strong jaw and chin were indications of strength. He was slender, not particularly tall, and striking[18] rather than handsome.

'Ezra?' Lynley prompted him.

Parrish's brown eyes darted from person to person in the room, as if he were waiting for someone to enter. 'Farmington. Our resident artist.[19] Doesn't every village have a resident artist, poet, novelist, or something? I thought that was a virtual requirement of country life[20].' Parrish shrugged narrow shoulders. 'Ezra's ours. Watercolours. The occasional oil.[21] Not bad, actually. He even sells some of them in a gallery in London. He used to come here for just a month or so each year, but he's become

1. De bonnes chaussures basses
2. des collants bleus assortis au tailleur
3. quel spectacle
4. marqua sa désapprobation d'un claquement de langue
5. s'avança nonchalamment vers
6. d'un ton familier
7. nouveau venu
8. s'asseoir
9. il estima
10. qu'il pouvait se joindre à eux
11. se souvint
12. avait la quarantaine
13. il avait la chance d'avoir des traits
14. la maturité bonifiait
15. qui se faisaient rares
16. nuancés de gris aux tempes
17. peignés vers l'arrière, dégageaient un front intelligent
18. séduisant
19. L'artiste du village.
20. quasi obligé, à la campagne
21. Une peinture à l'huile de temps à autre.

one of us now.' He smiled down at his drink. 'Dear, *dear* Ezra,' he mused[1].

Lynley was not about to be played[2] like a fish on the line[3]. 'What is it you'd like us to know about Ezra Farmington, Mr Parrish?'

Parrish's startled glance betrayed that he hadn't quite been expecting so direct an approach. 'Aside from the fact that he's just the teeniest bit of a village Lothario[4], there's what happened on the Teys place[5] that you ought to know.'

Lynley found Ezra's romantic inclinations to be neither here nor there[6], although obviously they were of interest to Parrish. 'What happened on the Teys place?' he asked, ignoring the other dangling line[7].

'Well ...' Parrish warmed to his topic[8] but a sad glance at his empty glass cooled the fires of the story[9].

'Sergeant,' Lynley said tonelessly[10], his eyes on the other man, 'would you get Mr Parrish another—?'

'Courvoisier,' Parrish said with a smile.

'And one for me.'

Havers obediently left the table. 'Nothing for her?' Nigel asked, face wrinkled with concern.

'She doesn't drink.'

'What a bore![11]' When Havers returned, Parrish treated her to[12] a sympathetic smile, took a genteel sip[13] of the Cognac, and settled down to his story[14]. 'As to Ezra,' he said, leaning into the table confidentially[15], 'it was a nasty little scene. The only reason I know about it is that I was out that way. Whiskers, you see.'

Lynley had gone in this direction once before. 'The musical[16] dog.'

'Pardon?'

'Father Hart told us that Whiskers liked to lie on the common and listen to you play the organ.'

1. dit-il, songeur
2. se laisser manipuler
3. un poisson pris à l'hameçon
4. un petit peu le séducteur du village
5. chez les Teys
6. importaient peu
7. l'autre perche tendue
8. se prépara à aborder le sujet
9. doucha son ardeur de conteur
10. d'une voix égale
11. Quelle barbe !
12. lui adressa
13. but une délicate gorgée
14. se mit à raconter
15. en se penchant sur la table, le ton confidentiel
16. mélomane

Parrish laughed. 'Isn't it the absolute devil?[1] I practise my fingers to the bone[2], dear ones, and my most enthusiastic audience[3] is a farm dog.' His words dealt with the matter[4] in a lambent fashion[5] – as if nothing on earth could really be more amusing. Yet Lynley could see it was a brittle performance[6], a façade made frangible[7] by the force of a current of bitterness that ran[8], swift and sure, just beneath the surface. Parrish was working at joviality[9] and rather too industriously[10].

'Well, there you have it,' he continued. He turned the snifter[11] in his hands, admiring the variety of colours that the Cognac produced as it caught the light. 'A virtual Sahara of musical appreciation in the village. In fact, the only reason I play at St Catherine's on Sundays is to please myself. God knows, no one else can tell[12] a fugue from a scherzo. D'you know that St Catherine's has the finest organ[13] in Yorkshire? Typical, isn't it? I'm sure Rome purchased it personally to keep the RCs[14] in control in Keldale. I'm C of E[15], myself[16].'

'And Farmington?' Lynley asked.

'Ezra? I don't think Ezra's religious at all. Except' – seeing no amused appreciation on Lynley's face – 'what you probably mean is what do I have to say about Ezra.'

'You've certainly read me[17], Mr Parrish.'

'Ezra.' Parrish smiled and took a drink, perhaps for courage, perhaps for solace[18]. It was difficult to tell. He lowered his voice momentarily, however; and, as he did so, a brief glimmer[19] of the real man[20] emerged, brooding[21] and moody[22]. But the chatty gossip[23] replaced him almost at once. 'Let me see, loves, it must have been about a month ago when William Teys ran Ezra off the farm[24].'

'Was he trespassing?[25]'

'Absolutely. But, according to Ezra, he has some sort of "artistic licence[26]" that allows him to tres-

1. N'est-ce pas absolument diabolique ?
2. Je répète à m'en user les doigts
3. mon public le plus enthousiaste
4. Il en parlait
5. avec un humour brillant
6. une pauvre prestation
7. fragilisée
8. une amertume qui sourdait
9. s'efforçait d'être jovial
10. laborieusement
11. petit verre
12. ne sait distinguer
13. le plus bel orgue
14. les catholiques
15. anglican
16. en ce qui me concerne
17. En effet
18. pour se réconforter
19. une brève lueur
20. de sa vraie personnalité
21. sombre
22. lunatique
23. le joyeux commérage
24. a chassé Ezra de sa ferme
25. Il s'était introduit dans la propriété ?
26. droit artistique

pass everywhere. And I do mean *everywhere*. He was doing what he calls "light studies[1]" of High Kel Moor. Your basic Rouen Cathedral sort of thing. Start a new picture every fifteen minutes.'

'I'm familiar with[2] Monet.'

'Then, you know what I mean. Well, the only way – let's say the quickest way – up to High Kel Moor is right through the woods[3] behind Gembler Farm. And the way to the woods—'

'Was across Teys' land[4],' Lynley finished.

'Exactly. I was trotting along the road[5] with Whiskers in tow[6]. He'd put in his usual appearance[7] on the common and, as it seemed late to let the old boy[8] find his own way home, I was taking him there myself. I had hoped our darling Stepha might be willing to do the job[9] in her Mini, but she was nowhere to be found. So I had to drag the old thing out there on these poor, stiff legs[10].'

'You don't own a car?'

'Not one that runs with any reliability[11], I'm afraid. Anyway, I got to the farm and there they were, right in the road, having the most god-awful row[12] I've ever seen. There was William in his jimjams[13]—'

'Excuse me?'

'His *pyjamas*, Inspector. Or was it his dressing-gown[14]?' Parrish squinted at[15] the ceiling and considered his own question. 'It was his dressing-gown. I remember thinking, "Lord, what hairy[16] legs old William has", when I saw him. Quite like a gorilla.'

'I see.'

'And Ezra was standing there, shouting at him, waving[17] his arms, and cursing in ways that must have made poor sainted William's[18] hair stand on end[19]. The dog got hot into the action[20] and took quite a piece out[21] of Ezra's trousers. While he was doing that, William ripped[22] three of Ezra's precious water-colours into shreds[23] and dumped[24] the rest of the portfolio right on to the verge[25]. It was dread-

1. des études sur la lumière
2. Je connais
3. à travers bois
4. Traversait les terres des Teys
5. Je filais sur la route
6. dans mon sillage
7. Il était venu, comme d'habitude
8. ce pauvre vieux
9. aurait voulu s'en charger
10. pauvres pattes raides
11. soit fiable
12. se disputant de la façon la plus minable
13. en pyj'
14. robe de chambre
15. loucha vers
16. poilues
17. agitant
18. de ce pauvre bigot de William
19. se dresser sur sa tête
20. s'est énervé
21. a arraché un bon morceau
22. a déchiré
23. en morceaux
24. jeté
25. bas-côté

ful.' Parrish looked down as he concluded his story, a mournful note to his voice[1], but when he lifted his head his eyes said clearly that Ezra had got what he'd long deserved[2].

1. le ton lugubre
2. ce qu'il méritait depuis longtemps

* * *

Lynley watched Sergeant Havers climb the stairs and disappear from view. He rubbed his temples and walked into the lounge, where a light at the far end of the room illuminated the bent head of Stepha Odell. She looked up from her book at his footsteps[3].

'Have we kept you up to lock the door?[4]' Lynley asked. 'I'm terribly sorry.'

She smiled and stretched her arms languidly[5] over her head. 'Not at all,' she replied pleasantly. 'I was nodding a bit[6] over my novel, however.'

'What are you reading?'

'A cheap romance.[7]' She laughed easily and got to her feet, which, he noticed, were bare. She had changed from her grey church dress into a simple tweed skirt and sweater[8]. A single freshwater pearl[9] on a silver chain hung between her breasts. 'It's my way of escaping. Everyone always lives happily ever after[10] in a romance novel.' He remained where he was, near the door. 'How do *you* escape, Inspector?'

'I don't, I'm afraid.'

'Then, what do you do about the shadows[11] in your life?'

'The shadows?'

'Chasing murderers down.[12] It can't be a pleasant job. Why do you do it?'

There was the question, he admitted, and knew the answer. *It's penance*[13]*, Stepha, an expiation for sins committed*[14] *that you couldn't understand.* 'I never stopped to think about it.[15]'

3. en entendant son pas
4. Vous a-t-on empêchée de fermer ?
5. s'étira mollement les bras
6. Je piquais du nez
7. Une histoire à l'eau de rose.
8. un pull
9. perle d'eau douce
10. est toujours très heureux à la fin
11. les ombres
12. Pourchasser les meurtriers.
13. par pénitence
14. pour expier des péchés
15. Je n'ai jamais pris le temps d'y penser.

'Ah.' She nodded thoughtfully and let it go[1]. 'Well, you've a package that's come[2]. Brought by a rather nasty[3] man from Richmond. He wouldn't[4] give me his name, but he smelt like a large digestive tablet[5].'

An apt[6] description of Nies, Lynley thought, as she went behind the bar. He followed. She had evidently been working in the lounge in the late afternoon, for the room was scented richly[7] with beeswax[8] and the yeasty smell of ale[9]. That combination took him right back to Cornwall, a ten-year-old boy hurriedly wolfing down pasties[10] in the kitchen of the Trefallen farm. Such delicacies they were to him[11], meat and onions folded into a flaky shell[12], fruit forbidden and unheard of[13] in the formal[14] dining-room of Howenstow. 'Common[15],' his father would snort contemptuously[16]. And indeed they were, which was why he loved them.

Stepha placed a large envelope on the counter. 'Here it is. Will you join me for a nightcap[17]?'

'Thank you. I'd like that.'

She smiled. He noticed how it curved[18] her cheeks, how the tiny lines[19] round her eyes seemed to vanish. 'Good. Sit down, then. You look exhausted[20].'

He went to one of the couches and opened the envelope. Nies had made no effort to put the material in any sort of order[21]. There were three notebooks of information, some additional photographs of Roberta, forensic reports identical to the ones he already had, and nothing whatsoever on[22] Whiskers.

Stepha Odell placed a glass on the table and sat opposite him, drawing her legs up into the seat of the chair[23].

'What happened to Whiskers?' Lynley asked himself. 'Why is there nothing about that dog?'

'Gabriel knows,' Stepha responded.

For a moment he thought it was some sort of village expression[24] until he recalled the constable's name. 'Constable Langston?'

1. n'insista pas
2. un paquet est arrivé pour vous
3. désagréable
4. n'a pas voulu
5. un gros cachet pour l'estomac
6. Une très bonne
7. sentait fortement
8. la cire d'abeille
9. la levure de bière
10. qui engloutissait des friands
11. Quel délice c'était, pour lui
12. pris dans une coque feuilletée
13. inconnu
14. solennelle
15. C'est vulgaire
16. grognait dédaigneusement
17. un dernier verre
18. modelait
19. rides
20. épuisé
21. pour classer les documents
22. absolument rien concernant
23. en repliant ses jambes sur le siège
24. une expression locale

She nodded, sipping her drink. Her fingers on the glass were long and slender[1], unencumbered by rings[2]. 'He buried Whiskers.'

'Where?'

She shrugged a shoulder and pushed her hair back off her face. Unlike the ugliness of the gesture of[3] Havers, in Stepha it was a lovely movement, chasing shadows away[4]. 'I'm not sure. I expect it was somewhere on the farm.'

'But why was no forensic study[5] done on the dog?' Lynley mused[6].

'I suppose they didn't need one. They could see how the poor thing died.'

'How?'

'His throat was slit[7], Inspector.'

* * *

He fumbled back through the material[8], looking for the pictures. No wonder[9] he had failed to see it before. Teys' body, sprawled right over[10] the dog's corpse[11], obscured the view. He considered the photograph.

'You see the problem now, don't you?'

'What do you mean?'

'Can you imagine Roberta slitting Whiskers' throat?' An expression of distaste[12] passed across Stepha's face. 'It's impossible. I'm sorry, but it's just impossible. Beyond that, no weapon was ever found[13]. Surely she didn't slit the poor animal's throat with an axe!'

As she spoke, Lynley found himself beginning to wonder for the first time exactly who the real target of the crime had been[14]: William Teys or his dog.

Suppose a robbery[15] had been in the works[16], he thought. The dog would need to be silenced[17]. He was old, certainly incapable of attacking someone,

1. fins
2. dépourvus de bagues
3. Loin d'être laid comme chez
4. qui repoussait les ombres
5. analyse médico-légale
6. se demanda Lynley
7. On lui a tranché la gorge
8. feuilleta à nouveau le dossier
9. Pas étonnant
10. étalé de tout son long sur
11. cadavre
12. dégoût
13. aucune arme n'a été retrouvée
14. qui était la véritable cible du meurtrier
15. qu'un cambriolage
16. en préparation
17. réduit au silence

but well enough able to make a din[1] if a foreign presence were found[2] in his territory.

So the dog would have to be dealt with[3]. But perhaps not quickly enough, so that when Teys rushed out[4] to the barn to see what the yelping was all about[5] he would have to be dealt with as well. Perhaps, thought Lynley, we have no premeditated[6] murder here, but a crime of an entirely different nature.

'Stepha,' he said thoughtfully. He reached in his pocket. 'Who is this?' He handed her the photograph that he and Havers had found in Roberta's chest of drawers.

'Where on earth did you get this?'

'In Roberta's bedroom. Who is it?'

'It's Gillian Teys, Roberta's sister.' She tapped the photograph lightly for emphasis[7], studying it as she spoke. 'Roberta must have kept this well hidden from William.'

'Why?'

'Because after Gillian ran off[8] she was dead to[9] William. He threw away her clothes, got rid of her books, and even destroyed every picture that she was in. Burnt her birth certificate[10] as well as everything else in a great bonfire[11] right in the middle of the yard[12]. How on earth,' she asked, more to herself than to him, her eyes on the photograph, 'did Roberta manage to save this[13]?'

'More important perhaps, *why* did she save it?'

'That's easy enough. Roberta adored Gillian. God knows why. Gillian was the great disaster in the family. She turned out quite wild.[14] She drank and swore and ran around like mad[15], having the time of her life[16], off to a party in Whitby one night, out with some hellion[17] God-knows-where the next[18]. Picking up men[19] and giving them a run for their money[20]. Then one night, some eleven years ago, she left. And she never came back.'

1. du vacarme
2. un inconnu s'était trouvé
3. il avait fallu s'occuper du chien
4. s'était précipité
5. ce qui provoquait les aboiements
6. avec préméditation
7. pour bien insister
8. se soit enfuie
9. morte aux yeux de
10. certificat de naissance
11. dans un grand feu
12. au beau milieu de la cour
13. à sauver celle-ci
14. Elle s'était bien dévergondée.
15. sortait comme une déchaînée
16. s'amusant comme une folle
17. sortant avec un bon à rien
18. le soir d'après
19. Séduisant des hommes
20. leur donnant du fil à retordre

Lynley caught[1] the word. 'Left? Or disappeared?[2]'

Stepha's body backed[3] into the chair. One of her hands rose to her throat, but she stopped the gesture as if it were betraying her. 'Left,' she said firmly.

He went along[4]. 'Why?'

'I imagine because she was at odds[5] with William. He was fairly straitlaced[6] and Gillian was nothing if not after a good time[7]. But Richard – her cousin – could probably tell you more. The two of them were rather thick[8] before he left for the fens.' Stepha got to her feet, stretched, and walked to the door, where she paused. 'Inspector,' she said slowly. Lynley looked up from the photograph, half-expecting her to say more about Gillian Teys. She hesitated. 'Would you like … anything else tonight?'

The light from the reception area behind her cast a glow[9] upon her hair. Her skin looked smooth and lovely. Her eyes were kind. It would be so easy. An hour of bliss[10]. Impassioned acceptance.[11] A simple, longed-for forgetting.[12] 'No, thank you, Stepha,' he made himself say[13].

The River Kel was a peaceful tributary[14] unlike many of the rivers that debouched frantically[15] from the hillsides[16] down into the dales. Silently, it wended its way through Keldale, flowing past[17] the ruined abbey on its way to the sea. It treated the village well, seldom overflowing in destruction[18], which was fortunate as the lodge and some village houses were built on its banks.

Olivia Odell had one of these houses, across the bridge from the lodge, with a sweeping view of the common and of St Catherine's Church. It was the finest[19] home in the village, with a lovely front garden and a lawn that sloped down to[20] the river.

It was still early morning when Lynley and Havers pushed open the gate, but the steady wailing of a child, coming from behind the house, told them that

1. releva
2. Partie ? Ou disparue ?
3. se cala
4. continua
5. en conflit
6. plutôt collet monté
7. ne pensait qu'à s'amuser
8. inséparables
9. formait un halo
10. d'extase
11. Un consentement passionné.
12. Ce pur oubli, ardemment désiré.
13. dit-il avec effort
14. paisible affluent
15. débouchaient avec frénésie
16. des flancs des coteaux
17. longeant
18. ses crues destructrices étaient rares
19. la plus belle
20. une pelouse en pente vers

the inhabitants were already up and about[1]. They followed the grief-stricken howling[2] to its source.

On the back steps[3] of the house sat the youthful mourner[4]. She was huddled in a ball of woe[5], head bent to her knees, a crumpled magazine photograph beneath her grubby[6] shoes. To her left sat her audience, a solemn male mallard[7] who watched her sympathetically. Upon her head was the ostensible[8] source of her grief, for she'd cut her hair – or, rather, somebody had – and had plastered it on to her skull[9] with grease. It once had been red[10] and, from the look of the locks escaping their confinement, decidedly curly[11]. But now, giving off the malodorous waft of cheap pomade[12], it was nothing but dreadful to behold[13].

Havers and Lynley exchanged a look. 'Good morning,' the inspector said pleasantly. 'You must be Bridie.'

The child looked up, grabbing[14] the photograph and clutching it to her chest in a motherly gesture[15]. The duck merely blinked.

'What's wrong?' Lynley asked kindly.

Bridie's defiant posture was completely deflated at[16] the gentle sound of the tall man's voice. 'I cut my hair!' she wailed. 'I saved my money to go to Sinji's but she said she couldn't make my hair go this way and she wouldn't cut it so I cut it myself and now look at me and Mummy's crying as well. I tried to straighten it all out[17] with this stuff of Hannah's[18] but it'll never come right!' She hiccuped pathetically[19] on the last word.

Lynley nodded. 'I see. It does look a bit awful, Bridie. Exactly what sort of effect were you going after[20]?' He quailed inwardly[21] at the thought of Hannah's black spikes.

'This!' She waved[22] the photograph at him, wailing anew.

1. debout
2. les hurlements de chagrin
3. les marches à l'arrière
4. la jeune pleureuse
5. recroquevillée de détresse
6. sales
7. colvert [canard] mâle
8. apparente
9. les avait plaqués sur son crâne
10. roux
11. franchement bouclés
12. exhalant des relents de Gomina bon marché
13. juste horrible à voir
14. saisissant
15. d'un geste maternel
16. perdit tout air de défi devant
17. de les rendre lisses
18. avec le truc d'Hannah
19. eut un hoquet pathétique
20. recherchais-tu
21. frémit intérieurement
22. agita

He took it from her and looked at the smiling, smooth-coiffured semblance[1] of the Princess of Wales, elegant in black evening gown[2] and diamonds, not a hair out of place. 'Of *course*,' he muttered.

Bereft of her picture[3], Bridie took comfort in the presence of her duck, slinging[4] an arm round him and pulling him to her side[5]. '*You* don't care[6], Dougal, *do* you?' she demanded of the bird. In reply, Dougal blinked and investigated[7] Bridie's hair for its edible propensities[8].

'Dougal the Duck?' Lynley enquired.

'Angus McDougal McDuck,' Bridie responded. The formal introduction made[9], she wiped her nose on the sleeve of her tattered[10] pullover and looked fearfully[11] over her shoulder at the closed door behind her. A single tear rolled down her cheek as she went on. 'An' he's hungry. But I can't go inside to get his food. All I got's these marshmallows[12]. They're all right for a treat[13], but his real food's inside and I can't go in.'

'Why not?'

' 'Cause Mummy said she didn't want to see me again till I'd done something about my hair and I don't know what to do!' The child began to cry again, real tears of anguish[14]. Dougal would apparently starve[15] – an unlikely prospect[16], considering his size[17] – unless some quick thinking were applied to the situation.

It appeared, however, that a plan of attack would be unnecessary, for at that moment the back door was jerked open angrily[18]. Olivia Odell took one look at[19] her daughter – her second only that day[20] – and burst into tears.

'I can't believe you would do it! I just can't believe it! Get in the house and wash your hair!' Her voice rose higher with[21] each word, climbing the peak to hysteria[22].

1. l'image souriante, aux cheveux bien lisses
2. en robe de soirée noire
3. Privée de sa photo
4. passant
5. l'attirant contre elle
6. Toi, tu t'en fiches
7. étudia
8. pour voir s'il y avait à manger
9. Ayant fait les présentations
10. en lambeaux
11. craintivement
12. de la guimauve
13. comme friandise
14. désespoir
15. mourir de faim
16. scénario peu probable
17. vu sa taille
18. ouverte avec colère
19. n'eut qu'à regarder
20. de la journée
21. montait à
22. approchant de l'hystérie

'But Dougal—'

'Take Dougal with you,' the woman said, weeping. 'But do as I say!' The duck was scooped into nine-year-old arms[1] and the two offenders[2] disappeared. Olivia tugged[3] a tissue[4] from the pocket of her cardigan, blew her nose[5], and smiled shakily[6] at the two adults. 'What a dreadful scene,' she said. But as she spoke she began to cry again and walked into the kitchen, leaving them standing at the open back door. She stumbled to the table and buried[7] her face in her hands.

Lynley and Havers looked at each other and, decision made, entered the house.

Unlike Gembler Farm, there was not the slightest doubt that this house was lived in. The kitchen was in total disarray[8]: the stove top[9] cluttered with pots and pans[10], appliances[11] gaping open[12] to be cleaned, flowers waiting to be put into water, dishes piled in the sink[13]. The floor was sticky[14] under their feet, the walls badly needed paint[15], and the entire room reeked with[16] the charcoal bouquet of burnt toast[17]. The offending source of this odour was lying on a plate, a sodden black lump[18] that looked as if it had been hastily extinguished[19] by a cup of tea.

Beyond the kitchen, what little they could see of the sitting-room indicated that its condition was much the same[20]. Housekeeping[21] was certainly not Olivia Odell's strong point. Neither was child-rearing[22], if the morning's confrontation was any indication.

'She's out of my control!' Olivia wept. 'Nine years old and she's out of my control!' She tore the tissue to shreds, looked dazedly[23] about for another, and, seeing none, cried harder still.

Lynley removed a handkerchief from his pocket. 'Take this,' he offered.

1. La gamine de neuf ans prit le canard dans ses bras
2. délinquants
3. sortit
4. mouchoir en papier
5. se moucha
6. fit un sourire tremblant
7. enfouit
8. sens dessus dessous
9. le dessus de la cuisinière
10. encombré de casseroles
11. l'électroménager
12. laissé ouvert, attendant d'être
13. de la vaisselle empilée dans l'évier
14. poisseux
15. avaient besoin d'un bon coup de peinture
16. empestait
17. la senteur de charbon de la tartine grillée
18. une masse noire et trempée
19. éteinte à la hâte
20. qu'il était dans le même état
21. Le ménage
22. L'éducation d'un enfant non plus
23. l'air hébété

'Ta[1],' she responded. 'Oh my God, what a morning!' She blew her nose, dried her eyes, ran her fingers through her brown hair, and looked at her reflection[2] in the toaster[3]. She moaned[4] when she saw herself, and her bloodshot[5] brown eyes filled again but didn't spill over[6]. 'I look fifty years old. Wouldn't Paul have laughed!' And then disjointedly[7], 'She wants to look like the Princess of Wales.'

'So she showed us,' Lynley responded impassively. He drew a chair out from the table, picked the newspapers off it[8], and sat down. After a pause, Havers did likewise[9].

'Why?' Olivia asked, directing the question more to the ceiling than to her companions. 'What have I done that my daughter believes the key to happiness is to look exactly like the Princess of Wales?' she squeezed her fingers into her forehead[10]. 'William would have known what to do. What a mess I am without him.[11]'

Wishing to avoid a fresh onslaught[12] of tears, Lynley spoke quickly to divert her. 'Little girls always have someone they admire, don't they?'

'Yes,' Olivia said. 'Oh, yes, how true that is.' She'd begun twisting[13] his handkerchief into an appalling little rope[14]. Lynley winced as he saw it mangled[15]. 'But I never seem to have the right thing to say to the child. Everything I try seems to end in hysterics. William always knew what to say and do. Whenever he was here, everything went smoothly[16]. But the moment he was gone[17], we'd begin to fight like cats and dogs[18]! And now he's really gone! What's to become of us?[19]' She didn't wait for an answer. 'It's her *hair*. She *hates* having red hair. She's hated it ever since she learned to speak. I can't understand it. Why is a nine-year-old girl so damned passionate[20] about her hair!'

'Redheads[21]', Lynley noted, 'are generally passionate about everything.'

1. Merci
2. reflet
3. grille-pain
4. gémit
5. rougis
6. retinrent leurs larmes
7. passant du coq à l'âne
8. en retira les journaux
9. de même
10. se pressa le front
11. Sans lui, je ne m'en sors pas.
12. un nouveau torrent
13. s'était mise à tordre
14. une épouvantable cordelette
15. de la voir malmener le mouchoir
16. tout se passait bien
17. dès qu'il était parti
18. comme des chiffonniers
19. Qu'allons-nous devenir ?
20. si obnubilée
21. Les rousses

'Oh, that's it! That's it! Stepha's quite the same. You'd think Bridie was her clone, not her niece.' She drew in a breath and sat up in her chair. Footsteps came running down the hall. 'Lord[1], give me strength,' Olivia murmured.

Bridie entered the room, a towel wrapped[2] precariously round her head, her pullover – which she hadn't bothered to remove in her haste to obey her mother's instructions – thoroughly soaked[3] round her shoulders and down most of her back[4]. She was followed by her duck, who walked like a seaman, with a peculiar rolling gait[5].

'He's crippled[6],' Bridie announced, noticing Lynley's inspection of the fowl[7]. 'When he swims, he jus' goes round in a big circle, so I don't let him swim unless I'm there. We took him swimming lots[8] last summer, though. In the river. We made a dam[9] just outside and he had ever so much fun. He'd plunk himself[10] in the water and go round and round. Huh, Dougal?' The mallard blinked his agreement[11] and searched on the floor for something to eat.

'Here[12], let me see you, MacBride,' her mother said. The daughter came forward, the towel was removed, the damage was surveyed[13]. Olivia's eyes welled with tears again[14] above her daughter's head. She bit her lip.

'Looks like it just needs a bit of a trim[15],' Lynley interposed hastily. 'What do you think, Sergeant?'

'A trim ought to do it[16],' Havers agreed.

'I think the thing to do, Bridie, is to give up on[17] the Princess of Wales idea. Now,' Lynley added as the child's bottom lip trembled, 'you've got to remember that your hair is curly. Hers is quite straight.[18] And when Sinji told you that she couldn't make it go in that style, she was telling you the truth.'

'But she's so pretty,' Bridie protested. Tears threatened once again.

1. Mon Dieu
2. une serviette entortillée
3. complètement trempée
4. presque partout dans le dos
5. étrange démarche chaloupée
6. Il est handicapé
7. volaille
8. plein de fois
9. un barrage
10. Il se laissait tomber
11. acquiesça d'un clignement d'œil
12. Voyons
13. on examina l'étendue des dégâts
14. se remplirent à nouveau de larmes
15. il faut juste égaliser un peu
16. Oui, ça devrait suffire
17. laisser tomber
18. Elle a les cheveux lisses.

'She is. Absolutely. But it would be a fairly strange world[1] if every woman were exactly like her, wouldn't it?

Believe me, there are many women who are very pretty and look nothing like her.'

'There are?' Bridie gave a longing[2] glance at the crumpled photograph again. A large smear of grease was sitting on[3] the Princess' nose.

'You can believe the inspector when he says that, Bridie,' Havers added, and her tone implied the rest: *He's a bit of an expert on the subject.*

Bridie looked from woman to man, sensing undercurrents[4] that she didn't understand. 'Well,' she announced, 'I s'pose I got to feed Dougal.'

The duck, at least, looked as if he approved.

The Odell sitting-room was only a slight improvement over[5] the kitchen. It was hard to believe that one woman and one child could produce such disarray[6]. Clothes lay piled over chairs as if mother and daughter were in the process of moving[7], knick-knacks[8] perched in unlikely positions[9] on the edges of tables and window-sills; an ironing-board[10] was set up in what looked like permanent residence; an upright piano[11] spat sheet music[12] on to the floor. It was havoc[13], with dust so thick[14] that it gave the air flavour[15].

Olivia appeared to be unaware of[16] the mess as she absently gestured them towards seats, but she looked about as she took her own[17] and sighed in unembarrassed resignation[18]. 'It's usually not this bad. I've been … it's been …' She cleared her throat and shook her head as if to get her thoughts in order. Once again the fingers went through the wispy, windblown-looking[19] hair. It was a girlish gesture, oddly incongruous to a woman who so plainly was no longer a girl. She had paper-fine skin and delicate features[20], but the ageing process was

1. un drôle de monde
2. envieux
3. Une grosse tache de graisse ornait
4. percevant des sentiments sous-jacents
5. à peine mieux que
6. un tel désordre
7. en plein déménagement
8. des bibelots
9. posés de façon incongrue
10. planche à repasser
11. un piano droit
12. déversait des partitions
13. le chaos
14. tellement de poussière
15. qu'elle imprégnait l'air
16. ignorer
17. en s'asseyant
18. l'air ouvertement résignée
19. décoiffés, comme ébouriffés par le vent
20. des traits fins

not dealing with her kindly[1]. She was lined and, although thin, her flesh lacked resiliency[2], as if she had lost too much weight[3] too quickly. Bones jutted[4] from her cheeks and wrists.

'You know,' she said suddenly, 'when Paul died, it wasn't this bad. I can't come to grips[5] with what's happened to me over[6] William.'

'The suddenness,' Lynley offered. 'The shock.'

She nodded. 'Perhaps you're right. My husband Paul was ill for several years. I had time to prepare myself. And Bridie, of course, was too young to understand. But William ...' She made an effort at control[7], fixing her eyes on the wall, sitting up tall[8]. 'William was such a presence in our lives, such a strength. I think we both started to depend on him and then he was gone. But it's selfish of me[9] to be reacting like this. How can I be so awful when there's Bobba to consider[10]?'

'Roberta?'

She glanced at him, then away. 'She always came here with William.'

'What was she like?'

'Very quiet. Very nice. Not an attractive girl. Heavy, you know. But she was always very good to[11] Bridie.'

'Her weight caused a problem between Richard Gibson and his uncle, though, didn't it?'

Olivia's brow furrowed[12]. 'A problem? How do you mean?[13]'

'Their argument over it.[14] At the Dove and Whistle. Will you tell us about it?[15]'

'Oh, *that*. Stepha must have told you. But that has nothing to do with William's death.' This as she saw[16] Sergeant Havers write a few lines in her notebook.

'One can never be sure. Will you tell us about it?'

A hand fluttered up[17] as if in protest but resettled in her lap[18]. 'Richard hadn't been back from

1. elle n'embellissait pas avec l'âge
2. ses chairs étaient flasques
3. de poids
4. Les os ressortaient
5. Je ne saisis pas
6. en ce qui concerne
7. pour se dominer
8. assise bien droite
9. égoïste de ma part
10. qu'il ne faut pas oublier
11. gentille avec
12. plissa le front
13. Comment ça ?
14. Leur dispute à cause de ça.
15. Pourriez-vous nous en parler ?
16. Ceci ajouté en voyant
17. se leva
18. se reposa sur ses genoux

the fens for long. He ran into us[1] at the Dove and Whistle. There were words. Silly. Over in a minute.[2] That's all.' She smiled vaguely.

'What sort of words?'

'It really had nothing to do with Roberta initially[3]. We were all sitting together at a table and William, I'm afraid, made a comment about Hannah. The barmaid[4]. Have you seen her?'

'Last night.'

'Then, you know she looks … different. William didn't at all approve of her, nor of the way her father deals with her[5]. You know – as if he's just amused by it all. So William said something about it. Something like, "Why her dad lets her walk about looking like a tart[6] is a mystery to me." That sort of thing. Nothing really serious. Richard was just a bit in his cups[7]. He'd a terrible set of scratches[8] on his face, so I think he'd been at it[9] with his wife as well. His mood was foul.[10] He said something about not being such a fool as to judge by appearances[11], that – as I recall[12] – an angel could be wearing a street-walker's guise[13] and the sweetest blonde-headed little face[14] could hide a whore[15].'

'And William took that to mean what?[16]'

She produced a tired smile. 'As a reference to[17] Gillian, his older daughter. Rather immediately, I'm afraid. He demanded to know what Richard meant by his remark. Richard and Gilly had been great friends, you see. I think – to avoid having to explain – Richard sidetracked[18] on to Roberta.'

'How?'

'As an example of not judging by appearances. Of course, it went on from there[19]. Richard demanded to[20] know why Roberta had been allowed to get into such an unattractive state. In turn, William demanded to know what he had meant by his insinuation about Gilly. Richard demanded that William

1. est tombé sur nous
2. Ça n'a pas duré plus d'une minute.
3. au début
4. serveuse
5. ni la façon dont son père s'occupe d'elle
6. vêtue comme une putain
7. un peu saoul
8. d'horribles égratignures
9. qu'il s'était disputé
10. Il était d'humeur féroce.
11. assez bête pour juger selon les apparences
12. si je me souviens bien
13. se déguiser en prostituée
14. la plus douce des petites blondes
15. une putain
16. l'a interprété comment ?
17. une allusion à
18. avait détourné le sujet
19. tout est parti de là
20. a voulu absolument

answer. William demanded that Richard answer. You know the sort of thing.'

'And then?'

She laughed. It was a tittering sound[1], like that of a trapped bird[2]. 'I thought they might fight. Richard said no child of his would ever be allowed to eat her way into an early grave[3] and that William ought to be ashamed[4] of the job he'd done as a father. William became so angry that he said something about Richard being ashamed of the job he was doing as a husband. He made a … well, a bit of a crude reference[5] to Madeline going unsatisfied[6] – she's Richard's wife, have you met her? – and frankly just when I thought Richard might truly hit[7] his uncle, instead he just laughed. He said something about being a fool to waste[8] his time worrying about Roberta and left us.'

'That was all?'

'Yes.'

'What do you suppose Richard meant?'

'By being a fool?' As if seeing the direction his question was taking her, she frowned. 'You want me to say that he felt he was being a fool because if Roberta died he'd get the farm.'

'Is that what he meant?'

'No, of course not. William rewrote his will[9] shortly after Richard returned from the fens. Richard knew very well that the farm had been left to him, not to Roberta.'

'But if you and William married, then the will would most likely have been rewritten once again. Isn't that true?'

Clearly, she saw the trap[10]. 'Yes, but … I know what you' re thinking. It was to Richard's advantage that[11] William should die before we could marry. But isn't that always the case when there's an inheritance involved[12]? And people don't generally kill

1. petit gazouillis étranglé
2. d'un oiseau pris au piège
3. creuser sa tombe à force de se goinfrer
4. avoir honte
5. une allusion grossière
6. qui n'aurait pas été comblée
7. allait vraiment frapper
8. de perdre
9. avait modifié son testament
10. le piège
11. dans l'intérêt de Richard si
12. en cas d'héritage

one another just because they're to inherit something in a will.'

'On the contrary, Mrs Odell,' Lynley objected politely, 'people do it all the time.'

'That wasn't the case here. I just think … well, that Richard's not very happy. And unhappy people say lots of things that they really don't mean[1] and do lots of things that they wouldn't otherwise do[2] just to try to forget their unhappiness, don't they?'

Neither Lynley nor Havers replied at once. Olivia moved restlessly[3] in her chair. Outside, Bridie's voice rose as she called to her duck.

'Did Roberta know about this conversation?' Lynley asked.

'If she did, she never mentioned it. When she was here, she mostly talked – in that low-voiced way of hers[4] – about the wedding. I think she was eager for[5] William and me to marry[6]. To have a sister in Bridie. To have what she once had with Gillian. She missed her sister dreadfully.[7] I don't believe she ever got over[8] Gillian's running away[9].' Her nervous fingers found a loose thread on the hem[10] of her skirt, and she twisted it compulsively[11] until it broke. Then she looked at it mutely[12], as if wondering how it came to be wrapped[13] round her finger. 'Bobba – that's what William always called her, and we did as well – would take Bridie off[14] so that William and I could have time alone. She and Bridie and Whiskers and that duck would go off together. Can you imagine what they looked like?' She smiled and smoothed the creases[15] in her skirt. 'They'd go to the river, across the common, or down to the abbey for a picnic. The four of them. And then William and I would be able to talk.'

'What did you talk about?'

'Tessa, mostly. Of course, it was a problem, but the last time he was here – the day of his death – he said it had finally been overcome[16].'

1. qu'ils ne pensent pas vraiment
2. qu'ils n'auraient jamais faites normalement
3. s'agita
4. de sa voix basse
5. qu'il lui tardait que
6. qu'on se marie, William et moi
7. Sa sœur lui manquait terriblement.
8. qu'elle se soit jamais remise
9. de la fugue
10. un fil qui pendait de l'ourlet
11. de façon obsessionnelle
12. en silence
13. comment il avait bien pu s'enrouler
14. emmenait Bridie
15. lissa les faux plis
16. réglé

'I'm not certain that I understand,' Lynley remarked. 'What kind of a problem? Emotional, you mean? An unwillingness to come to terms with her death[1]?'

Olivia had been looking out the window, but she turned to them upon the last word. *'Death?'* she asked, perplexed. 'Tessa's not dead, Inspector. She deserted[2] William a short time after Roberta was born. He'd hired a detective[3] to find her so that he could have their marriage annulled[4] by the Church, and Saturday afternoon he came to tell me she'd been found at last.'

'York,' the man said. 'And I'm not obliged to tell you anything more. I've yet to be[5] paid for my services, you know.'

Lynley gripped the telephone in his hand. He could feel the anger burning in his chest. 'How does a court order sound?[6]' he asked pleasantly.

'Listen here, old chap[7], don't try to pull that kind of shit on me[8]—'

'Mr Houseman, may I remind you that, in spite of what you may think, you are *not* part of a Dashiell Hammett novel[9] .' Lynley could just picture[10] the man, feet up on his desk[11], a bottle of Bourbon in the filing drawer[12], a gun tossed from hand to hand[13] as he balanced the telephone receiver[14] on his shoulder. He wasn't too far from the truth.

Harry Houseman looked out the grimy[15] window of his office above Jackie's Barber Shop in Richmond's Trinity Church Square. A light rain[16] was falling, not enough to clean off his window, just enough to emphasize its filth[17]. What a dreary day[18], he thought. He'd intended to spend it on a drive to the coast – a little lady in Whitby was only too eager[19] to do some serious private investigating with him – but this kind of weather didn't put him in the mood[20]. And God knows he needed to

1. Du mal à accepter sa mort
2. a quitté
3. engagé un détective privé
4. pour faire annuler leur mariage
5. Je n'ai toujours pas été
6. Que diriez-vous d'une injonction du juge ?
7. Écoutez-moi, mon vieux
8. de me la faire
9. [cf. le Faucon maltais]
10. visualisait très bien
11. les pieds sur son bureau
12. le tiroir de son caisson
13. à jongler avec son arme
14. le combiné du téléphone en équilibre
15. crasseuse
16. pluie fine
17. pour en souligner la crasse
18. sale journée
19. ne demandait pas mieux
20. lui coupait l'envie

be in the mood more and more these days before anything happened in the land down under[1]. He grinned, showing a badly capped front tooth[2]. It added a piratical dimension[3] to his otherwise mundane appearance[4]: dull[5] brown hair, muddy-coloured[6] eyes, cadaverous skin, and the incongruity of full, sensual lips.

He played with a well-chewed pencil[7] on the top of his scarred desk. His eyes caught the thin-lipped glance[8] of his wife's shrewish[9] face peering moodily out at him[10] from the photograph nearby. He reached out with his pencil and[11] toppled it over, face down[12].

'I'm sure we can reach some sort of mutual agreement[13],' Houseman said into the phone. 'Let me see. Miss Doalson?' A suitable pause for dramatic effect.[14] 'Do I have time today to … Well, cancel[15] *that*. It can certainly wait until I see …' Back to the phone. 'What did you say your name was?'

'We aren't going to see each other,' Lynley responded patiently. 'You're going to give me the address in York and that's going to be the end of our relationship[16].'

'Oh, I don't see how I can—'

'Certainly you do.' Lynley's voice was steel[17]. 'Because, as you said, you haven't been paid yet. And in order for you ever to get paid once the estate is settled[18] – which may, incidentally[19], take years if we don't get to the bottom of this[20] – you're going to have to give me Tessa Teys' address.'

A pause for consideration. 'What is that, Miss Doalson?' the infuriating voice asked in saccharine tones[21]. 'On the other line? Well, put him off, will you?' A martyred sigh.' I can see, Inspector, that you're not an easy man to deal with. We all have to make a living, you know.'

'Believe me, I know,' Lynley replied curtly[22]. 'The address?'

1. au-dessous de la ceinture
2. dévoilant une incisive mal refaite
3. un côté pirate
4. son allure banale
5. ternes
6. terreux
7. un crayon rongé
8. l'air pincé
9. acariâtre
10. l'observant, l'air mauvais
11. Il tendit le bras et, avec son crayon,
12. la fit tomber côté photo
13. parvenir à un accord
14. Ménageant une pause pour faire son petit effet.
15. annulez
16. nos relations s'arrêteront là
17. sans appel
18. quand la succession sera réglée
19. soit dit en passant
20. si nous n'allons pas au bout de cette affaire
21. sur un ton mielleux
22. sèchement

'I'll just have to find it in my files. May I give you a ring[1] in … say[2], an hour or so?'

'No.'

'Well, good *God*, man—'

'I'm on my way to Richmond.'

'No, no, that won't be necessary. Just wait a moment, old chap.' Houseman leaned back in[3] his chair, eyeing[4] the grey sky for a minute. He reached over to his dented filing cabinet[5], opening and closing a few drawers for effect. 'What's that, Miss Doalson?' he called. 'No, put her off till[6] tomorrow, will you? I don't care if she's weeping *buckets*[7], sweetheart, I don't have time to spend with her today.' He picked a scrap of memo paper[8] off his desk. 'Ah, *here* it is, Inspector,' he said and gave Lynley the address. 'But don't expect her to welcome you with open arms[9], will you?'

'I don't particularly care how she welcomes me, Mr Houseman. Good—'

'Oh, but you ought to, Inspector. Just a bit, you know. Hubby went mad[10] when he heard the news. Thought he'd strangle *me* right on the spot[11], so God knows what he'll do when Scotland Yard shows up[12]. He's one of those scholarly types[13], big words and thick specs[14]. But trust me, Inspector, that man is deep[15]. There's an animal inside him.'

Lynley's eyes narrowed. It was a cast upon the waters[16], an expert manoeuvre. He wanted to swim past it[17] but admitted defeat. 'What are you talking about? What news did he hear?'

'The news about hubby number one, of course.'

'What are you trying to tell me, Houseman?'

'That Tessa Teys is a bigamist[18], old boy,' Houseman finished with delight[19]. 'Married up with number two without seeing to the formal bye-byes to our[20] William. Can you imagine her surprise when I popped up[21] on her doorstep?'

1. vous rappeler
2. disons
3. se radossa à
4. fixant
5. son placard cabossé
6. remettez-la à
7. pleure comme une fontaine
8. prit un bout de papier
9. à ce qu'elle vous accueille à bras ouverts
10. Son petit mari était furieux
11. sur place
12. va débarquer
13. du genre intello
14. mots ronflants et grosses lunettes
15. obscur
16. un truc pour l'appâter
17. passer outre
18. bigame
19. en se délectant
20. sans prendre la peine de divorcer d'avec
21. je me suis pointé

The house wasn't at all what he had expected. Women who desert husband and children should somehow end up in tenement buildings[1] pungent with the odours of garlic[2] and urine. They should daily subdue a bucking, quarrelsome conscience[3] with liberal applications of soporific gin[4]. They should be faded[5] and worn[6], their looks[7] quite destroyed by the ravages of shame. Whatever they should be, Lynley was certain they shouldn't be Tessa Teys Mowrey.

He'd parked in front of the house, and they stared at it silently until Havers finally spoke. 'Not exactly gone downhill[8], has she?' she asked.

They'd found it easily, a new, middle-class neighbourhood[9] a few miles from the city centre, the kind of place where houses have numbers as well as coy little names[10]. The Mowreys' home was called Jorvik View. It was the concrete reality of every mediocre dream: a façade of brick covered the poured-block[11] construction; red tiles[12] swept up[13] to form steep gables[14]; white-curtained bay windows[15] showed off[16] sitting- and dining-rooms on either side of a polished front door. A single-car, attached garage[17] was topped by a white iron-fenced roof terrace[18], and a door opened on to this from the upper floor of the house. It was on this terrace that they had their first glimpse[19] of Tessa.

She came out of the door, blonde hair blowing lightly in the breeze, to water potted plants[20]: spider chrysanthemums, dahlias, and marigolds[21] that made an autumn wall of colour against the white iron. She saw the car and hesitated, watering-can poised in mid-air[22], appearing every bit[23] in the late-morning light as if Renoir had captured her[24] by surprise.

And she looked, Lynley noted grimly[25], not a day older than her photograph taken nineteen years before and religiously enshrined[26] at Gembler Farm.

'So much for the wages of sin[27],' he muttered.

1. finir dans des logements sociaux
2. empestant l'ail
3. noyer leur conscience rebelle et vindicative
4. à grands coups de gin
5. fanées
6. marquées
7. leur beauté
8. Sa situation ne s'est pas vraiment dégradée
9. quartier bourgeois
10. des petits noms
11. en béton coulé
12. des tuiles
13. relevées
14. des pignons abrupts
15. des baies vitrées
16. laissaient voir
17. Un petit garage attenant
18. terrasse de toit ceinte de fer forgé blanc
19. le premier aperçu
20. arroser des plantes en pots
21. des soucis
22. l'arrosoir figé à mi-course
23. tout à fait
24. l'avait peinte
25. avec sévérité
26. conservée
27. Comme quoi il n'y a pas forcément de rançon du péché

8

'Maybe there's a portrait in the attic[1],' Havers replied.

Lynley glanced at her in surprise. Thus far[2] today, she had been so markedly diligent[3] about behaving appropriately[4], about co-operating completely and promptly with his every order[5], that to hear her break away from that[6] and say something amusing was a bit of a shock. A nice one, in fact. 'Honours to you[7], Sergeant,' he chuckled[8]. 'Let's see what Mrs Mowrey has to say.'

She met them at the front door, looking from one to the other in confusion and – was it veiled just behind the eyes? – a touch of fear[9]. 'Good morning,' she said. Down from the roof terrace, she looked at least more like a woman approaching middle age[10]. But the hair was still sunny-blonde[11], the figure slight, the skin lightly freckled and virtually unlined[12].

Lynley showed her his warrant card[13]. 'Scotland Yard CID. May we come in, Mrs Mowrey?'

She looked from Lynley to Havers' grim face and back again. 'Of course.' Her voice was quite even, polite and warm. But there was a hesitation, rigidity in her movements, that suggested strong emotion withheld[14].

She led them to the left, through an open door that took them into the sitting-room, where she ges-

1. au grenier [portrait qui, comme pour Dorian Gray, prend les marques de la vieillesse et de la déchéance morale, tandis qu'elle-même reste jeune et belle]
2. Jusqu'ici
3. s'était nettement appliquée
4. correctement
5. le moindre de ses ordres
6. l'entendre y déroger
7. Bravo
8. dit-il avec un petit rire
9. un soupçon de peur
10. qui allait vers la cinquantaine
11. blonds lumineux
12. presque sans rides
13. sa carte de police
14. contenue

tured wordlessly at the furniture, beckoning them to sit[1]. It was a well-furnished, tasteful[2] room, with pieces of a modern design[3], pine and walnut that mingled[4] with subdued[5] autumn colours. A clock was ticking[6] somewhere, light and rapid like a racing pulse[7]. Here was none of the riotous[8] disorder of Olivia Odell nor the mechanical precision of Gembler Farm. Rather, this room was obviously the gathering place[9] for a congenial[10] family, with informal[11] photographs displayed, souvenirs of trips, and a stack of boxed games[12] and cards shelved[13] among books.

Tessa Mowrey chose a chair in the farthest corner where the light was weakest[14]. She sat down on its edge, her back upright, her legs crossed, her hands folded in her lap. She wore a plain gold wedding band[15]. She didn't ask why Scotland Yard had come calling[16]. Rather, she followed Lynley with her eyes as he walked to the mantel[17] and took note of the photographs that were its display[18].

'Your children?' he asked. There were two of them, a girl and a boy, pictures taken on a family holiday in St Ives. He recognized the familiar sweep of the bay[19], the grey and white buildings on the shore[20], and the assortment of boats left beached[21] at low tide[22].

'Yes,' she responded. She volunteered nothing else. Quiescent[23], she awaited the inevitable. The silence continued. Lynley allowed it to do so[24]. Eventually, sheer nervousness compelled her to go on.[25]

'Has Russell telephoned you?' There was an edge of despair in her voice. It was dull-sounding[26], as if she'd experienced the full range of grief[27] and there was nothing left in her, no depth of emotion to plummet further[28]. 'I thought he might. Of course, it's been three weeks. I'd begun to hope he was only punishing me till we sorted everything out[29].'

1. les invitant à s'asseoir
2. meublée avec goût
3. des éléments modernes
4. en pin et en noyer, qui se mêlaient
5. sobres
6. On entendait le tic-tac d'une pendule
7. un cœur battant à tout rompre
8. extrême
9. l'espace de vie
10. chaleureuse
11. non guindées
12. jeux de société
13. sur les étagères
14. la lumière était la plus faible
15. une simple alliance en or
16. lui rendre visite
17. vers le dessus de la cheminée
18. qui y étaient exposées
19. la forme familière de la baie
20. rivage
21. amarrés
22. marée basse
23. Passive
24. le fit durer
25. Elle était si nerveuse qu'elle finit par demander :
26. morne
27. toutes les souffrances possibles
28. où s'enfoncer
29. jusqu'à ce qu'on s'explique

1. remua, mal à l'aise

She stirred uneasily[1] when Sergeant Havers took out her notebook. 'Oh, must you?' she asked faintly.

'I'm afraid so,' Lynley replied.

2. les serra plus fort

'Then, I'll tell you everything. It's best.' She looked down at her hands and tightened their grip on each other[2].

3. espèce

4. série de gestes

5. les bras servant

6. geste rapide pour se rajuster

7. un mouvement de recul pour parer un choc psychologique

8. épreuve

9. par le simple biais

10. enlacés

Odd, Lynley thought, how as members of the same species[3] we inevitably rely on the same set of gestures[4] for our nonverbal signals of distress. A hand raised to the throat, arms cradling[5] the body protectively, a quick adjustment of clothing[6], a flinching to ward off a psychic blow[7]. Tessa, he saw, was gathering strength now to get through this ordeal[8], as if one hand could give the other a transfusion of courage through the simple expedient[9] of fingers intertwined[10]. It seemed to work. She looked up, her expression defiant.

11. Je venais d'avoir 16 ans

'I had just turned sixteen[11] when I married him. Can you understand what it's like to be married to a man eighteen years older than yourself when you're only sixteen? Of course you can't. No one can. Not even Russell.'

'You didn't want to stay on at school?'

12. a eu des problèmes de dos

13. pour que je ne prenne pas de retard

'I'd planned to. But I'd left school to help on the farm for a few weeks when Dad's back went bad[12]. It was only a temporary arrangement. I was supposed to return in a month. Marsha Fitzalan gave me work to do so that I wouldn't fall behind[13]. But I fell behind, and there was William.'

'How do you mean?'

14. bélier

15. [héros du roman *Les Hauts de Hurlevent*, d'Emily Brontë]

16. venant enfin chercher Cathy

17. pour moi

'He'd come to buy a ram[14] from Dad. I took him out to see it. William was … very handsome. I was romantic. He was Heathcliff[15] come to claim Cathy at last[16], as far as I was concerned[17].'

18. était un peu inquiet

'Surely your father had some concern[18] about his sixteen-year-old daughter wanting to marry? And to marry a man so much older than herself?'

'He did. Mother as well. But I was stubborn[1], and William was responsible, respectable, and strong. I think they believed that if they didn't let me marry him, I would turn out wild[2] and go desperately bad[3] in one way or another. So they gave their consent, and we married.'

'What happened to the marriage?'

'What *does* a sixteen-year-old girl know about marriage, Inspector?' she asked in answer. 'I wasn't even certain[4] how babies got themselves born[5] when I married William. You'd think a farm girl would have a bit more sense[6], but you have to remember that I spent most[7] of my free time with the Brontës. Charlotte, Anne, and Emily were always a bit vague when it came down to the[8] details. But I found out quickly enough. Gillian was born before my seventeenth birthday. William was thrilled[9]. He adored her. It was as if his life began the moment he saw Gilly.'

'Yet a number of years passed[10] before you had a second child.'

'That's because Gilly changed everything between us.'

'How?'

'Somehow[11] she – this tiny, fragile baby – made William discover religion and nothing was quite the same[12] after that.'

'I've somehow got the impression he was always religious.'

'Oh, no. Not till Gillian. It was as if he couldn't quite be a good enough father, as if he had to purify his soul[13] to be worthy of a[14] child.'

'How did he do it?'

She laughed shortly at the memory, but the sound was regretful and unamused[15]. 'The Bible, confession, daily communion. Within a year of our marriage, he became the backbone[16] of St Catherine's and a devoted[17] father.'

1. entêtée
2. je me dévergonderais
3. je tournerais très mal
4. Je savais à peine
5. venaient au monde
6. de bon sens
7. Je passais le plus clair
8. quant aux
9. enchanté
10. Il s'est pourtant écoulé plusieurs années
11. Je ne sais pourquoi,
12. n'était plus vraiment pareil
13. son âme
14. pour être digne d'un enfant
15. empreint de regrets et sans gaieté
16. le pilier
17. attentionné

'And there you were, a teenager, trying to live with a baby and a saint.'

'That's exactly what it was like.[1] Except that I didn't have to worry so much[2] about the baby. I wasn't quite good enough to care[3] for William's child. Or perhaps not holy enough[4] because, at any rate[5], he mostly cared for her himself.'

'What did you do?'

'I retreated to[6] my books.' She had sat nearly motionless[7] through the initial part of their conversation, but now she moved restlessly, getting up and pacing across[8] the room to look out the bay window where York Minster[9] loomed in the distance[10]. But, instead of the cathedral, Lynley guessed that Tessa saw the past. 'I dreamt that William would become Mr Darcy[11]. I dreamt that Mr Knightley[12] would sweep me off my feet[13]. I hoped that any day[14] I might meet Edward Rochester[15] if I only believed enough that my dreams were real.' She crossed her arms in front of her as if that could ward off the pain of that time. 'I wanted desperately to be loved. How I wanted to be loved! Can you possibly understand that, Inspector?'

'Who couldn't understand?' Lynley replied.

'I thought that if we had a second child, we would each have someone special to love. So I … I seduced William back to our bed[16].'

'Back?'

'Oh, yes, back. He'd left me shortly after Gilly was born and had begun to sleep elsewhere[17]. On the couch, in the sewing[18]-room, anywhere but with me[19].'

'Why?'

'He used as an excuse the fact that Gilly's birth had been so hard on me[20]. He didn't want me to become pregnant[21] and go through the torture again.'

'There are contraceptives—'

1. C'était exactement ça.
2. tellement à me préoccuper
3. pour prendre soin
4. pas assez pure
5. de toute façon
6. Je me suis retranchée dans
7. immobile
8. en faisant les cent pas
9. la cathédrale d'York
10. se dressait au loin
11. [l'amoureux de l'héroïne d'Orgueil et préjugés, de Jane Austen]
12. [l'amoureux de l'héroïne d'Emma, de Jane Austen]
13. ferait ma conquête
14. d'un jour à l'autre,
15. [l'amoureux de l'héroïne de Jane Eyre, de Charlotte Brontë]
16. J'attirai à nouveau William dans notre lit
17. ailleurs
18. de couture
19. partout, sauf avec moi
20. m'avait tellement éprouvée
21. que je retombe enceinte

'William's Catholic, Inspector. There are no contraceptives.' She turned from the window to face them again. The light bled colour from her cheeks[1], effaced eyebrows and lashes[2], and deepened the creases[3] from nose to mouth. If she sensed this[4], she made no move to avoid it. Rather[5], she remained, as if willing to allow her age to be exposed[6]. She went on.

'But I really think, looking back on it[7], that it was sex, not conception, that frightened William. At any rate, I got him back to my bed eventually[8]. And, eight years after Gilly, Roberta was born.'

'If you had what you wanted – a second baby to love – why did you leave?'

'Because it began again. All of it. She wasn't mine anymore[9] than Gillian had been. I loved my little girls, but I wasn't allowed near them[10], not the way I wanted to be[11]. I had nothing.' Although her voice quavered[12] on the last word, she drew herself in[13], cradling her body tighter, and found control. 'All I had once again was Darcy. My books.'

'So you left.'

'I woke up one morning just a few weeks after Roberta was born and I knew that if I stayed I would shrivel to nothing[14]. I was nearly twenty-five. I had two children I wasn't allowed to love and a husband who had begun to consult the Bible before dressing[15] in the morning. I looked out the window, saw the trail leading[16] to High Kel Moor, and knew I would leave that day.'

'Didn't he try to stop you?'

'No. Of course, I wanted him to[17]. But he didn't. I walked out of the door and out of his life[18], carrying just one case[19] and thirty-four pounds[20]. I came to York.'

'He never came to see you? Never tried to follow you?'

1. draina la couleur de ses joues
2. les sourcils et les cils
3. creusa les sillons
4. le perçut
5. Au contraire
6. elle cherchait à ce que son âge se voie
7. avec le recul
8. en fin de compte
9. pas plus
10. on ne me laissait pas en approcher
11. comme je le voulais
12. se brisa
13. se recroquevilla
14. j'allais dépérir
15. avant même de s'habiller
16. le chemin conduisant
17. j'aurais bien voulu
18. je suis sortie de sa vie
19. une seule valise à la main
20. livres sterling

She shook her head. 'I never told him where I was. I just ceased to exist. But I'd ceased to exist so many years before for William that what did it matter?'

'Why didn't you divorce him?'

'Because I never intended to[1] marry again. I came to York longing for an education[2], not a husband. I planned to work for a while, to save money[3], to go to London or even emigrate to the States[4]. But six weeks after I arrived in York, everything changed. I met Russell Mowrey.'

'How did you meet?'

She smiled at the memory.[5] 'They'd fenced off[6] part of the city when they began the Viking digs[7].'

'Yes, I recall that.'

'Russell was a graduate student[8] from London. He was part of the excavation team[9]. I'd stuck my head through a bit of a hole in the fence to have a look at the work. And there was Russell. His first words to me were, "Jesus, a Norse goddess[10]!" and then he blushed to the roots of his hair[11]. I think I fell in love with him then. He was twenty-six years old. He wore spectacles that kept slipping down his nose[12], absolutely filthy[13] trousers, and a university jersey[14]. When he walked over to speak to me, he slipped in the mud and fell directly on to his bottom[15].'

'Not much of a Darcy[16],' Lynley said kindly.

'No. So much more. We were married four weeks later.'

'Why didn't you tell him about William?'

She knotted her brows, appeared to be searching for[17] words that would enable them[18] to understand. 'Russell was an innocent. He had such … such an image of me. He saw me as a kind of Viking princess, a snow queen[19]. How could I tell him I had two children and a husband that I'd left on a farm in the dales?'

'What would have changed if he'd known?'

1. je ne comptais pas du tout
2. avec l'idée de chercher à m'instruire
3. d'économiser de l'argent
4. États-Unis
5. Le souvenir la fit sourire.
6. bloqué l'accès à
7. les fouilles viking
8. étudiant de 2e/3e cycle
9. l'équipe de fouilles
10. déesse scandinave
11. a rougi jusqu'à la racine des cheveux
12. qui n'arrêtaient pas de glisser de son nez
13. très sales
14. un pull de son université
15. il est tombé sur les fesses
16. Rien de très Darcy
17. semblant chercher
18. leur permettraient
19. reine des neiges

'Nothing, I suppose. But at the time I believed *everything* would have. I believed that he wouldn't want me if he knew, that he wouldn't be willing to wait for me through a divorce[1]. I'd been looking for love, Inspector. And finally here it was. Could I take a chance[2] that it might escape me?'

'But you're only two hours from Keldale here. Were you never worried that William might one day show up[3] in your life? Even as a chance encounter[4] in the street?'

'William never left the dales. Not once[5] in the years that I knew him. He had everything there: his children, his religion, his farm. Why on earth[6] would he ever come to York? Besides, I thought at first that we'd go to London. Russell's family is there. I'd no idea that he'd want to settle[7] here. But here we stayed. We had Rebecca five years later. Then William eighteen months after that.'

'William?'

'You can imagine how I felt when Russell wanted to call him William. It's his father's name. What could I do but agree?[8]'

'And you've been here, then, for nineteen years?'

'Yes,' she replied. 'First in a small flat[9] in the city centre, then a terraced[10] house near Bishopthorpe Road, and last year we bought this house. We'd … saved for so long[11]. Russell did two jobs and I've my job at the museum as well. We've been' – she blinked back[12] her first tears – 'so happy. God, so happy. Until now. You've come for me[13], haven't you? Or have you brought me word[14]?'

'No one's told you? You haven't read about it?[15]'

'Read about it? Has something …? He isn't …?' Tessa looked from Lynley to Havers. It was obvious that she saw something in their faces, for her own face flashed fear[16] before she went on. 'The night Russell left, he was terribly angry. I thought that if

1. le temps que j'obtienne le divorce
2. le risque
3. débarque un jour
4. Ou juste de le croiser par hasard
5. Pas une seule fois
6. Pourquoi diable
7. qu'il voudrait s'installer
8. Comment aurais-je pu refuser ?
9. appartement
10. mitoyenne
11. économisé depuis si longtemps
12. ravala
13. venez me chercher
14. venez me donner des nouvelles
15. Vous ne l'avez pas vu dans les journaux ?
16. eut un éclair de frayeur

only I said nothing, did nothing, it would work itself out[1]. He'd come home and—'

Lynley suddenly understood that they were talking about two entirely different things. 'Mrs Mowrey,' he said, 'do you not know about your husband?'

Her eyes widened[2], growing dark with apprehension. 'Russell,' she whispered[3]. 'He left that Saturday the investigator found me[4]. Three weeks ago. He's not been home since.[5]'

'Mrs Mowrey,' Lynley said carefully, 'William Teys was murdered[6] three weeks ago. On Saturday night between ten and midnight. Your daughter Roberta was charged[7] with the crime.'

If they had thought she might faint[8], they were wrong. She stared at them[9] without speaking for nearly a minute, then turned back to the window. 'Rebecca will be home soon,' she said tonelessly. 'She comes home for lunch. She'll ask about[10] her father. She does every day. She knows something's wrong, but I've managed to keep most of it from her[11].' A trembling hand touched her cheek. 'I know Russell's gone to London. I haven't phoned his family because, of course, I didn't want them to know anything was wrong. But I know he's gone to them in London. I *know*.'

'Do you have a photograph of your husband?' Lynley asked. 'His family's London address?'

She swung on him[12]. 'He wouldn't![13]' she cried passionately. 'This is a man who has *never* lifted his hand to strike[14] one of his own children! He was angry – yes, I've said that – but his anger was with *me*[15], not with William! He wouldn't have gone, he couldn't have—' She began to cry, horribly, shedding what were probably[16] her first tears in three agonizing weeks[17]. Pressing her forehead against the window glass[18], she wept bitterly[19], as if she would never be consoled.

1. ça s'arrangerait tout seul
2. s'écarquillèrent
3. chuchota-t-elle
4. le samedi où ce détective m'a retrouvée
5. Il n'est pas rentré depuis.
6. a été assassiné
7. est accusée
8. qu'elle allait s'évanouir
9. les fixa
10. des nouvelles de
11. lui cacher l'essentiel
12. lui fit face
13. Il ne ferait jamais ça !
14. levé la main sur
15. c'est contre moi qu'il était en colère
16. versant probablement
17. en trois semaines de souffrance
18. la vitre
19. pleura amèrement

Havers got to her feet and left the room. Good God, where is she going? Lynley wondered, half-expecting a repeat of her disappearing act[1] in the pub last night. But she returned moments later with a pitcher[2] of orange juice and a glass.

'Thank you, Barbara,' he said.

She nodded, shot him a diffident smile[3], and poured the woman a glass of the liquid.

Tessa Mowrey took it but, rather than drink, she clutched it as if it were a talisman. 'Rebecca mustn't see me like this. I've got to pull myself together.[4] Must be stronger than this.' She saw the glass in her hand, took a sip[5], and grimaced. 'I can't abide[6] tinned[7] orange juice. Why do I have it in the house? Oh, Russell says that it's not that bad[8]. I suppose it isn't, really.' When she turned back to Lynley, she looked, he saw, every single day of[9] her forty-three years. 'He did not kill William.'

'That's what everyone in Keldale says of Roberta.'

She flinched. 'I don't think of her as my daughter. I'm sorry. I never knew her.[10]'

'She's been placed in a mental asylum, Mrs Mowrey. When William was found, she claimed[11] to have killed him.'

'Then, if she's *admitted* to[12] the crime, why have you come to see me? If she says she killed William, then certainly Russell …' Her voice drifted off[13]. It was as if she had suddenly heard her own words and realized how eager she was[14] to trade[15] daughter for husband.

He could hardly blame her[16]. Lynley thought of the barn stall, the ornate Bible, the photograph albums, the cool silence of the melancholy[17] house. 'Did you never see Gillian again?' he asked abruptly, waiting for a sign, the smallest indication[18] that Tessa knew of Gillian's disappearance. There was none.

'Never.'

1. à ce qu'elle disparaisse à nouveau, comme
2. un pichet
3. lui fit un timide sourire
4. Il faut que je me ressaisisse.
5. gorgée
6. Je déteste
7. en boîte
8. ce n'est pas si mauvais
9. il vit qu'elle faisait tout à fait
10. Je ne l'ai jamais connue.
11. a déclaré
12. reconnaît avoir commis
13. s'éteignit
14. l'enthousiasme qu'elle mettait
15. à échanger
16. difficilement le lui reprocher
17. triste
18. le moindre indice

'She never contacted you in any way?'

'Of course not. Even if she'd wanted to, William wouldn't have allowed it, I'm sure.'

Probably not, thought Lynley. But once she ran off[1], once she cut the ties[2] with her father, why had she not sought[3] her mother then?

'Religious fanatic,' Havers declared decisively[4]. She shoved her hair back behind her ears and gave her attention to[5] the photograph she held. 'But *this* one's not half bad[6]. She did OK on her second time round[7]. Too bad she didn't bother with a divorce.[8]' Russell Mowrey smiled up at her from the photograph Tessa had given them. He was a nice-looking man in a three-piece suit[9], wife on his arm. Easter Sunday.[10] Havers put it in the manila folder and gave herself back[11] to the passing scenery[12]. 'At least we know why Gillian left.'

'Because of the father's religion?'

'That's the way I see it,' Havers replied. 'Obviously, a combination of that and the second baby. There she'd been, for eight years the centre of her father's life – Mum doesn't appear to have counted for much[13] – when all of a sudden a new baby arrives. It's supposed to be Mummy's, but Dad doesn't trust[14] Mummy to do right by her children[15], so he takes this one over[16] as well. Mummy leaves and Gillian follows[17].'

'Not exactly, Havers. She waited eight years to go wherever she went[18].'

'Well, you can't expect her to have run off when she was eight years old! She bided her time[19], probably hating little Roberta every second for stealing her dad.'

'That doesn't make sense.[20] First you say that Gillian left because she couldn't abide her father's religious fanaticism. Then you say she left because she'd lost his love to[21] Roberta. Now, what is it? She

1. après sa fugue
2. avoir coupé les liens
3. n'avait-elle pas cherché à revoir
4. d'un ton catégorique
5. examina
6. n'est pas si mal
7. la deuxième fois
8. Dommage qu'elle n'ait pas pris la peine de divorcer.
9. en costume trois pièces
10. Un dimanche de Pâques.
11. s'intéressa à nouveau
12. au paysage qui défilait
13. avoir eu beaucoup d'importance
14. ne fait pas confiance à
15. pour s'occuper correctement de ses enfants
16. prend celle-là en charge
17. fait de même
18. avant d'aller on ne sait où
19. a attendu le bon moment
20. Ce n'est pas cohérent.
21. parce qu'il lui préférait

either loves him and wants to be his favourite again, or she can't abide his religious devotion and feels she has to escape. You can't have it both ways.[1]'

'It's not black and white!' Havers protested loudly. 'These things never are!'

Lynley glanced at her, amazed by the affront in her voice[2]. Her stubby[3] features looked like paste. 'Barbara—'

'I'm sorry! Dammit![4] I'm doing it all over again! Why do I bother? I'm no *good* at this. I *always* do it. I never—'

'Barbara,' he interrupted firmly.

She stared straight ahead. 'Yes, sir?'

'We're discussing the case, not arguing[5] before a court of law[6]. It's fine to have an opinion. I want you to, in fact. I've always found it extremely helpful to talk a case over with someone.' But it was more than that, really. It was arguing, laughing, hearing the sweet voice say *Oh, you think you're right, Tommy, but I shall prove you wrong*[7]*!* He felt loneliness settle on him like a cold, wet shroud[8].

Havers moved restlessly in her seat. With no music playing, the tension was screaming to be heard[9].

'I don't know what it is,' she said at last. 'I get into the fray[10] and forget what I'm doing.'

'I understand.' He let the matter drop, his eyes following the meandering pattern[11] that the stone walls made on the hillside across the dale[12] from the road on which they travelled.

He thought about Tessa. He knew that he was trying to understand her and that he was ill-equipped to do so[13]. Nothing in his life of Cornwall and Howenstow, of Oxford and Belgravia, even of Scotland Yard, explained the paucity of[14] experience of life on a remote farm[15] that would drive[16] a girl of sixteen to believe that her only future[17] lay in immediate marriage[18]. And yet surely that was the foundation of what had happened. No romantic interpretation

1. C'est l'un ou c'est l'autre.
2. son ton offensé
3. épais
4. Bon sang !
5. on n'est pas en train de s'affronter
6. au tribunal
7. je vais démontrer que tu as tort
8. un voile humide et froid
9. était plus que palpable
10. Je me lance dans la bagarre
11. tracé sinueux
12. les versants des coteaux
13. qu'il n'était pas armé pour le faire
14. la maigre
15. dans une ferme perdue
16. qui avait pu amener
17. son unique avenir
18. c'était de se marier tout de suite

of the facts at hand[1] – no reflections upon[2] Heathcliff, no matter how apt[3] – could hide the real explanation. The drudgery and sheer ennui[4] of those weeks when she had been forced to stay home and help out had made an otherwise simple Yorkshire farmer[5] look arresting[6] by comparison. Thus, she merely moved[7] from one trap into another[8]. Married at sixteen, a mother before her seventeenth birthday. Wouldn't any woman have wanted to escape such a life? Yet, if that was the case, why marry again in such a hurry?

Havers broke into his thoughts[9]. An underlying note of urgency in her voice[10] made Lynley glance at her curiously. Tiny beads of sweat[11] stood out on her forehead. She swallowed noisily. 'What I can't see is the … Tessa's shrine. The woman walks out on him[12] – not that she[13] didn't appear to have every right to – and he sets up a virtual Taj Mahal of photographs in a corner of the sitting-room.'

It suddenly dawned on Lynley.[14] 'How do we know *William* set up[15] the shrine?'

Havers came to her own quick terms with the knowledge[16]. 'Either of the girls could have done it,' she responded.

'Who do you imagine?'

'It had to be[17] Gillian.'

'As a bit of revenge?[18] A little daily reminder[19] to William that Mummy'd run off? A little knife inserted between the ribs[20] since[21] he'd started to favour[22] Roberta?'

'Bet on it[23], sir,' Havers agreed.

They drove on for several miles before Lynley spoke again. 'She could have done it, Havers. Something tells me she was desperate enough.'

'Tessa, d'you mean?'

'Russell was gone that night. She says she took aspirin and went directly to bed, but no one can verify it[24]. She could have gone to Keldale.'

1. en présence
2. aucune référence à
3. aussi pertinente soit-elle
4. Les corvées et l'ennui mortel
5. un simple fermier du Yorkshire
6. paraître captivant
7. n'avait fait que passer
8. d'un piège à un autre
9. interrompit sa réflexion
10. Son ton relativement pressant
11. De petites perles de sueur
12. le quitte
13. non pas qu'elle
14. Lynley eut une révélation.
15. que c'est William qui a installé
16. envisagea rapidement l'hypothèse inverse
17. Forcément
18. En représailles ?
19. rappel quotidien
20. couteau dans la plaie
21. puisque
22. à préférer
23. À tous les coups
24. le confirmer

'Why kill the dog?'

'He wouldn't have known her.[1] He wasn't there nineteen years ago. Who was Tessa to him[2]? A stranger.'

'But decapitate her first husband?' Havers frowned. 'Would have been easier to divorce him, I'd think[3].'

'No. Not for a Catholic.'

'Even so[4], Russell's a better candidate if you ask me. Who knows where he went?' When Lynley didn't reply, she added, 'Sir?'

'I …' Lynley hesitated, studying the road ahead. 'Tessa's right. He's gone to London.'

'How can you be certain of that?'

'Because I think I saw him, Havers. At the Yard.'

'So he did go to turn her in[5]. I suppose she knew all along[6] that he would.'

'No. I don't think so.'

Havers offered a new thought. 'Well, then there's Ezra.'

Lynley flashed her[7] a smile. 'William in his jim-jams in the middle of the road ripping up[8] Ezra's watercolours while Ezra curses him to hell and back[9]? We *could* have a motive for murder there. I don't think an artist would take lightly[10] to having someone rip up his work.'

Havers opened her mouth, stopped. She reflected for a moment. 'But it wasn't his pyjamas.'

'Yes, it was.'

'It wasn't. It was his dressing-gown[11]. Remember? Nigel said his legs reminded him of a gorilla[12]. So what was he doing in his dressing-gown? It was still light out.[13] It wasn't time for bed[14].'

'Changing for dinner, I dare say. He's up in his room, looks out the window, sees Ezra trespassing[15], and comes charging into the yard[16].'

'I suppose that could be it.'

'What else?'

'Exercising[17], perhaps?'

1. Il ne la connaissait pas.
2. pour lui
3. à mon avis
4. Tout de même
5. est bien allé la dénoncer
6. a toujours su
7. lui lança
8. et qui déchire
9. le traite de tous les noms
10. prenne à la légère
11. peignoir
12. un gorille
13. Il faisait encore jour dehors.
14. l'heure d'aller se coucher
15. qui s'invite sur sa propriété
16. il fonce dans la cour
17. Il faisait de la gym

'Deep knee-bends in his underwear?[1] That's hard to picture[2].'

'Or … perhaps with Olivia?'

Lynley smiled. 'Not if everything we've heard about him is true. William sounds to me like a strictly after-marriage man[3]. I don't think he'd try any funny business[4] with Olivia beforehand[5].'

'What about Nigel Parrish?'

'What about him?'

'Walking the dog back[6] to the farm out of the goodness of his heart[7], like a card-carrying member[8] of the RSPCA[9]? Doesn't that whole story seem a bit off[10] to you?'

'It does. But do you really think Parrish would want to get his hands dirty with a bit of William Teys' blood? Not to mention his head rolling across the stall floor.'

'To be honest, he seems the type to faint at the sight[11].'

They laughed, a first shared communication[12]. It dropped almost immediately into an uncomfortable[13] silence at the sudden realization[14] that they could become friends.

The decision to go to Barnstingham Mental Asylum grew out of Lynley's belief[15] that Roberta held[16] all the cards in the current game they were playing[17]: the identity of the murderer, the motive behind the crime, and the disappearance of Gillian Teys. He'd stopped an hour out of York to make the arrangements[18] by telephone, and now, pulling the car to a stop[19] on the gravel drive in front of the building, he turned to Barbara.

'Cigarette?' He offered his gold case.

'No, sir. Thank you.'

He nodded, glanced at the imposing building, then back at her. 'Rather[20] wait here, Sergeant?' he asked as he lit his cigarette with the silver lighter.

1. Des exercices de flexion en sous-vêtements ?
2. difficile à imaginer
3. être du genre « jamais avant le mariage »
4. qu'il tenterait le coup
5. avant le mariage
6. Ramener le chien
7. par bonté d'âme
8. un adhérent
9. de la SPA
10. un peu foireuse
11. du genre à s'évanouir s'il voyait ça
12. se sentant complices pour la première fois
13. gêné
14. car ils prenaient soudain conscience
15. fut motivée par la conviction de Lynley
16. détenait
17. de la partie qui se jouait
18. pour tout organiser
19. arrêtant la voiture
20. Vous préférez

He took a few moments about replacing[1] all the impedimenta of his habit[2].

She watched him with speculative eyes. 'Why?'

He shrugged casually[3]. Too casually, she noted. 'You look fagged out[4]. I thought you might want a bit of a rest.'

Fagged out. It was his public-school-fop act.[5] She'd begun to notice how he used it occasionally to serve the need[6] of the moment. He'd dropped it earlier. Why was he picking it up[7] now?

'If we're talking about exhaustion[8], Inspector, *you* look just about ready to drop[9]. What's up?'

He examined himself in the mirror at her words, his cigarette dangling[10] from his lips, his eyes narrowed against[11] the smoke, part[12] Sam Spade[13], part Algernon Moncrieff[14]. 'I do look a sight.[15]' He busied himself about his appearance for a moment: straightening his tie, examining his hair, brushing at nonexistent lint[16] on the lapels of his jacket. She waited. Finally he met her eyes. The fop[17], as well as the other personae[18], was gone. 'The farm upset you a bit yesterday,' he said frankly. 'I have an idea that what we'll find in here is going to be a hell of a lot worse than the farm.'

For a moment she couldn't take her eyes from his[19], but she pressed her hand to the door and flung it open. 'I can deal with it[20], sir,' she said abruptly and got out into the brisk autumn air.

'We've kept her confined[21],' Dr Samuels was saying to Lynley as they walked down the transverse passage[22] that ran straight through[23] the building from east to west.

Barbara followed behind them, relieved to find that Barnstingham was not exactly what she had pictured when she first heard the words *mental asylum*. It was really not very hospital-like at all, an English baroque building laid out on cross-axes[24].

1. Il prit le temps de remettre en place
2. tous ses accessoires de fumeur
3. d'un air détaché
4. lessivée
5. Encore ce style très smart.
6. selon les besoins
7. recommençait-il
8. En parlant d'épuisement
9. que vous allez vous écrouler
10. pendant
11. plissés pour éviter
12. mi
13. [le privé, dans le Faucon maltais]
14. [le dandy spirituel, dans De l'importance d'être constant]
15. En effet, j'ai une sale tête.
16. brossant des pellicules invisibles
17. dandy
18. personnage
19. le fixa sans parvenir à détacher son regard
20. Ça va aller
21. à l'isolement
22. couloir
23. traversait tout
24. avec un plan en croix

1. étages
2. des pilastres cannelés reposant sur des socles
3. le mot d'ordre
4. les moulures
5. épaisse
6. moquette
7. rouille clair
8. sombres et moroses
9. l'école flamande
10. semblaient volontiers s'en excuser
11. eu un instant de faiblesse
12. qui montait
13. Rien ne lui échappait.
14. s'engagèrent dans
15. apaisants
16. des paysages de Constable [peintre romantique de la campagne anglaise]
17. s'entendait au loin
18. cause lui aussi
19. n'aurait jamais deviné
20. évoquait
21. barbu
22. à l'aise
23. à cheval ou en randonnée
24. qu'à sonder des esprits dérangés
25. bien fait, les membres déliés
26. rasé de près
27. ne valait pas la sienne
28. très fort sur un court de tennis

They had entered through a front hall that rose two storeys[1], with fluted pilasters standing on plinths[2] against the walls. *Light* and *colour* were the operative words[3] here, for the room was painted a calming shade of peach, the decorative plasterwork[4] was white, the ankle-thick[5] carpeting[6] was merely a shade off rust[7], and while the portraits were dark and moody[8], of the Flemish school[9], their subjects managed to look suitably apologetic about the fact[10].

All this was a relief, for when Lynley had first mentioned the need to see Roberta, to come to this place, Barbara had become quite faint[11], that old insidious panic setting in[12]. Lynley had seen it, of course. Damn the man. He didn't miss a trick.[13]

Now that she was inside the building, she felt steadier, a feeling that improved once they left the great central hall and began their journey down[14] the passage. Here conviviality expressed itself in soothing[15] Constable landscapes[16] and vases of fresh flowers and quiet voices in the air. The sound of music and singing came from a distance[17].

'The choir,' Dr Samuels explained. 'Here, it's just this way.'

Samuels himself had been a secondary source[18] of both surprise and relief. Outside the walls of the hospital, Barbara wouldn't have known[19] he was a psychiatrist. *Psychiatrist* somehow conjured up[20] images of Freud: a bearded[21] Victorian face, a cigar, and those speculative eyes. But Samuels had the look of a man who was more at home[22] on horseback or hiking[23] across the moors than probing disturbed psyches[24]. He was well built, loose limbed[25], and clean shaven[26], with a tendency, Barbara guessed, to be less than patient with anyone whose intelligence did not match his own[27]. He was probably the devil on a tennis court[28] as well.

She'd begun to feel quite at ease with the hospital when Dr Samuels opened a narrow door – funny how it had been concealed[1] by some panelling – and led them into the new wing of the building. This was the locked ward[2], looking and smelling exactly as Barbara had supposed a locked ward would. The carpeting was a very dark, serviceable[3] brown. The walls were the colour of sun-baked sand, unadorned[4] and broken only by doors into which small windows were set at eye level[5]. The air was filled with[6] that medicinal smell of antiseptics and detergents and drugs[7]. And it was cut by[8] a low moaning[9] that seemed to come from nowhere and everywhere. It could have been the wind. It could have been anything.

Here it is, she told herself. The place for psychos[10], for girls who decapitate daddies, for girls who murder. Lots of things are murder, Barb.

'There's been absolutely nothing since her original statement[11],' Dr Samuels was saying to Lynley. 'She's not catatonic. She's merely said what she intends to say, I think.' He glanced at the clipboard he was carrying. ' "I did it. I'm not sorry!" On the day the body was found. She's not spoken since.'

'There's no medical cause? She's been examined?'

Dr Samuels' lips tightened[12] in offence[13]. It was clear that this Scotland Yard intrusion bordered on insult[14], and if he had to impart information[15] it would be minimal at best[16].

'She's been examined,' he said. 'No seizure, no stroke.[17] She can speak. She chooses not to.[18]'

If he was bothered[19] by the clipped nature[20] of the doctor's response, Lynley didn't let it show. He was used to encountering attitudes like the psychiatrist's, attitudes proclaiming that the police were antagonists to be thwarted[21] rather than allies to be helped. He slowed his steps[22] and told Dr Samuels about Roberta's cache of food[23]. This, at least,

1. dissimulé
2. l'aile des personnes à l'isolement
3. facile à entretenir
4. sable brûlé par le soleil, unis
5. à hauteur d'yeux
6. L'atmosphère respirait
7. de médicaments
8. on percevait
9. un gémissement
10. les dingues
11. sa première déclaration
12. pinça les lèvres,
13. signe qu'il prenait ça mal
14. frisait l'insulte
15. communiquer des informations
16. au mieux, le strict minimum
17. Pas de crise, pas d'attaque.
18. Mais elle refuse.
19. contrarié
20. la réticence
21. qu'il fallait contrecarrer
22. ralentit le pas
23. stocks clandestins

caught[1] the man's attention. When he next spoke, his words walked the line[2] between frustration and deeper thought[3].

'I don't know what to tell you, Inspector. The food could, as you guess, be a compulsion. It could be a stimulus or a response. It could be a source of gratification[4] or a form of sublimation. Until Roberta's willing to give us something to go on[5], it could be damn well anything.'

Lynley shifted to another area[6]. 'Why did you take her from[7] the Richmond police? Isn't that a bit irregular?'

'Not when the responsible party's signed her in[8],' Dr Samuels replied. 'We're a private hospital.'

'The responsible party. Was that Superintendent Nies?'

Samuels shook his head impatiently. 'Not at all. We don't take people at random[9] from the police.' He scanned Roberta's chart[10]. 'It was ... let me see where ... Gibson, Richard Gibson. He names himself[11] as her closest relative[12]. He's the one who got the court to agree[13] and filled in the paperwork[14].'

'Richard Gibson?'

'That's the name on the form[15], Inspector,' Samuels replied tersely[16]. 'He's signed her in for treatment pending the trial[17]. She's in therapy daily. There's no progress yet, but that isn't to say there never will be any.'

'But why would Gibson—?' Lynley was speaking more to himself than to the other two, but Samuels went on, perhaps on the assumption[18] that he was being addressed[19].

'She's his cousin, after all. And the sooner she's better, the sooner the trial. That is, unless she's proved incompetent[20] to stand trial at all[21].'

'And in that case,' Lynley finished, his eyes fixed grimly on the doctor's face, 'she's in for life[22], isn't she?'

1. retint
2. hésitaient
3. réflexion
4. plaisir
5. plus d'indices
6. changea de sujet
7. l'avez-vous retirée à
8. c'est la personne responsable qui a demandé son admission
9. au hasard
10. la fiche
11. Il se désigne
12. son plus proche parent
13. qui a eu l'accord du juge
14. rempli tous les papiers
15. formulaire
16. sèchement
17. en attendant le procès
18. pensant
19. qu'on s'adressait à lui
20. qu'elle ne soit déclarée irresponsable
21. et ne soit pas jugée du tout
22. elle sera internée à vie

'Until she recovers[1].' Samuels led them up to a heavy, locked door. 'She's just in here. It's unfortunate that she has to be alone, but considering the circumstances[2] ...' He gestured with his hands, unlocked the door, and swung it open. 'Roberta, you've visitors,' he said.

He'd chosen Prokofiev – *Romeo and Juliet* – and the music had begun almost immediately when he started the car. Thank God, Barbara thought brokenly[3]. Thank God. Let[4] the music of violins, cellos[5] and violas[6] drive thought away[7], drive memory away, drive everything completely, irreversibly away so that there is no existence but that of audition[8], so that she needn't think of the girl in the room and, even more frightening[9], of the man in the car.

Even staring steadfastly[10] ahead, she could still see his hands on the wheel, could see the gold hair[11] on them – lighter even than the hair on his head – could see each finger, note its movement, as he guided the car back to Keldale.

When he leaned forward[12] to make an adjustment in the sound[13], she could see his profile. He was very lightly tanned[14]. Gold and brown. Skin, hair, and eyes. Straight, classical nose. The firm line of jaw.[15] A face that spoke clearly[16] of tremendous inner strength[17], of resources of character that she couldn't comprehend.

How had he done it?

She'd been by a window, not looking out but, rather, staring fixedly at the wall, a lummox of a girl[18] nearly six feet tall who must have weighed well over fifteen stone[19]. She sat on a stool[20], her back hunched over in an arc of defeat[21], and she rocked[22].

'Roberta, my name is Thomas Lynley. I've come to talk to you about your father.'

1. sa guérison
2. vu les circonstances
3. dans l'agitation de ses réflexions
4. Que
5. des violoncelles
6. des altos
7. chasse la pensée
8. pour que seule reste l'écoute [de la musique]
9. plus effrayant encore
10. résolument
11. poils blonds
12. se pencha
13. pour régler le son
14. légèrement bronzé
15. La mâchoire fermement dessinée.
16. qui reflétait clairement
17. une grande force intérieure
18. une fille pataude
19. bien plus de 90 kg
20. tabouret
21. le dos voûté, vaincue
22. se balançait

The rocking continued. The eyes looked at nothing, saw nothing. If she heard at all, she gave absolutely no sign[1].

Her hair was filthy, foul-smelling[2]. It was pulled back from her broad, moon-shaped face[3] with an elastic band, but greasy tendrils[4] had escaped imprisonment and hung forward stiffly[5], kissing on her neck the pockets of flesh that encased in their folds[6] the incongruous ornament of a single, slender gold chain.

'Father Hart came to London, Roberta. He's asked us to help you. He says he knows you didn't hurt anyone.'

Nothing. The broad face was expressionless. Suppurating pimples[7] covered cheeks and chin. Bloated skin[8] stretched over layers of fat[9] that had long ago erased[10] whatever definition her features might have had. She was dough-like[11], grey and unclean[12].

'We've been talking to a great many people in Keldale. We've seen your cousin Richard, and Olivia, and Bridie. Bridie cut her hair, Roberta. She's made quite a mess of it, unfortunately, in an effort to look like the Princess of Wales. Her mother was quite upset[13] about it. She said how good you always were to Bridie.'

No response. Roberta was dressed in a too-short skirt that revealed white, flabby[14] thighs[15] upon which the flesh, dotted by[16] red pustules, quivered[17] when she rocked. There were hospital slippers on her feet, but they were too small, and her sausage toes hung out[18], their uncut nails curling round them[19].

'We've been to the house. Have you read all those books? Stepha Odell said that you'd read them all. We were amazed at how many you have. We saw the pictures of your mother, Roberta. She was lovely, wasn't she?'

1. n'en laissa rien voir
2. sentaient mauvais
3. de son large visage rond
4. des boucles grasses
5. rebiquaient, raides
6. les plis de chair qui emprisonnaient
7. Des boutons purulents
8. La peau bouffie
9. des couches de graisse
10. gommé depuis longtemps
11. informe
12. sale
13. très contrariée
14. flasques
15. des cuisses
16. parsemée de
17. tremblotait
18. ses orteils boudinés dépassaient
19. les ongles trop longs commençant à s'enrouler

Silence. Her arms hung at her sides.[1] Her enormous breasts[2] strained against[3] the cheap material[4] of her blouse. Its buttons struggled to hold the thin garment closed as the pressure of the rocking continued, each movement causing the flesh to heave to and fro[5] in a rebarbative pavane.

'I think this may be a bit difficult for you to hear, Roberta, but we saw your mother today. Do you know that she lives in York? You have another brother and sister there. She told us how much your father loved you and Gillian.'

The movement ceased. The face neither acknowledged nor changed, but the tears began. They were silent, ugly[6] rivers of mute[7] pain dipping and plunging through the crevices of fat[8], climbing the peaks of acne[9]. With the tears came the mucus[10]. It began its descent from her nose in a slimy cord[11], touched her lips, and crawled on to her chin[12].

Lynley squatted[13] before her. He removed a snowy[14] handkerchief from his pocket and wiped her face clean[15]. He took her pulpy[16], lifeless[17] hand in his own and pressed it firmly.

'Roberta.' There was no response. 'I'll find Gillian.' He stood, folded the elegant, monogrammed linen square[18], and returned it to his pocket.

What had Webberly said? Barbara thought. *There's a lot you might learn from working with Lynley.*

And now she knew. She couldn't look at him. She couldn't meet his eyes[19]. She knew what would be there, and the thought of its existence in this man she had been determined to believe was an absolute fop of an upper-class snob chilled her[20] entirely.

He was supposed[21] to be the man who danced in nightclubs, who dispensed sexual favours, laughter, and good cheer, who moved effortlessly in a gilt-edged world[22] of money and privilege[23]. But he was not supposed to be – never supposed to be[24] – the man she had seen today.

1. Elle avait les bras ballants
2. poitrine
3. était trop serrée dans
4. tissu
5. les chairs ballottées à chaque mouvement
6. affreuses
7. muette
8. voguant dans les crevasses de graisse
9. escaladant les points d'acné
10. la morve
11. un filet visqueux
12. rampa sur son menton
13. s'accroupit
14. blanc immaculé
15. lui essuya le visage
16. replète
17. inerte
18. le carré de lin brodé à ses initiales
19. croiser son regard
20. la glaçait
21. censé
22. les sphères dorées
23. des privilèges
24. sûrement pas censé être

He'd stepped neatly out of the mould[1] she'd created and destroyed it without a backward glance[2]. She had to fit him back into it[3] somehow. If she didn't, the fires within her[4] that for so many years had kept her alive[5] would be swiftly extinguished[6]. And then, she knew well, she would die in the cold[7].

That was the thought that carried her to Keldale, longing to fly from his presence[8]. But when the Bentley made the final turn into the village, she knew immediately that there would be no quick escape. For Nigel Parrish and another man were having a violent quarrel upon the bridge, directly in the path[9] of the car.

1. bel et bien quitté le moule
2. sans se retourner
3. Il fallait qu'elle l'y recase
4. qui la consumaient et
5. l'avaient maintenue en vie
6. vite éteints
7. de froid
8. en attendant de fuir sa présence
9. au beau milieu du chemin

9

Organ music seemed to be blasting[1] from the very trees[2]. It swelled to[3] crescendos, faded[4], and roared out[5] again: a baroque combination of chords, rests, and flourishes[6] that made Lynley think that at any moment the phantom[7] himself would come swinging down from the opera chandeliers. At the appearance of the Bentley, the two men parted[8], the one shouting a final violent imprecation at Nigel Parrish before he stalked off[9] in the direction of the high street.

'I think I'll have a word[10] with our Nigel,' Lynley remarked. 'No need for you to come, Havers. Go have a bit of a rest.'

'I can certainly—'

'That's an order, Sergeant.'

Damn him. 'Yes, sir.'

Lynley waited until Havers had disappeared into the lodge before he walked back across the bridge to the strange little cottage that sat on the far side[11] of the common. It was, he thought, a more than curious structure. The front of the building was trellised[12] by late[13] roses. Unrestrained, they spread out[14] like an encroaching wilderness towards[15] the narrow windows on either side[16] of the door. They climbed the wall, crowned the lintel majestically[17], and travelled upward to begin their glory on

1. sortir à plein volume
2. des arbres mêmes
3. montait en
4. s'atténuait
5. rugissait
6. d'accords, de silences et de fioritures
7. fantôme de l'Opéra
8. se séparèrent
9. de s'éloigner, d'un pas raide
10. que je vais aller causer
11. qui était à l'autre bout
12. recouvert
13. tardives
14. On les laissait s'étendre
15. des plantes sauvages gagnant
16. de chaque côté
17. couronnaient le linteau avec majesté

the roof[1]. They were a solid blanket[2] of disturbing colour – blood-red – and they flooded[3] the air with a scent so rich[4] as to be virtually miasmal[5]. The entire effect was one step short of[6] obscene.

Nigel Parrish had already retreated inside, and Lynley followed him, pausing[7] in the open doorway to survey[8] the room. The source of the music that continued to soar[9] round them was a speaker system[10] that beggared belief[11]. Enormous amplifiers[12] sat in all four corners[13], creating at the centre a vortex of sound. Other than an organ, a tape recorder[14], a receiver, and a turntable[15], there was nothing in the room save a threadbare carpet[16] and a few old chairs.

Parrish switched off the tape-recorder that had been the source of the sound. He rewound the tape[17], removed it from the machine, and replaced it in its container. He took his time about it all, giving every movement a precision which told Lynley that he knew very well that the other man was standing at the door. It was none the less a nice performance.

'Mr Parrish?'

A start[18] of surprise. A swift turn. A welcoming smile breaking over the features[19]. But he couldn't hide the fact that his hands were shaking. As Lynley saw this, so apparently did Parrish, for he stuffed them[20] into the pockets of his tweed trousers.

'Inspector! A social call[21], I hope? Sorry you had to come upon[22] that little scene with Ezra.'

'Ah. So that was Ezra.'

'Yes. Honey-haired, honey-tongued[23] little Ezra. Dear boy thought "artistic licence" gave him access to my back garden to study the light on the river. Can you imagine such cheek[24]? Here I was fine-tuning my psyche[25] with Bach when I glanced out the window and saw him setting up shop[26]. Blast his pretty little heart.[27]'

1. pour amorcer leur splendeur sur le toit
2. formaient une couverture unie
3. saturaient
4. d'un parfum si fort
5. qu'il formait presque un brouillard
6. en était presque
7. s'arrêtant un instant
8. observer
9. à résonner à plein volume
10. sonorisation
11. incroyable
12. baffles
13. aux quatre coins
14. magnétophone
15. une platine
16. tapis tout élimé
17. rembobina la cassette
18. sursaut
19. masquant ses traits
20. car il les fourra
21. simple visite de courtoisie
22. que vous soyez tombés sur
23. mielleux
24. insolence
25. J'étais là, à me mettre mentalement en phase
26. en train d'installer son matériel
27. Quel type pénible !

'It's a bit late in the afternoon to be setting up for a painting,' Lynley remarked. He wandered to the window. Neither the river nor the garden could be seen from the room. He reflected on the nature of Parrish's lie[1].

'Well, who knows what goes on in the minds of these great magicians of the paintbrush[2]?' Parrish said lightly. 'Didn't Whistler[3] paint the Thames[4] in the middle of the night?'

'I'm not sure Ezra Farmington's in Whistler's league[5].' Lynley watched Parrish take out a packet of cigarettes and struggle to light one[6] with fingers that wouldn't co-operate. He crossed the room and offered the flame of his lighter.

Parrish's eyes met his and then hid themselves behind a thin veil of smoke. 'Thanks,' he said. 'Beastly little[7] scene. Well, I haven't welcomed you to Rose Cottage. A drink? No? I hope you don't mind if I indulge[8].' He disappeared into an adjoining[9] room. Glass rattled.[10] There was a long pause followed by the sounds of bottles and glassware[11] again. Parrish emerged, a respectable inch of whisky[12] in a tumbler[13]. His second or third, Lynley speculated[14].

'Why do you drink at the Dove and Whistle?'

The question caught Parrish off guard[15]. 'Do sit down, Inspector. I need to, and the thought of you towering over me[16] like Nemesis himself makes me positively limp with fear[17].'

It was an excellent stall tactic[18], Lynley thought. But two could play at that game. He walked over to the stereo and took his time over an inventory[19] of Parrish's tapes: a considerable collection of Bach, Chopin, Verdi, Vivaldi, and Mozart, with an adequate representation of modernists as well. Parrish indulged a wide range of musical tastes[20], he concluded. He crossed the room to one of the heavy, stuffed chairs and meditated on the black oak beams that spanned the ceiling[21].

1. mensonge
2. pinceau
3. [peintre américain, symbolisme/impressionnisme]
4. la Tamise
5. soit du niveau de Whistler
6. lutter pour en allumer une
7. Lamentable
8. si je m'en sers un
9. adjacente
10. Bruits de verre.
11. de verre
12. un whisky bien tassé
13. un verre
14. estima
15. par surprise
16. l'idée que vous soyez là à me toiser
17. me tétanise
18. manœuvre dilatoire
19. pour faire l'inventaire
20. avait des goûts musicaux très variés
21. les poutres noires, en chêne, couvrant le plafond

'Why do you live in this village in the middle of nowhere? A man with your musical taste and talent would obviously be happier in a more cosmopolitan environment, wouldn't he?'

Parrish laughed shortly. He smoothed a hand over[1] his perfectly combed hair. 'I think I like the other question better. Have I a choice on which one to answer?'

'The Holy Grail is only round the corner[2]. But you walk to the other end of the village on – what was it? – your tired old legs to drink in the other pub in St Chad's Lane. What's the attraction?[3]'

'Absolutely nothing. Well, I could say it's Hannah, but I doubt if you'd believe me. The truth is I prefer the Dove's atmosphere. There's something unholy[4] about getting roaring drunk[5] just opposite a church, isn't there?'

'Avoiding someone at the Holy Grail?' Lynley asked.

'Avoiding …?' Parrish's eyes slipped from Lynley to the window. A full-headed rose was kissing the glass[6] with enormous lips. The petals had begun to curl back[7]. Stigma, style, anther[8], and filament had blackened[9]. It should have been picked. It would die soon. 'Good heavens, no. Whom would I avoid? Father Hart, perhaps? Or the dear, deceased[10] William? He and the priest used to tipple a few[11] once or twice a week there.'

'You didn't care much for[12] Teys, did you?'

'No, not much. Holier-than-thou's[13] have never been in my line[14]. I don't know how Olivia abided[15] the man.'

'Perhaps she wanted a father for Bridie.'

'Perhaps. God knows the child could use some parental influence[16]. Even dour[17] old William was probably better than nothing. Liv is hopeless[18] with her. I'd take it on myself[19] but, to be frank, I don't

1. lissa de la main
2. juste au coin de la rue
3. Qu'est-ce qui vous y attire ?
4. Cela a quelque chose de profane
5. de se saouler à mort
6. caressait la vitre
7. à être trop ouverts
8. Les stigmates, le style, l'anthère
9. noirci
10. défunt
11. s'en jetaient un ou deux derrière la cravate
12. Vous n'aimiez guère
13. Les culs bénis
14. n'ont jamais été mon genre
15. supportait
16. a besoin d'une éducation parentale
17. austère
18. ne s'en sort pas
19. Je pourrais m'en charger

much care for children. And I don't like ducks at all.'

'But you're close to[1] Olivia anyway?'

Parrish's eyes showed nothing. 'I went to school with her husband, Paul. What a man *he* was! Rip-roaring, good-time[2] Paul.'

'He died four years ago, is that correct?'

Parrish nodded. 'Huntington's chorea.[3] At the end he didn't even recognize his wife. It was horrible. For everyone. Changed everyone's life to see him die that way.' He blinked several times and gave his attention to his cigarette and then to his fingernails[4]. They were well manicured, Lynley noted. The man went on with another bright smile. It was his defensive weapon[5], his way of denying any[6] emotion that might seep through the surface of[7] his thin-shelled indifference[8]. 'I suppose the next question is where was *I* on the fatal night? I'd love to trot out an alibi for you[9], Inspector. In bed with the village tart[10] would be nice. But I'm afraid that I didn't know our blessed[11] William would encounter an axe that evening, so I sat here playing my organ. Quite alone.[12] But I must clear myself[13], mustn't I? So I suppose I should say that anyone who heard me could verify the story.'

'Like today perhaps?'

Parrish ignored the question and finished off[14] his drink. 'Then when I was done[15] I skipped off to bed[16]. Again, unfortunately, very much alone.'

'How long have you lived in Keldale, Mr Parrish?'

'Ah. Back to the original thought[17], are we? Let me see. It must be nearly seven years.'

'Before that?'

'Before that, Inspector, I lived in York. I was a music teacher at a prep school. And, no, if you're going to go delving into my past[18] for tasty little items[19], I was not dismissed[20]. I left by choice. I wanted the

1. proche d'
2. Ce sacré bon vivant de
3. De la maladie de Huntington.
4. ongles
5. arme de défense
6. nier toute
7. susceptible de percer
8. fragile indifférence
9. vous débiter un alibi
10. la putain du village
11. ce sacré
12. Tout seul.
13. me laver de tout soupçon
14. finit
15. j'en ai eu assez de jouer,
16. j'ai filé au lit
17. Nous revoilà à votre première idée
18. fouiller dans mon passé
19. à la recherche de détails savoureux
20. renvoyé

country. I wanted some peace.' His voice rose slightly[1] on the last word.

Lynley got to his feet. 'Let me give you some now. Good evening to you.'

As he left the cottage, the music resumed[2] – muted this time[3] – but not before the discordant noise of glass breaking on stone[4] told him the manner in which Nigel Parrish celebrated his departure[5].

'I hope you don't mind, but I've booked you[6] into Keldale Hall[7] for dinner,' Stepha Odell said. She cocked[8] her bright head to one side and regarded Lynley thoughtfully[9]. 'Yes, I think I did just the right thing[10]. You look as if you need that tonight.'

'Am I becoming gaunt before your eyes?[11]'

She closed a ledger[12] and shelved it[13] behind the reception desk. 'Not at all. The food's excellent, of course, but that isn't why I've booked you there. The hall is one of our biggest diversions[14]. It's run by the local eccentric[15].'

'You have everything here, don't you?'

She laughed. 'All the pleasures that life affords[16], Inspector. Would you like a drink, or are you still on duty?'

'I wouldn't say no to a pint of Odell's.'

'Good.' She led him into the lounge and busied herself behind the bar. 'Keldale Hall is run by the Burton-Thomas family. I use that last word quite loosely[17], of course. Mrs Burton-Thomas has half a dozen or more young people working for her[18], and she stubbornly insists[19] that they all call her aunty. It's part of the cloud of eccentricity in which she likes to move[20], I should imagine.'

'Sounds a Dickensian[21] group,' Lynley remarked.

She pushed his ale across the bar and pulled a smaller one for herself. 'Just wait till you meet them. And meet them you shall, for Mrs Burton-Thomas always takes dinner with her guests[22]. When I rang

1. monta légèrement
2. reprit
3. atténuée, cette fois
4. le bruit dissonant du verre brisé sur la pierre
5. avait fêté son départ
6. je vous ai réservé une table
7. manoir
8. inclina
9. pensivement
10. je crois que j'ai bien fait
11. Je maigris à vue d'œil ?
12. un registre
13. le rangea sur une étagère
14. une de nos meilleures distractions
15. l'excentrique du coin
16. Tous les plaisirs de la vie
17. avec libéralité
18. emploie une demi-douzaine de jeunes gens
19. veut à toute force
20. dans lequel elle aime évoluer
21. à la Dickens
22. dîne toujours avec ses clients

her to book you in, she was beside herself with the idea of[1] Scotland Yard dining at her table. No doubt she'll poison[2] someone just to see you at work[3]. The pickings are going to be rather slim[4], however. She said she has only two couples there now: an American dentist and two "hoochiesmoochie types[5]", to use her expression.'

'It sounds just the kind of evening I'm longing for[6].' He walked to the window, glass in hand, and looked down the winding lane[7] that was Keldale Abbey Road. He couldn't see much of it, for it curved to the right and disappeared into the dusk[8].

Stepha came to join him. They didn't speak for some moments. 'I expect you've seen Roberta,' she said gently at last.

He turned, thinking to find her watching him, but she wasn't. Instead her eyes were on the glass of ale she held. She turned it slowly in the palm[9] of her hand, as if all her concentration were centred on its balance[10] and the total necessity of not spilling a drop[11] 'How did you know?'

'She was quite tall as a child, I remember. Almost as tall as Gillian. A big girl.' With a hand dampened by the moisture[12] of the glass, she brushed a few hairs from her brow. Her fingers left a misty streak[13] on her skin. She rubbed it off[14] impatiently. 'It happened quite slowly, Inspector. First she was just filled out[15] – chubby[16], I suppose. Then she was … what you saw today.' The shudder[17] that passed through her body spoke volumes[18]. And as if she realized what her reaction implied, she went on. 'That's horrible of me, isn't it? I have rather a despicable aversion to ugliness.[19] Frankly, I don't much like that about myself.'

'But you didn't answer me.'

'I didn't? What did you ask?'

'How you knew I'd seen Roberta.'

1. surexcitée à l'idée que
2. Elle va sûrement empoisonner
3. au travail
4. Elle n'aura pas beaucoup de choix
5. tourtereaux qui se bécotent
6. que je rêve de passer
7. le chemin en lacet
8. crépuscule
9. paume
10. à le garder en équilibre
11. de ne pas en renverser une goutte
12. mouillée par la buée
13. une traînée luisante
14. la fit disparaître en frottant
15. s'est juste un peu enveloppée
16. rondouillarde
17. frisson
18. était révélateur
19. J'ai une regrettable aversion pour la laideur.

A dull flush[1] crept into[2] Stepha's cheeks. She shifted her weight[3] from one foot to the other and looked so ill-at-ease[4] that Lynley was sorry he had pressed her[5].

'It doesn't matter,' he said.

'It's just that ... you look a bit different than you did this morning. More weighted down[6]. And there are lines at the corners of your mouth.' The flush deepened[7] on her beautiful skin. 'They weren't there before.'

'I see.'

'So I wondered if you'd seen her.'

'But you knew without asking.'

'Yes, I suppose I did. And I wondered how you can bear[8] to look at the ugliness of other people's lives as you do[9].'

'I've done it for some years. One gets used to it[10], Stepha.' The big man strangled[11] as he sat at his desk, the dirty girl[12] dead with the needle in her arm[13], the savage mutilation of a young man's corpse[14]. Did one ever really get used to man's dark side[15]?

Her eyes met his with surprising directness[16]. 'But surely it must be like looking at hell[17].'

'A bit.'

'Then, have you never wanted to run from it[18]? Run away madly[19] in the other direction? Never? Not once[20]?'

'One can't run for ever.'

She turned from him, moving her eyes back to the window. 'I can[21],' she murmured.

A sharp rap[22] on the door caused Barbara to stub out[23] her third cigarette. She looked around in a panic, opened the window, and rushed to the lavatory[24], where she flushed the incriminating evidence down the toilet[25]. A second rap and Lynley's voice called her name.

1. Une rougeur diffuse
2. gagna
3. se balança
4. parut si mal à l'aise
5. d'avoir insisté
6. accablé
7. La rougeur s'accentua
8. supporter
9. comme vous le faites
10. On s'y fait
11. étranglé
12. la paumée
13. une aiguille dans le bras
14. cadavre
15. au côté obscur des hommes
16. franchise
17. des visions de l'enfer
18. de fuir tout ça
19. comme un fou
20. une seule fois
21. Moi, si
22. coup sec
23. écraser
24. se précipita vers les toilettes
25. tira la chasse d'eau sur la pièce à conviction

She went to the door. He hesitated, glancing over her shoulder curiously before he spoke. 'Ah, Havers,' he said. 'Apparently Miss Odell has seen fit[1] to find us a more edible repast[2] this evening. She's booked us into Keldale Hall.' He consulted his watch. 'In an hour.'

'What?' Barbara cried out in involuntary horror. 'I haven't … I can't … I don't think …'

Lynley raised an eyebrow. 'Please don't go all Helen on me[3] and say you've nothing to wear[4], Havers.'

'But I haven't!' she protested. 'You go alone. I'll get something at the Dove and Whistle.'

'Considering your reaction to last night's fare[5], do you think that's wise[6]?'

A blow below the belt.[7] Blast him. 'I don't care much for chicken. I never have.'

'Wonderful. I understand[8] the cook at the hall is a bit of a gourmet. I doubt if[9] anything with feathers[10] will even put in an appearance[11]. Unless, of course, Hannah's waiting on tables[12].'

'But I simply can't—'

'It's an order, Havers. In an hour.' He turned on his heel.

Damn him! She slammed the door loud enough[13] to signal her displeasure[14]. Wonderful! What an evening to look forward to[15]: fumbling aimlessly[16] with sixteen pieces of silverware[17]; wineglasses everywhere; waiters and waitresses removing knives and forks before one even had a chance[18] to decide what to do with them. Chicken and peas at the Dove and Whistle sounded like heaven compared to that.

She strode to the wardrobe[19] and yanked it open[20]. Divine. Now what *shall* it be for an evening of mingling elegantly with society[21]? The brown tweed skirt and matching[22] pullover? The jeans and hiking boots? What about the blue suit, to remind him of Helen? Ha! Who could ever remind him of Helen,

1. a jugé bon
2. quelque chose de plus mangeable
3. ne me faites pas le coup d'Helen,
4. prétendant que vous n'avez rien de mettable
5. au menu d'hier
6. que ce soit raisonnable
7. Un coup en dessous de la ceinture.
8. Apparemment,
9. Je doute que
10. le moindre gibier à plumes
11. fasse une apparition
12. qu'Hannah fasse le service
13. claqua la porte assez fort
14. marquer son mécontentement
15. en perspective
16. à ne savoir que faire
17. seize couverts en argent
18. avant même d'avoir pu
19. l'armoire
20. l'ouvrit sans ménagement
21. à côtoyer la bonne société
22. assorti

with her impeccable wardrobe[1], her well-cut hair, her manicured hands, her lyrical voice?

She yanked a white wool shirtwaist[2] from the wardrobe and tossed it[3] on to the rumpled[4] bed. It really was almost amusing. Would people actually think she was his date[5]? Apollo taking Medusa to dine? How would he handle[6] the stares and the gibes[7]?

One hour later, as good as his word[8], he knocked on her door. She looked in the mirror, her stomach churning[9]. Oh God, the dress was *awful*. She resembled a white-garbed barrel[10] with legs. She jerked open the door and glared at him[11] furiously. He was dressed to the absolute teeth.[12]

'Do you always carry clothes like that around with you?' she demanded, incredulous.

'Just like the Boy Scouts.' He smiled. 'Shall we go?'

He escorted her gallantly down the stairs and into the night, where he opened the car door for her and tucked her[13] within the tooled leather comfort of the[14] Bentley. The born gentleman, she thought derisively[15]. On automatic pilot. Get him into his Lord of the Manor outfit and[16] forget Scotland Yard.

As if he read her mind, he turned to her before starting the car. 'Havers, I'd like to give the case a rest[17] for the evening.'

What on earth would they have to talk about if the murder of Teys was going to be taboo? 'All right,' she replied, brusquely.

He nodded and turned the ignition key[18]. The big car purred to life[19]. 'I love this part of England,' he said as they set off down Keldale Abbey Road. 'You haven't been told that I'm an unabashed[20] Yorkist, have you?'

'A Yorkist?'

'The Wars of the Roses[21]. We're deep in their country now.[22] Sheriff Hutton's not far from here and Middleham's practically within shouting distance[23].'

1. ses tenues impeccables
2. robe chemisier
3. la jeta
4. froissé
5. invitée pour la soirée
6. réagirait-il
7. aux railleries
8. comme promis
9. l'estomac retourné
10. un tonneau vêtu de blanc
11. le dévisagea
12. Il était d'une élégance parfaite.
13. l'installa
14. dans le confort tout cuir de la
15. avec dérision
16. Dès qu'il met sa panoplie de châtelain, il
17. qu'on ne parle pas de l'affaire
18. clé de contact
19. démarra en ronronnant
20. incorrigible
21. guerre des Deux-Roses [guerre de succession anglaise au XVe s. entre les maisons York, rose blanche, et Lancastre, rose rouge]
22. au beau milieu de leur territoire.
23. à côté

'Oh.' Wonderful. A discourse on history. Her entire knowledge[1] of the Wars of the Roses began and ended with the[2] conflict's name.

'Naturally, I know one's really obliged to think badly[3] of the Yorks. They *did*, after all, do away with[4] Henry VI.' He tapped his fingers reflectively against the wheel. 'Except I can never help thinking that there was a justice in that. Pomfret[5] and all: Richard II being murdered by his very own cousin. Killing Henry seems to have closed the circle[6] of the crime.'

She pleated[7] the white dress between her fingers and sighed, defeated. 'Look, sir, I'm no good at this sort of thing. I … well, I'd do much better[8] at the Dove and Whistle. If you'd please just—'

'*Barbara.*' He pulled abruptly to the verge.[9] He was looking at her, she knew, but she stared ahead into the darkness and counted the moths[10] that danced in the car's headlamps[11]. 'Would you just for an evening be what you are[12]? *Whatever* you are.'

'What's that supposed to mean?' God, how shrewish[13] she sounded.

'It means that you may drop the act[14]. Or at least that I wish you would.'

'What act?'

'Just be what you are.'

'How dare you[15]—'

'Why do you pretend not to smoke[16]?' he interrupted.

'Why do *you* pretend to be such a public-school fop?' She hadn't intended the words to be so shrill[17]. At first, as if evaluating her comment[18], he didn't respond.

There was silence. Then he threw back his head and laughed. '*Touché*. Shall we call a truce[19] for the rest of the evening and go on despising each other[20] with the dawn[21]?'

1. Tout ce qu'elle savait
2. se résumait au
3. d'avoir une opinion négative
4. Après tout, ils se sont débarrassés d'
5. [château où Richard II fut assassiné]
6. bouclé la boucle
7. plissa
8. je m'en sortirais mieux
9. Il s'arrêta brusquement sur le bas-côté.
10. compta les papillons de nuit
11. phares
12. être vous-même
13. revêche
14. arrêter de jouer un rôle
15. osez-vous
16. faites-vous semblant de ne pas fumer
17. aussi véhéments
18. sa remarque
19. Si nous faisions une trêve
20. recommencer à nous mépriser
21. demain dès l'aube

1. malgré elle
2. toute crainte d'ordre vestimentaire
3. n'avait su apaiser
4. mitée
5. haut froncé
6. châle à perles
7. jeté autour de ses épaules
8. élastiques
9. en écaille
10. peigne [à chignon]
11. toisa Lynley
12. Ils n'avaient pas le même look
13. aux éclats
14. peu nombreux
15. vous m'avez évité le meurtre
16. faisant passer Barbara devant lui
17. Vous allez vite comprendre.
18. aux arômes des différentes viandes qui rôtissaient
19. Je n'ai pas révélé
20. remettant son châle en place d'un coup d'épaule
21. Elle les mena à
22. la lueur des bougies projetait des ombres
23. Ne se caressent pas
24. Adorables.

She glared at him a moment, then, in spite of herself[1], smiled. She knew she was being manipulated, but it didn't seem to matter. 'All right,' she said reluctantly. But she noticed that neither of them had answered the other's question.

They were welcomed into Keldale Hall by a woman who put to rest every sartorial fear[2] of Barbara's that Lynley had not been able to assuage[3]. She was dressed in a moth-eaten[4] skirt of indeterminate colour, a gypsy blouse[5] decorated with stars, and a beaded shawl[6] that she had slung round her shoulders[7] like an Indian blanket. Her grey hair was gathered tightly into two elastic bands[8], one on each side of her neck, and to complete the ensemble she had perched an elaborate tortoise-shell[9] Spanish comb[10] on the top of her head.

'Scotland Yard?' she asked and looked Lynley over[11] with a critical eye. 'God, they didn't package 'em that way[12] when *I* was young.' She laughed uproariously[13]. 'Come in! We're a small party[14] tonight, but you've saved me from murder[15].'

'How's that?' Lynley asked, ushering Barbara ahead of him[16].

'I've an American couple that I'd love to kill. But we'll leave that. You'll understand soon enough.[17] We're gathered in here.' She led them across the massive stone hall, scented with the assorted meats that were roasting[18] in the kitchen nearby. 'I haven't breathed a word[19] that you're Scotland Yard,' she confided loudly, shouldering her beadwork back into place[20]. 'When you meet the Watsons, you'll know why.' On through[21] the dining-room, where candlelight was casting shadows[22] on the walls. A linen-covered table was set with china and silver. 'The other couple are newlyweds. Londoners. I like 'em. Don't paw each other[23] in public the way so many newlyweds do. Very quiet. Very sweet.[24] I expect they don't like to draw attention to themselves because the man's crippled. Wife is a lovely little creature[1], though.'

Barbara heard Lynley's swift intake of breath[2]. Behind her, his steps slowed and then stopped altogether[3]. 'Who are they?' he asked hoarsely[4].

Mrs Burton-Thomas turned round at the entrance to the oak hall. 'Name of Allcourt-St James.' She threw open the door. 'Here's more company for us!' she announced.

Barbara was intensely aware[5] of the photographic quality[6] of the scene. A fire burned brilliantly[7], hissing[8] as the flames devoured the coal. Comfortable chairs were gathered round it. At the far end of the room, touched by shadows[9], Deborah St James was bent over a piano, leafing through[10] a family album with delight. She looked up with a smile. The men rose to their feet. And the picture froze.

'*Lord*,' Lynley whispered – prayer, curse, resignation.

At his tone, Barbara looked at him, and it came with a sudden jolt of recognition[11]. How ridiculous that she hadn't seen it before. Lynley was in love with the other man's wife.

'Hi there! That's one heckuva nice-lookin' suit[12],' Hank Watson said. He extended his hand to Lynley. It was fat, slightly sweaty[13], like shaking hands with a warm, uncooked[14] fish. 'Dentistry,' he announced. 'Here for the ADA[15] convention[16] in London. Tax write-off to the s-k-y.[17] This is JoJo, my wife.'

Somehow the introductions were muddled through[18].

'Champagne before dinner is my rule[19],' Mrs Burton-Thomas said. 'Before breakfast as well, if I have *my* way[20]. Danny, bring the juice[21]!' she shouted, in the general direction of the doorway, and a few

1. une très jolie petite
2. retenant son souffle
3. complètement
4. la voix rauque
5. perçut très bien
6. la dimension photographique
7. flambait de tout son éclat
8. crépitant
9. presque dans l'ombre
10. feuilletant
11. tout s'expliqua d'un coup
12. Voilà un sacré beau costard
13. moite
14. cru
15. des dentistes américains
16. congrès
17. Entièrement déductible des impôts.
18. on parvint à faire les présentations
19. est d'usage ici
20. si on me laisse faire
21. le mousseux

moments later a girl came into the room, burdened with an ice bucket[1], champagne, and glasses.

'What line-a work you in[2], fella?' Hank asked Lynley as the glasses went around. 'I thought Si here was some sort-a college[3] professor type. Gave me the jumping hee-haws[4] when he said he was a dead-body man[5].'

'Sergeant Havers and I work for Scotland Yard,' Lynley responded.

'Say-hey[6], JoJo-bean. Did you hear that, woman?' He looked at Lynley with new interest. 'You here on the baby gig[7]?'

'The baby gig?'

'Three-year-old case.[8] Guess the trail's kinda cold[9] now.' Hank winked in the direction of Danny, who was putting the bottle of champagne into the bucket of ice. 'Dead baby in the abbey? *You* know.'

Lynley didn't know anything, didn't want to know anything. He couldn't have answered if his life had depended upon it. He found that he didn't know what to do with himself, where to cast his eyes[10], what to say. He was only conscious of Deborah.

'We're here on the decapitation gig[11],' Havers responded politely, miraculously.

'De-cap-i-ta-tion?' Hank crowed[12]. 'This is one jumping area of the country![13] Don't you think so, Bean?'

'Sure is,' his wife said, nodding in solemn affirmation[14]. She fingered the long strand of white beads[15] she wore and looked hopefully in the direction of the silent St Jameses.

Hank hunched forward[16] in his chair, dragging it closer[17] to Lynley's. 'Well, give us the poop!' he demanded.

'I beg your pardon?'

'The p-o-o-p. The verified, certified poop.' Hank slapped the arm[18] of Lynley's chair. 'Who did it, fella?' he demanded.

1. seau à glace
2. Vous faites quoi, comme boulot
3. d'université
4. M'a foutu la chair de poule
5. qu'il s'occupait de cadavres
6. Dis donc
7. l'affaire du bébé
8. Une affaire d'il y a 3 ans.
9. la piste est un peu froide
10. où poser son regard
11. pour l'affaire de la décapitation
12. exulta
13. Ça n'arrête pas, dans le coin !
14. en acquiesçant solennellement
15. rang de perles blanches
16. se courba en avant
17. le traînant pour se rapprocher
18. tapa sur l'accoudoir

It was too much. The appalling little man screwing his face up in excitement[1] was too much to bear. He was wearing a saffron polyester suit[2], a matching shirt in a floral print[3], and round his neck hung a heavy gold chain with a medallion that danced on the thick hair of his chest. A diamond the size of a walnut[4] glittered[5] on his finger, and he flashed white teeth[6] made even whiter by his burnt sienna tan[7]. His bulbous nose flexed its nostrils[8] blackly[9].

'We're not entirely sure,' Lynley replied seriously. 'But you fit the description[10].'

Hank stared at him, bug-eyed[11]. '*I* fit the description?' he croaked[12]. Then he peered at Lynley closely[13] and broke into a grin. '*Damn* you Brits![14] I just can't get the hang of[15] your humour! But I'm gettin' better, right, Si?'

Lynley finally looked at his friend and found him smiling. Amusement danced in St James' eyes. 'Absolutely,' Si replied.

As they drove in the darkness back to the lodge, Barbara studied Lynley furtively, realizing that until this evening it had been entirely unthinkable to her that a man such as he[16] could ever have been unsuccessful in love[17]. Yet here on the outskirts[18] of the village was the undeniable evidence of that fact: Deborah.

There had been at the hall a horrified moment with the three of them staring at one another before she had come forward, a tentative[19] smile on her face, a hand outstretched in greeting.

'Tommy! Whatever are you doing[20] in Keldale?' Deborah St James had asked.

He'd been at an absolute loss.[21] Barbara saw it and intervened. 'An investigation,' she replied.

Then the horrible little American had thrown himself into their midst[22] – it was a merciful

1. le visage froncé d'excitation
2. un costume en polyester couleur safran
3. à fleurs
4. aussi gros qu'une noix
5. scintillait
6. son grand sourire montrait des dents d'une blancheur
7. peau très bronzée
8. contractait ses narines
9. d'un air menaçant
10. vous correspondez au portrait
11. les yeux exorbités
12. articula
13. regarda Lynley attentivement
14. Sacrés rosbifs !
15. J'ai toujours du mal à saisir
16. comme lui
17. malheureux en amour
18. aux abords
19. hésitant
20. Mais que fais-tu donc
21. Il avait été incapable de dire un mot.
22. s'était imposé

intervention[1], really – and the other three began to breathe evenly[2] once more.

Still, St James had remained in his place by the fire[3], greeting his friend politely but making no other movement, his eyes for the most part[4] following his wife. If he was concerned about Lynley's unexpected arrival, if jealousy stirred in him[5] at the man's blatant feelings[6], his face betrayed nothing[7].

Of the two, Deborah had been more obviously distressed[8]. Her colour was high[9]. Her hands had clasped and unclasped repeatedly[10] in her lap. Her eyes had moved restlessly[11] between the two men, and she hadn't concealed her relief when Lynley suggested their departure at the earliest opportunity[12] after the meal's conclusion[13].

Now he was pulling the car in front of the lodge and switching off the ignition. He leaned back and rubbed his eyes. 'I feel as if I could sleep for a year. How do you suppose Mrs Burton-Thomas is going to get rid of that dreadful dentist?'

'Arsenic?'

He laughed. 'She'll have to do something. He was talking as if staying another month were the dearest thing to his heart[14]. What an appalling man!'

'Not exactly the son one wants to run into on a honeymoon,' she admitted. She wondered if he would pick up the conversational thread[15], if he would say anything about St James and Deborah and the awkward coincidence[16] that had flung them into his path[17]. Indeed, she wondered further[18] if he would say anything at all about how he had come to position himself[19] on the worst possible side[20] of this unusual love triangle.

Instead of replying, however, he got out of the car and slammed the door. Barbara watched him shrewdly[21] as he came to her side. Not a ripple[22] appeared on the surface of his calm. He was in firm control. If anything at all,[23] the fop was back.

1. une intervention salutaire
2. à mieux respirer
3. était resté à sa place, près du feu
4. essentiellement
5. si la jalousie le tenaillait
6. face aux sentiments flagrants de l'autre
7. ne trahissait rien
8. désemparée
9. Elle avait les joues rouges
10. Elle serrait et desserrait ses mains sans cesse
11. sans arrêt
12. à la première occasion
13. fin
14. lui tenait vraiment à cœur
15. s'il suivrait le fil de la conversation
16. cette drôle de coïncidence
17. sur son chemin
18. même
19. comment il avait pu se retrouver
20. du pire côté
21. l'observa attentivement
22. Pas la moindre crispation
23. Peut-être même que

The lodge door opened and a square of light framed[1] Stepha Odell. 'I thought I heard your car,' she said. 'You've a visitor, Inspector.'

Deborah gazed at her reflection in the mirror. He'd said absolutely nothing since coming into their room, merely walking over to[2] the fire and sitting in the chair, the brandy glass in his hand. She'd watched him, not sure what to say, afraid to penetrate the wall of his sudden isolation[3]. *Don't go that way*[4], *Simon*, she'd wanted to shout. *Don't cut yourself off from me.*[5] *Don't go back to that darkness.* But how could she say it and risk having Tommy thrown up in her face[6]?

She ran[7] the water into the bathroom basin and dismally watched its flow[8]. What was he thinking, alone in that room? Was he haunted[9] by Tommy? Did he wonder if she closed her eyes when they made love so she could dream of him? He never once had asked. He never once had questioned. He simply accepted whatever she said[10], whatever she gave. So what could she say or give to him now, with her past and Tommy's between them?

She splashed her face[11] repeatedly, dried it, turned off the water, and forced herself to walk back into the bedroom. Her heart sank[12] when she saw that he'd gone to bed. His heavy leg-brace[13] lay on the floor near the chair, and his crutches leaned[14] against the wall next to the bed. The room was dark. But in the dying light of the fire she saw that he was still awake[15], sitting up in fact, with the pillows[16] behind him, watching the glow of the embers[17].

She walked to the bed and sat down. 'I'm in a welter[18],' she said.

He felt for[19] her hand. 'I know. I've been sitting here trying to think how I might help you. But I don't know what to do.'

1. un carré de lumière encadra
2. se dirigeant simplement vers
3. de son isolement soudain
4. Ne fais pas ça
5. Ne te coupe pas de moi
6. qu'il lui jette Tommy au visage
7. fit couler
8. la regarda s'écouler, lugubrement
9. hanté
10. tout ce qu'elle disait
11. se passa de l'eau sur le visage
12. Le cœur lui manqua
13. prothèse
14. ses béquilles étaient appuyées
15. ne dormait pas
16. oreillers
17. les braises rougeoyer
18. Je ne sais que faire
19. Il chercha

'I hurt him, Simon. I never intended to[1], but it happened all the same[2], and I can't seem to forget it. When I see him, I feel so responsible for his pain. I want to make it go away. I … I suppose I'*d* feel better then. Less guilty[3] about it all.'

He touched her cheek and traced[4] the line of her jaw. 'If it were only that easy[5], my love. You can't make it go away. You can't help him. He's got to do it alone, but it's hard because he's in love with you. And the fact that you're wearing a wedding ring doesn't change that[6], Deborah.'

'Simon—'

He wouldn't let her finish. 'What bothers me[7] is seeing the effect he has on you. I see your guilt. I want to take it away, and I don't know how. I wish that I did. I don't like to see you feeling so wretched[8].'

She searched his face, finding comfort[9] and peace in the familiar battle[10] of its lines and angles. Utterly unhandsome.[11] A catalogue[12] of agonies lived through and conquered[13] and lived through again. Her heart swelled with[14] love for him. Her throat tightened[15] with the emotion's sudden intensity.

'Have you actually been sitting in this darkness[16] worried about me? How like you[17], Simon.'

'Why do you say that? What did you think I was doing?'

'Tormenting yourself with … things in the past.'

'Ah.' He drew her[18] into his arms, resting his cheek on the top of her head. 'I won't lie to you, Deborah. It's not easy for me, knowing that Tommy was your lover[19]. If it had been some other man, I could have attributed to him all sorts of faults[20] to convince myself that he wasn't worthy of you[21]. But that's not the case, is it? He is a good man. He does deserve you. And no one knows that better than I.'

'So you *are* haunted by it. I thought as much.[22]'

1. Ce n'était pas mon intention
2. quand même
3. Moins coupable
4. suivit
5. Si seulement c'était aussi simple
6. n'y change rien
7. Ce qui me dérange
8. te voir si malheureuse
9. du réconfort
10. le déchaînement familier
11. Totalement dépourvu de beauté.
12. série
13. peines vécues et surmontées
14. se gonfla d'
15. Sa gorge se serra
16. resté assis dans le noir
17. C'est tout toi
18. l'attira
19. a été ton amant
20. défauts
21. digne de toi
22. Je m'en doutais.

'Not haunted. Not at all.' His fingers moved lightly down her hair to caress her throat and slip the nightdress[1] from her shoulders. 'I was at first.[2] I'll admit that. But frankly, the very first time[3] we made love, I realized that I never had to think of you and Tommy again. If I didn't want to. And now' – she could feel his smile – 'every time I look at you, I'm reminded most decidedly of the present[4], not of the past. And then I find that I want to undress you, breathe the fragrance of your skin[5], kiss your mouth and breasts and thighs[6]. In fact, the distraction's becoming quite a problem[7] in my life.'

'In mine as well.'

'Then, perhaps, my love,' he whispered, 'we should concentrate all our energies on seeking[8] a solution.' Her hand slid under the covers. He caught his breath[9] at her touch[10]. 'That's a good beginning,' he admitted and brought his mouth to hers[11].

1. faire glisser la chemise de nuit
2. Au début, oui.
3. la toute première fois
4. je me place résolument dans le présent
5. sentir l'odeur de ta peau
6. tes seins et tes cuisses
7. devient un vrai problème
8. à trouver
9. retint sa respiration
10. contact
11. joignit sa bouche à la sienne

10

The visitor was Superintendent Nies. He was waiting in the lounge, three empty pint glasses[1] on a table nearby and a cardboard carton[2] at his feet. He was standing, not sitting, a man wary and watchful[3] and never relaxed. His lips thinned[4] at the sight of Lynley, and his nostrils pinched[5] as if he smelt something foul. He was contempt personified[6].

'You wanted *everything*, Inspector,' he snapped. 'Here it is.' He gave the carton a sharp kick[7], not so much to move it as to direct[8] the other man's attention to it.

No one stirred. It was as if the raw hatred[9] behind Nies' words immobilized them all[10]. Next to her, Barbara felt Lynley's tension tightening his muscles like a whipcord[11]. His face, however, was without expression as he took the measure of[12] the other man.

'This *is* what you wanted, isn't it?' Nies persisted nastily[13]. He picked up the carton, dumping its contents[14] on to the carpet. 'I expect, when you ask for everything, that you do mean everything, Inspector. Something about you tells me you're a man of your word[15]. Or were you hoping that I'd send it all with[16] someone else so you might avoid having any further chats[17] with me?'

1. verres de bière vides
2. un carton
3. méfiant et sur le qui-vive
4. se pincèrent
5. se serrèrent
6. le mépris personnifié
7. un grand coup de pied
8. mais plutôt pour attirer
9. la haine farouche
10. les avaient tous pétrifiés
11. la lanière d'un fouet
12. tandis qu'il jaugeait
13. l'air mauvais
14. déversant son contenu
15. un homme de parole
16. je vous ferais passer le tout par
17. d'autres conversations

Lynley's eyes dropped to the objects on the floor. A woman's clothing[1], by their appearance.

'Perhaps you've had too much to drink,' he suggested.

Nies took a step forward[2]. Blood rushed[3] to his face. 'You'd like to think that, wouldn't you? You'd like to see me giving it over to drink[4], in my cups with flaming regret[5] for having you in the nick[6] for a few days over Davenport's death. Not exactly the digs[7] his precious lordship was used to, were they?'

Barbara had never recognized so acutely[8] one man's need to strike another or the atavistic savagery[9] that often drove that need to completion[10]. She saw it in Nies now, in his posture, in his hands with their talon-like[11] fingers halfway drawn into a fist[12], in the cords that stood out on his neck[13]. What she couldn't understand was Lynley's reaction. After the initial flash of tension, he'd become unnaturally unperturbed. That seemed to be the source of Nies' increasing rage.

'Have you solved this case[14], Inspector?' Nies sneered. 'Made any arrests? No, of course not. Not without having all the facts. So let me give you a few and save you a little time. Roberta Teys killed her father. She chopped off[15] his miserable head, sat herself down, and waited to be discovered. And no bloody evidence you can dig out of the blue[16] is *ever* going to prove this case otherwise[17]. Not for Kerridge. Not for Webberly. Not for anyone. But you have a fine time digging for it, laddie[18]. You'll get nothing more from me. Now, get out of my way.'

Nies shoved past them, flung open[19] the outer door, and stormed[20] to his car. It roared into life[21]. He ground the gears viciously[22] and was gone.

Lynley looked at the two women. Stepha was very pale, Havers was stoic, but both clearly expected some kind of response from him. He found he

1. Des vêtements de femme
2. fit un pas en avant
3. afflua
4. me mettre à boire
5. me saouler, rongé par le remords
6. de vous avoir gardé à l'ombre
7. le genre de piaule
8. aussi précisément
9. cette violence atavique
10. faisait passer à l'acte
11. griffus
12. formant presque un poing
13. les tendons qui saillaient de son cou
14. résolu cette affaire
15. a tranché
16. sortie de nulle part
17. ne pourra prouver le contraire
18. mon petit gars
19. les bouscula en passant, ouvrit violemment
20. se précipita
21. démarra en rugissant
22. passa les vitesses comme une brute

1. Quels que soient les démons motivant
2. aurait volontiers étiqueté
3. paranoïaque
4. l'impression
5. qu'on va craquer
6. à force d'efforts et d'épuisement
7. tout près de craquer
8. l'examen
9. de fulminer
10. laisser Nies se défouler
11. le fixa bêtement
12. l'étendit à plat
13. un imprimé pastel
14. col marin
15. manchettes blanches
16. avait une énorme tache brune
17. s'étendait, irrégulière
18. en était tacheté
19. si une étiquette le spécifiait
20. linon [lin ou coton fin]
21. de grandes chaussures noires à talons
22. le long de la tranche
23. la semelle gauche rejoignait
24. Un jupon

couldn't make one. Whatever devils were driving[1] Nies' behaviour, he didn't care to discuss them. He longed to hang labels[2] on the man: *paranoid*[3], *psychopath, madman* came to mind. But he knew too well what it felt like[4] to be brought to the breaking point[5] through sheer endeavour and exhaustion[6] during a case. Lynley could see that Nies was a hair's-breadth from breaking[7] under the stress of the Scotland Yard scrutiny[8] of his competence. So if it gave the man even a moment's relief to rail wildly[9] about their run-in five years ago, he was more than happy to give Nies free rein[10].

'Would you get the Teys file from my room, Sergeant?' he asked Havers. 'You'll find it on the chest of drawers.'

Havers gawked at him[11]. 'Sir, that man just—'

'It's on the chest of drawers,' Lynley repeated. He crossed the room to the heap of garments on the floor, picked up the dress, and laid it like a collapsed tent[12] across the couch. It was a pale pastel print[13] with a white sailor collar[14] and long sleeves that ended in upturned white cuffs[15].

The left sleeve of the garment was heavily stained with a solid mass of brown[16]. Another solid mass formed an irregular pool[17] from thighs to knees. The bottom of the skirt was speckled with it[18]. Blood.

He fingered the material and recognized the texture without looking to see if a label revealed it[19]: a delicate lawn[20].

Shoes had been part of the package as well: large black high-heeled pumps[21] with mud encrusted along the ridge[22] where left sole met[23] shoe body. These too were flecked with the same brown substance. Petticoat[24] and underclothes completed the lot.

'That's her church dress,' Stepha Odell said and added tonelessly, 'She had two. One for winter and one for spring.'

'Her best dress?' Lynley asked.

'As far as I know.'

He was beginning to understand the villagers' stubborn refusal[1] to believe that the girl had committed the crime. With each new piece of information, it made less and less sense[2]. Havers returned with the file, her face without expression. Before he began leafing through it, he was convinced that the information he wanted wouldn't be there. It wasn't.

'Damn the man,' Lynley muttered fruitlessly[3] and looked at Havers. 'He's given us no analysis of the stains.'

'He'd have to have done them[4], wouldn't he?' Havers asked.

'He's done them. But he has no intention of giving them to us. Not if that would make our job easier.' Lynley uttered an oath[5] beneath his breath and swept the garments back into their cardboard container.

'What's to do?[6]' Havers asked.

Lynley knew the answer. He needed St James: the mechanical precision of his highly trained[7] mind, the quick, clean certainty of his finely wrought skill[8]. He needed a laboratory where tests could be made and a forensic expert he could trust who would make them. It was a maddening[9], circular sort of problem because in any direction the trail curved unquestionably[10] back to St James.

He regarded the open carton at his feet and gave himself the ephemeral pleasure[11] of cursing[12] the man from Richmond. Webberly was wrong, he thought. I'm the last person he should have involved in this. Nies reads[13] the London condemnation too clearly. He sees in me his single[14] serious mistake.

1. refus entêté
2. cela avait de moins en moins de sens
3. vainement
4. Il les a forcément analysées
5. jura
6. Que faire ?
7. très entraîné
8. la finesse de son savoir-faire
9. qui le rendait fou
10. la piste le ramenait indiscutablement
11. s'offrit le plaisir fugace
12. de maudire
13. interprète
14. unique

He considered his options.[1] He could turn the case over[2] to another DI: MacPherson could certainly come sailing[3] into Keldale and have the matter taken care of[4] within two days. But MacPherson was caught up in[5] the Ripper murders. It would be inconceivable to move him from the one case where his expertise was so desperately needed simply because Nies couldn't come to terms with[6] his past. He could telephone Kerridge in Newby Wiske. Kerridge, after all, was Nies' superior officer. But to have Kerridge involved, chomping at the bit[7] to make up[8] for the Romanivs in any way he could, was even more absurd. Besides, Kerridge didn't have the paperwork, the results of the lab tests, the depositions. All he had was an overwhelming[9] hatred of Nies and an inability to get along[10] with the man. The entire situation was an irritating, howling[11], political maelstrom of thwarted ambition[12], error, and revenge. He was sick of it[13].

A glass was placed before him on the table. He looked up into Stepha's serene eyes. 'A bit of Odell's is called for[14], I think.'

He laughed shortly. 'Sergeant,' he said, 'would you care to indulge?'

'No, sir,' she replied, and just when he thought she would go on in her former, exasperating I'm-on-duty manner[15], she added, 'but I could do with a smoke[16], if you don't mind.'

He handed her his gold case and silver lighter. 'Have[17] as many as you like.'

She lit her cigarette. 'Got all dressed up[18] to chop off Dad's head? It doesn't make sense.'

'The dress does[19],' Stepha said.

'Why?'

'Because it was Sunday. She was ready for church.'

Lynley and Havers looked up, realizing simultaneously the import of[20] Stepha's words. 'But Teys was killed on Saturday night,' Havers said.

1. Il envisagea les possibilités qui s'offraient à lui.
2. transmettre le dossier
3. rappliquer
4. régler la question
5. pris par
6. ne parvenait pas à assumer
7. brûlant
8. d'avoir sa revanche
9. dévorante
10. bien s'entendre
11. énorme
12. ambitions contrariées
13. en avait assez
14. s'impose
15. persister avec son « je suis en service »
16. je fumerais bien une cigarette
17. Prenez-en
18. Elle s'était mise sur son trente et un
19. Pour la robe, si
20. ce qu'impliquaient

'So Roberta must have got up as usual on Sunday morning, put her church clothes on, and waited for her father.' Lynley eyed[1] the dress heaped in the carton. 'He wasn't in the house, so she probably assumed[2] he was somewhere on the farm. She wouldn't worry, of course, because he'd be back in time to take her to church. He probably never missed church in his life. But when he didn't show up[3], she began to get worried. She went out to look for him.'

'And she found him in the barn,' Havers concluded. 'But the blood on her dress – how do you think it came to be[4] there?'

'I'd guess she was in shock. She must have picked up[5] the body and cradled it[6] in her lap.'

'But he had no head! How could she—'

Lynley went on. 'She lowered the body back[7] down to the floor and, still in shock, sat there until Father Hart came and found her.'

'But, then, why say she killed him?'

'She never said that,' Lynley replied.

'What do you mean?'

'What she said was, "I did it. I'm not sorry." ' Lynley's voice held a note of decision.

'That sounds like a confession to me.'

'Not necessarily.' He ran his fingers round the edges[8] of the stain on the dress and tested the spacing[9] of the spatters[10] on the skirt. 'But it does sound like something.'

'What?'

'That Roberta knows quite well[11] who murdered her father.'

Lynley awoke with a jolt[12]. Early-morning light filtered into the room in delicate bands that streaked across the floor to the[13] bed. A chill breeze[14] blew back the curtains and carried upon it the pleasant sounds of waking birds and the distant cries

1. fixa
2. alors elle a sans doute cru
3. il ne venait pas
4. à votre avis, comment est-il arrivé
5. a dû soulever
6. l'a tenu
7. a redéposé le corps
8. passa les doigts sur le contour
9. évalua l'espacement
10. des éclaboussures
11. sait très bien
12. se réveilla en sursaut
13. en délicats rubans striant le sol jusqu'au
14. Un petit vent glacé

of sheep. But none of this touched his awareness[1]. He lay in the bed and knew only[2] depression, overwhelming desperation[3], and the burning of desire. He longed to turn on his side and find her there, her wealth of hair[4] spread across the bedclothes, her eyes closed in sleep. He longed to arouse her to wakefulness[5], his mouth and tongue feeling the subtle[6], familiar changes in her body that betrayed[7] her desire.

He flung back[8] the covers. *Madness*, he thought. He began pulling on clothing mindlessly[9], furiously, any article[10] that first came to hand[11]. Escape was the exigency.

He grabbed an Aran sweater[12] and ran from the room, thundering down[13] the stairs and out into the street. There, he finally noticed the time. It was half-past six.

A heavy mist[14] lay[15] on the dale, swirling[16] delicately round the edges of buildings and blanketing[17] the river. To his right the high street was shuttered[18], abandoned. Not even the greengrocer was setting his boxes out on to the pavement. Sinji's windows were darkened, the Wesleyan chapel was barred[19], and the tea room looked back at him with blank disinterest.

He walked to the bridge, wasted five minutes restlessly tossing pebbles[20] into the river, and was finally distracted by the sight of the church.

On its hillock, St Catherine's looked peacefully down upon[21] the village, the very exorcist he needed for[22] the demons of his past. He began to walk towards it.

It was a proud little church. Surrounded by trees and an ancient, crumbling[23] graveyard, it lifted its splendid Norman exterior to the sky. Its apse[24] housed[25] a semi-circle of stained-glass windows[26], while its bell tower[27] at the opposite end played host[28] to a whispering band[29] of doves[30]. For a mo-

1. ne l'atteignait vraiment
2. ne ressentait que
3. le désespoir
4. son opulente chevelure
5. la réveiller en l'excitant
6. subtils
7. trahissaient
8. repoussa
9. à enfiler sans réfléchir
10. vêtement
11. lui tombant sous la main
12. un pull irlandais
13. descendant quatre à quatre
14. brume
15. couvrait
16. tourbillonnant
17. masquant
18. avait les volets fermés
19. fermée [avec une barre]
20. agité, à jeter des galets
21. veillait paisiblement sur
22. exactement ce qu'il lui fallait pour chasser
23. vieux et en ruine
24. abside
25. arborait
26. vitraux
27. clocher
28. abritait
29. groupe
30. colombes

ment he watched them rustling[1] at the edges of the roof, then he walked up the gravel path to the lych gate[2]. He entered, and the peace of the graveyard settled round him.

Idly[3], he began to wander among[4] the graves, looking at tombstones[5] made barely legible[6] by the ravages of time. The yard was overgrown with weeds[7] and grass, dampened by morning mist. Gravestones bent into thick vegetation. Moss flourished[8] on surfaces that never saw sun, and trees sheltered[9] final resting-places[10] of people long forgotten.

A curious group of twisting[11] Italian cypresses[12] arched over a few toppled[13] tombstones some distance from the church. Their contortions were mystifying[14], oddly humanoid, as if they were attempting to protect the graves beneath them. Intrigued, he walked in their direction and saw her.

How completely like her[15] to have rolled up the legs[16] of her faded blue jeans, to have removed her shoes and plunged barefoot[17] into the tall, damp growth[18] so as to capture[19] the graves in the best angle and light. How like her as well to be utterly oblivious to her surroundings[20]: oblivious to the streak of mud that snaked from ankle to calf[21], to the torn crimson leaf[22] that had somehow become tangled[23] in her hair, to the fact that he stood less than ten yards away and drank in[24] her every movement and longed quite hopelessly for her to be again what she once had been in his life.

The low ground fog[25] hid and revealed in alternate patches[26]. The early sunlight weakly dappled[27] the stones. An inquisitive bird watched with bright eyes from a grave nearby. He was only dimly aware of this, but he knew that with her camera she would capture it all.

He looked for St James. Surely the man would be sitting somewhere nearby, fondly[28] watching his

1. froufrouter
2. porche du cimetière
3. Nonchalamment
4. se promener parmi
5. pierres tombales
6. presque effacées
7. mauvaises herbes
8. La mousse prospérait
9. protégeaient
10. les dernières demeures
11. tordus
12. cyprès
13. écroulées
14. déconcertantes
15. Cela lui ressemblait tellement
16. d'avoir relevé le bas
17. pieds nus
18. la végétation haute et trempée
19. saisir
20. inconsciente de ce qui l'entourait
21. serpentait de la cheville au mollet
22. la feuille morte pourpre
23. s'était prise
24. buvait du regard
25. Le brouillard au ras du sol
26. par places
27. tachetait
28. avec adoration

wife work. But he was nowhere in sight. She was very much alone.

He felt immediately as if the church had betrayed him with its early promise of comfort and peace. *It's no good, Deb*, he thought as he watched her. *Nothing makes it go away. I want you to leave him. Betray him. Come back to me. It's where you belong.*[1]

She looked up, brushed her hair off[2] her face, and saw him. He knew from her expression that he might as well[3] have said everything aloud. She read it at once.

'Oh, Tommy.'

Of course she wouldn't pretend[4], wouldn't fill the awkward moment[5] with amusing chatter[6] that, Helen-like, would serve to get them through[7] the encounter. Instead she bit her lip, looking very much as if he had struck her, and turned back to her tripod[8], making unnecessary adjustments[9].

He walked to her side. 'I'm so sorry,' he said. She continued to fumble uselessly with her equipment, her head bent, her hair hiding her face. 'I can't get past it.[10] I try to see my way clear[11], but it's just no good.' Her face was averted[12]. She seemed to be examining the pattern of the hills. 'I tell myself that it's ended the right way for us all, but I don't believe that. I still want you, Deb.'

She turned to him then, her face quite white, her eyes gleaming with tears. 'You *can't*. You've got to let that go.'

'My mind accepts that, but nothing else does.' A tear escaped and descended her cheek. He put out his hand to wipe it away but remembered himself[13] and dropped his arm to his side. 'I woke up this morning so desperate[14] to make love with you again that I thought if I didn't get out of the room at once I should begin clawing at the walls in[15] pure adolescent frustration. I thought the church would be a balm[16] to me. What I didn't think was that you

1. C'est là qu'est ta place.
2. écarta les cheveux de
3. c'était comme s'il
4. qu'elle ne ferait pas comme si de rien n'était
5. qu'elle ne meublerait pas cet instant de gêne
6. bavardage
7. pourrait les aider à passer
8. trépied
9. pour faire des réglages inutiles
10. Je n'arrive pas à passer à autre chose.
11. J'essaie de m'en sortir
12. s'était détourné
13. il se reprit
14. avec un besoin si criant
15. j'allais en griffer les murs de
16. baume

would be wandering round its graveyard at dawn.' He looked at her equipment. 'What are you doing here? Where's Simon?'

'He's still at the hall. I … I woke up early and came out to see the village.'

It didn't ring true.[1] 'Is he ill?' he asked sharply.

She scanned the branches of the cypresses. A shallowness in Simon's breathing[2] had immediately awakened her shortly before six. He was lying so still[3] that for one horrifying moment[4] she thought he was dying. He was drawing in each breath[5] carefully, and she knew all at once that his only thought had been not to awaken her. But when she reached for his hand, his fingers closed bruisingly round her own[6]. 'Let me get your medicine[7],' she whispered, and had done so, and then had watched his determined face as he battled to be master of the pain[8]. 'Can you … for an hour, my love?' It was the part of his life that brooked no companion[9]. It was the part of his life she could never share[10]. She had left him.

'He had … there was some pain this morning.'

Lynley felt the full impact of Deborah's words. He understood so well everything that they implied. 'Christ, there's no escaping it[11], is there?' he asked bitterly. 'Even *that's* part of the miserable account[12].'

'No!' Raw horror tore[13] her voice. 'Don't say that! Don't you ever![14] Don't you do that to yourself! It isn't your fault!' Having spoken so quickly, really without thinking of the impression that her words would have upon Lynley, it was suddenly as if she had said too much – far more than she had intended to say – and she went back to fumbling with her camera, taking it apart[15] this time detaching lens[16] from body[17] and body from tripod, putting everything away[18].

He watched her. Her movements were jerky[19], like an old-time motion picture run[20] at the wrong speed. Perhaps sensing this and realizing what her

1. Cela ne sonnait pas juste.
2. Le souffle trop court de Simon
3. allongé, si immobile
4. l'espace d'un terrible instant,
5. inspirait
6. serrèrent les siens à lui faire mal
7. tes médicaments
8. pour maîtriser sa douleur
9. qui ne souffrait aucune compagnie
10. qu'elle ne partagerait jamais
11. il n'y a donc pas d'échappatoire
12. fait partie de cette triste histoire
13. brisa
14. Ne dis jamais ça !
15. le démontant
16. retirant l'objectif
17. boîtier
18. remballant tout
19. saccadés
20. un vieux film qu'on passe

discomfort revealed, she stopped what she was doing, her head bent, one hand at her eyes. Her hair was caught in a shaft[1] of sunlight. It was the colour of autumn. Summer's death.

'Is he still at the hall? Did you leave him there, Deb?' It wasn't that he wanted to[2] know but that she needed to tell him. Even now he couldn't let that need go unanswered[3].

'He wanted … it was the pain. He doesn't want me to see it. He thinks he's protecting me if he makes me leave.' She looked up at the sky, as if for some sort of sign[4]. The delicate muscles worked[5] in her throat. 'Being cut out[6] like this. It's so hard. I *hate* it.'

He understood. 'That's because you love him.'

She stared at him for a moment before she replied. 'I do. I do love him, Tommy. He's half of myself. He's part of my soul.[7]' She put a tentative hand on his arm, a mere whisper of a touch[8]. 'I want you to find someone to love you like that. It's what you need. It's what you deserve. But I … I can't be that someone for you. I don't even want to be.'

His face blanched[9] at her words. His spirit despaired[10] at the finality behind them[11]. Seeking composure[12], he found a distraction in the grave at their feet. 'Is this the source of your morning's inspiration?' he asked lightly.

'Yes.' She deliberately matched her tone to his[13]. 'I've heard so much about the baby in the abbey that I thought I'd have a peep[14] at its grave.'

' "As Flame to Smoke,"[15] ' he read. 'Bizarre epitaph for a child.'

'I'm rather attached to Shakespeare,' a thin voice said behind them. They swung round.[16] Father Hart, looking like a spiritual gnome in his cassock and surplice[17], stood on the gravel path a few feet away, hands folded demurely[18] over his stomach.

1. rayon
2. Non qu'il voulût
3. ignorer ce besoin
4. comme y cherchant un signe
5. se crispèrent
6. Être repoussée
7. Il fait partie de mon âme.
8. l'effleurant à peine
9. blêmit
10. Son courage faiblit
11. devant leur caractère irrévocable
12. Pour reprendre contenance
13. adopta le même ton que lui
14. que je jetterais un coup d'œil
15. « Comme la flamme la fumée » [dans Périclès, de Shakespeare]
16. Ils firent volte-face.
17. en soutane et surplis
18. modestement

He'd managed to come upon them noiselessly, like an apparition taking its form from[1] the mist.

'Left to my own devices[2], I always think Shakespeare's just the thing[3] for a grave. Timeless. Poetic. He gives life and death meaning.' He patted the pockets of his cassock and brought out a packet of Dunhills, lighting one absently and pinching the match[4] between his fingers before pocketing it. It was a dream-like movement, as if he were unaware that he was doing it at all.

Lynley noticed the yellowed pallor[5] of his skin and the rheumy quality[6] of his eyes. 'This is Mrs St James, Father Hart,' he said gently. 'She's taking photographs of your most famous grave.'

Father Hart stirred from his reverie[7]. 'Most famous...?' Puzzled[8], he looked from man to woman before his eyes fell on the grave and clouded[9]. His cigarette burned, ignored, between his stained fingers. 'Oh, yes. I see.' He frowned. 'What a horrible thing to have done to an infant, leaving it out naked in the cold to die[10]. I needed special permission to bury the poor thing here.'

'Special permission?'

'She was unbaptized[11]. But I call her Marina.' He blinked quickly, moving on to other things. 'But if it's famous graves that you've come to see, Mrs St James, then what you really want is the crypt.'

'Sounds like something from Edgar Allan Poe,' Lynley remarked.

'Not at all. It's a holy[12] place.' The priest dropped his cigarette to the path and crushed it out[13]. He stooped unselfconsciously[14] for the extinguished butt[15], put it into his pocket, and began to walk in the direction of the church. Lynley picked up Deborah's camera equipment, and they followed.

'It's the burial place of[16] St Cedd[17],' Father Hart was saying. 'Do come in. I was just getting ready for daily Mass[18] but I'll show it to you first.' He un-

1. se matérialisant dans
2. Si on me laisse faire
3. convient parfaitement
4. pinçant l'allumette
5. pâleur jaunâtre
6. l'aspect chassieux
7. sortit de sa rêverie
8. Perplexe
9. s'assombrirent
10. l'abandonner toute nue, pour qu'elle meure de froid
11. n'était pas baptisée
12. sacré
13. l'écrasa
14. se baissa sans complexe
15. pour ramasser le mégot éteint
16. là qu'est enterré
17. [moine qui évangélisa l'est de l'Angleterre au VIIe s.]
18. la messe du jour

locked the doors of the church with an enormous key and motioned them inside[1]. 'Weekday Mass is a bit of a bygone[2] now. No one much[3] bothers unless it's a Sunday. William Teys was my only consistent daily attendant[4], and with William gone[5] … well, I've found myself more often than not saying Mass in an empty church during the week.'

'He was a close friend of yours[6], wasn't he?' Lynley asked.

The priest's hand wavered[7] over the light-switch[8]. 'He was … like a son.'

'Did he ever talk to you about the trouble he had sleeping[9]? About his need for sleeping pills[10]?'

The hand wavered again. The priest hesitated. It was too long a pause, Lynley decided, and adjusted his position[11] in the dim light to see the old man's face more clearly. His eyes were on the light-switch but his lips moved as if in prayer[12].

'Are you all right, Father Hart?'

'I … yes, fine. I just … so often the memory of him.' The priest pulled himself up[13] with an effort, like someone drawing the scattered pieces[14] of a puzzle into one disjointed[15] pile. 'William was a good man, Inspector, but a troubled spirit. He … he never spoke to me about having difficulty sleeping, but it doesn't surprise me at all to hear it.'

'Why?'

'Because unlike so many troubled souls[16] who drown themselves[17] in alcohol or escape their difficulties some other way, William always faced them head on[18] and did the best he could. He was strong and decent[19], but his burdens were tremendous[20].'

'Burdens like Tessa leaving and Gillian running away?'

On the[21] second name, the priest's eyes closed. He swallowed with difficulty: it was a rasping[22] sound. 'Tessa hurt him. But Gillian devastated him[23]. He was never the same once she'd gone.'

1. leur fit signe d'entrer
2. appartient passé
3. Plus grand monde
4. le seul à y assister tous les jours
5. maintenant qu'il n'est plus là
6. un ami proche
7. hésita
8. interrupteur
9. ses troubles du sommeil
10. de somnifères
11. changea de place
12. remuaient comme s'il priait
13. se ressaisit
14. rassemblant les pièces éparses
15. grossière
16. contrairement à tant d'âmes en peine
17. qui se noient
18. leur faisait toujours front
19. comme il faut
20. il avait de lourds fardeaux
21. Au
22. rauque
23. Gillian, ce fut dévastateur

'What was she like?[1]'

'She … she was an angel, Inspector. Sunshine.' The shaking hand moved quickly to the lights and switched them on[2], and the priest gestured towards[3] the church. 'Well. What do you think of it?'

It was decidedly not the expected[4] interior of a village church. Village churches tend to be[5] small, square, purely functional affairs[6] with an absence of colour, line, or beauty. This was none of that.[7] Whoever had built it had cathedrals in mind[8], for[9] two great pillars[10] at the west end had been intended[11] to bear a more tremendous weight[12] than that of St Catherine's roof.

'Ah, so you've noticed,' Father Hart murmured, following the direction of Lynley's gaze from pillars to apse. 'This was to have been[13] the site of the abbey; St Catherine's was to have been the great abbey church. But a conflict among the monks resulted in[14] the other location[15] by Keldale Hall. It was a miracle.'

'A miracle?' Deborah asked.

'A real miracle. If they'd built the abbey here, where the remains of St Cedd are, it would all have been destroyed in the time of Henry VIII. Can you imagine destroying the very church where St Cedd lay buried[16]?' The priest's voice managed to convey his complete revulsion. 'No, it was an act of God that brought about the disagreement[17] among the monks. And since the foundation[18] for this church was already laid[19] and the crypt complete, there was no reason to disinter[20] the body of the saint. So they left him here with just a small chapel.' He moved with painful slowness to a stone stairway that led from the main aisle[21] down[22] into darkness. 'It's just this way,' he beckoned them[23].

The crypt was a second tiny church deep within[24] the main church of St Catherine's. It was a vault[25], arched[26] in Norman style, and pillared with col-

1. À quoi ressemblait-elle ?
2. les alluma
3. montra d'un geste
4. prévisible
5. sont traditionnellement
6. bâtiments
7. Celle-ci, pas du tout.
8. à l'esprit
9. car
10. piliers
11. étaient destinés
12. à supporter un poids bien supérieur
13. aurait dû être
14. a entraîné
15. le choix de l'autre emplacement
16. reposait
17. la main de Dieu qui a créé la dissension
18. comme les fondations
19. faites
20. d'exhumer
21. qui partait de l'allée principale
22. et aboutissait
23. il leur fit signe de le suivre
24. au cœur de
25. caveau
26. aux voûtes

umns that had meagre ornamentation[1]. At its far end, a simple stone altar[2] was adorned with[3] two candles and a crucifix, and along its sides stones from an earlier version of the church – crossheads and cross shafts[4] and pieces from vesicular[5] windows – lay preserved for posterity. It was a damp and musty[6] place, poorly lit[7] and smelling of loam[8]. Green mould[9] clung to the walls.

Deborah shivered. 'Poor man. It's so cold here. One would think he might prefer to be buried somewhere in the sun.'

'He's safer[10] here,' the priest answered. He moved reverently to the altar rail[11], knelt, and spent the next few moments in meditation.

They watched him. His lips moved and then he paused for a moment as if in communion with an unknown god. His prayer completed[12], he smiled angelically and got to his feet.

'I speak to him daily,' Father Hart whispered, 'because we owe him everything[13].'

'Why is that?' Lynley asked.

'He saved us. The village, the church, the life of Catholicism here in Keldale.' As he spoke, the priest's face began to glow[14].

Lynley thought fleetingly[15] of Montressor[16] and restrained himself from looking for[17] the mortar[18] and bricks. 'The man himself or the relics?' he asked.

'The man, his presence, his relics, all of it.' The priest flung out[19] his arms and encompassed[20] the crypt, and his voice rose in zealous jubilation. 'He gave them courage to keep their faith[21], Inspector, to remain true to[22] Rome, during the terrible days of the Reformation[23]. The priests hid here then. The stairway was covered with a false floor[24], and the village priests remained in hiding[25] for years. But the saint was with them all the time, and St Catherine's never fell to the[26] Protestants.' There were tears in his eyes. He fumbled for his handkerchief.

1. dépouillées
2. autel
3. orné de
4. les bras et les montants de croix
5. en forme de trèfle
6. humide et sentant le renfermé
7. mal éclairé
8. le terreau
9. Des moisissures vertes
10. plus en sécurité
11. la clôture de l'autel
12. achevée
13. lui devons tout
14. s'illumina
15. eut une vision
16. [meurtrier qui emmure vivante sa victime, dans une nouvelle d'Edgar Poe]
17. s'empêcha de chercher
18. mortier
19. ouvrit grand
20. engloba
21. foi
22. fidèles à
23. Réforme [sous Henri VIII]
24. plancher
25. sont restés cachés
26. n'est jamais tombée aux mains des

'You ... I'm ... please excuse me. When I talk about Cedd ... to be so privileged[1] to have his relics here. To be in communion with him. I'm not quite sure you could understand.'

To be on a first-name basis[2] with an early[3] Christian saint was obviously too much for the old man. Lynley sought[4] a diversion. 'The confessionals above look like Elizabethan carvings[5],' he said kindly. 'Are they?'

The man wiped his eyes, cleared his throat[6], and gave them a shaky[7] smile. 'Yes. They weren't originally intended for confessionals. That's why they have such a secular theme[8]. One doesn't generally expect to see young men and women entwined in dance[9] on the woodcarving in a church, but they're lovely, aren't they? I think the light in that part of the church is too poor[10] for the penitents to see the doors clearly. I expect some of them think it's a depiction of the Hebrews[11] left on their own[12] while Moses went up to Sinai.'

'What *does* it depict?' Deborah asked as they followed the little priest up the stairs and into the larger church once again.

'A pagan bacchanal[13], I'm afraid,' he replied. He smiled apologetically[14] as he said it, bid them good morning[15], and disappeared through a carved door near the altar.

They watched it close behind him. 'What an odd little man. How do you know him, Tommy?'

Lynley followed Deborah out of the church into the light. 'He brought us all the information on the case. He found the body.' He told her briefly about the murder, and she listened as she always had, her soft green eyes never moving from[16] his face.

'Nies!' she cried when he had completed the tale. 'How dreadful for you! Tommy, how completely unfair[17]!'

1. quel privilège
2. Être à tu et à toi
3. ancien
4. voulut tenter
5. des sculptures
6. s'éclaircit la voix
7. tremblant
8. leur décor est si profane
9. enlacés dans une danse
10. faible
11. que cela représente les Hébreux
12. laissés seuls
13. bacchanale païenne
14. eut un sourire d'excuse
15. prit congé
16. rivés sur
17. quelle injustice

It was like her, he thought, to cut to the quick of the matter[1], to see beneath the surface to the issue that plagued him[2] at the heart of the case.

'Webberly thought my presence might make him more co-operative, God knows how,' he said drily[3]. 'Unfortunately, I seem to be having the opposite effect[4] on the man.'

'But how awful for you! After what Nies put you through[5] in Richmond, why did they assign you to[6] this case? Couldn't you have turned it down[7]?'

He smiled at her white-faced indignation[8]. 'We're not usually given that option, Deb. May I drive you back to the hall?'

She responded in an instant. 'Oh, no, you don't need to. I've—'

'Of course. I wasn't thinking.' Lynley set down[9] her camera case[10] and bleakly[11] watched the doves grooming and settling themselves[12] on the bell tower of the church. Her hand touched his arm.

'It isn't that,' she said gently. 'I've a car just over there. You probably didn't notice it.'

Now he saw the blue Escort parked under a chestnut that was blanketing[13] the ground with crisp[14] autumn leaves. He picked up her case and carried it to the car. She followed some paces behind[15].

She unlocked the boot and watched as he put the case inside. She took more time than was necessary to arrange it in a safe travelling position for the short mile back[16] to the hall. And then, because it could no longer be avoided, she looked at him.

He was watching her, making a passionate study of[17] her features as if she were about to vanish for ever[18] and all he would have left[19] was the image in his mind.

'I remember the flat in Paddington,' he said. 'Making love to you there in the afternoon.'

'I haven't forgotten that, Tommy.'

1. ça lui ressemblait bien, pensait-il, de trouver le cœur du problème
2. du problème qui l'empoisonnait
3. sèchement
4. l'effet inverse
5. t'as fait subir
6. t'ont-ils confié
7. refuser
8. en la voyant blême d'indignation
9. posa
10. sac de photographe
11. l'air abattu,
12. lustrer leurs plumes et s'installer
13. jonchait
14. craquantes
15. légèrement en retrait
16. une position stable pour le court trajet de retour
17. scrutant ardemment
18. disparaître à jamais
19. que tout ce qui lui resterait

Her voice was tender. For some reason[1] that did nothing but hurt him further[2]. He looked away. 'Will you tell him you saw me?'

'Of course I will.'

'And what we talked about? Will you tell him of that?'

'Simon knows how you feel[3]. He's your friend. So am I.'

'I don't want your friendship, Deborah,' he said.

'I know. But I hope you will[4] some day[5]. It'll be there when you do.'

He felt her fingers on his arm again. They tightened, then loosened[6] in farewell[7]. She opened the car door, slipped inside[8], and was gone.

Alone, he walked back towards the lodge, feeling the cloak of desolation[9] settle more firmly round his shoulders. He had just reached the Odell house when the garden door opened and a little figure hurtled determinedly down[10] the steps. She was followed moments later by her duck.

'You wait there, Dougal!' Bridie shouted. 'Mummy put your new food in the shed[11] yesterday.'

The duck, unable to navigate[12] the steps anyway, sat patiently waiting as the child tugged open[13] the shed door and disappeared inside. She was back in a moment, lugging[14] a large sack behind her. Lynley noticed that she wore a school uniform, but it was badly rumpled[15] and not particularly clean.

'Hello, Bridie,' he called.

Her head darted up.[16] Her hair, he noticed, had been managed somewhat more expertly[17] since yesterday's fiasco. He wondered who had done it.

'Got to feed Dougal,' she said. 'Got to go to school today as well. I hate school.'

He joined her in the yard. The duck watched his approach warily[18], one brown eye on him and the other on the promised breakfast. Bridie poured[19] a

1. Bizarrement,
2. il en eut encore plus de peine
3. ce que tu ressens
4. que tu en voudras,
5. un jour
6. relâchèrent leur étreinte
7. en signe d'adieu
8. se glissa à l'intérieur
9. une chape de désespoir
10. dévala résolument
11. la remise
12. incapable de gravir
13. tirait le battant pour ouvrir
14. traînant
15. horriblement froissé
16. Elle redressa la tête d'un coup.
17. un peu arrangés
18. le regarda s'approcher, l'air méfiant
19. versa

gargantuan[1] portion on to the ground and the duck flapped his wings[2] eagerly[3].

'OK, Dougal, here you go,' Bridie said. She lifted the bird lovingly from the steps and placed him on the damp ground, watching fondly[4] as he plunged head first into the food. 'He likes breakfast best[5],' she confided to Lynley, taking an accustomed place[6] on the top step. She rested her chin on her knees[7] and gazed adoringly at the mallard. Lynley joined her on the step.

'You've fixed[8] your hair quite nicely,' he commented. 'Did Sinji do it for you?'

She shook her head, eyes still on duck. 'Nope.[9] Aunt Stepha did it.'

'Did she? She did a very nice job.'

'She's good at stuff like that[10],' Bridie acknowledged[11] in a tone that indicated there were other things that Aunt Stepha was not at all good at. 'But now I have to go to school. Mummy wouldn't let me go yesterday. She said it was "too humiliating for words[12]".' Bridie tossed her head scornfully[13]. 'It's my hair, not hers,' she added, practically.

'Well, mothers have a way of[14] taking things a bit personally. Haven't you noticed?'

'She could've taken it the way Aunt Stepha did. *She* just laughed when she saw me.' She hopped off the steps[15] and filled a shallow pan[16] with water. 'Here, Dougal,' she called. The duck ignored her. There was a chance the food might be taken away if he did not eat it all as fast as he could. Dougal was a duck who never took chances[17]. Water could wait. Bridie rejoined Lynley. Companionably[18], they watched as the duck gorged himself[19]. Bridie sighed. She was inspecting the scuffed tops[20] of her shoes and she rubbed at them ineffectually[21] with a dirty finger. 'Don't know why I have to go to school anyway. William never did[22].'

'Never?'

1. gargantuesque
2. battit des ailes
3. avec enthousiasme
4. avec adoration
5. Le petit déjeuner est son repas préféré
6. sa place habituelle
7. posa le menton sur ses genoux
8. Tu as arrangé
9. Nan.
10. douée pour ces trucs-là
11. reconnut
12. bien trop humiliant
13. dédaigneusement
14. ont tendance à
15. sautilla au bas des marches
16. une écuelle peu profonde
17. qui ne prenait jamais de risques
18. Assis tranquillement côte à côte
19. se gobergeait
20. le dessus râpé
21. les frotta sans résultat
22. n'y est jamais allé

'Well … not after he was twelve years old. If Mummy'd married William I wouldn't've had to go to school. Bobba didn't go[1].'

'Ever?'

Bridie adjusted her information[2]. 'William never made her go[3] after she was sixteen. I don't know what I'll do if I have t' wait till I'm sixteen. Mummy'll make me go. She wants me to go to university, but I don't want to.'

'What would you rather do?'

'Take care of Dougal.'

'Ah. Not that he doesn't look like the picture of complete health, Bridie, but ducks don't live for ever[4]. It's always nice to have something to fall back on[5].'

'I can always help Aunt Stepha.'

'At the lodge?'

She nodded. Dougal had finished his breakfast and was now beak deep[6] into the water pan. 'I tell Mummy that, but it's no use[7]. "I don't want you spending your life at that lodge." ' She did a disconcertingly fair imitation[8] of Olivia Odell's distracted voice[9]. She shook her head darkly. 'If William and Mummy had married, it would all be different. I could leave school and do all my learning[10] at home. William was awfully clever[11]. He could have taught me. He would have. I know it.'

'How do you know it?'

' 'Cause he always would read to me and Dougal[12].' The duck, hearing his name, waddled contentedly back to them[13] in his peculiar, lopsided fashion[14]. 'Mostly Bible stuff[15], though.' Bridie polished one shoe on the back of her sock. 'I don't much like the Bible. Old Testament[16] especially. William said it was because I didn't understand it, and he told Mummy I ought to have religious 'structions[17]. He was real nice and explained stories to

1. n'y allait pas
2. rectifia
3. ne l'a jamais forcée à y aller
4. éternellement
5. sur quoi compter
6. plongeait le bec
7. cela ne sert à rien
8. une imitation étonnamment réussie
9. voix préoccupée
10. apprendre
11. super intelligent
12. nous faisait toujours la lecture, à Dougal et à moi
13. revint vers eux, content, en se dandinant
14. de sa démarche bancale
15. des trucs de la Bible
16. L'Ancien Testament
17. recevoir une éducation religieuse

me, but I didn't understand 'em very well. It's mostly 'cause no one ever got in trouble[1] for their lies[2].'

'How's that?' Lynley sought fruitlessly[3] through his own limited religious instruction for successful biblical liars[4].

'Everybody was always lying with[5] other people. Least[6], that's what the stories said. And no one ever got told it was wrong[7].'

'Ah. Yes. Lying.' Lynley studied the mallard, who was examining his shoelaces[8] with a knowing beak[9]. 'Well, things are a bit symbolic in the Bible,' he said breezily[10]. 'What else did you read?'

'Nothing. Just the Bible. I think that's all William and Bobba ever read. I tried to like it, but I didn't. I didn't tell William that 'cause he was trying to be nice, and I didn't want to be rude[11]. I think he was trying to get to know me[12],' she added wisely[13]. ' 'Cause if he married Mummy, I'd be round all the time[14].'

'Did you want him to marry your mummy?'

She scooped the bird up[15] and placed it on the step between them. With a level, dispassionate look[16] at Lynley, Dougal began grooming his shining feathers.

'Daddy read to me,' Bridie said in answer. Her voice was a shade lower[17] and her concentration on her shoe tops was total. 'And then he went away.'

'Went away?' Lynley wondered if this was a euphemism for his death.

'He went away one day.' Bridie rested her cheek on her knee, pulled the bird to her side[18], and stared at the river. 'He didn't even say goodbye.' She turned and kissed the duck's smooth head. He pecked at her cheek in return.[19] 'I would've said goodbye,' she whispered.

1. personne n'était jamais puni
2. pour avoir menti
3. chercha en vain
4. des menteurs bibliques impénitents
5. [Bridie confond « mentir à » et « coucher avec »]
6. En tout cas,
7. on ne leur disait jamais que c'était mal
8. lacets
9. d'un bec de connaisseur
10. d'un ton enjoué
11. impolie
12. de mieux me connaître
13. avec sagesse
14. j'aurais toujours été là
15. récupéra l'oiseau
16. regard franc et placide
17. un ton plus bas
18. attira l'oiseau contre elle
19. Il lui bécota la joue en retour.

'Would you use the word *angel* or *sunshine* to describe someone who drank, swore, and ran around[1] like mad?' Lynley asked.

Sergeant Havers looked up from her morning eggs, stirred[2] sugar into her coffee, and thought about it. 'I suppose it depends on your definition of rain[3], doesn't it?'

He smiled. 'I suppose so.' He pushed his plate away from him and regarded Havers thoughtfully. She wasn't looking half bad[4] this morning: there was a hint of colour[5] on her eyelids[6], cheeks, and lips, and her hair had a noticeable curl to it[7]. Even her clothes had distinctly improved[8], for she wore a brown tweed skirt and matching pullover which, even if they weren't exactly the best colour for her skin tone[9], at least were a marked improvement over[10] yesterday's ghastly blue suit.

'Why the question?' she asked.

'Stepha described Gillian as wild[11]. A drinker.'

'Who ran around like mad.'

'Yes. But Father Hart said she was sunshine[12].'

'That *is* peculiar.'

'He said Teys was devastated when she ran away.'

Havers knotted her thick eyebrows[13] and, without thinking about how the action redefined their relationship[14], poured Lynley a second cup of coffee. 'Well, that does explain why her photos are gone, doesn't it? He'd devoted[15] his life to his children and look at his reward for the effort[16]. One of the two vanishes into the night.'

The last four words struck a chord in Lynley. He rummaged through the file[17] on the table between them and brought out[18] the picture of Russell Mowrey that Tessa had given them.

'I'd like you to take this round the village[19] today,' he said.

1. courait après les hommes
2. touilla
3. votre définition de la pluie
4. avait meilleure allure
5. une touche de couleur
6. paupières
7. faisaient plus souples
8. s'étaient vraiment améliorés
9. pour son teint
10. constituaient une nette amélioration par rapport
11. comme une dévergondée
12. un rayon de soleil
13. fronça ses épais sourcils
14. à la façon dont cela changeait leurs relations
15. consacré
16. voyez comment il en est récompensé
17. fouilla dans tout le dossier
18. en sortit
19. que vous fassiez le tour du village avec ça

Havers took the photograph, but her expression was quizzical[1]. 'But you said he was in London.'

'Now, yes. Not necessarily[2] three weeks ago. If Mowrey was here then, he would have had to ask someone for directions[3] to the farm. Someone would have had to see him. Concentrate on the high street and the patrons[4] of the pubs. You might go to the hall as well. If no one's seen him—'

'We're back to Tessa[5], then,' she finished.

'Or someone else with a motive. There seem to be several.'

Madeline Gibson answered the door to Lynley's knock[6]. He'd climbed his way over[7] two quarrelling children in the war-torn[8] front garden, manoeuvred past a broken tricycle and a dismembered doll[9], and avoided a plate of congealing[10] fried eggs[11] on the front steps. She surveyed all this with a bored glance[12] and adjusted[13] an emerald green peignoir over high, pointed breasts[14]. She wore nothing under it and made no secret of the fact[15] that he couldn't have arrived at a more inconvenient time[16].

'Dick,' she called, her sultry[17] eyes on Lynley, 'put it back in your trousers[18]. It's Scotland Yard.' She gave him a lazy smile and held the door open wider. 'Do come in, Inspector.' She left him in the tiny entryway among the toys and the dirty clothes and strolled[19] to the stairwell[20]. 'Dick!' she called again. She turned, folded[21] her arms across her breasts, and kept her eyes on Lynley. A smile played over her features. A well-formed[22] knee and thigh showed themselves between the folds[23] of thin satin.

There was movement above them, a man's mumbling[24], and Richard Gibson appeared. He clattered noisily to the bottom[25] of the stairs and caught sight of his wife. 'Jesus Christ, put on some clothes, Mad,' he said.

1. perplexe
2. Pas forcément
3. de lui indiquer le chemin
4. clients
5. Cela nous ramène à Tessa
6. lorsque Lynley frappa
7. avait enjambé
8. ravagé
9. poupée démembrée
10. figés
11. œufs sur le plat
12. d'un regard blasé
13. réajusta
14. sur ses seins hauts et pointus
15. ne lui cacha pas
16. qu'il ne pouvait plus mal tomber
17. boudeurs
18. tu peux te la remballer
19. s'en fut d'un pas traînant
20. au pied de l'escalier
21. croisa
22. bien galbés
23. les plis
24. un homme qui grommelait
25. descendit en claquant des pieds

'You didn't want them on[1] five minutes ago,' she replied, looked him over with a knowing smile[2], and made her way deliberately – revealing as much of her slim body as possible – up the stairs.

Gibson watched her with wry amusement[3]. 'You should see what she's like when she *really* wants it[4],' he confided. 'She's just teasing now.[5]'

'Ah. Yes. I see.'

The farmer laughed through his nose[6]. 'At least it keeps her happy, Inspector. For a while.' He scrutinized the chaos of the cottage and added, 'Let's go out in front.'

Lynley thought the front garden was even less appealing a place for their encounter[7] than the malodorous cottage, but he held his tongue[8] and followed the other man.

'Go in to[9] your mother,' Gibson ordered his two wrangling[10] children. With his foot, he pushed the plate to the edge of the front step. In a moment, the family's mangy cat[11] appeared from the tangle of dry and dying bushes[12] and began to devour the remains[13] of the eggs and toast. It was the greedy, surreptitious eating of a scavenger[14], and it reminded Lynley of the woman upstairs.

'I saw Roberta yesterday,' he said to Gibson. The other man had sat down on the step and was lacing[15] his work shoes tightly[16].

'How was she? Any improvement?'

'No. When we first met, you didn't mention the fact that you'd signed[17] Roberta into the asylum, Mr Gibson.'

'You didn't ask, Inspector.' He finished with the boots and got to his feet. 'Did you expect me to leave her with the police[18] in Richmond?'

'Not especially. Have you arranged for a solicitor[19] as well?'

Gibson, Lynley saw, wasn't a man who expected the police to concern themselves with the legal

1. Tu ne voulais pas que j'en porte
2. un sourire entendu
3. l'air narquois
4. a vraiment envie
5. Là, elle est juste taquine
6. eut un rire nasillard
7. encore moins agréable pour causer
8. se garda de le dire
9. auprès de
10. en train de se battre
11. le chat galeux
12. fouillis de buissons desséchés et mourants
13. les restes
14. Il mangeait comme un charognard, avide et furtif
15. laçait
16. fermement
17. que vous aviez fait admettre
18. aux mains de la police
19. contacté un avocat

representation[1] of confessed murderesses[2]. The question surprised him. His eyelids quivered and he spent a moment tucking[3] his flannel shirt into his blue jeans. He took his time about answering.

'A solicitor? No.'

'Intriguing that you'd make arrangements to have her put into hospital[4] but not make arrangements for[5] her legal interests. Convenient as well, wouldn't you say?'

A muscle worked in Gibson's jaw. 'No, I wouldn't say.'

'Can you explain yourself, then?'

'I don't think I need to explain myself to you,' Gibson said tersely. 'But it seems to me that Bobby's mental problems were a wee bit more pressing[6] than her legal ones[7].' His swarthy[8] skin had darkened.

'Indeed. And if she's found incompetent[9] to stand trial[10] – as no doubt she will be – you're in a good position, aren't you?'

Gibson faced him. 'By God, I am, yes,' he retorted[11] angrily. 'Free to take the damn farm, free to have the damn house, free to screw my damn wife[12] on the dining-room table if I want. And all without Bobby hulking about[13]. That's what you want to hear, isn't it, Inspector?' He thrust his face forward belligerently[14], but when Lynley offered no reaction to this aggression, he backed away[15]. His words, however, were no less angry. 'I've just about had it with[16] people believing I'd hurt Bobby, with people believing Madeline and I would be only too happy to see her put away for life[17]. You think I don't know that's what everyone believes? You think Madeline doesn't know it?' He laughed bitterly.' No, I *didn't* get her a solicitor. I got one myself.[18] And if I can get her certified[19] mentally incompetent, I intend to do so. Do you think that's worse than seeing she ends up in prison?'

1. s'inquiète du défenseur
2. meurtrières passées aux aveux
3. à rentrer
4. pour qu'elle soit hospitalisée
5. que vous n'ayez pas veillé à
6. un tantinet plus urgents
7. ses problèmes judiciaires
8. basanée
9. si elle est déclarée irresponsable
10. et donc dispensée de passer en jugement
11. rétorqua
12. libre de baiser ma foutue femme
13. sans la grosse Bobby dans mes pattes
14. Il approcha la tête, menaçant
15. il recula
16. J'en ai plus qu'assez, que
17. internée à vie
18. J'en ai déjà un à moi.
19. la faire déclarer

'So you think she did kill[1] her father?' Lynley asked.

Gibson's shoulders sagged[2]. 'I don't know what to think. All I know is Bobby's not the same girl that I knew when I left Keldale. *That* girl wouldn't have hurt a fly[3]. But this new girl … she's a stranger.'

'Perhaps that has to do with Gillian's disappearance.'

'*Gillian?*' Gibson laughed incredulously. 'I'd say Gilly's leaving was a relief to all concerned[4].'

'Why?'

'Let's just say Gilly was advanced for her years[5], shall we?' He glanced back at the house. 'Let's just say she'd have made[6] Madeline look like the Virgin Mary. Am I making myself clear?'

'Perfectly. Did she seduce you?'

'You *are* direct, aren't you? Give me a fag[7] and I'll tell you about it.' He lit the cigarette that Lynley offered from his case and looked off into the fields[8] that began just across the unpaved street. Beyond them, the trail to[9] High Kel Moor weaved into the trees[10]. 'I was nineteen years old when I left Keldale, Inspector. I didn't want to leave. God knows that was the last thing I wanted to do. But I knew if I didn't there'd be hell to pay eventually[11].'

'But you slept with your cousin Gillian before you left?'

Gibson snorted[12]. 'Hardly.[13] *Slept* isn't exactly the word I'd use with a girl like Gilly. She wanted control and she had it, Inspector. She could do things to a man … better than a high-class tart[14]. She made me crazy just about four times a day.'

'How old was she?'

'She was twelve when she first locked her eyes on me[15] in an uncousinly fashion[16], thirteen the first time she … performed. Then for the next two years she drove me wild[17].'

'Are you telling me you left to escape her?'

1. qu'elle a vraiment tué
2. s'affaissèrent
3. fait de mal à une mouche
4. un soulagement pour tous les intéressés
5. était précoce
6. qu'à côté d'elle
7. une clope
8. regarda au loin, vers les champs
9. le sentier menant à
10. serpentait entre les arbres
11. cela finirait mal
12. ricana
13. Pas vraiment.
14. mieux qu'une putain de haut vol
15. la première fois qu'elle m'a lancé un regard
16. qui ne s'adressait pas au cousin
17. m'a rendu dingue

'I'm hardly that noble. I left to escape William. It was only a matter of time[1] before he caught her going at me[2]. I didn't want that to happen to either of us. I wanted it to end.'

'Why did you never just speak to William about it?'

Gibson's eyes widened. 'As far as he was concerned, neither of those girls could do anything wrong. How was I supposed to tell him that Gilly, the proverbial apple of his eye[3], was rubbing up to me[4] like a cat in heat[5] and taking me on[6] like a whore[7]? He'd never have believed it. Half the time, I didn't myself.'

'She left Keldale a year after you, didn't she?'

He tossed his cigarette into the street. 'That's what they tell me,' he replied.

'Did you ever see her again?'

Gibson's eyes slid away. 'I never did,' he replied. 'And it was a blessing[8].'

Marsha Fitzalan was a bent, withered[9] woman with a face that reminded Lynley of the kind on American dolls carved from apples[10]: it was a mass of delicate wrinkles[11] that traced a pattern[12] across[13] her cheeks up to[14] her eyes. These were blue. They danced in her face with interest and amusement and told[15] anyone who looked at her that the body was indeed old but the heart and the mind had not changed from youth[16].

'Good morning,' she smiled, and then with a look at her watch, 'or nearly afternoon. You're Inspector Lynley, aren't you? I thought you might be by sooner or later[17]. I've lemon pie[18] made.'

'For the occasion?[19]' Lynley asked.

'Indeed[20],' she replied. 'Come in.'

Although she lived in one of the council houses in St Chad's Lane, its appearance couldn't have been more different from the Gibsons'. The front gar-

1. Ce n'était qu'une question de temps
2. qu'il ne la surprenne en train de me faire des choses
3. la légendaire prunelle de ses yeux
4. se frottait contre moi
5. une chatte en chaleur
6. m'entreprenant
7. putain
8. c'est une chance
9. voûtée et parcheminée
10. sculptées dans les pommes
11. rides
12. dessinaient un motif
13. depuis
14. jusqu'à
15. montraient
16. depuis sa jeunesse
17. que vous viendriez tôt ou tard
18. de la tarte au citron
19. Exprès pour moi ?
20. Mais oui

den was planted, parterre-like[1], with neat patterns of flowers[2]: in the spring and summer there would be alyssum and primrose[3], snapdragons[4] and geraniums. They had been trimmed back[5] for the coming of winter, the soil turned over lovingly[6] round each plant. On two of the stepping[7] stones leading to the door, birdseed[8] had been fashioned into small, accessible piles[9], and a set of metal windchimes[10] hung near a window, its six notes still managing to be heard[11] over the din[12] of the Gibson children next door.

The contrast to the Gibsons' small cottage continued indoors[13], where the smell of potpourri in the air reminded Lynley of long afternoons spent in his grandmother's bedroom at Howenstow. The tiny sitting-room was comfortably if inexpensively[14] furnished[15] and two of its walls were lined from floor to ceiling[16] with books. A small table under the single window was covered by a collection of photographs, and several needlepoint tapestries[17] hung above an ancient television set.

'Will you come into the kitchen, Inspector?' Marsha Fitzalan asked. 'I know it's dreadful to entertain[18] in the kitchen, but I've always been far more comfortable there[19]. My friends tell me it's because I grew up on[20] a farm, and the life of a farm always centres itself in[21] the kitchen, doesn't it? I suppose I never got over that. Here, please sit at the table. Coffee and pie? You do look hungry. I imagine you're a bachelor[22]. Bachelors never eat as well as they should, do they?'

Again there was the memory of his grandmother, that unmistakable security[23] of unconditional love. As he watched her busily putting together a tray[24], her hands sure and unshaking, Lynley knew for a certainty[25] that Marsha Fitzalan held[26] the answer.

'Can you tell me about Gillian Teys?' he asked.

1. découpé en rectangles
2. de fleurs formant des motifs soignés
3. des alysses et des primevères
4. des gueules-de-loup
5. coupées
6. la terre retournée avec amour
7. de seuil
8. des graines pour les oiseaux
9. disposées en petits tas accessibles
10. carillons à vent
11. perceptibles
12. malgré le tapage
13. persistait à l'intérieur
14. mais très simplement
15. meublé
16. recouverts du sol au plafond
17. des broderies
18. recevoir
19. je m'y suis toujours sentie plus à l'aise
20. j'ai grandi dans
21. se passe beaucoup à
22. célibataire
23. ce sentiment de sécurité caractéristique
24. s'affairant à garnir un plateau
25. avec certitude
26. avait

1. Ce sera avec grand plaisir.
2. l'être le plus adorable
3. que j'aie jamais rencontré

Her hands stopped. She turned to him with a smile. 'Gilly?' she said. 'What a pleasure that shall be.[1] Gillian Teys was the loveliest creature[2] I've ever known[3].'

11

She returned to the table and placed the tray between them. It was an unnecessary nicety[1]. The kitchen was so tiny that only a few steps were needed to move across the room, yet still she preserved the semblance of gentility[2] and countered[3] the claustrophobia of poverty[4] by using the tray. It was covered with a piece of old lace[5] upon which rested fine bone china[6]. Both plates were chipped[7], but the cups and saucers had somehow managed the years unscathed[8].

Autumn leaves in a pottery jug[9] served to decorate the plain pine table[10], and on to its surface Marsha Fitzalan set everything out carefully: plates, cutlery, and linen[11]. She poured the steaming[12] coffee into their cups and added sugar and milk to her own before she began to speak.

'Gilly was exactly like her mother. I taught Tessa[13] as well. Of course, it betrays[14] my age dreadfully to admit to that. But there you have it[15]. Nearly everyone in the village passed through my classroom, Inspector.' Her eyes twinkled[16] as she added, 'Except Father Hart. He and I are of the same generation.'

'I should never have guessed[17],' Lynley said solemnly.

She laughed. 'Why is it that truly charming men always know when a woman is fishing for a

1. un raffinement inutile
2. une aisance apparente
3. luttait contre
4. de la pauvreté
5. un morceau de vieille dentelle
6. sur lequel était disposée de la porcelaine fine
7. ébréchées
8. traversé les années sans dommage
9. un pichet en poterie
10. la table en pin brut
11. serviettes
12. fumant
13. Tessa a été mon élève
14. trahit
15. c'est ainsi
16. pétillèrent
17. Je ne l'aurais jamais cru

compliment[1]?' She dug into[2] her pie enthusiastically, chewed appreciatively[3] for a few moments, and then continued. 'Gillian was the mirror image[4] of her mother. She had that same lovely blonde hair, those beautiful eyes, and that same wonderful spirit. But Tessa was a dreamer[5] and Gillian was a bit more of a realist, I should say. Tessa's head was always in the clouds. She was all romance[6]. I think that's why she chose to marry so young. She was determined that life was all about being swept off one's feet by[7] a tall, dark hero, and William Teys certainly fitted the image[8].'

'Gillian wasn't worried about being swept off her feet?'

'Oh, no. I don't think the thought of men ever entered Gilly's head[9]. She wanted to be a teacher. I can remember her coming by in the afternoons, curling up on the floor[10] with a book. How she loved the Brontës! That child must have read *Jane Eyre* six or seven times by her fourteenth birthday[11]. She, Jane, and Mr Rochester were all rather intimate acquaintances[12], as I recall[13]. And she loved to talk about everything she read. But it wasn't just chatter[14]. She talked about characters[15], motivations, meanings[16]. She would say, "I shall have to know these things when I'm a teacher, Miss Fitzalan." '

'Why did she run away?'

The old woman studied the bronze leaves in the jug. 'I don't know,' she replied slowly. 'She was such a good child. There was never a problem that she couldn't seem to solve[17] with that quick mind of hers[18]. I honestly don't know what happened.'

'Could she have been involved with a man? Perhaps someone she was running after?'

Miss Fitzalan dismissed[19] the idea with a movement of her hand. 'I don't believe Gillian was interested in men yet. She was a bit slower to mature[20] than the other girls were.'

1. recherche la flatterie
2. entama
3. mâcha avec plaisir
4. la copie conforme
5. rêveuse
6. très romantique
7. c'était de tomber follement amoureuse d'
8. correspondait tout à fait
9. que Gillian se soit jamais souciée des hommes
10. lovée par terre
11. avant ses quatorze ans
12. étaient intimement liés
13. si je me souviens bien
14. que du bavardage
15. personnages
16. du sens
17. qu'elle ne sache résoudre
18. cet esprit vif qu'elle avait
19. rejeta
20. moins mature

'What about Roberta? Was she much like her sister?'

'No, Roberta was like her father.' She stopped suddenly and frowned. '*Was.* I don't want to talk about her in the past tense[1] like that. But she seems to have died[2].'

'She does, doesn't she?[3]'

The woman looked as if she appreciated his concurring with her[4]. 'Roberta was big like her father, very solid and silent. People will tell you she had no personality at all, but that's not true. She was simply excruciatingly shy[5]. She had her mother's romantic disposition[6], her father's taciturnity[7]. And she lost herself[8] in books.'

'Like Gillian?'

'Yes and no. She read like Gillian, but she never spoke about what she read. Gillian read to learn. Roberta, I think, read to escape.'

'Escape what?'

Miss Fitzalan fussily straightened[9] the lace that covered the old tray. Her hands, Lynley saw, were spotted with age[10]. 'The knowledge of being deserted[11], I should guess.'

'By Gillian or by her mother?'

'By Gillian. Roberta worshipped[12] Gillian. She never knew[13] her mother. You can imagine what it must have been like having Gilly for an older sister[14]: so lovely, so lively[15], so intelligent. Everything Roberta wasn't and wished she could be[16].'

'Jealousy?'

She shook her head. 'She wasn't jealous of Gilly. She loved her. I should think it hurt Roberta dreadfully when her sister left. But unlike Gillian, who would have talked about her pain – Lord knows, Gilly talked about anything and everything[17] – Roberta internalized it[18]. I remember, in fact, the poor child's skin after Gilly left. Funny that I would still remember that.'

1. au passé
2. on dirait qu'elle est morte
3. On dirait, en effet.
4. qu'il soit du même avis
5. atrocement timide
6. le tempérament romantique
7. l'air taciturne
8. était plongée
9. redressa nerveusement
10. avaient des taches de vieillesse
11. La conscience d'avoir été abandonnée
12. vénérait
13. n'a pas connu
14. comme sœur aînée
15. si pleine de vie
16. aurait voulu être
17. de tout et n'importe quoi
18. l'intériorisait

Lynley thought of the girl he had seen in the asylum and was not surprised that the teacher would remember the condition[1] of Roberta's skin. 'Acne?' he asked. 'She would have been young for that.'

'No. She broke out into[2] the most dreadful rash[3]. I know it was nerves[4], but when I spoke to her about it, she blamed it on[5] Whiskers.' Miss Fitzalan dropped her eyes and toyed[6] with her fork, making delicate patterns[7] in the crumbs[8] on her plate. Lynley waited patiently, convinced there was more. Finally she went on[9]. 'I felt so inadequate[10], Inspector, such a failure[11] as a friend and as a teacher that she couldn't talk to me about what had happened to Gilly. But she just couldn't talk, so she blamed it all on being allergic to her dog.'

'Did you speak to her father about it?'

'Not at first. William had been so crushed[12] by Gillian's running off that he wasn't the least bit approachable[13]. For weeks it seemed the only person he would talk to at all was Father Hart. But in the end, frankly, I felt I owed it to[14] Roberta. After all, the child was only eight years old. It wasn't her fault that her sister had run away. So I went out to the farm and told William I was worried about her, especially considering the pathetic story she'd made up[15] about the dog.' She poured herself more coffee and sipped it as she brooded over[16] that long-ago[17] visit. 'Poor man. I certainly needn't have worried about his reaction. I think he must have felt terribly guilty about having[18] ignored Roberta, because he drove to Richmond directly and bought three or four different kinds of lotion to put on her skin. It may well have been[19] that all the poor girl needed was her father's attention, because the rash went away after that.'

But nothing else did, Lynley thought. In his mind he saw the lonely little girl in the gloomy[20] farmhouse, surrounded by the ghosts[21] and voices of

1. l'état
2. a eu
3. éruption
4. que c'était nerveux
5. a dit que c'était de la faute de
6. joua
7. dessinant de délicats motifs
8. miettes
9. poursuivit
10. si peu à la hauteur
11. si nulle
12. si accablé
13. qu'il n'était pas du tout accessible
14. que je devais bien ça à
15. qu'elle avait inventée
16. le buvait, tout en se remémorant
17. lointaine
18. coupable d'avoir
19. Peut-être qu'en fait
20. lugubre
21. entourée des fantômes

the past, living her life in grim sterility[1], taking her nourishment[2] from books.

Lynley unlocked the back door and let himself[3] into the house. It was unchanged[4], as cold and airless as it had been before. He went through the kitchen to the sitting-room, where Tessa Teys smiled at him tenderly from her corner[5] shrine, looking young and infinitely vulnerable. He imagined Russell Mowrey raising his head from his excavation[6] and seeing that lovely face framed in a gap in the fence[7]. It was easy to see why Mowrey had fallen in love. It was easy to see why he would be in love still.

Not a thousand ships[8] but one enraged husband, Lynley thought. *Is it possible, Tessa? Or did you see your world shatter[9] in one afternoon and know you couldn't bear to build it again[10]?*

He turned from the shrine and ran up the stairs. No, the answer had to be in the house. It had to be Gillian.

He went first to her bedroom, but its vacuity[11] told him nothing. The bed stared up at him wordlessly, its covering unblemished[12]. The rug held no footprints[13] leading back into the past. The wallpaper covered[14] no long-held[15] secrets. It was as if a young girl had never lived in the room, had never breathed her liveliness and spirit into the air. And yet something … something of Gillian lingered[16], something he had seen, something he could feel.

He walked to the window and looked, unseeing[17], at the barn. *She was wild, ungoverned. She was an angel, sunshine. She was a cat in heat. She was the loveliest creature I've ever seen.* It was as if there were no real Gillian at all, but only a kaleidoscope that, juggled before viewing[18], appeared different to each person who gazed into it[19]. He longed to believe that the answer was in the room, but when he

1. aride et austère
2. se nourrissant
3. entra
4. telle quelle
5. du coin de la pièce
6. levant la tête de son chantier
7. encadrée dans un trou de la clôture
8. [comme Hélène, pour laquelle partit la flotte grecque contre Troie ; citation d'une tragédie de Christopher Marlowe]
9. s'écrouler
10. n'aviez pas le courage de tout reconstruire
11. le vide qui y régnait
12. avec son dessus-de-lit intact
13. Aucune trace de pas sur le tapis
14. ne recelait
15. lointains
16. subsistait
17. sans voir
18. tourné dans tous les sens avant d'y mettre l'œil
19. regardait à travers

turned from the window he saw nothing but furniture, wallpaper, and rug.

How could someone be wiped so completely out[1] of the life of the family in which she had lived for sixteen years? It was inconceivable. Yet it had been done.[2] Or had it?[3]

He walked to Roberta's room. Gillian couldn't have faded from her sister's life so completely. The love was there. The bond was strong.[4] Everyone, at least, no matter what they had said about Gillian, agreed upon that[5]. His gaze roamed[6] from window to wardrobe to bed. He considered this last: it was her hiding-place for food, why not for Gillian as well?

Steeling himself to[7] the sight and the smell of the putrefaction, Lynley pulled back the mattress. The stench rose[8] like an undulating wave[9].

He glanced about, looking for a way to make the job at hand easier[10] but finding nothing that would do. The light in the room was poor, and, unpleasant as it would be, there was nothing for it but[11] to drag the entire mattress off[12] and rip the box spring apart[13]. Grunting with the effort[14], he jerked mattress and bedding on to the floor[15] and then went to the window. He threw it open and stood for a moment sucking in the fresh air[16] before turning back to the bed. He climbed on to the box spring and planned his attack, ignoring his queasiness[17]. *Come on, old boy. Isn't this why you got into police work? Buck up, now.*[18] *Give it one big pull.*

He did so, and the rotting material[19] – that thin layer of sanity[20] – came apart in his hands, exposing the madness beneath it. Mice scattered[21] in all directions, leaving diminutive tracks[22] through the decaying fruit. One sow-like rodent[23] nursed[24] her litter of clutching, blind offspring[25] in a bed of women's dirty underclothes. And an angry cloud of moths[26], disturbed from their slumber[27], burst out

1. si totalement gommé
2. C'était pourtant le cas.
3. Et si ce n'était pas ça ?
4. Leur lien était solide.
5. s'accordait là-dessus
6. erra
7. Se préparant à affronter
8. L'odeur fétide remonta
9. par vagues
10. se faciliter le travail
11. il fallait se résoudre à
12. retirer le matelas
13. éventrer le sommier
14. Grognant sous l'effort
15. envoya par terre le matelas et les draps
16. à inspirer l'air pur
17. nausée
18. Allez, courage.
19. la matière en décomposition
20. cette pellicule de normalité
21. Des souris jaillirent
22. de minuscules traces
23. Telle une truie, une femelle
24. nourrissait
25. sa portée de petits, aveugles et agrippés
26. mites
27. dans leur sommeil

into the light, flinging themselves upwards into Lynley's face.

Startled, he reeled back[1], managed to keep from crying out[2], and quickly made his way to the bathroom, where he took a moment to splash water on his face. He looked at himself in the mirror and laughed soundlessly. *Good thing you skipped lunch*[3]. *After that, you may well skip eating for the rest of your life.*

He sought a towel on which to dry his face. There was none on the rack[4], but he caught a glimpse of a dressing-gown hanging on the back of the bathroom door. He swung it shut. Its broken hasp lock[5] grated against the frame like a shriek[6]. He dried his face on the hem of the garment[7], fingered the lock meditatively, and after a moment, a new thought triggered[8], he left the room.

The box of keys was where he had seen it before, at the back of the top shelf of Teys' wardrobe. He took it out and dumped it on to the bed. Teys would have[9] put Gillian's things in a trunk[10] somewhere. In the attic[11], perhaps. And the keys would be here. He searched through them fruitlessly[12]. They were all door keys, the old-fashioned key-hole variety[13], a strange collection of rusting, metallic mementoes[14]. He threw them back into their box in disgust and cursed the blind determination[15] of the man who had wiped one daughter's existence off the face of the earth[16].

Why? he wondered. What kind of anguish was it that had driven[17] William Teys to deny[18] the existence of the child he so loved? What could she possibly have done to bring him to such an act of destruction? And at the same time provoke her sister to such an impotent[19] yet desperate act of preservation as the simple hiding of a photograph.

He knew what came next. *The attic's a blind*[20], *old boy. Back to her bedroom. You know it's there.*

1. recula en chancelant
2. à ne pas crier
3. que tu n'aies pas déjeuné
4. porte-serviette
5. Son loquet, cassé,
6. crissa contre le chambranle
7. bord du vêtement
8. une autre idée lui étant venue
9. avait dû
10. une malle
11. Au grenier
12. sans succès
13. pour serrure classique
14. souvenirs
15. maudit la résolution aveugle
16. de la surface de la terre
17. Quelle sorte d'angoisse avait pu conduire
18. à nier
19. impuissant
20. un leurre

Maybe not in the mattress, but you know it's there. He shuddered at the thought of what other surprises waited like spectres in that sepulchral room[1].

As he was gathering his shattered defences[2] for another assault, the sound of whistling[3], joyful and unrestrained, came to him from outside. He went to the window.

A young man was walking down the trail from High Kel Moor, an easel[4] over his shoulder and a wooden case in his hand. It was time, Lynley decided, to meet Ezra.

His first thought was that the other man was not as young as he looked from a distance. It must have been the hair, Lynley thought, which was a rich, deep blond[5] and worn much longer than was the current fashion[6]. Up close[7], Ezra looked very much what he was: a man somewhere in his thirties, wary about this meeting[8] with the detective from Scotland Yard. The wariness came through[9] in the careful stance[10]; it also came through in the swiftly veiled eyes[11], the kind of eyes that changed colour with the clothing he wore[12]. They were deep blue now, as was the man's shirt, which was streaked with[13] paint. He had stopped whistling the moment he saw Lynley come out of the house and climb nimbly over[14] the pasture wall.

'Ezra Farmington?' he said pleasantly[15].

Farmington halted. His features put Lynley in mind of the Delacroix painting of Frédéric Chopin. Here were the same sculpted lips; the shadow of a cleft[16] in the chin; the dark brows – much darker than the hair; the nose that was dominant but not detractive[17].

'That's right,' he said, noncommittally[18].

'Doing some painting on the moor today?'

'Yes.'

'Nigel Parrish tells me you do light studies.'

1. chambre funèbre
2. Alors qu'il rassemblait son courage mis à mal
3. quelqu'un qui sifflotait
4. un chevalet
5. d'un blond chaud et intense
6. que ne le voulait la mode
7. De près
8. méfiant à l'idée de cette rencontre
9. transparaissait
10. la prudence de son attitude
11. l'opacité soudaine de ses yeux
12. selon ses vêtements
13. striée de
14. escalader avec agilité
15. aimablement
16. fossette
17. ne le desservait pas
18. avec réserve

The name got a reaction. The eyes became guarded.[1] 'What else does Nigel tell you?'

'That he saw William Teys run you off[2] his property. You seem to be making free use of it[3] now.'

'With Gibson's permission.' The words were terse[4].

'Indeed? He didn't mention it.' Lynley gazed serenely in the direction of the trail. It was steep and rocky[5], ill-maintained[6], not the place for a country hike[7]. An artist would have to be most sincere about his endeavours[8] to bother climbing up to the high moor[9] at all. He turned back to the other man. The afternoon breeze that rustled through the pasture[10] ruffled[11] Farmington's blond hair appealingly so that the sun struck its highlights[12]. Lynley began to understand why he wore it long. 'Mr Parrish tells me that Teys destroyed some of your work.'

'Does he also tell you what the hell *he* was doing out here that night?' Farmington demanded. 'No, blast his eyes[13], I'll be *damned* if he does.[14]'

'According to him, he was bringing Teys' dog back to the farm.'

The artist's face mirrored his disbelief[15]. 'Bringing the *dog* back to the farm? What a laugh!' He savagely drove[16] the pointed legs of his easel into the soft earth[17]. 'Nigel really knows how to manipulate the facts[18], doesn't he? Let me guess what he told you. That Teys and I were having a bloody fine row[19] in the middle of the road when up he popped[20], innocently walking the poor, blind dog home.' Farmington ran one hand through his hair in agitation. His body was so tense that Lynley wondered if he would start swinging his fists[21]. 'Christ, that man will drive me to do something mad.'

Lynley lifted an eyebrow in interest. The other man read the expression.

'And I suppose *that* is a confession of guilt, Inspector? Well, I suggest you trot back to[22] Nigel and ask him what *he* was doing wandering down Gem-

1. Le regard se fit prudent.
2. vous chasser de
3. d'en user librement
4. brusques
5. abrupte et rocheux
6. mal entretenu
7. se promener
8. franchement motivé
9. jusqu'en haut de la lande
10. qui bruissait dans la prairie
11. ébouriffait
12. frappait ses mèches claires
13. maudit soit-il
14. ça m'étonnerait !
15. refléta son incrédulité
16. Il enfonça violemment
17. terre meuble
18. déformer la réalité
19. on se disputait violemment
20. il s'est pointé
21. à cogner
22. que vous refiliez voir

bler Road that night. Believe me, that dog could have found his way back[1] from Timbuktu, if he'd wanted to.' He laughed. 'That dog was a damn sight smarter[2] than Nigel. Not that that means much.'

Lynley wondered at the source of[3] Farmington's anger. The passion was real, without doubt. Yet it was out of all proportion to the subject at hand[4]. The man was like a taut bowstring[5] upon which undue pressure was being exerted[6]. An ounce more, and he would snap[7].

'I saw your work at Keldale Lodge. The way you painted the abbey put me in mind of Wyeth. Was that deliberate[8]?'

Ezra relaxed a tightly balled fist[9]. 'That was done years ago. I was floundering for style.[10] I didn't trust my instincts[11] so I copied everyone else's. I'm surprised Stepha still has it hanging[12].'

'She said you did it to pay for your board one autumn.'

'That's right. I paid for almost everything like that in those days. If you look hard enough, you'll see my crap[13] hanging in every shop in town. I even bought toothpaste[14] that way.' It was a derisive statement[15], an indication of contempt, but directed at himself[16], not at Lynley.

'I like Wyeth,' Lynley went on. 'There's a simplicity to his work[17] that I find refreshing. I like simplicity. The clarity of line and image. Details.'

Farmington folded his arms. 'Are you always this obvious[18], Inspector?'

'I try to be[19],' Lynley responded with a smile. 'Tell me about your argument with William Teys.'

'And if I refuse?'

'You may, of course. But I'd wonder why. Have you something to hide, Mr Farmington?'

Farmington shifted on the balls of his feet[20]. 'I've nothing to hide. I was on the moor that day and came down towards dark. Teys must have seen me

1. aurait su retrouver son chemin
2. bien plus intelligent
3. se demanda d'où venait
4. c'était complètement disproportionné
5. une corde de violon tendue
6. soumise à trop forte pression
7. casser
8. intentionnel
9. ouvrit son poing serré
10. J'avais du mal à trouver mon style.
11. Je ne me fiais pas à mon instinct
12. accroché au mur
13. mes croûtes
14. du dentifrice
15. un constat plein de dérision
16. envers lui-même
17. dans son œuvre
18. aussi transparent
19. Je m'efforce de l'être
20. se balança sur la pointe des pieds

from a window. Hell, I don't know. He caught up with me[1] here on the road. We had it out.[2]'

'He destroyed some of your work.'

'It was crap anyway[3]. It didn't matter.'

'I was always under the impression that artists like to have control over their own creations rather than give it to other people. Wouldn't you agree?' Lynley immediately saw that he'd struck tender flesh[4], for Farmington stiffened[5] involuntarily. His eyes moved to the low sun in the sky. He didn't respond immediately.

'I'd agree,' he said finally. 'Yes, by God, I'd agree.'

'Then, when Teys took it upon himself[6]—'

'*Teys?*' Ezra laughed. 'I didn't care what Teys did. I told you, what he'd destroyed was pure crap anyway. Not that he'd have known the difference. Any man who'd play Souza full blast[7] for an evening's entertainment[8] hasn't got a whole lot of taste, as far as I'm concerned.'

'Souza?'

'The god-awful stars-and-stripes piece[9]. Christ, you'd think he was entertaining a house full of flag-waving[10] Americans. And then to have the cheek to howl at me[11] for disturbing his peace by tiptoeing across his land[12] to get to the trail. I laughed at him. That's when he went for[13] my paintings.'

'What did Nigel Parrish do while all this was going on?'

'Nothing. Nigel had seen what he'd come to see, Inspector. He'd done his bit of sleuthing[14]. He could rest an easy man[15] that night.'

'And on other nights?'

Farmington picked up his easel. 'If there's nothing more, I'll be on my way[16].'

'No, there *is* one thing more.'

Farmington pivoted to face him. 'What?' he demanded.

1. m'a rattrapé
2. On s'est expliqués.
3. de la merde, de toute façon
4. qu'il avait touché un point sensible
5. se raidit
6. s'est permis
7. qui passe du Souza à fond
8. pour se distraire le soir
9. [Le compositeur de] l'affreux hymne américain
10. agitant des drapeaux
11. avoir le culot de me hurler dessus
12. en traversant ses terres sur la pointe des pieds
13. là qu'il s'en est pris à
14. était venu nous épier
15. dormir tranquille
16. je vais y aller

'What were you doing the night William Teys died?'

'I was at the Dove and Whistle.'

'And after time was called[1]?'

'Home in bed. Sleeping it off.[2] Alone.' He tossed his hair off his face[3]. It was an odd, distinctly feminine[4] gesture. 'Sorry I didn't take Hannah with me, Inspector. She'd be quite an alibi[5], but I've never gone in for the whips and chains routine[6].' He climbed over the stone wall and strode angrily down the road.

'It was, as they say in American detective films[7], a total bust[8].' Sergeant Havers tossed the photograph on to the table in the Dove and Whistle and dropped wearily[9] into a chair opposite him.

'Which means, I suppose, that no one has ever seen Russell Mowrey in this lifetime[10]?'

'And, unless we can believe in reincarnation, no one has ever seen him at all. Tessa, however, was widely recognized. A few lifted eyebrows. A few pointed[11] questions.'

'What was your response?'

'I was suitably vague[12], murmuring a lot of interesting Latin adages to get me through[13] difficult moments. I was fine until I tried out *caveat emptor*[14]. Somehow it didn't have that ring of authority[15] the other phrases had.'

'Would you care to drown your disappointment[16] in a drink, Sergeant?' he asked.

'Just tonic water,' she responded and, seeing his expression, added, 'Really. I don't drink much, sir. Honest[17],' with a smile.

'I've spent a rather fascinating day, 'Lynley told her when he returned with her drink. 'An encounter with Madeline Gibson, all hotly[18] *déshabillée* in an emerald négligé with absolutely nothing at all underneath[19].'

1. la fin du service
2. Au lit, en train de cuver.
3. rejeta ses cheveux en arrière
4. très féminin
5. ferait un bon alibi
6. le fouet et les chaînes, ça n'a jamais été mon truc
7. les films policiers
8. un fiasco
9. s'affala
10. dans cette vie
11. insistantes
12. Je suis restée vague, comme il convenait
13. pour me sortir des
14. [en droit, « c'est à l'acheteur de se méfier et de s'informer »]
15. cette aura d'autorité
16. Souhaitez-vous noyer votre déception
17. Vraiment
18. de façon provocante
19. rien dessous

'The life of a policeman is rotten[1],' Havers noted.

'And Gibson upstairs at the absolute ready[2]. I was a welcome guest[3].'

'I can imagine.'

'I've learnt the most today about Gillian, however. She was a sunshine angel, a cat in heat, or the loveliest creature ever seen. It depends who's reporting the details[4]. Either the woman's a chameleon or some of these people are taking considerable trouble[5] to make it look that way.'

'But why?'

'I don't know. Unless, of course, they have a vested interest[6] in keeping her as mysterious as possible.' He swallowed the rest of his ale and leaned back in his chair[7], stretching his tired muscles[8]. 'But the real atmosphere today was at Gembler Farm, Havers.'

'Why's that?'

'I was hot on the trail[9] of Gillian Teys. Picture it[10], please. Something told me it was all in Roberta's room. So I threw myself into the investigation with a passion[11], ripped off the top of her mattress box spring, and fairly lost myself on the spot[12].' He described the sight.

Havers made a grimace of distaste[13]. 'Glad I missed that.[14]'

'Oh, have no fear. I was far too discomposed to put the bed back together[15]. So I shall need your assistance tomorrow. Shall we say directly after[16] breakfast?'

'Sod you.[17]' She grinned.

It was obviously teatime when they arrived at the cottage on the corner of Bishop Furthing Road. It was a late tea, however, probably sliding itself right into dinner[18], for Constable[19] Gabriel Langston answered the door, holding tightly in his hand a plate weighted down with a variety[20] of food. Cold

1. pourrie
2. fin prêt
3. le bienvenu
4. de qui donne l'info
5. se donnent beaucoup de mal
6. un intérêt personnel
7. se radossa
8. en étirant ses muscles fatigués
9. J'étais aux trousses
10. Imaginez
11. avec frénésie
12. je me suis décomposé sur-le-champ
13. dégoût
14. Contente d'avoir raté ça.
15. pour remettre le lit en ordre
16. tout de suite après
17. Salaud.
18. glissant plutôt vers le dîner
19. l'agent
20. surchargée d'un assortiment

chicken legs[1], cheese, fruit, and cake jockeyed for position[2] on a brown pottery dish.

Langston seemed very young for a policeman but aptly named Gabriel[3], for he was slightly built, with thinning yellow hair the consistency of spun glass[4], baby-smooth skin[5], and features that looked undeveloped[6], as if the bones were too soft[7] beneath them.

'I sh-sh-should've s-seen you at once,' he stammered[8], blushing heavily[9] on cheeks and neck. 'Wh-when you ar-arrived. But I was to-told you'd c-come to m-me if you n-needed anything.'

'Nies told you, no doubt,' Lynley guessed. The other man nodded awkwardly[10] and gestured them into his home.

The table was laid out for one[11] and the constable hastily set his meal down on it, wiped his hand on his trousers, and extended it to Lynley. 'N-nice to m-meet you b-both. S-sorry about ...' He blushed darker and gestured helplessly at his mouth[12] as if there were something he could have done about his speech impediment[13]. 'T-tea?' he said eagerly.

'Thank you. I'd love a cup. What about you, Sergeant?'

'Yes, thank you,' Havers replied.

The man nodded in obvious relief[14], smiled, and disappeared into an undersized[15] kitchen off[16] the room in which they stood. The cottage, they could see, was strictly a one-person affair[17], not much more than a bed-sitting room[18]. But it was conscientiously clean[19] – swept, polished, and dusted[20]. Only the faint odour of wet dog[21] marred it[22]. The source of this lay on a chewed and stringy rag rug[23], toasting himself before a single-bar electric fire set into a small stone fireplace. He was a white Highland terrier, and he lifted his chin, blinked at them seriously, and yawned[24], revealing a long pink tongue.

1. Des cuisses de poulet froid
2. en vrac
3. portait bien son prénom
4. d'une texture de verre filé
5. une peau de bébé
6. faisaient pas finis
7. si les os étaient trop mous
8. bégaya
9. rougissant fortement
10. acquiesça gauchement
11. Le couvert était mis pour une personne
12. montra sa bouche d'un air désolé
13. problème d'élocution
14. visiblement soulagé
15. petite
16. donnant sur
17. n'était conçu que pour une personne
18. qu'un studio
19. d'une propreté méticuleuse
20. balayé, ciré, dépoussiéré
21. une vague odeur de chien mouillé
22. gâchait l'ensemble
23. un tapis en lirette filasse
24. bâilla

This done, he turned his nose happily back to the electric blaze.

Langston returned with a tray in his hands and another terrier at his heels[1]. This was a livelier[2] version of the first, for it threw itself[3] upon Lynley in excited greeting.

'H-here, *down*![4]' Langston ordered as sharply[5] as his gentle voice would allow[6]. The dog obeyed reluctantly, then scampered across the room[7] to join the other in a heap by the fire. 'Th-they're g-good lads, Inspector. S-sorry.'

Lynley waved off the apology[8] as Langston poured the tea. 'Go on with your meal, Constable. Havers and I are out prowling a bit late[9] this evening. We can talk while you eat.'

Langston didn't look as if he believed this was possible, but he dug into his food with a shy duck of his head[10].

'I understand that Father Hart rang you directly after he found William Teys' body,' Lynley began. When the man nodded eagerly[11], he went on. 'Roberta was still there when you arrived?' Another nod. 'Did you bring Richmond in immediately? Why was that?' Lynley regretted the question the moment he asked it. Stupid clod[12], he thought, wondering what it would be like for the man to have to agonize his way[13] through questioning witnesses[14], especially those like Father Hart who seemed to float between two distinct planes of existence[15].

Langston was staring at his plate, attempting to formulate an answer.

'I expect that was the quickest way to go about it[16],' Havers offered[17]. Langston nodded gratefully.

'Did Roberta speak to anyone at all?' Langston shook his head. 'Not to you? Not to anyone from Richmond?' Again, the negative. Lynley glanced at Havers. 'Then, she only spoke to Father Hart.' He considered the situation. 'Roberta was sitting on the

1. sur les talons
2. plus fringante
3. car il se jeta
4. couché !
5. aussi sévèrement
6. le lui permettait
7. gambada à travers la pièce
8. le tranquillisa d'un geste
9. on s'est mis en chasse un peu tard
10. en rentrant timidement la tête
11. vivement
12. Pauvre crétin
13. devait endurer
14. pour interroger les témoins
15. niveaux de l'existence
16. que ça irait plus vite comme ça
17. suggéra

overturned pail, the axe was nearby, the dog was under Teys. But the weapon used to slit[1] the dog's throat was missing[2]. Is that correct?' A nod. Langston bit into his third chicken leg, his eyes on Lynley. 'What happened to the dog?'

'I ... b-buried h-him.'

'Where?'

'Out the b-back.[3]'

Lynley leaned forward. 'Behind this cottage? Why? Did Nies tell you to do so?'

Langston swallowed, rubbed his hands on his trousers. He looked miserably at his two companions by the fire and, seeing themselves the focus of his attention, they[4] wagged their tails supportively[5]. 'I ...' It was embarrassment rather than his speech that stopped him this time. 'I love d-dogs,' he said. 'D-didn't want th-them to burn old Wh-Whiskers. He ... was a p-pal o' the l-lads[6].'

'Poor man,' Lynley murmured when they were on the street again. Darkness was falling quickly. Somewhere a woman's voice rose, calling to a child. 'No wonder[7] he brought in Richmond.'

'What could have possessed him, becoming[8] a police constable?' Havers demanded as they crossed to the lodge.

'I expect he never thought he'd come across a murder[9]. At least not one like this. Who would expect it in a place like Keldale? God knows, before this Langston's most serious duty[10] was probably patrolling[11] the village and checking shop doors to see they[12] were locked at night.'

'Then, what's next?[13]' Havers asked. 'We won't have the dog till the morning.'

'True.' Lynley flipped open his watch[14]. 'That gives me twelve hours to talk[15] St James into abandoning[16] his honeymoon for the thrill of the chase[17]. What do you think, Havers? Have we a chance?'

1. ayant servi à trancher
2. avait disparu
3. Derrière.
4. ceux-ci, voyant qu'il les regardait
5. remuèrent la queue en signe de soutien
6. ami avec mes chiens
7. Pas étonnant
8. Qu'est-ce qui lui a pris de devenir
9. qu'un meurtre lui tomberait dessus
10. sa mission la plus importante
11. faire des rondes dans
12. de vérifier que les portes des boutiques
13. Bon, et maintenant ?
14. ouvrit sa montre
15. convaincre
16. d'abandonner
17. pour le plaisir de la chasse

'Will he have to choose between the dead dog and Deborah?'

'Afraid so.[1]'

'I think we'll need a miracle, sir.'

'I'm good at that,' Lynley said grimly[2].

It would have to be the white shirtwaist again. Barbara took it out of the wardrobe and looked at it critically[3]. A different belt and[4] it wouldn't look bad. Or perhaps a scarf[5] at the throat. Had she brought a scarf? Even one for the head could be tied some way[6] to give a touch of colour, to change the outfit[7] somehow, to make it look a bit different. Humming beneath her breath[8], she rummaged through her things. They were tossed into the chest of drawers in a heap[9], but she found what she was looking for easily enough. A scarf of red and white check[10]. A bit like a tablecloth[11], but it couldn't be helped.

She went to the mirror and saw her reflection with a start of pleased surprise[12]. The country air had whipped colour[13] into her cheeks and her eyes had sparkle to them[14]. It was being useful that did it, she decided.

She had enjoyed her day in the village alone. It was the first time a DI had allowed her to do something all by herself[15]. It was the first time a DI had assumed she had brains[16]. She felt bolstered[17] by the experience and realized how much her confidence[18] had been destroyed by her humiliating return to uniform. What a horrible time that had been in her life: the seething anger boiling over into[19] incomprehensible rage, the festering sore of unhappiness[20], the knowledge of being evaluated by others as not good enough, not up to snuff[21].

Snuff[22]: the image of Jimmy Havers' little pig eyes looked back at her from the mirror. Her eyes were his. She turned from the glass.

1. Hélas !
2. l'air sombre
3. d'un œil critique
4. Avec une autre ceinture,
5. foulard
6. en le nouant d'une certaine façon
7. l'ensemble
8. Fredonnant dans sa barbe
9. en tas
10. à carreaux rouges et blancs
11. Il faisait un peu nappe
12. et sursauta, agréablement surprise
13. insufflé de la couleur
14. de l'éclat
15. toute seule
16. estimait qu'elle était intelligente
17. se sentit renforcée
18. sa confiance en elle
19. cette colère bouillonnante muée en
20. l'insatisfaction, cette plaie purulente
21. de ne pas être à la hauteur
22. [rappel : c'est aussi le tabac à priser]

Everything was going to be better now. She was on her way, and nothing could stop her. She would sit for[1] the inspector's exam[2] again. She would pass[3] this time. She knew it.

She stepped out of[4] her tweed skirt, struggled out[5] of the pullover, and kicked off her shoes[6]. Of course, no one had given her any information about Russell Mowrey, but everyone had taken her quite seriously[7] in her questioning. Everyone had seen her for[8] what she was: a representative of New Scotland Yard. A fine representative: competent, intelligent, insightful[9]. It was what she had needed. Now she could really be part of the case.

She completed her dressing[10], tied the scarf jauntily[11] round her throat, and descended the stairs to meet Lynley.

He was in the lounge, standing before the watercolour of the abbey, lost in thought[12]. Behind the bar, Stepha Odell watched him. They might have been part of a painting themselves. The woman stirred first[13].

'A drink before you leave, Sergeant?' she asked pleasantly.

'Thank you, no.'

Lynley turned. 'Ah, Havers,' he said, absently rubbing his temples. 'Are you ready for another assault on Keldale Hall?'

'Quite[14],' she replied.

'Then, we're off[15].' He nodded a detached goodnight to[16] the other woman and, hand on Barbara's elbow, guided her from the room. 'I've been meditating on our best approach,' he said once they were in the car. 'You'll have to keep that dreadful American couple engaged in conversation[17] long enough for me to have a word[18] with St James. Can you do that? I hate to abandon anyone to such a fate[19], but if good old Hank hears me, I have the most appal-

1. passerait
2. l'examen pour être inspecteur
3. l'aurait
4. retira
5. s'extirpa
6. enleva ses chaussures d'un coup de pied
7. très au sérieux
8. l'avait prise pour
9. perspicace
10. finit de s'habiller
11. prestement
12. perdu dans ses pensées
13. bougea la première
14. Absolument
15. allons-y
16. salua d'un air détaché
17. tenir la jambe à ces affreux Américains
18. pour que j'aie le temps de parler à
19. à un tel sort

ling suspicion that he'll demand[1] to be part of the case himself.'

'No problem, sir,' Barbara replied. 'I'll keep him enthralled.[2]'

He glanced at her suspiciously. 'How?'

'I'll have him talk about himself.[3]'

In response, Lynley laughed, suddenly looking younger and far less fatigued. 'That should do it, all right.'

'Now, lookit, Barbie,' Hank said with a wink, 'if it's investigating[4] you and Tom are up to in this burg[5], then you oughta get yourselfs hooked up[6] in *this* place for a nighter two[7]. Whatsay, JoJo-bean? This place j-u-m-p-s after dark[8], huh?'

They were taking their post-prandial drinks[9] in the oak hall. Hank, wearing blinding white[10] trousers, an embroidered south-of-the-border shirt[11] open to the waist[12], and the requisite[13] gold chain, leered at[14] Barbara knowingly. He stood as if hoping to become at one[15] with the garlands[16] and cherubs[17] of the carved chimney-piece[18]. One hand was resting on a stylized stone primrose, the fingers curling round a generous measure of brandy[19]: his third or fourth. The other hand was at his waist, the thumb cocked into the loop[20] of his trousers. It was quite a pose.

His wife sat in a high-backed chair, directing her mournfully apologetic gaze[21] alternately between Deborah and Barbara. Lynley and St James, Barbara noted with satisfaction, had managed to effect a disappearance[22] in the direction of the stone hall almost immediately after dinner, and Mrs Burton-Thomas had dozed off noisily[23] on a well-padded couch[24] nearby. Barbara reflected upon the uneven quality[25] of Mrs Burton-Thomas' snores[26] and decided the woman was faking it[27]. She couldn't

1. exigera
2. Je vais le captiver.
3. Je le ferai parler de lui.
4. pour une enquête
5. êtes dans ce bled
6. vous devriez loger
7. une ou deux nuits
8. Ça bouge, ici, le soir
9. leur verre d'après-dîner
10. d'un blanc aveuglant
11. chemise mexicaine brodée
12. déboutonnée jusqu'à la taille
13. qui va avec
14. lorgnait
15. comme s'il voulait se confondre avec
16. guirlandes
17. les angelots
18. manteau de la cheminée
19. tenant une bonne dose de cognac
20. le pouce dans un passant
21. regardant de son air morne et navré
22. à s'esquiver
23. s'était assoupie bruyamment
24. sofa bien rembourré
25. l'irrégularité
26. ronflements
27. simulait

blame her. Hank had been holding forth[1] for a good quarter-hour.

Barbara cast a quick look at Deborah to see how she was dealing with her husband's sudden desertion of her to Hank's clutches[2]. The other woman's face, crossed by fire and shadow, was tranquil, but when she felt Barbara's eyes on her, a mischievous[3] smile touched her lips for an instant. She knows perfectly well what's happening, Barbara decided, and liked Deborah for the generosity implied behind[4] her acceptance of the fact.

As Hank was opening his mouth to continue his description of the after-dark j-u-m-p-s at Keldale Hall, Lynley and St James rejoined them by the fire.

'Now, you gotta get the pitcher here[5],' Hank was continuing. 'I go to the window two nights ago to shut out[6] that damned screeching[7]. Ever hear peacocks[8] make such a ruckus[9], Debbie?'

'*Peacocks?*' Deborah asked. 'Good heavens, Simon, it wasn't the baby in the abbey at all! Did you lie to me?'

'I was obviously misled[10],' St James replied. 'It sounded remarkably like a baby to me. Are you telling me we warded off evil[11] for nothing?'

'Like a *baby*?' Hank demanded, incredulous. 'You must be lost in the throes of l-u-v[12], Si. That was a peacock screeching fit to beat the band[13]' He sat down, knees spread apart[14], his arms resting on his chunky thighs[15]. 'So I go to the window to either shut the thing or give the old heave-ho to a shoe[16] and kill that damn bird. I'm one helluva shot[17]. Did I tell you that? No? Well, we got this alley in Laguna, see, where the queers hang out[18].' He waited to see if he would once again have to explain the denizens[19] of Laguna Beach to his audience[20], but they were caught in the grip of his pictorial pun[21]. He went on happily. 'And I get puhlenty[22] of

1. pérorait
2. les griffes
3. malicieux
4. que révélait
5. imaginez la scène
6. ne plus entendre
7. ces cris d'enfer
8. des paons
9. un tel raffut
10. Apparemment, je me suis trompé
11. que nous avons repoussé le mal
12. en plein câlin
13. à tout casser
14. genoux écartés
15. larges cuisses
16. balancer une godasse
17. super bon tireur
18. se baladent [exhibant tous leurs attributs]
19. aux habitants
20. auditoire
21. sous l'emprise de son jeu de mots imagé
22. plein [insistance sur « plenty »]

practice[1] heaving shoes out at them, lemme tell you. Whatsay,[2] Bean? Truth[3] or not?'

'Truth, honey,' JoJo replied. 'He can hit *anything*,' she swore to the others.

'I have no doubt,' Lynley said grimly.

Hank flashed his capped teeth[4]. 'So, here I am at the window, ready to heave it, see, when what I notice is a heckuva lot more 'an some bird[5].'

'Someone else screeching?' Lynley enquired.

'Hell, no. The bird was there all right[6], but I got an eyeful-a[7] something else!' He waited for them to ask what it was. There was polite silence. 'OK, OK!' He laughed. He lowered his voice. 'Danny and that fella[8], what's-is-name, Ira … Hezekiah …'

'Ezra?'

'Yep[9]! And they are liplocked[10] like I never s-e-e-n. Whew! "You two gonna come up for air?[11]" I yell.' He howled appreciatively.

Polite smiles all around. JoJo gazed from one face to another like a puppy eager to be loved[12].

'Only, this is the best part.' Hank lowered his voice again. 'What we got on our hands isn't Danny at all. But it's Ezra all right.' He smiled triumphantly. Their complete attention was his at last.[13]

'More brandy, Deborah?' St James asked.

'Thank you.'

Hank squirmed forward in his seat[14]. 'But he's gettin' it on with *Angelina*[15]! Can you *see* it?' He barked with laughter[16] and pounded his knee[17]. 'This Ezra's busier than a rooster[18] in a hen-house[19], fellas. I don't know what he's got, but he sure likes spreading it around[20]!' He slurped at his drink. 'I made a few pointed remarks to Angelina in the a.m.[21], but that girl is *deep*. Not a twitch of the e-y-e.[22] I'm telling you, Tom, if it's action you're looking for, you oughta get yourself down *here*.' He sighed with satisfaction and fingered his heavy gold chain.

1. d'entraînement
2. Hein,
3. Vrai
4. exhiba ses dents mal refaites
5. c'est autre chose qu'un oiseau
6. bien là
7. je me suis rincé l'œil avec
8. ce type
9. Ouais
10. en train de se rouler un patin
11. vous comptez l'ouvrir pour respirer ?
12. un chiot réclamant de l'amour
13. Ils étaient enfin totalement attentifs.
14. se tortilla vers l'avant de son fauteuil
15. c'est Angelina qu'il se tape
16. éclata d'un énorme rire
17. se tapa le genou
18. coq
19. poulailler
20. en faire profiter tout le monde
21. le lendemain matin
22. Elle n'a pas bougé un cil.

'L-u-v. Wonderful thing, huh? Nothing messes with the mind[1] like l-u-v. Bet you can attest to *that*, Si, huh?'

'I've been distraught[2] for years,' St James acknowledged.

Hank brayed[3]. 'Cotcher heart pretty young[4], did she?' He pointed a knowing finger at Deborah[5]. 'After him for a while, huh?'

'Since childhood[6],' she replied smoothly.

'*Childhood?*' Hank crossed the room to slosh more[7] brandy into his glass. Mrs Burton-Thomas snored loudly as he passed her. 'You two're school sweethearts[8] like me and the Bean, I'll bet. Remember it, Bean? A little you-know-what[9] in the back of the Chevy[10]. You got drive-in movies here?'

'I think that's a phenomenon endemic to your country[11],' St James replied.

'Say what?[12]' Hank shrugged and fell back into his seat. Brandy splashed out[13] on to his white trousers. He ignored it. 'So you met in school?'

'No. We were formally introduced[14] at my mother's house.' St James and Deborah exchanged innocent glances.

'Hey, she set you two up[15], I bet. The Bean and I met on a blind date[16], too! We got something in common, Si.'

'Actually, I was born in his mother's house,' Deborah added politely. 'But I grew up mostly in Simon's house in London.'

Hank's face fell. These were dangerous waters.[17] 'Did you catch that, Bean? You two related? Cousins or something?' Visions of haemophiliacs[18] languishing behind closed doors clearly danced[19] in his head.

'Not at all. My father is Simon's … well, what would you call Dad?' She turned to her husband. 'Footman, servant, butler[20], valet?'

'Father-in-law,' St James replied.

1. Rien ne tourneboule
2. Je suis éperdu d'amour
3. rit comme un âne
4. Elle vous a séduit tout jeune
5. désigna Deborah d'un air entendu
6. l'enfance
7. se reverser du
8. amoureux depuis l'école
9. Un petit câlin
10. à l'arrière de la Chevrolet
11. propre à votre pays
12. Hein ?
13. déborda
14. présentés en bonne et due forme
15. a organisé votre rencontre
16. rendez-vous arrangé
17. On arrivait en terrain miné.
18. hémophiles
19. se bousculaient visiblement
20. Valet, domestique, majordome

'Did you catch that, Bean?' Hank said in awe[1]. 'This is *some* romance[2].'

It was sudden, unexpected[3]. She was trying to adjust[4]. Lynley's was turning out to be such[5] a multifaceted character[6], like a diamond cut by a master jeweller[7]; in every situation a new surface glittered that she had never seen before.

In love with Deborah. All right, certainly. That was understandable. But in love with the daughter of St James' *servant*? Barbara struggled to assimilate the information. How had it ever happened to him? she wondered. He had always seemed to be in such complete control of his life and his destiny. How had he ever *allowed* it to happen?

She now saw his peculiar behaviour at St James' wedding in an entirely new light[8]. Not anxious to be rid of *her* as soon as he could, but anxious to be away[9] from a source of considerable pain: the nuptial happiness of a woman he loved with another man.

At least she understood now why of the two men Deborah had chosen St James. Obviously, she'd never even been given a choice[10], for Lynley would never have allowed himself to speak to her of love. To do this would ultimately have led him to speak of marriage, and Lynley would never marry the daughter of a servant. It would shake[11] his family tree to its very roots[12].

Yet he certainly must have wanted to make Deborah his wife, and how he must have suffered, watching St James placidly break the ridiculous code of social behaviour[13] that held Lynley immobilized[14].

What had St James said? *Father-in-law.* In four short syllables he had coolly wiped away[15] every class distinction that might ever have separated him from his wife.

1. impressionné
2. Ça, c'est une belle histoire d'amour
3. inattendu
4. réviser son jugement
5. Il s'avérait que la personnalité de Lynley
6. avait de multiples facettes
7. joaillier
8. sous un tout autre jour
9. désireux de s'éloigner
10. n'avait jamais eu le choix
11. ébranlerait
12. jusqu'aux racines
13. rompre le code ridicule des convenances
14. retenait Lynley
15. froidement balayé

No wonder she loves him, Barbara realized suddenly.

She glanced warily at Lynley as they drove back to the lodge. What must it be like for him[1], knowing[2] that he had lacked[3] the courage to tell Deborah that he wanted her, knowing that he'd put his family and his title before his love? How he must hate himself! What regret he must feel! How horribly lonely he must really be[4]!

He felt her looking at him. 'You did nice work today, Sergeant. Especially at the hall. Keeping Hank at bay[5] for a quarter of an hour shall get you a citation[6], rest assured[7].'

She felt absurdly warmed[8] by the praise[9]. 'Thank you, sir. St James agreed to help?'

'He did indeed.'

He did indeed, Lynley thought. He let out his breath sharply[10] in[11] self-derision and tossed the file on to the bedside[12] table. He dropped his spectacles on top of it, rubbed his eyes[13], and adjusted[14] the pillows behind his back.

Deborah had spoken to her husband. Lynley could see that. They'd already discussed what his response would be when he was asked to assist[15]. It was a simple one: 'Of course, Tommy. What can I do?'

How like both of them! How like Deborah to have seen in their conversation that morning all of his concerns[16] about the case. How like her to have paved the way[17] for him to ask St James' help. And how like St James to have agreed without hesitation, for any hesitation would have aroused the guilt[18] that always lay like a dangerous wounded[19] tiger between them.

He leaned back against the pillows and closed his eyes wearily, allowing his mind in its exhaustion to drift back to the past[20]. He gave himself to the[21]

1. Qu'est-ce que cela doit lui faire
2. de savoir
3. n'avait pas eu
4. Il devait se sentir bien seul
5. En maintenant Hank à distance
6. vous vaudra des félicitations officielles
7. soyez-en sûre
8. réconfortée
9. le compliment
10. souffla brusquement
11. en signe d'
12. de chevet
13. se frotta les yeux
14. arrangea
15. on lui demanderait son aide
16. toutes ses préoccupations
17. d'avoir préparé le terrain
18. aurait réveillé le sentiment de culpabilité
19. blessé
20. remonter dans le passé
21. s'abandonna aux

bewitching[1] visions of a former[2] happiness that remained unclouded by grief or pain.

The lovely Thais by his side,
Sate[3] like a blooming[4] Easter bride,
In flow'r of youth[5] and beauty's pride[6].
Happy, happy, happy pair[7]!
None but the brave deserves the fair.[8]

Dryden's words came from nowhere[9], unbidden[10] and unwanted[11]. He swallowed them down[12] and demanded that they recede[13] into his mind, an effort that took every ounce of[14] his concentration and prevented him from hearing[15] the door open and the footsteps cross to the[16] bed. He was quite unaware[17], in fact, of the presence in the room until a cool hand touched his cheek gently. His eyes flew open[18].

'I think you need an Odell's, Inspector,' Stepha whispered.

1. ensorcelantes
2. révolu
3. [forme ancienne de « sat »]
4. rayonnante
5. Dans la fleur de sa jeunesse
6. et l'orgueil de sa beauté
7. heureux couple
8. Seul un brave mérite la belle.
9. surgirent à l'improviste
10. spontanés
11. involontaires
12. les ravala
13. leur ordonna de s'estomper
14. toute
15. l'empêcha d'entendre
16. parvenir jusqu'au
17. ne perçut rien
18. s'ouvrirent d'un coup

12

Nonplussed[1], he stared at her. He waited for his smooth[2] persona[3] to click into place[4], for the arrival of that illusory man who laughed and danced and had a quick-witted answer[5] for everything. But nothing happened. Stepha's appearance in his room, materializing for all he knew[6] out of nowhere, seemed to have destroyed his only line of defence, and all that was left in his repertoire of engaging behaviours[7] was the ability to meet, without wavering[8], her beautiful eyes.

He needed to give reality to the moment, to make her something he hadn't dreamt up[9] from the mist of his dispirited memory[10], so he reached out[11] and touched the fall[12] of her hair. *Soft*, he thought wonderingly. She caught his hand and kissed the palm[13], the wrist. Her tongue lightly traced the length[14] of his fingers. 'Let me love you tonight. Let me drive away[15] the shadows.'

She spoke on the merest breath of a whisper[16], and he wondered if her voice were a part of the dream. But her smooth hands played across[17] his cheeks and jaw and throat, and when she bent to him and he tasted the sweetness of her mouth, felt the caress of her tongue, he knew she was part of a searing[18] reality, a present calmly laying siege to[19] the castellated walls[20] of his past.

1. Perplexe
2. sans souci
3. personnage
4. s'installe en un déclic
5. une repartie
6. en apparence
7. d'attitudes charmantes
8. de pouvoir croiser, sans flancher
9. de faire qu'elle ne soit pas un être fictif
10. sorti de sa mémoire embrumée de déprime
11. tendit le bras
12. cascade
13. paume
14. suivit doucement la ligne
15. dissiper
16. dans un murmure
17. elle promena ses mains douces sur
18. impitoyable
19. qui assiégeait calmement
20. les murs fortifiés

He wanted to flee from the onslaught[1], to escape to that haven of bliss-charged remembrance[2] that had kept him well armoured[3] in the year that had passed, a year during which all desire had been absent, all longing dead[4], all life incomplete. But she allowed no evasion, and as she purposefully[5] destroyed the ramparts that shielded him[6] he felt once again not a sweet liberation but that terrifying need to possess another person, body and soul[7].

He *couldn't*. He wouldn't allow it to happen. He desperately sought out[8] last shattered defences[9], uselessly willing back into being[10] an insensate[11] creature who no longer lived. In its place was reborn[12] – quiet and vulnerable – the man who had been there, inside, all along.

'Tell me about Paul.'

She raised herself on one elbow, touched her[13] finger to[14] his lips, traced their shape. The light struck her hair, her shoulders, her breasts. She was fire and cream, scented[15] almost imperceptibly with the sweetness of Devon violets.

'Why?'

'Because I want to know about you. Because he was your brother. Because he died.'

Her eyes moved from his. 'What did Nigel say?'

'That Paul's death changed everyone.'

'It did.'

'Bridie said that he went away, that he never said goodbye.'

Stepha lowered herself[16] next to him, into his arms. 'Paul killed himself, Thomas,' she whispered. Her body trembled on the words. He held her closer[17]. 'Bridie's not been told. We say he died of Huntington's, and he did, in a way. It was Huntington's that killed him. Have you ever seen people with the disease? St Vitus' dance.[18] They've no control over their bodies. They twitch[19] and stagger[20] and

1. fuir l'assaut
2. cet éden de souvenirs extatiques
3. bien protégé
4. toute aspiration avait disparu
5. consciencieusement
6. qui l'abritaient
7. âme
8. chercha désespérément
9. des restes de résistance
10. tentant, en vain, de redevenir
11. insensible
12. ressuscita
13. posa le
14. sur
15. un mélange de roux et de blancheur laiteuse, parfumée
16. s'allongea
17. resserra son étreinte
18. La danse de Saint-Guy.
19. se tordent
20. titubent

leap[1] and fall. And then their minds go at the last[2]. But not Paul. By *God*, not Paul.' Her voice caught[3]. She drew in a breath. His hand found its way to her hair and he pressed his lips to the top of her head.

'I'm sorry.'

'He had just enough mind left[4] to know that he no longer recognized his wife, no longer knew the name of his child, no longer had any control over his body. He had just enough mind left to decide it was time for him to die[5].' She swallowed. 'I helped him. I had to. He was my twin[6].'

'I didn't know that.'

'Nigel didn't tell you?'

'No. Nigel's in love with you, isn't he?'

'Yes.' She answered without artifice[7].

'Did he come to Keldale to be near you?'

She nodded. 'We were all at university together: Nigel, Paul, and I. I might have married Nigel at one time[8]. He was less mad then, less angry. I'm the source of his madness, I'm afraid. But I'll never marry now.'

'Why not?'

'Because Huntington's is a hereditary disease[9]. I'm a carrier[10]. I don't want to pass it on[11] to a child. It's bad enough[12] seeing Bridie every day and thinking every time she stumbles[13] or drops[14] something that she's got the bloody disease herself. I don't know what I'd do if I had a child of my own. Probably drive myself mad with worry[15].'

'You don't have to have children. Or you could adopt.'

'Men say that, of course. Nigel does all the time. But there's no point to marriage[16] as far as I'm concerned[17] if I can't have my own child. My own healthy child.[18]'

'Was the baby in the abbey a healthy child?'

1. sautent
2. à la fin, ils perdent l'esprit
3. se brisa
4. était juste assez lucide
5. qu'il était temps qu'il meure
6. frère jumeau
7. sans ambages
8. à une époque
9. maladie héréditaire
10. porteuse
11. la transmettre
12. déjà assez dur
13. qu'elle trébuche
14. fait tomber
15. devenir folle d'inquiétude
16. à quoi bon se marier,
17. en ce qui me concerne,
18. Mon propre enfant bien portant.

She drew herself up to look at him. 'On duty[1], Inspector? An odd time and place[2] for it, wouldn't you say[3]?'

He smiled wryly[4]. 'Sorry. Reflex action[5], I'm afraid.' And then he added, unrepentant[6], 'Was she?'

'Wherever did you hear about the baby in the abbey? No, don't tell me. Keldale Hall.'

'I understand it was a bit of a legend come true[7].'

'Of sorts.[8] The legend – fanned[9] by the Burton-Thomases at every opportunity[10] – is that sometimes one can hear a baby cry from the abbey at night. The reality, I'm afraid, is much as you'd expect. It's a trick of wind[11] when it's blowing with just the right force[12] from the north through a crack[13] in the wall between the north transept and the nave[14]. It happens several times a year.'

'How do you know?'

'When we were teenagers, my brother and I camped there for a fortnight one spring until we'd tracked the sound down[15]. Of course, we didn't disappoint the Burton-Thomases by telling them the truth. But, to be honest, even that wind doesn't sound a great deal like[16] a baby.'

'And the real baby?'

'Ah, back to that, are we?' She rested[17] her cheek on his chest. 'I don't know much about it. It was just over three years ago. Father Hart found her, managed to stir up a great deal of local outrage[18] about her, and it fell to[19] Gabriel Langston to sort it all out[20]. Poor Gabriel. He never was able to discover anything at all. The furore died down[21] after a few weeks. There was a funeral that everyone of conscience attended[22] and that was the end of it, I'm afraid. It was all rather grim.'

'And you were glad when it was over?'

'I was. I don't like grimness[23]. I don't want it in my life. I want life filled with laughter and wild, crazy joy.'

1. Vous êtes en service
2. Drôle d'endroit et de moment
3. ne croyez-vous pas
4. ironiquement
5. Un réflexe
6. récidivant pourtant
7. devenue réalité
8. Si on veut.
9. ravivée
10. dès qu'ils le peuvent
11. un effet du vent
12. avec pile la force nécessaire,
13. venant du nord, à travers une fissure
14. la nef
15. que nous ayons identifié le bruit
16. ne ressemble guère aux pleurs d'
17. posa
18. susciter l'indignation de la paroisse
19. c'est
20. qui a dû s'en dépatouiller
21. L'agitation est retombée
22. auquel ont assisté ceux dotés d'une conscience
23. ce qui est sinistre

'Perhaps you're afraid of feeling anything else.'

'I am. But I'm mostly afraid of ending up lost like Olivia, of loving someone so much and then having that person[1] ripped out of my life[2]. I can't bear to be near her any longer.[3] After Paul died, she went into a fog bank[4] and never emerged. I don't want to be like that. Ever.' She spoke the last word on a hard note of anger, but when she raised her head, her eyes shone with tears[5]. 'Please. Thomas,' she whispered, and his body responded with the quicksilver[6] flame of desire.

He pulled her to him roughly[7], felt her heat and passion[8], heard her cry of pleasure, felt the shadows drift away.

'What about Bridie?'

'What do you mean?'

'She's like a little lost soul. Just Bridie and that duck.'

Stepha laughed. She curled on her side[9], her smooth back[10] a pleasant pressure against him. 'Bridie's special, isn't she?'

'Olivia seems oddly detached from her. It's as if Bridie's growing up[11] without parents at all.'

'Liv wasn't always that way. But Bridie's like Paul. So exactly like. I think it hurts Olivia even to see her[12]. She's not really over[13] Paul yet. I doubt she ever will be.'

'Then, why on earth was she going to remarry?'

'For Bridie's sake.[14] Paul was a very strong father. Olivia seems to have felt duty-bound[15] to replace him with someone else. And William was eager[16] to be the replacement, I suppose.' Her voice was growing sleepy[17]. 'I don't quite know what she thought it was going to be like for herself. But I think she was more interested in getting Bridie under control. It would have worked well, too. William was very good to Bridie. So was Roberta.'

1. pour ensuite me le voir
2. arracher
3. Je ne supporte plus de m'en approcher.
4. a disparu dans un banc de brouillard
5. brillaient de larmes
6. très vive
7. avec rudesse
8. son ardente excitation
9. se lova de côté
10. la douceur de son dos exerçant
11. grandissait
12. qu'Olivia souffre rien qu'en la voyant
13. ne s'est pas vraiment remise de la mort de
14. Dans l'intérêt de Bridie.
15. s'être sentie obligée
16. très désireux
17. de plus en plus ensommeillée

'Bridie says you are as well.'

She yawned[1]. 'Does she? I fixed[2] her hair, poor little pumpkin[3]. I'm not certain I'm good at anything else.'

'You chase ghosts away[4],' he whispered. 'You're very good at that[5].' But she was asleep.

He awoke to find the reality[6] this time. She lay[7], child-like, curled with her knees drawn up[8], with both of her fists under her chin. She was frowning with her dream[9], and a strand[10] of hair was caught between her lips. He smiled at the sight.

A glance at his watch told him it was nearly seven. He bent and kissed her bare[11] shoulder. She awoke at once, coming fully awake[12] in an instant, not the least bit confused about[13] where she was. She raised her hand, touching his cheek, pulling him down to her[14].

He kissed her mouth, then her neck, and heard the delicate change in her breathing that signalled her pleasure when he reached her breast. His hand slid the length[15] of her body. She sighed.

'Thomas.' He lifted his head. Her cheeks were flushed, her eyes bright. 'I must go.'

'Not just yet.[16]'

'Look at the time.'

'In a moment.' He bent to her, felt her hands in his hair.

'You … I … Oh Lord.' She laughed as she realized how her body was betraying her.

He smiled. 'Go if you must, then.'

She sat up[17], kissed him a last time, and crossed to[18] the bathroom. He lay there, filled with a contentment that he had thought was entirely lost to him, and listened to the familiar noises she made. He found himself wondering how he'd survived the last year of isolation. Then she was returning to him, smiling, running his hairbrush[19] through her

1. bâilla
2. lui ai arrangé
3. la pauvre mignonne
4. Tu fais fuir les fantômes
5. très douée
6. se réveilla face à la réalité
7. était allongée
8. en chien de fusil
9. Un rêve lui fronçait les sourcils
10. une mèche
11. nue
12. tout éveillée
13. sachant tout de suite
14. l'attirant contre elle
15. glissa le long
16. Pas tout de suite.
17. se rassit
18. alla à
19. passant sa brosse

tangled[1] hair. She reached for her grey dressing-gown and began to put it on, lifting one arm gracefully as she did so.

And it was in that movement in the early-morning light that he saw the unmistakable evidence on her body that she had borne a child[2].

Barbara finally got up when she heard Lynley's door open and close softly. She'd been lying on her side, her eyes fixed desperately upon a single spot on the wall, her teeth grinding together so fiercely[3] that her entire jaw ached[4]. She had willed conscious feeling into absolute death[5] for the last seven hours, ever since the first moment when she'd heard them together in his room.

She walked now to the window on legs that felt numb[6]. She stared stonily[7] out into the Keldale morning. The village seemed lifeless, a place without colour or sound. How appropriate[8], she thought.

The real agony was the bed: the unmistakable[9], rhythmic creaking[10] of his bed. It went on and on[11] until she wanted to scream, to pound[12] her fists against the wall to bring it to an end[13]. But the silence that fell just as suddenly was worse. It beat against her eardrums[14] in angry pulsations that she finally came to recognize as the pounding of her heart. And then the bed again, endlessly. And the woman's muffled cry[15].

She put a dry, hot hand on to the windowpane[16] and felt with listless[17] surprise the damp, cool glass. Her fingers slipped, left streaks. She examined them meticulously.

So much for his unrequited love[18] for Deborah, Barbara thought acidly. Christ, I must have been absolutely out of my mind! When had he ever been more than what he'd been last night: a real stud[19], a bona-fide bull[20], a hard, hot stallion of a man[21] who

1. emmêlés
2. été enceinte
3. les dents si violemment serrées
4. toute la mâchoire lui faisait mal
5. annihilé toute sensation consciente
6. les jambes engourdies
7. froidement
8. Tout à fait de circonstance
9. caractéristique
10. grincement
11. Ça avait duré encore et encore
12. cogner
13. pour que ça s'arrête
14. lui frappait les tympans
15. le cri étouffé
16. la vitre
17. indifférente
18. Tu parles d'un amour sans retour
19. un vrai tombeur
20. un authentique taureau
21. étalon en rut

had to prove his virility between the legs of every woman he met.

Well, you proved it last night, Inspector. Took her directly up to heaven three or four times, didn't you? You've got solid gold talent, all right.

She laughed soundlessly[1], mirthlessly[2]. It was a pleasure, really, to discover that he was just what she'd always assumed him to be: an alley cat[3] on the prowl for[4] any female in heat[5], cleverly disguised under a refulgent veneer[6] of upper-class breeding. But what a thin veneer it was after all! Scratch the surface of the man[7] and the truth oozed out[8].

The bath began running noisily in the next room, a rushing of water that sounded to Barbara like a burst of applause[9]. She stirred, turned from the window, and made her decision about how to face the day.

'We're going to have to take the house apart[10] one room at a time,' Lynley said.

They were in the study. Havers had gone to the bookshelves and was sullenly[11] flipping through a dog-eared[12] Brontë. He watched her. Other than monosyllabic, expressionless replies[13] to every remark he'd made at breakfast, she had said nothing at all. The fragile thread[14] of communication they had established between them seemed to be utterly broken[15]. To make matters worse[16], she'd returned to her hideous light blue suit and ridiculous coloured tights[17].

'Havers,' he said sharply. 'Are you listening to me?'

Her head turned with slow insolence. 'To every word ... Inspector.'

'Then, start with the kitchen.'

'One of the two places where a little woman belongs[18].'

'What's that supposed to mean?'

'Not a thing.' She left the room.

1. sans bruit
2. sans joie
3. chat de gouttière
4. à l'affût de
5. en chaleur
6. sous un vernis resplendissant
7. Si on grattait un peu,
8. ressortait
9. l'éclat d'applaudissements
10. passer la maison au peigne fin
11. l'air morne
12. aux pages cornées
13. des réponses inexpressives
14. Le fil ténu
15. s'être bel et bien rompu
16. Pour ne rien arranger
17. collants
18. où cantonner une bonne femme

His eyes followed her, perplexed. What in God's name had got into the woman?[1] They had been working so well together, but now she was acting as if she could hardly wait[2] to throw it all away[3] and return to uniform. It made no sense. Webberly was offering her a chance to redeem herself[4]. Given that, why would she deliberately attempt to prove justifiable every prejudice held against her by[5] the other DIs at the Yard? He muttered an oath[6] and summarily dismissed her[7] from his thoughts.

St James would be in Newby Wiske by now, the corpse of the dog wrapped in a polythene shroud[8] in the boot of the Escort and Roberta's clothing in a cardboard carton on the rear seat. He would perform the post-mortem[9], supervise the tests, and report the results with his usual efficiency[10]. Thank God. St James' involvement would ensure that at least something in the case was handled[11] correctly.

Chief Constable Kerridge of the Yorkshire Constabulary had been only too delighted[12] to hear that Allcourt-St James would be coming to use their well-equipped lab. Anything, Lynley thought, to put another nail in Nies' coffin[13]. He shook his head in disgust, went to William Teys' desk, and opened the top drawer.

It held no secrets. There were scissors, pencils, a wrinkled[14] map of the county[15], a typewriter ribbon[16], and a roll of tape[17]. The map caused a flurry of short-lived interest[18] and he unfolded it eagerly: perhaps it marked out[19] a careful search for Teys' older daughter. But it was unmarred by any cryptogrammic message[20] that indicated the location of[21] a missing girl[22].

The other drawers were as devoid of pertinent facts[23] as the first: a pot of glue[24], two boxes of unused[25] Christmas cards, three packets of photographs taken on the farm, account[26] books,

1. Mais bon sang, qu'avait-elle tout à coup ?
2. elle n'avait de cesse
3. tout saborder
4. se racheter
5. de justifier tous les préjugés qu'avaient contre elle
6. jura dans sa barbe
7. la chassa sommairement
8. un linceul en polyéthylène
9. ferait l'autopsie
10. son efficacité habituelle
11. géré
12. plus que ravi
13. pour enfoncer Nies un peu plus
14. toute froissée
15. carte du comté
16. ruban de machine à écrire
17. rouleau de Scotch
18. suscita un bref intérêt
19. retraçait-elle
20. vierge de tout message mystérieux
21. où se trouvait
22. une jeune fille disparue
23. aussi dénués d'éléments pertinents
24. colle
25. vierges
26. de compte

records of lambing[1], a roll of ageing breath-mints[2]. But nothing of Gillian.

He leaned back in the chair. His eyes fell on the bookstand and the Bible it held. Struck by a thought, he opened it to the previously marked page. 'And Pharaoh[3] said unto[4] Joseph, "For as much as[5] God hath showed thee all this, there is none so discreet and wise as thou art[6]. Thou shalt be over[7] my house, and according unto thy word shall all my people be ruled[8]: only in the throne will I be greater than thou." And Pharaoh said unto Joseph, "See, I have set thee over[9] all the land of Egypt." And Pharaoh took off his ring from his hand, and put it on Joseph's hand, and arrayed him in vestures[10] of fine linen, and put a gold chain about his neck; and he made him to ride in the second chariot which he had; and they cried before him, "Bow the knee[11]" and he made him ruler over[12] all the land of Egypt.'[13]

'Seeking guidance from the Lord?[14]'

Lynley looked up. Havers was leaning against the study door, her shapeless[15] body silhouetted[16] sharply by the morning light, her face a blank[17].

'Have you finished the kitchen?' he asked.

'Thought I'd take a break[18].' She sauntered into[19] the room. 'Got a smoke on you?'

He handed her his cigarette case absently and went to the bookshelves, running his eyes over them[20], seeking a volume of Shakespeare. He found it and began looking.

'Is Daze a redhead[21], Inspector?'

It took a moment for the odd question to strike him[22]. When he looked up, Havers was back at the door, running her fingers meditatively against the wood, apparently indifferent to whatever answer he might give. 'I beg your pardon?'

She flipped open the cigarette case and read its inscription. 'Darling Thomas. We'll always have Par-

1. des registres d'agnelage
2. vieilles pastilles à la menthe
3. Pharaon
4. à
5. Puisque
6. personne qui soit aussi intelligent et aussi sage que toi
7. Je t'établis sur
8. mon peuple t'obéira
9. te donne le commandement de
10. le revêtit
11. À genoux
12. lui donna le commandement de
13. [Genèse, chap. 41]
14. Vous cherchez conseil auprès du Seigneur ?
15. informe
16. découpé
17. le visage fermé
18. faire une pause
19. entra nonchalamment
20. les parcourant des yeux
21. rousse
22. pour qu'il voie le saugrenu de la question

is, won't we? Daze.' Coldly, she met his eyes. It was then that he noticed how pale she was, how the skin beneath her eyes was dark with fatigue[1], how the gold case shook in her hand. 'Aside from her rather hackneyed use[2] of Bogart, is she a red-head?' Havers repeated. 'I only ask because you seem to prefer them. Or is the truth that anyone will do[3]?'

Horrified, Lynley realized too late what the change in her was[4] and his own responsibility for having brought it about[5]. There was nothing he could say. There was no quick answer he could give. But he could tell at once that none was necessary, for she had every intention[6] of continuing without his response.

'Havers—'

She held up a hand to stop him. She was deathly white[7]. Her features looked flat[8]. Her voice was tight. 'You know, it's really poor form[9] not to go to the woman's room for your trysts[10], Inspector. I'm surprised you didn't know that. With *your* experience I should think that a little social nicety[11] like that would be the last thing you'd forget. Of course, it's just a small lapse[12], and it probably doesn't really bother a woman at all, not when it's compared with the ecstatic experience of fucking you[13].'

He recoiled[14] from the brutal ugliness that her tone gave[15] the word. 'I'm sorry, Barbara,' he said.

'Why be sorry?' She forced a guttural laugh. 'No one thinks about listeners in the heat of passion[16]. I know I never do.' She gave a brittle[17] smile. 'And it certainly was the old heat of passion last night, wasn't it? I couldn't believe it when you two started banging away on a second go[18]. And so *soon*! Lord, you barely gave it a rest[19].'

He watched her move to the shelf and run a finger along the spine[20] of a book. 'I didn't know you could hear us. I apologize, Barbara. I'm terribly sorry.'

1. noire de cernes
2. À part sa citation éculée
3. n'importe qui fait l'affaire
4. en quoi son attitude avait changé
5. dans quelle mesure il en était responsable
6. car elle était bien décidée
7. d'une blancheur cadavérique
8. tristes
9. mal élevé
10. pour ses rendez-vous galants
11. subtilité mondaine
12. impair
13. baiser avec vous
14. eut un mouvement de recul
15. l'intonation brutale et hideuse qu'elle donnait
16. dans le feu de l'action
17. caustique
18. avez remis le couvert
19. vous aviez à peine repris haleine
20. le dos

She swung back to him quickly. 'Why be sorry?' she repeated, her voice louder this time. 'You aren't on duty twenty-four hours a day. And, besides, it's not really your fault, is it? How were you to know Stepha would howl like a banshee[1]?'

'None the less, it was never my intention to hurt your feelings[2]—'

'You haven't hurt my feelings at all!' She laughed shrilly. 'Where on earth did you get an idea like *that*? Let's say you've merely piqued my interest[3]. As I listened to you sending Stepha to the moon[4] – was it three times or four? – I wondered if Deborah used to howl as well.'

It was a wild shot in the dark[5], but the barb had gone home[6]. He knew that she saw it, for her face blazed[7] with triumph. 'That's hardly your concern[8], is it?'

'Of course not! I know that! But during your second session with Stepha – it *was* at least an hour, wasn't it? – I couldn't help thinking about poor old Simon. He must have to struggle like hell[9] to follow *your* act[10].'

'You've certainly done your homework[11], Havers. I'll say that much for you. And when you take off the gloves[12], you do shoot to kill[13]. Or am I mixing my[14] metaphors?'

'Don't you patronize me.[15] Don't you dare!' she shouted. 'Just who the hell do you think you are?'

'Your superior officer, for a start[16].'

'Oh, that's right, Inspector. Now's the time to pull rank[17]. Well, what shall I do? Shall I get to work in here? Don't *mind* if I'm not quite up to par[18]. I didn't *sleep* well last night.' She pulled a book angrily from the shelf. It toppled[19] to the floor. He could see she was struggling not to cry.

'Barbara...' She continued to pull books down, to turn the pages savagely, to drop them to the floor. They were mildewed and damp[20], filling the

1. allait crier tout ce qu'elle pouvait
2. vous blesser
3. simplement piqué ma curiosité
4. au septième ciel
5. un coup au hasard
6. il fit mouche
7. rayonna
8. ne vous regarde pas vraiment
9. doit avoir bien du mal à
10. être aussi performant que vous
11. Beau travail
12. ne prenez pas de gants
13. vous ne ratez pas votre cible
14. je mélange les
15. Épargnez-moi votre condescendance.
16. pour commencer
17. d'user de votre grade
18. pas très en forme
19. il tomba
20. moisis et humides

air with the unpleasant odour of neglect. '*Listen* to me. You've done good work so far. Don't be foolish now.'

She pivoted, trembling. 'What's *that* supposed to mean?'

'You have a chance to be back in CID. Don't throw it away because you're angry with me.'

'I'm not angry with you! I don't give a *shit* about you.[1]'

'Of course not. I didn't mean to imply that you did.[2]'

'We both know why I was assigned to you anyway. They wanted a woman on the case and they knew I was *safe*[3].' She spat the word out[4]. 'The minute this is over[5], I'm back on the street.'

'What are you talking about?'

'Come on, Inspector, I'm not stupid. I've looked in a few mirrors.'

He was astonished at the implication behind her words[6]. 'Do you think you've been brought back[7] to CID because Webberly believes I'd take any other female officer to bed[8]?' She didn't respond. 'Is that what you think?' he repeated. The silence continued. '*Dammit*[9], Havers—'

'It's what I know!' she shouted. 'But what Webberly doesn't know is that *any* blonde or brunette is safe with you these days, not just pigs[10] like me. It's redheads you've a taste for, redheads like Stepha, replacements for the one that you've lost.'

'That has *nothing* to do with this conversation!'

'It has everything to do with it! If you weren't so desperate to have Deborah back, you wouldn't have spent half the night pounding Stepha into pulp[11] and we wouldn't be having this whole bleeding discussion[12]!'

'Then, let's drop it, shall we? I've apologized. You've made your feelings and beliefs – bizarre

1. Je m'en fous, de vous.
2. Je n'ai pas voulu prétendre le contraire.
3. que moi, je ne risquais rien
4. avait articulé avec mépris
5. Dès que cette affaire sera bouclée
6. de ce que ses paroles impliquaient
7. qu'on vous a réintégrée
8. coucherais avec n'importe quel autre officier femme
9. Mais nom de Dieu
10. les mochetés
11. à vous acharner sur Stepha
12. cette discussion à la con

as they are – absolutely clear. I think we've said enough.'

'Oh, that's damned convenient to call *me* bizarre,' she cried bitterly. 'What about you? You won't marry[1] a woman because her father's in service[2], you watch your very own friend fall in love with her instead, you spend the rest of your life racked with misery over it[3], and then you decide to call *me* bizarre.'

'Your facts aren't quite straight[4],' he said icily.

'Oh, I've got all the facts I need. And when I string them together[5], *bizarre* is just the word I'd use to describe them. Fact one: you're in love with Deborah St James, and don't bother to deny it[6]. Fact two: she's married to someone else. Fact three: you obviously had a love affair[7] with her, which leads us inescapably to fact four: you *damn* well could have married her but you chose not to and you're going to pay for that stupid narrow-minded[8] upper-class[9] decision for the rest of your bleeding goddam life!'

'You seem to have a great deal of confidence in my fatal attraction for women. Any woman who sleeps with me is only too willing to[10] become my wife. Is that correct?'

'Don't you laugh at me!' she shrieked, her eyes squeezed shut in rage[11].

'I'm not laughing at you. I'm also not spending another moment[12] discussing this with you.' He started for[13] the door.

'Oh, that's it! Run away! That's just what I'd expect of you, Lynley! Go have it off with[14] Stepha again! Or what about Helen? Does she pop a red wig on[15] so you can get it up[16]? Does she let you call her *Deb*?'

He felt anger like a current shooting through[17] his veins. He drove himself towards calm[18] by looking at his watch. 'Havers, I'm going to Newby Wiske to see the results of St James' tests.

1. ne voulez pas épouser
2. est un domestique
3. malade de chagrin
4. Vos éléments ne correspondent pas tout à fait à la réalité
5. je les mets bout à bout
6. n'essayez pas de dire le contraire
7. une liaison
8. bornée
9. typique de la haute société
10. ne demande qu'à
11. fermant les yeux de rage
12. une minute de plus
13. se dirigea vers
14. Allez donc vous faire
15. se met une perruque rousse
16. pour vous faire bander
17. s'engouffrant dans
18. parvint à garder son calme

1. Ce qui vous laisse environ
2. susceptible de me conduire
3. un tel don
4. à partir de rien
5. cela ne devrait pas vous poser de problème
6. vous pourrez vous considérer comme virée
7. et en finir
8. savourer un plaisir d'avance
9. du A gravé
10. du côté visible
11. était encore en vie
12. à lui
13. le regarda partir, sidérée
14. admettant lentement
15. le châtier
16. dénigrer
17. l'avait emporté sur
18. un instant d'égarement

That gives you about[1] – shall we say – three hours to tear this house apart and find me something – *anything*, Havers – that leads me[2] to Gillian Teys. Since you have such a remarkable ability[3] to gather facts out of thin air[4], that should prove to be no problem whatsoever for you[5]. If, however, you have nothing to report within three hours, consider yourself sacked[6]. Is that clear?'

'Why not sack me right now and have done with it[7], then?' she shrilled.

'Because I like to look forward to my pleasures[8].' He walked over to her, took his cigarette case from her limp hand. 'Daze is a blonde,' he said.

She snorted. 'I find *that* hard to believe. Does she wear a red wig for those intimate moments?'

'I don't know.' He turned the cigarette case over in his hand so that the old ornate A engraved[9] on its cover was face up[10]. 'But it's an interesting question. If my father were still alive[11], I'd ask him. This was his[12]. Daze is my mother.' He picked up the volume of Shakespeare and left.

Barbara stared after him[13], motionless, waiting for the pounding of her blood to stop, slowly coming to terms with[14] the terrible enormity of what she had done.

You've done good work so far … You have a chance to be back in CID. Don't throw it away because you're angry with me.

And isn't that exactly what she had done? The need to rage at him, to castigate him[15], to rail against[16] his attraction to a beautiful woman had overcome[17] every good intention that she had ever possessed in setting to work on the case. What in God's name had come over her?

Was she jealous? Had there been one insane moment[18] when she had been so foolish as to think that Lynley might ever look at her and not see her for what she truly was: a plain, dumpy woman, angry at the world, bitter and friendless[1] and terribly alone? Had she possibly harboured a secret hope[2] that he might come to care for her[3]? Is that what had driven her to attack him this morning? The thought was patently[4] absurd.

It couldn't be. It wasn't possible. She knew enough about him not to be *that* ignorant.

She felt drained[5]. It was this house, she decided. It was having to come and work in this dwelling-place of ghouls[6]. Five minutes here and she was ready to snap and snarl[7], to climb the walls, to tear wildly at[8] her hair.

She went to the study door and looked across the sitting-room to Tessa's shrine. The woman smiled at her kindly. But wasn't there just a touch of victory[9] in her eyes? Wasn't it as if Tessa had known all along that she could do nothing but fail once she walked into this house and felt its silence and chill[10]?

Three hours, he'd said. Three hours to find the secret of Gillian Teys.

She laughed bitterly at the thought, tasting the sound in the empty air[11]. He knew that she would fail, that he would have the enjoyment[12] of sending her back to London, back to uniform, back to disgrace. So what was the point of[13] trying at all? Why not leave now rather than give him the pleasure?

She threw herself down on the sitting-room couch. Tessa's image watched her sympathetically. But… what if she could[14] find Gillian? What if, where Lynley himself had failed, she was able to succeed? Would it really matter then if he sent her back to the streets? Wouldn't she know, once and for all[15], that she was good for something, that she could have been part of a working team?

It was a thought. She picked idly at[16] the worn upholstery[17] of the couch. The sound of her fingers

1. amère et sans amis
2. nourri l'espoir secret
3. en venir à l'aimer
4. manifestement
5. à bout de forces
6. ce lieu macabre
7. aboyer et gronder
8. s'arracher violemment
9. un petit air victorieux
10. son atmosphère glaçante
11. et en apprécia le bruit dans le vide
12. plaisir
13. à quoi bon
14. et si elle était capable de
15. une bonne fois pour toutes
16. tirailla pensivement
17. le revêtement usé

1. qui frottaient sur les fils
2. le bruissement et le grattement des souris
3. aux marges
4. qui prend corps
5. le plus animé
6. s'était dispersée
7. il ne restait que les habitués
8. accoudés au
9. un demi à la main
10. plongeur
11. débattant à voix forte des
12. poulain de trois ans
13. sur lequel
14. de sa paie de la semaine
15. administra à son café
16. sa dose de sucre habituelle
17. cuillerée
18. écœurant
19. sucrer [=abuser] le diable lui-même [citation d'Hamlet]
20. pour me remettre
21. À charge de revanche
22. Plutôt deux fois qu'une.
23. s'est vidé de son sang
24. dont la lame faisait env. 13 cm

scratching at the threads[1] was the only noise in the house. Except for the rustling and burrowing of mice[2] at the edge[3] of her consciousness, like a half-formed[4] thought.

She looked at the stairway reflectively.

They sat at a table in the corner of the Keys and Candle, Newby Wiske's central and most thriving[5] pub. Most of the lunch-time crowd had thinned out[6] and, aside from themselves, only the regulars remained[7], hunched over the[8] bar to nurse pints of bitter[9].

They pushed their plates to one side of the table, and Deborah poured the coffee that had just been placed before them. Outside, the cook and the dishwasher[10] dumped rubbish into the bin, arguing loudly over the[11] merits of a three-year-old[12] who would be running at Newmarket and in whom[13] the cook had evidently invested a considerable sum of his most recent week's wages[14].

St James ministered to[15] his coffee with his usual amount of sugar[16]. Lynley spoke after the fourth teaspoonful[17] was dumped absently into the cup.

'Does he count?'

'Not that I've ever noticed,' Deborah replied.

'St James, that's appalling[18]. How can you stand it?'

'Just sugaring "o'er the devil himself[19]",' his friend replied. He pulled the test results towards him. 'I need to do something to recover[20] from the smell of that dog. You owe me for this one[21], Tommy.'

'In spades.[22] What do you have?'

'The animal bled to death[23] from a wound in the neck. It appeared to have been inflicted with a knife the blade of which was five inches[24] long.'

'Not a pocket-knife, then.'

'I should guess a kitchen knife. A butcher's knife. Something along that line[1]. Did forensics see to all the knives on the farm?'

Lynley fingered through the material from the file he had brought with him. 'Apparently. But the knife in question was nowhere to be found[2].'

St James looked thoughtful. 'That's intriguing. It almost suggests ...' He paused, brushing aside[3] the idea. 'Well, they have the girl admitting to killing her father, they have the axe sitting[4] right there on the floor—'

'With no fingerprints on it,' Lynley interjected.

'Given.[5] But unless the RSPCA wants to make a case[6] for cruelty to[7] animals, there's no real necessity to have the weapon that killed the dog.'

'You're starting to sound like Nies.'

'Perish the thought.[8]' St James stirred his coffee and was about to apply more sugar to it[9] when, with a beatific smile, his wife moved the bowl out of his reach[10]. He grumbled good-naturedly[11] and continued his conversation. 'However, there was something else. Barbiturates.[12]'

'What?'

'Barbiturates,' St James repeated. 'They showed up[13] in the drug screen[14]. Here.' He passed the toxicology report across the table.

Lynley read it, amazed. 'Are you telling me the dog was drugged?'

'Yes. The amount of residual drug that showed up in the tests indicates that the animal was unconscious when his throat was slit.'

'Unconscious!' Lynley scanned the report[15] and tossed it down on the table. 'Then, he couldn't have been killed to silence him.'

'Hardly.[16] He wouldn't have been making a sound.'

'Was there enough barbiturate to kill him? Had someone attempted to kill him with the drug and

1. de ce genre
2. n'a pas été retrouvé
3. écartant
4. posée
5. Accordé.
6. ne veuille monter un dossier
7. cruauté envers
8. J'espère bien que non.
9. y rajouter du sucre
10. mit le bol hors de portée
11. avec bienveillance
12. Des barbituriques.
13. sont apparus
14. au dépistage de substances
15. consulta le rapport
16. Certes non.

then, having botched it[1], decided to take a knife to the poor creature[2]?'

'That's possible, I suppose. Except that with everything you've told me about the case, it doesn't make much sense.'

'Why not?'

'Because this unknown person would have had to get into the house first, get the drug, administer it to the dog, wait for it to do the trick[3], realize that it wasn't going to kill him, go back for[4] a knife, and finish the job off[5]. What was the dog doing all this time? Co-operatively waiting to have his throat slit? Wouldn't he have been barking, raising the devil[6]?'

'Wait. You're too far ahead of me[7]. Why would the person have to go into the house for the drug?'

'Because it was the very same[8] drug that William Teys had taken, and he kept his sleeping pills in the house, not in the barn, I should think[9].'

Lynley assimilated this. 'Perhaps someone brought it with him.'

'Perhaps. I suppose the person could have administered it to the dog, waited for it to take effect, slit the dog's throat, and waited for Teys to come out to the barn.'

'Between ten and midnight? What would Teys be doing in the barn between ten and midnight?'

'Looking for the dog?'

'Why? Why the barn? Why not in the village where the dog always went? Why look for him at all, in fact? Everyone says that the dog wandered freely[10]. Why would he have suddenly been worried about him on this one night[11]?'

St James shrugged. 'What Teys was up to[12] is a moot point[13], if your attention is fixed on finding the killer of the animal. Only one person could have killed that dog – Roberta.'

1. comme ça avait raté
2. d'attaquer la pauvre bête au couteau
3. attendre qu'elle agisse
4. retourner chercher
5. finir le boulot
6. fait un raffut du diable
7. vas trop vite pour moi.
8. exactement la même
9. à mon avis
10. allait et venait en toute liberté
11. ce soir-là en particulier
12. Ce que mijotait Teys
13. secondaire

Outside the pub, St James spread the tent-like dress over the boot of Lynley's car, oblivious[1] of the curious stares[2] of a group of elderly[3] tourists who passed, in pursuit of pictorial souvenirs[4], cameras slung[5] round their necks. He pointed to[6] the stain on the inside elbow[7] of the left sleeve[8], to the pool-like stain[9] between waist and knees, and to the same substance on the right, white cuff[10].

'All of these test as the[11] dog's blood, Tommy.' He turned to his wife. 'My love, will you demonstrate? As you did in the lab? On this bit of lawn[12]?'

Deborah co-operatively[13] dropped to her knees[14], resting back on her heels[15]. Her rich, umber[16] dress billowed out[17] and spread on the ground like a mantle[18]. St James moved behind her.

'A willing[19] dog would make this easier to imagine, but we'll do our best. Roberta – who had access to her father's sleeping pills, I should guess – would have given the dog the drug earlier. In his dinner, perhaps. She would have had to make sure the animal stayed in the barn. It wouldn't have done[20] to have had the creature keel over[21] in the village somewhere. Once the dog was unconscious, she would kneel down[22] on the ground just as Deborah has done. Only that particular posture could give us the stains in the precise places they appear on her dress. She would lift[23] the dog's head and hold it in the crook of her arm[24].' He gently bent[25] Deborah's arm to demonstrate. 'Then, with her right hand, she would cut the dog's throat.'

'That's insane[26],' Lynley said hoarsely[27]. '*Why?*'

'Wait a moment, Tommy. The dog's head is turned away from her[28]. She drives[29] the knife into his throat, which results in the pool of blood on the skirt of her dress. She pulls the knife upward with her right hand until the job is done.' He pointed to specific areas on Deborah's dress. 'We have blood on the elbow where the head was cradled, blood on

1. sans prêter attention
2. aux regards curieux
3. âgés
4. en quête de souvenirs à photographier
5. suspendus
6. pointa du doigt
7. à l'intérieur du coude
8. manche gauche
9. la tache en forme de mare
10. poignet
11. D'après les tests, toutes proviennent du
12. ce coin de pelouse
13. coopérative,
14. s'accroupit
15. en gardant les talons au sol
16. ocre
17. se gonfla
18. une cape
19. qui serait bien disposé
20. Il ne fallait pas
21. que l'animal s'effondre
22. a dû s'agenouiller
23. a dû soulever
24. dans le creux du bras
25. plia doucement
26. complètement fou
27. la voix rauque
28. est tournée de l'autre côté
29. plonge

the skirt where it poured[1] from the neck, and blood on the right sleeve and cuff from where she drove the knife in and continued the path of the slash[2].' St James touched his wife's hair lightly. 'Thank you, my love.' He helped her to her feet[3].

Lynley walked back to the car and examined the dress. 'Frankly, it doesn't make a great deal of sense. Why on earth would she do it? Are you saying the girl dressed herself up on a Saturday night in her best Sunday clothes, calmly went out to the barn, and slit the throat of a dog she'd loved since childhood?' He looked up. '*Why?*'

'I can't answer that. I can't tell you what she was thinking, only what she had to have done[4].'

'But couldn't she have gone out to the barn, found the dog dead, and, in her panic, picked him up, cradled him, and got the blood all over herself then?'

There was a fractional pause[5]. 'Possibly. But unlikely.'

'But it's possible. It *is* possible?'

'Yes. But unlikely, Tommy.'

'What scenario do *you* have, then?'

Deborah and St James exchanged uneasy glances[6] in which Lynley saw that they had discussed the case and were of a mutual opinion they were reluctant to share[7]. 'Well?' he demanded. 'Are you saying that Roberta killed her dog, that her father came to the barn and discovered the deed[8], that they got into a tremendous row[9], and then she beheaded him[10]?'

'No, no. It's quite possible Roberta didn't kill her father at all. But she was definitely present[11] when it happened. She had to have been.[12]'

'Why?'

'Because his blood is all over the bottom of her dress[13].'

'Perhaps she went to the barn, found his body, and fell to her knees in shock.'

1. a coulé
2. elle a prolongé l'entaille
3. l'aida à se relever
4. ce qu'elle a dû faire
5. une pause infime
6. un regard gêné
7. qu'ils hésitaient à partager
8. son forfait
9. qu'ils se sont horriblement disputés
10. qu'ensuite elle l'a décapité
11. forcément là
12. C'est obligé.
13. recouvre le bas de sa robe

St James shook his head. 'That idea doesn't wash.[1]'

'Why not?'

He pointed to the garment on the back of the car. 'Look at the pattern[2]. Teys' blood is in splatters[3]. You know what that means as well as I. It only got there one way.[4]'

Lynley was silent for a moment. 'She was standing by[5] when it happened,' he concluded.

'She had to have been. If indeed she didn't do it herself, then she was standing right there[6] when someone else did.'

'Is she protecting someone, Tommy?' Deborah asked, seeing the expression on Lynley's face.

He didn't reply at once. He was thinking of patterns[7]: patterns of words, patterns of images, patterns of behaviour[8]. He was thinking of what a person learns, and when he learns it, and when it emerges into practical use[9]. He was thinking of knowledge and how it ultimately[10], inevitably combines with experience and points to what is incontrovertible truth[11].

He roused himself[12] to answer the question with one of his own[13]. 'St James, what would you do, how far would you go, to save Deborah?' It was a dangerous query[14]. Its risk was deadly. These were waters[15], perhaps, best left unexplored[16].

' "Forty thousand brothers"[17]? Is that where we are with it now?' St James' voice was unchanged, but the angles of his face were a warning[18], finely drawn and grim[19].

'How far would you go?' Lynley insisted.

'Tommy, don't!' Deborah put out her hand, a gesture to stop him from going any further, to stop him from doing irreparable damage to the delicate crystal of their friable[20] peace.

'Would you hold back the truth?[21] Would you lay down your life? How far would you go to save Deborah?'

1. Cette hypothèse n'est pas crédible
2. le dessin que ça fait
3. a fait comme des éclaboussures
4. Il n'y a qu'une seule explication.
5. se tenait à proximité
6. elle était présente
7. Il pensait aux modèles
8. de comportement
9. c'est mis en pratique
10. finalement
11. la vérité incontestable
12. se secoua
13. en en posant une autre
14. question
15. C'était un terrain où
16. il valait mieux ne pas s'aventurer
17. [... ne pourraient aimer Ophélie autant que moi, Hamlet]
18. valaient un avertissement
19. tirés et graves
20. fragile
21. Tu cacherais la vérité ?

1. ses quelques taches de rousseur
2. une lutte dans une tombe à Elseneur [entre Hamlet et Laërte, frère d'Ophélie]
3. essentielle
4. l'ampleur
5. Ne transformons pas
6. en suicide pur et simple
7. fouillé dans toutes ses cassettes
8. d'un peu plus tonifiant
9. par-dessus le vacarme
10. Imagine-les un peu
11. sautillant dans les bois
12. continuelle
13. convenait à son humeur
14. aussi accablé
15. d'aller au fond du problème
16. atavique
17. hydre [de Lerne]
18. tranchée impitoyablement
19. haineuse
20. la simple routine lui suffisait
21. pour parvenir au cœur du mal

St James looked at his wife. The colour had completely drained from her face; her sprinkling of freckles[1] danced across her nose; her eyes were haunted with tears. And he understood. This was no grappling in an Elsinore grave[2], but the question primeval[3].

'I'd do anything,' he replied, his eyes on his wife. 'By God, yes, I would. I'd do anything.'

Lynley nodded. 'People generally do, don't they, for the ones they love most.'

He chose Tchaikovsky: Symphony No. 6, *Pathétique*. He smiled as the swelling[4] of the first movement filled the car. Helen would never have allowed it.

'Darling Tommy, absolutely *not*! she would have protested. 'Let's not drive[5] our mutual depression right into suicide[6]!' Then she would have resolutely rooted through all of his tapes[7] to find something suitably uplifting[8]: invariably Strauss, played at full volume with Helen making her usual assortment of amusing remarks over the din[9]. 'Just picture them[10], Tommy, flitting through the woods[11] in their little tutus. It's positively religious!'

Today, however, the heavy theme of '*Pathétique*' with its relentless[12] exploration of man's spiritual suffering suited his mood[13]. He couldn't remember the last time he had felt so burdened[14] by a case. It felt as if a tremendous weight, having nothing whatsoever to do with the responsibility of getting to the bottom of the matter[15], were pressing upon his heart. He knew the source. Murder – its atavistic[16] nature and ineffable consequences – was a hydra[17]. Each head, ruthlessly cut off[18] in an effort to reach the 'prodigious dog-like body' of culpability, left in its place two heads more venomous[19] than the last. But unlike so many of his previous cases, in which mere rote sufficed[20] to see him sear his way to the core of evil[21] – stopping the flow of blood, allowing no further growth[1], and leaving him personally untouched by the encounter[2] – this case spoke to him far more intimately. He knew instinctively that the death of William Teys was merely one of the heads of the serpent[3], and the knowledge that eight others waited to do battle with him – and, more than that, that he had not even come to know the true nature of the evil he faced – filled him with a sense of trepidation[4]. But he knew himself well enough to know that there was more to[5] his desolation and despair than the death of a man in a Keldale barn.

There was Havers to be dealt with[6]. But beyond[7] Havers there was the truth. For underneath her bitter, unfounded accusations, her ugliness and hurt, the words she spoke rang with veracity[8]. Had he not indeed spent the last year of his life fruitlessly seeking[9] a replacement for Deborah? Not in the way Havers had suggested, but in a way far more dishonest[10] than an inconsequential coupling[11] in which two bodies meet, experience momentary pleasure[12], and separate to lead their individual lives[13], untouched and unchanged by the encounter. That, at least, was an expression of some sort[14], a giving of the moment[15] no matter how brief[16]. But for the last year of his life he had given nothing to anyone.

Behind his behaviour, wasn't the reality that he had maintained his isolated celibacy[17] this last, long year not because of Deborah but because he had become high priest in a religion of one[18]: a celebrant[19] caught up in devotion to[20] the past? In this twisted[21] religion, he had held up[22] every woman in his life to unforgiving scrutiny[23] and had found each one wanting[24] in comparison to Deborah, not the real Deborah but a mystical goddess[25] who lived only in his mind.

He saw now that he had not wished to forget the past, that he had done everything instead to keep it

1. empêchant tout nouveau développement
2. s'en sortant indemne
3. [l'hydre]
4. d'inquiétude
5. qu'il n'y avait pas que
6. dont il fallait qu'il s'occupe
7. au-delà de
8. avaient l'accent de la vérité
9. à rechercher vainement
10. malhonnête
11. accouplement sans importance
12. prennent un plaisir fugace
13. pour reprendre leur vie respective
14. cela exprimait quelque chose
15. le don du moment présent
16. même si c'était bref
17. célibat solitaire
18. le grand prêtre d'un dieu unique
19. un officiant
20. célébrant
21. fausse
22. soumis
23. à un examen implacable
24. médiocre
25. une déesse mystique

alive, as if his intention had always been to make it, not Deborah, his bride. He was sick at heart.

With the sickness came the realization that there were facts to be faced about Stepha as well. But he could not bring himself to them[1]. Not yet.

As the final movement of the symphony came to a close[2], he turned down the winding[3] road from the moors into Keldale. Autumn leaves flew from under the car's wheels, leaving a cloud of red, gold, and yellow billowing[4] behind him, promising winter[5]. He pulled up in front of the lodge and spent a moment gazing at the windows, numbly wondering[6] how and when he was going to piece together the fragments[7] of his life.

Havers must have been watching for him[8] from the lounge, for she came to the door as soon as he switched off the car's ignition[9]. He groaned and steeled himself to[10] another confrontation, but she gave him no chance[11] to make preliminary remarks.

'I've found Gillian,' she announced.

1. ne pouvait s'y résoudre
2. arrivait à son terme
3. en lacets
4. tourbillonnant
5. annonciateur de l'hiver
6. se demandant, hébété
7. recoller les morceaux
8. le guetter
9. coupa le contact de la voiture
10. se raidit en prévision d'
11. ne lui laissa pas le temps

13

She had somehow survived the morning. The dreadful row[1] with Lynley followed by the horrors of Roberta's bedroom had served to wear down[2] her anger and wretchedness[3], abrading them both[4] into a dull detachment[5]. She knew he was going to sack her anyway. She certainly deserved it. But, before he did, she would prove to him that she could be a decent[6] DS. In order to do that, however, there was this one last meeting to get through[7], this one last[8] opportunity to show her stuff[9].

She watched Lynley's eyes roam over[10] the unusual collection of items[11] spread out on one of the tables in the lounge: the album containing the defaced family pictures[12], a dog-eared and well-thumbed[13] novel, the photograph from Roberta's chest of drawers, the additional one of the two sisters, and a collection of six yellowed newspaper pages[14], all folded and shaped to the identical size[15], seventeen by twenty-two inches[16].

Lynley absently felt[17] in his pocket for his cigarettes, lit one[18], and sat down on the couch. 'What is this, Sergeant?' he asked.

'I think these are the facts on Gillian,' she responded. Her voice was carefully modulated, but a slight quaver[19] in it caught his attention. She cleared her throat to hide it.

1. dispute
2. permis de calmer
3. sa tristesse
4. les réduisant
5. à une morne indifférence
6. correcte
7. il fallait supporter de le voir une dernière fois
8. toute dernière
9. de quoi elle était capable
10. parcourir
11. objets
12. les photos de famille défigurées
13. corné, lu et relu
14. pages de journal jaunies
15. pliées en un même format
16. env. 43 cm x 55 cm
17. chercha machinalement
18. en alluma une
19. un léger chevrotement

'You're going to need to enlighten me[1], I'm afraid,' he said. 'Cigarette?'

Her fingers itched to feel[2] the cylinder of tobacco; her body ached for[3] the soothing smoke[4]. But she knew, if she lit one, it would betray her shaking hands[5]. 'No, thank you,' she replied. She took a breath, kept her eyes on his noncommittal[6] face, and went on. 'How does your man Denton line your chest of drawers?'

'With some sort of paper, I should guess. I've never noticed.'

'But it isn't newspaper, is it?' She sat down opposite him, squeezing her hands into fists in her lap[7], feeling the sharp crescent pain[8] of nails biting palms[9]. 'It wouldn't be, because the newsprint would come off[10] on your clothes.'

'True.'

'So I was intrigued when you mentioned that Roberta had lined the drawers with newspapers. And I remembered Stepha saying that Roberta used to come every day for[11] the *Guardian*.'

'Until Paul Odell died. Then she stopped.'

Barbara pushed her hair back behind her ears. It was quite unimportant, she told herself, if he didn't believe her, if he laughed at the conclusions she had drawn[12] after nearly three hours in that horrible room. 'Except that I don't think the reason she stopped coming for the *Guardian* had anything to do with Paul Odell. I think it was Gillian.'

His eyes drifted to the newspapers and Barbara saw him take in[13] what she herself had noticed: that Roberta had lined the drawers with the classified section[14]. Moreover, although there were six pieces of newspaper on the table, they were duplicates of only two pages of the *Guardian*, as if something memorable[15] had appeared in a single issue[16], and Roberta had collected that day's edition[17] from the villagers to keep as souvenirs.

1. Il va falloir éclairer ma chandelle
2. Ça la démangeait de toucher
3. réclamait
4. l'apaisement que procure la fumée
5. trahirait le tremblement de ses mains
6. impassible
7. les poings serrés sur ses genoux
8. l'empreinte douloureuse
9. des ongles enfoncés dans les paumes
10. l'encre déteindrait
11. prendre
12. qu'elle avait tirées
13. qu'il était en train de voir
14. petites annonces
15. d'extraordinaire
16. dans un seul numéro
17. récupéré l'édition de ce jour-là

'The personal column[1],' Lynley murmured. 'By God, Havers, Gillian sent her a message.'

Barbara pulled one of the sheets towards her and ran her finger down the column. ' "R. Look at the advert.[2] G," ' she read. 'I think that's the message.'

'Look at the advertisement[3]? What advertisement?'

She reached for a representation[4] of the second saved[5] page. 'This one, I think.'

He read it. Dated nearly four years previously[6], it was a small, square announcement of[7] a meeting in Harrogate, a panel discussion[8] involving a group from an organization called Testament House. The members of the panel[9] were listed, but Gillian Teys was not among them. Lynley looked up, his brown eyes frankly quizzical[10].

'You've lost me[11], Sergeant.'

Her eyebrows lifted in surprise. 'Aren't you familiar with Testament House? Never mind, I keep forgetting that you haven't been in uniform in years[12]. Testament House is run[13] out of[14] Fitzroy Square by an Anglican priest[15]. He used to teach at university but evidently one day one of his students asked him why he wasn't bothering to practise[16] what he preached[17] – feeding the hungry and clothing the naked[18] – and he decided that was something in his life that he ought to address[19]. So he started Testament House.'

'Which is?'

'An organization that collects runaways[20]. Teenaged prostitutes – both male and female – drug abusers[21] of every colour and shape, and everyone else under the age of twenty-one who's hanging about aimlessly[22] in Trafalgar Square or Piccadilly or in any of the stations just waiting to be preyed on[23] by a pimp[24] or a whore. He's been doing it for years. The uniformed police all know him. We always took kids to him.'

1. La rubrique des messages personnels
2. Regarde la pub.
3. publicité
4. un exemplaire
5. conservée
6. Datant de presque 4 ans
7. encart annonçant
8. réunion-débat
9. participants
10. franchement perplexes
11. Je ne vous suis pas
12. depuis des années
13. dirigée
14. à
15. prêtre anglican
16. mettre en pratique
17. prêchait
18. nourrir ceux qui ont faim et vêtir ceux qui sont nus
19. auquel il devait s'atteler
20. qui recueille les fugueurs
21. les drogués
22. traînant sans but
23. à la merci
24. d'un souteneur

'He's the Reverend George Clarence that's listed here, I take it?'

She nodded. 'He goes out on fund-raising tours[1] for the organization.'

'Do I understand you to mean[2] that you believe Gillian Teys was picked up[3] by this group in London?'

'I ... Yes, I do.'

'Why?'

It had taken her ages[4] to find the advertisement, ages longer to decipher its significance[5], and now everything – most especially her career, she admitted – depended upon Lynley's willingness to believe[6]. 'Because of this name.' She pointed to the third on the list of panellists[7].

'Nell Graham?'

'Yes.'

'I'm completely in the dark.[8]'

'I think *Nell Graham* was the message Roberta was waiting for. She faithfully searched[9] the paper each day for years, waiting to see what had happened to her sister. *Nell Graham* told her. It meant Gillian had survived.'

'Why Nell Graham? Why not' – he glanced at the other names – 'Terence Hanover, Caroline Paulson, or Margaret Crist?'

Havers picked up the battered novel from the table. 'Because none of those were born of one of the Brontës[10].' She tapped the book. '*The Tenant of Wildfell Hall*[11] is about Helen Huntington, a woman who breaks the social code[12] of her time and leaves her alcoholic husband to start a new life. She falls in love with a man who knows nothing about her past, who knows only the name she has chosen for herself[13]: Helen Graham, *Nell* Graham, Inspector.' She finished and waited in agony[14] for his response[15].

When it came, nothing could have surprised her more, could have disarmed her more quickly. '*Bravo*,

1. en tournée pour lever des fonds
2. Dois-je comprendre
3. a été recueillie
4. une éternité
5. pour en déchiffrer le sens
6. veuille bien la croire
7. des participants
8. Je ne vois pas du tout.
9. Elle a fidèlement examiné
10. n'a été créé par une des Brontë
11. [La Recluse de Wildfell Hall, par Anne Brontë]
12. qui rompt avec les codes
13. qu'elle s'est choisi
14. torturée d'angoisse
15. sa réaction

Barbara,' he said softly, his eyes lit[1] and a smile breaking over[2] his face. He leaned forward earnestly.[3] 'What's your theory on how she came to be involved with this group?'

The relief was so tremendous[4] that Barbara found she had begun trembling from head to toe[5]. She took a ragged breath[6] and somehow found her voice[7]. 'My … I suspect that Gillian had enough money to get to London but that it ran out fairly soon[8]. They may have picked her up off the street[9] somewhere or in one of the stations.'

'But wouldn't they return her to her father?'

'That's not how Testament House works[10]. They encourage the kids to go home or at least to phone their parents and let them know they're all right, but no one is forced to do it. If they choose to stay at Testament, they just have to obey the rules[11]. No questions asked.[12]'

'But Gillian left home at sixteen. If she is Nell Graham, she would have been twenty-three when she was on this panel in Harrogate. Does it make sense that she would have stayed with Testament House for all those years?'

'If she had no one else, it makes perfect sense[13]. If she wanted a family, they were her best bet[14]. At any rate[15], there's only one way we can know for sure[16]—'

'Talk to her,' he finished promptly. He got to his feet. 'Get your things together.[17] We'll leave in ten minutes.' He rooted through[18] the file and took out the photograph of Russell Mowrey and his family. 'Give this to Webberly when you get to London,' he said as he scribbled[19] a message on the back.

'When I get to London?' Her heart sank.[20] He was giving her the sack, then. He'd as much as promised that[21] after their encounter at the farm. It was, indeed, all she could expect.

1. le regard lumineux
2. apparaissant sur
3. Il se pencha avec intérêt.
4. Son soulagement fut si énorme
5. de la tête aux pieds
6. Elle reprit son souffle à grand peine
7. parvint à retrouver sa voix
8. qu'elle en a manqué assez vite
9. dans la rue
10. fonctionne
11. en observer les règles
12. On ne pose pas de questions.
13. c'est tout à fait plausible
14. ils représentaient la meilleure solution
15. De toute façon
16. de nous en assurer
17. Faites vos bagages.
18. fouilla dans
19. en griffonnant
20. Elle eut le cœur lourd.
21. Il l'avait plus ou moins promis

Lynley looked up, all business. 'You found her, Sergeant. You can bring her back to Keldale. I think Gillian's the only way we're going to get through to[1] Roberta. Don't you agree?'

'I … What about …?' She stopped herself, afraid to believe the meaning behind his words. 'You don't want to phone Webberly? Have someone else …? Go there yourself?'

'I've too many things to see to[2] here. You can see to Gillian. If Nell Graham *is* Gillian. Hurry up. We've got to get to York so you can catch the train.'

'But … how should I? What approach should I use? Should I simply—?'

He waved her off. 'I trust[3] your judgement, Sergeant. Just bring her back as quickly as you can.'

She unclenched[4] her hands, aware of the numbing relief sweeping over her. 'Yes, sir,' she heard her voice whisper[5].

He tapped his fingers against the steering wheel[6] and regarded the house cresting[7] its smooth slope of lawn[8]. By driving like the devil[9], he had managed to get Havers on the three o'clock train[10] for London and now he sat in front of the Mowrey home, trying to decide how best to approach the woman inside. Wasn't the truth, after all, better than the silence? Had he not at least learned that?

She met him at the door. The wary glance that she cast back over her shoulder[11] told him he was far less welcome than when they had previously met[12]. 'My children are just home from school,' she said in explanation and stepped outside, pulling the door shut behind her. She drew her cardigan firmly round her slender body[13]. It was like the body of a child. 'Have you … Is there word about[14] Russell?'

He reminded himself that he couldn't have expected her to ask about her daughter. Tessa, of all people, had said goodbye to the past[15], had made a

1. d'atteindre
2. à gérer
3. fais confiance à
4. desserra
5. s'entendit-elle murmurer
6. le volant
7. surplombant
8. la pelouse en pente douce
9. En roulant comme un dératé
10. mettre Havers au train de 15 h
11. lança par-dessus son épaule
12. qu'à leur précédente rencontre
13. autour de son corps menu
14. Avez-vous des nouvelles de
15. Si quelqu'un avait dit adieu à son passé, c'était bien Tessa

surgical cut[1] and walked away cleanly[2]. 'You need to involve the police, Mrs Mowrey.'

She paled. 'He couldn't. He didn't.'

'You must telephone the police.'

'I can't. I *can't*,' she whispered fiercely[3].

'He's not with his relatives[4] in London, is he?' She shook her head briefly, once, and kept her face averted[5]. 'Have they heard from him at all?[6]' Again, the same response. 'Then, isn't it best to find out where he is?' When she didn't reply, he took her arm and led her gently towards the drive[7]. 'Why did William keep all those keys?'

'What keys?'

'There was a box of them on the shelf in his wardrobe[8]. But there are no keys anywhere in the rest of the house. Do you know why?'

She bent her head, put a hand to her brow[9]. 'Those. I'd forgotten,' she murmured. 'I … It was because of Gillian's tantrum[10].'

'When was this?'

'She must have been seven. No, she was nearly eight. I remember because I was pregnant with[11] Roberta. It was one of those situations that come up out of nowhere[12] and are blown out of all proportion[13], the kind that families laugh about later when the children are grown[14]. I remember William said at dinner, "Gilly, we'll read from the Bible tonight." I was sitting there – daydreaming[15] probably – and expected her to say, "Yes, Papa," as she always did. But she decided that she wouldn't read the Bible that night, and William decided just as definitely[16] that she would. She became absolutely hysterical about it[17], ran to her room and locked the door.'

'And then?'

'Gilly had never disobeyed her father before. Poor William simply sat there, astonished[18]. He didn't seem to know how to handle it.[19]'

'What did you do?'

1. qui avait fait une coupure bien nette
2. disparu complètement
3. farouchement
4. chez des parents à lui
5. le visage toujours tourné de l'autre côté
6. Ont-ils eu de ses nouvelles ?
7. l'allée
8. sur l'étagère de son armoire
9. porta la main à son front
10. esclandre
11. enceinte de
12. venues d'on ne sait où
13. qui dégénèrent
14. ont grandi
15. en train de rêvasser
16. tout aussi catégorique,
17. Cela l'a rendue totalement hystérique
18. stupéfait
19. Il n'avait pas l'air de savoir quoi faire.

'Nothing that helped particularly, as I recall. I went to Gilly's room, but she wouldn't let me in. She'd only scream that she wouldn't read the Bible any longer and that no one could make her[1]. Then she threw things at the door. I ... I went back down to William.' She looked at Lynley with an expression that combined both perplexity and admiration as she went on[2]. 'You know, William never scolded her[3]. That wasn't his way. But he later took the keys[4] from all the doors. He said if the house had burned down[5] that night and he hadn't been able to get to[6] Gilly because she'd locked her door, he would never have forgiven himself.'

'Did they go back to reading[7] the Bible after that?'

She shook her head. 'He never asked Gilly to read the Bible after that.'

'Did he read it with you?'

'No. Just alone.'

A girl had come to the door as they spoke, a piece of bread in her hand and a thin line of jam[8] traced across her upper lip[9]. She was small like her mother but with her father's dark hair and intelligent eyes. She watched them curiously.

'Mummy,' she called. Her voice was sweet and clear[10]. 'Is anything wrong? Is it Daddy?'

'No, darling,' Tessa called back hastily[11]. 'I'll be in[12] in a moment.' She turned to Lynley.

'How well did you know[13] Richard Gibson?' he asked her.

'William's nephew? As well as anyone could have known Richard, I suppose. He was a quiet[14] boy but immensely likeable[15], with a wonderful sense of humour, as I recall. Gilly quite adored him. Why do you ask?'

'Because William left the farm to him[16], not to Roberta.'

Her brow furrowed.[17] 'But why not to Gilly?'

1. personne ne l'y forcerait
2. tandis qu'elle poursuivait
3. il ne la grondait jamais
4. ensuite, il a retiré les clés
5. brûlé
6. entrer chez
7. Ont-ils repris la lecture de
8. trace de confiture
9. sur la lèvre supérieure
10. douce et claire
11. répondit précipitamment
12. J'arrive
13. Vous connaissiez bien
14. tranquille
15. adorable
16. lui a légué la ferme
17. Elle fronça les sourcils.

'Gillian ran away from home when she was sixteen, Mrs Mowrey. No one ever heard from her again.'

Tessa drew in a breath[1]. It was sharp and quick, like the reaction to an unexpected blow[2]. Her eyes fixed themselves on Lynley.

'No,' she said. It was not so much denial as disbelief[3].

He continued. 'Richard had been gone for a time as well. To the fens. There's a chance[4] that Gillian followed him there and then perhaps went on to London.'

'But why? Whatever happened? What could have happened?'

He considered how much to tell her[5]. 'I've got the impression,' he said, spacing[6] the words delicately, 'that she was involved with Richard somehow[7].'

'And William found out? If that's the case, he would have torn Richard limb from limb[8].'

'Suppose he did find out and Richard knew what his reaction would be. Would that be enough for Richard to leave the village?'

'I should think so.[9] But it doesn't explain why William left the farm to him and not to Roberta, does it?'

'It was apparently a bargain he'd struck[10] with Gibson. Roberta would continue to live there for her lifetime[11] with Richard and his family, but the land would go to the Gibsons.'

'But certainly Roberta would marry some day. It hardly seems fair.[12] Surely William would have wanted the land to remain in the immediate family, to be passed on[13] to his grandchildren – if not to Gilly's children, then to Roberta's.'

Even as she spoke[14], Lynley realized[15] what a vast chasm[16] the nineteen years of her absence had caused[17]. She knew nothing of Roberta, nothing of the girl's hidden storehouse of food[18], nothing

1. eut un han de surprise
2. un choc inattendu
3. plus de l'incrédulité que du déni
4. Il se peut
5. jusqu'où il pouvait aller
6. en détachant
7. qu'elle avait plus ou moins une liaison avec Richard
8. taillé Richard en pièces
9. Plutôt, oui.
10. un marché qu'il avait conclu
11. toute sa vie
12. Cela ne semble pas très juste
13. qu'elle soit transmise
14. En l'écoutant
15. prit conscience de
16. l'ampleur de l'abîme
17. créé
18. garde-manger

of her vacant, rocking catatonia[1]. Roberta was just a name to her mother, a name who would marry, have children, grow old. She was not at all real. She did not actually exist[2].

'Did you never think about them?' he asked her. She looked down at her feet, employing in the act[3] an intensity that suggested all of her concentration was centred on the smooth, rusty suede[4] of her shoes. When she didn't reply, he persisted. 'Did you never wonder how they were[5], Mrs Mowrey? Did you never imagine what they looked like or how they'd grown up?'

She shook her head once, sharply[6]. And when she answered him at last, in a voice so controlled that it spoke volumes[7] on the emotion she had spent on the subject[8], she kept her eyes on the minster in the distance. 'I couldn't let myself do that, Inspector. I knew they were safe. I knew they were well. So I let them die. I had to[9] if I wanted to survive. Can you understand?'

A few days ago, he would have said no. And that would have been the truth of the matter[10]. But that was not the case now. 'Yes,' he replied. 'I do understand.' He nodded to her in farewell[11] and walked back to his car.

'Inspector...' He turned, his hand on the door handle. 'You know where Russell is, don't you?'

She read the answer in his face, but she listened instead to the lie[12]. 'No,' he responded.

Ezra Farmington lived directly across from the[13] Dove and Whistle in the council house that abutted against[14] Marsha Fitzalan's. Like hers, its front garden was planted and cared for, but with less detailed concern[15], as if the man had started out with the best of intentions, but they, along with the plants[16], had become the worse for wear[17]. Bushes were thriving[18] but overgrown[19], weeds were

1. son air absent et de son balancement catatonique
2. n'existait pas vraiment
3. y mettant
4. le daim couleur rouille
5. comment elles allaient
6. sèchement
7. ça en disait long
8. que tout ça lui avait coûté
9. Il le fallait
10. la simple vérité
11. prit congé d'un hochement de tête
12. préféra entendre le mensonge
13. juste en face du
14. jouxtant
15. avec moins de minutie
16. tout comme les plantes, ces bonnes intentions
17. dépéri
18. Les arbustes étaient florissants
19. non taillés

assaulting[1] the flower beds[2], dead annuals[3] needed to be uprooted and discarded[4], and a small patch of lawn was looking long enough to be considered a potential source of fodder[5].

Farmington was not at all pleased to see him. He opened the door to Lynley's knock and placed his body squarely[6] in the frame[7]. Over his shoulder Lynley saw that the other man had been going through his work, for dozens of watercolours were spread upon the sitting-room couch and scattered on the floor. Some were torn into shreds, others were crumpled into tight, angry balls[8], still others[9] were abandoned to meet their fate under foot[10]. It was a haphazard purging[11] of artistic effort, however, because the artist himself was more than halfway drunk[12].

'Inspector?' Farmington asked with deliberate politeness.

'May I come in?'

The man shrugged. 'Why not?' He opened the door wider and gestured Lynley inside with a lackadaisical sweep[13]. ' 'Scuse the mess. Just cleaning out the crap.'

Lynley stepped over several paintings. 'From four years ago?' he asked blandly.

It was the right choice of time. Farmington's face told him so in the sudden flare of nostrils[14] and the movement of lips.

'What's that s'posed to mean?' He was just on the edge of slurring his words[15], and, perhaps noticing this himself, he sought control visibly.

'What time was it when you and William Teys argued[16]?' Lynley asked, ignoring the man's question.

'Time?' Ezra shrugged. 'No idea. Drink, Ins … Inspector?' He smiled glassily[17] and stiffly[18] crossed the room to pour himself a tumbler[19] of gin. 'No? You don't mind if I …? Thank you.' He gulped back a mouthful[20], coughed, and laughed, swiping at[21]

1. les mauvaises herbes envahissaient
2. plates-bandes
3. des plantes annuelles, mortes,
4. retirées et jetées
5. envisager d'en faire du fourrage
6. fermement
7. dans l'encadrement
8. froissées et comprimées en boules sous la colère
9. d'autres encore
10. prêtes à être piétinées
11. une purge aléatoire
12. plus qu'à moitié saoul
13. d'un grand geste indolent
14. la dilatation soudaine de ses narines
15. commençait à avoir du mal à articuler
16. vous êtes disputés
17. l'œil vitreux
18. avec raideur
19. un verre
20. en avala une bonne gorgée
21. frappant

his mouth so savagely with his wrist that the movement was as good as a blow[1]. 'Pulin' wimp[2]. Can' even handle a drink.'

'You were coming down from High Kel Moor. That's not a walk you would make in the dark, is it?'

' 'Course not.'

'And you heard music from the farmhouse?'

'Ha!' He waved his glass[3] at Lynley. 'Whole screamin' *band*[4]. In ... spector. Thought I was in the middle of a flipping[5] parade.'

'Did you see only Teys? No one else?'

'Are we counting sweet Nigel bringing the doggie[6] home?'

'Aside from Nigel.'

'Nope.[7]' He lifted his glass and drained it. 'Course, Roberta was proba'ly inside the house changing the records[8], poor fat slob[9]. She wasn't much good for anything else. 'Cept[10]' – his bleary eyes twinkled[11] – 'swinging an axe[12] and sending Papa into the great beyond[13].' He laughed at his comment. 'Like Lizzie Borden[14]!' he added and laughed louder still.

Lynley wondered why the man was being deliberately repugnant, wondered what was motivating him to go to such great lengths[15] to develop and then display a side of his character[16] so ugly as to be[17] intolerable. Hatred and anger were the foundation here and a contempt so virulent that it was like a third person in the room. Farmington was obviously a talented man and yet a man blindly bent upon[18] destroying the single creative force that gave his life meaning[19].

As he clutched at himself with callous nonchalance[20] and stumbled in the direction of the lavatory, Lynley looked at the paintings he left behind and saw the source of the man's despair in the studies the artist could not bring himself to[21] destroy.

They were done from every possible angle, in charcoal[22], pencil, pastels, and paint. They

1. quasiment un coup de poing
2. Mauviette
3. agita son verre
4. Toute une satanée fanfare
5. putain de
6. ramenant le chienchien
7. Nan.
8. occupée à changer les disques
9. cette pauvre grosse souillon
10. Sauf
11. ses yeux troubles brillèrent
12. pour balancer sa hache
13. dans l'au-delà
14. [accusée de double meurtre à la hache, États-Unis, 1892]
15. se donner tant de mal
16. dévoiler une facette
17. hideuse au point d'être
18. qui s'acharnait aveuglément
19. donnant du sens à sa vie
20. avec nonchalance, l'air dur
21. se résoudre à
22. au fusain

chronicled[1] movement, passion, and desire, and bore witness to the anguish[2] of the artist's soul. They were all of Stepha Odell.

When Lynley heard the man's returning footsteps, he forced his eyes[3] from the work and his mind away from the implication[4]. Instead, he made himself look at Farmington and in doing so he saw the other man clearly for the first time: womanizer[5] and hypocrite, using past pain as an excuse for present behaviour. He saw that Farmington was at best his own mirror image, his second self, the man, indeed, he could choose to become.

From King's Cross Station, Barbara took the Northern Line to Warren Street. Fitzroy Square was only a few minutes' walk[6] from there. She spent that time meditating on a plan of attack. It was clear that Gillian Teys was involved in this situation up to her neck[7], but that was going to be extremely difficult to prove. If she was smart enough[8] to disappear from sight[9] for eleven years, certainly she was smart enough to have a cast-iron alibi[10] for the night in question. It seemed to Barbara that the best approach – if indeed Gillian was Nell Graham and if she could be located[11] using the scant information[12] they had – was to give her no choice, arrest her if necessary, in order to get her back to Keldale that night. She thought about everything that had been said about Gillian: about her delinquent behaviour, her sexual licence[13], and her ability to hide both under an exterior of angelic refinement[14]. There was only one way to deal with someone that[15] clever. Be tough, be aggressive, be absolutely ruthless[16].

Fitzroy Square – a tidily renovated patch[17] of Euston – was an unusual spot to find a home for stray teenagers[18]. Twenty years before, when the square had still been a post-war[19] rectangle of sagging[20] buildings, grubby pavements[21], and empty window-

1. contaient
2. témoignaient de l'angoisse
3. se força à détourner les yeux
4. à ne pas penser à ce que cela impliquait
5. coureur de jupons
6. à quelques minutes de marche
7. impliquée jusqu'au cou
8. assez intelligente
9. de la circulation
10. un alibi en béton
11. si elle pouvait la localiser
12. le peu d'information
13. débauche
14. un abord angélique et raffiné
15. d'aussi
16. sans pitié
17. un îlot soigneusement rénové
18. un foyer pour adolescents fugueurs
19. d'après-guerre
20. affaissés
21. de trottoirs sordides

boxes[1], a home for the flotsam and jetsam[2] of London life would be what one would expect to find. But now, when the entire face[3] of the square was crisp and new[4], when the lovely green[5] in the centre was carefully fenced off against vagrants[6], when every building was freshly painted and every burnished door gleamed[7] in the fading light of the day, it was hard to believe that society's forgotten and unwanted[8], frightened and pained still lived here.

Number 11 was the home of Testament House, a Georgian building, its front covered with scaffolding[9]. A rubbish bin overflowing with[10] plaster, empty paint tins, cardboard cartons, and tarpaulins[11] gave evidence to the fact that Testament House was joining its neighbours in an architectural renaissance. The front door stood open, and from within came the sound of music, not the rowdy[12] rock-and-roll one might have expected from a gathering place for runaway teenagers, but the delicate strains[13] of classical guitar and the kind of quiet that spoke of an audience[14] held spellbound[15]. However, those on this week's kitchen duty[16] were not taking part in the recital above stairs, Barbara guessed, for even outside the air was rich with the aroma of tomato sauce and spices, sure indication of the evening's fare[17].

She walked up the two steps and entered the building. The long hallway was covered with an old red runner[18], worn so thin[19] in places[20] that the wood of the floor beneath showed through[21]. Walls were bare of decoration[22] save bulletin boards[23] that held employment information, messages received, and announcements posted[24]. A table of classes[25] at the university on Gower Street was given the most prominent position[26], with large cardboard arrows[27] pointing to it encouragingly. Nearby clinics, drug programmes, and Family Planning offices[28] were advertised for inhabitants[29], and the

1. de rebords de fenêtres nus
2. un refuge pour toutes les épaves
3. toute la physionomie
4. flambant neuve
5. espace vert
6. clôturé pour dissuader les clochards
7. les portes lustrées miroitaient
8. les laissés-pour-compte
9. d'échafaudages
10. débordant de
11. de bâches
12. bruyant
13. les accords délicats
14. auditoire
15. captivé
16. de service à la cuisine
17. menu
18. tapis de couloir
19. si élimé
20. par endroits
21. se voyait au travers
22. nus
23. à part des panneaux d'affichage
24. des affichettes
25. Une liste de cours
26. placée le plus en évidence
27. flèches en carton
28. centres de planning familial
29. pour les résidents

telephone number of a suicide hotline was printed repeatedly on tear-off sheets[1] at the bottom of the board. Most of them, Barbara noted, were gone.

'Hello,' a voice called cheerfully. 'Need some help?'

Barbara turned to find a plump middle-aged woman leaning over the reception counter, pushing a pair of hornrimmed[2] spectacles[3] to the top of her clipped[4] grey hair. Her smile was welcoming, but it faded immediately when her eyes fell upon the warrant card[5] that Barbara produced. Above them, the intricate[6] music continued.

'Is there some sort of trouble?' the woman asked. 'I suppose you want Mr Clarence.'

'No,' Barbara replied.' That may not be necessary. I'm looking for this young woman. Her name is Gillian Teys, but we think she may be using the name Nell Graham.' She handed over the photograph, a gesture she knew would be unnecessary, for the moment she[7] had said the name the other woman' s expression had altered and revealed[8].

None the less, she looked at the photograph cooperatively. 'Yes, this is Nell,' she said.

In spite of having been so certain, Barbara felt a surge of triumph[9]. 'Can you tell me how to locate her? It's quite important that I find her as soon as possible.'

'She's not in trouble, is she?'

'It's important that I find her,' Barbara said again.

'Oh, yes, of course. I suppose you can't tell me. It's only that ...' The woman fingered her chin nervously. 'Let me get Jonah,' she said impulsively. 'This is his concern.[10]'

Before Barbara could reply, the woman was running up the stairs. In a moment the guitar music stopped abruptly to a storm of protesting voices[11] and then laughter. That was followed by the sound of footsteps. The hushed voice[12] of the receptionist was met by a man's response[13].

1. des feuillets détachables
2. à monture d'écaille
3. lunettes
4. coupés court
5. son regard se posa sur la carte de police
6. élaborée
7. dès qu'elle
8. changé et l'avait trahie
9. triompha intérieurement
10. Cela le concerne.
11. sous un torrent de protestations
12. Au chuchotement
13. répondit une voix masculine

When he came into sight on the stairway, Barbara saw that he was the musician, for he carried a fine guitar over his shoulder. He was far too young to be the Reverend George Clarence, but he wore clerical garb[1] and his marked resemblance to the founder[2] of Testament House indicated to Barbara that this must be the man's son. For here were the same chiselled[3] features, the same broad expanse of forehead[4], the same quick glance that assimilated and evaluated within an instant[5]. Even his hair was the same, parted on the left[6], with an unruly tuft[7] that no comb could discipline. He was not a big man, probably no more than five feet eight inches tall[8], and his build was slight[9]. But there was something about the way he held his body that indicated the presence of an inner core of strength[10] and self-confidence[11].

He strode down the hall and extended his hand. 'Jonah Clarence,' he said. His grip was firm. 'Mother tells me you're looking for Nell.'

Mrs Clarence had removed her spectacles from their perch[12] on the top of her head. She chewed on the earpiece[13] unconsciously as she listened to their conversation, her brow creased and her eyes moving back and forth between them as they spoke.

Barbara handed him the photograph. 'This is Gillian Teys,' she said. 'Her father was murdered three weeks ago in Yorkshire, and she's going to have to come with me for some questioning.'

Clarence greeted the statement[14] with no strong visible reaction beyond what appeared to be an inability to take his eyes[15] from Barbara's face. But he made himself do so, made himself look at the picture. Then his eyes met his mother's. 'It's Nell.'

'Jonah,' she murmured. 'My dearest ...' Her voice was laced with compassion[16].

Clarence handed the photograph back to Barbara but spoke to his mother. 'It had to happen one day, didn't it?' he said. His tone was coloured by emotion[17].

1. portait une tenue de pasteur
2. le fondateur
3. ciselés
4. front large
5. en un instant
6. avec une raie à gauche
7. un épi indomptable
8. dans les 1,76 m
9. d'apparence frêle
10. d'une force intérieure
11. de confiance en soi
12. de leur perchoir
13. mâchouillait le bout d'une des branches
14. accueillit cette déclaration
15. de détacher son regard
16. pleine de compassion
17. teintée d'émotion

'Darling, shall I …? Do you want to …?'

He shook his head. 'I was just about to leave anyway,' he said, and looked at Barbara. 'I'll take you to Nell. She's my wife.'

* * *

Lynley gazed at the painting of Keldale Abbey and wondered why he had been so blind to its[1] message. The painting's beauty lay in its utter simplicity[2], its devotion to detail[3], its refusal to distort or romanticize[4] the crumbling ruin, to make it anything other than what it was: a vestige of time dead[5], waiting to be devoured by time to come.

Skeletal walls arched[6] against a desolate sky[7], straining to lift themselves out of the inevitable end[8] that waited for them on the ground below. They fought against ferns[9] that grew stubbornly out of barren[10] crevices[11]; wild flowers that bloomed[12] on the edge of transept walls; grass that grew thickly[13] and mingled with wild parsley[14] on the very stones where monks had once knelt in prayer[15].

Steps led to nowhere. Curving stairways that once had carried the devoted[16] from cloister to parlour[17], from day room to court, now sank into moss-covered oblivion[18], submitting to changes that did not make them ignoble, but merely moulded them[19] into a different shape and a purpose changed[20].

Windows were gone. Where long ago stained glass[21] had proudly enclosed presbytery and choir[22], nave and transept, nothing remained but gaping holes[23], gazing sightlessly out on to a landscape which rightfully[24] proclaimed that it alone had ascendancy[25] in the battle with time.

How did one really define the remains[26] of Keldale Abbey? Was it the plundered ruin[27] of a glorious past or a tumbling promise[28] of what the future could be? Wasn't it all, Lynley thought, the definition?

1. aussi incapable d'en déceler le
2. résidait dans son extrême simplicité
3. culte du détail
4. déformer ou idéaliser
5. d'une époque révolue
6. Des murs squelettiques s'arquaient
7. un ciel de désolation
8. l'issue fatale
9. des fougères
10. stériles
11. fissures
12. écloses
13. l'herbe dense qui poussait
14. se mêlait au persil sauvage
15. s'agenouillaient autrefois pour prier
16. les fervents
17. parloir
18. s'enfonçaient dans la mousse et l'oubli
19. se contentaient de les modeler
20. une autre raison d'être
21. des vitraux
22. entouraient fièrement le presbyterium et le chœur
23. que des trous béants
24. à raison
25. lui seul aurait le dessus
26. les vestiges
27. ruines pillées
28. la promesse croulante

He stirred at the sound of a car stoppping at the lodge, of doors opening and the murmur of voices, of uneven footsteps approaching. He realized that darkness was falling in the lounge and switched on one of the lamps just as[1] St James entered the room. He was alone, as Lynley had known he would be.

They faced each other across a short expanse[2] of inoffensive carpeting, across a virtual chasm[3] created and maintained by one man's guilt[4] and another man's pain. They both knew and recognized these components[5] of their history, and, as if to escape them, Lynley went behind the bar and poured each of them a whisky. He crossed the room and handed it to his friend.

'Is she outside?' he asked.

'She's gone to the church. Knowing Deborah, to have one last look at the graveyard, I expect. We're off tomorrow.'

Lynley smiled. 'You've been braver[6] than I. Hank would have driven me off[7] within[8] the first five minutes. Are you fleeing to the lakes?[9]'

'No. To York for a day, then back to London. I'm to be in court to testify[10] on Monday morning. I need a bit of time to complete a fibre analysis[11] before then.'

'Rotten luck[12] to have had so few days.'

'We've the rest of our lives. Deborah understands.'

Lynley nodded and looked from St James to the windows in which they saw themselves reflected[13], two men so entirely different from each other, who shared an afflicted past[14] and who could, if he chose, share a full, rich future. It was all[15], he decided, in the definition. He tossed back[16] the rest of his drink.

'Thank you for your help today, St James,' he said finally, extending his hand. 'You and Deborah are wonderful friends.'

1. au moment où
2. de part et d'autre d'une petite zone
3. un abîme virtuel
4. la culpabilité de l'un
5. admettaient ces composantes
6. plus courageux
7. m'aurait fait fuir
8. dès
9. Fuyez-vous vers les lacs ?
10. Je dois être au tribunal pour témoigner
11. pour terminer une analyse de fibres
12. Ce n'est pas de chance
13. leurs propres reflets
14. un passé d'affliction
15. Tout tenait
16. but d'un trait

Jonah Clarence drove them to Islington in his delapidated[1] Morris. It wasn't a very long drive[2], and he was quiet for every moment of it, his hands on the wheel[3] showing white knuckles[4] that betrayed his distress.

They lived in a peculiar little street called Keystone Crescent, directly off Caledonian Road. Blessed with[5] two takeaway food stores[6] at its head – exuding the multi-cultural odours[7] of frying egg rolls[8], falafel, and fish and chips – and a butcher's shop at its foot in Pentonville Road, it was located in an area of town that was arguing between[9] industrial and residential. Dressmaking factories[10], car-hire firms[11], and tool companies[12] gave way to streets which were trying very hard to become fashionable.

Keystone Crescent was just that, a crescent[13] lined on one side with a concave and on the other with a convex terrace of houses. All were fenced by identical wrought iron, and where once diminutive gardens[14] had bloomed, concrete paving[15] provided additional parking for cars.

The buildings were sooty brick[16], two storeys tall[17], topped by dormer windows[18] and a thin scalloping of ornamentation[19] at the roofline[20]. Each building had its own basement flat[21], and while some of the houses had recently been refurbished[22] in keeping with the[23] neighbourhood effort towards chic, the one in front of which Jonah Clarence parked his car was definitely shabby[24], whitewashed and decorated with green woodwork[25] at one time, but grimy[26] now, with two unlidded dustbins[27] standing in front of it.

'It's this way,' he said tonelessly.

He opened the gate and led her down a set of narrow, steep steps to the door of a flat. Unlike the building itself, which was in sad disrepair[28], the door was sturdy[29], freshly painted, with a

1. déglinguée
2. trajet
3. le volant
4. des jointures
5. Avec ses
6. boutiques de plats à emporter
7. aux senteurs multiculturelles
8. pâtés impériaux
9. à mi-chemin entre
10. Des usines de confection
11. des sociétés de location de voitures
12. des entreprises d'outillage
13. rue en arc de cercle
14. minuscules jardinets
15. un revêtement en béton
16. en brique noire de suie
17. à deux étages
18. surmontées de lucarnes
19. feston décoratif
20. la base du toit
21. appartement en sous-sol
22. rénovées
23. conformément au
24. vraiment miteuse
25. boiseries
26. crasseuses
27. poubelles sans couvercle
28. très délabré
29. robuste

brass knob[1] gleaming in its centre. He unlocked and opened it, gesturing Barbara inside.

She saw at once that a great deal of care had gone into the decorating of the little home, as if the occupants wanted to drive a very firm wedge[2] between the exterior grubbiness of the building and the crisp, clean loveliness of what existed within it. Walls were freshly painted; floors were covered with colourful rugs; white curtains hung in windows which housed a splendour of plants[3]; books, photograph albums, a humble stereo system[4], a collection of phonograph records[5], and three pieces of antique pewter[6] occupied a low shelving unit[7] that ran along one wall. There were few pieces of furniture, but each one had been clearly selected for its workmanship[8] and beauty.

Jonah Clarence set his guitar carefully down on a stand[9] and went to the bedroom door. 'Nell?' he called.

'I was just changing, darling. Out in a moment,' a woman's voice replied cheerfully.

He looked at Barbara. She saw that his face had become grey and ill. 'I'd like to go in—'

'No,' Barbara said. 'Wait here. Please, Mr Clarence,' she added when she read his determination to go to his wife.

He sat down on a chair, moving painfully, as if he had aged years[10] in their brief twenty-minute acquaintance[11]. He fixed his eyes on the door. Behind it, brisk movement accompanied light-hearted humming[12], a lilting rendition[13] of 'Onward, Christian Soldiers[14]'. Drawers opened and closed. A wardrobe door creaked[15]. There was a pause in the humming as footsteps approached. The song finished, the door opened, and Gillian Teys returned from the dead[16].

She looked exactly like her mother, but her blonde hair was quite short, almost like a boy's, and gave

1. heurtoir en cuivre
2. créer un hiatus
3. abritaient de superbes plantes
4. une modeste chaîne Hi-Fi
5. disques
6. trois objets en vieil étain
7. un bloc d'étagères basses
8. pour sa facture
9. support
10. avait énormément vieilli
11. depuis leur rencontre, 20 mn avant
12. un fredonnement enjoué
13. une interprétation chantante
14. [hymne, XIXe]
15. grinça
16. revint d'entre les morts

her the appearance of being ten years old, something that carried over to[1] her manner of dress. She wore a plaid pleated skirt[2], a dark-blue pullover, and black shoes and knee socks[3]. She might have been on her way home from school.

'Darling, I—' She froze[4] when she saw Barbara. 'Jonah? Is something …?' Her breathing seemed to stop. She groped for the doorknob[5] behind her.

Barbara took a step forward. 'Scotland Yard, Mrs Clarence,' she said crisply. 'I'd like to ask you some questions.'

'Questions?' Her hand went to her throat.[6] Her blue eyes darkened. 'What about?'

'About Gillian Teys,' her husband replied. He hadn't moved from his chair.

'Who?' she asked in a low voice.

'Gillian Teys,' he repeated evenly[7]. 'Whose father was murdered in Yorkshire three weeks ago, Nell.'

She backed into the door[8] stiffly. 'No.'

'Nell—'

'No!' Her voice grew louder. Barbara took another step forward. 'Stay away from me![9] I don't know what you're talking about! I don't know any Gillian Teys!'

'Give me the picture,' Jonah said to Barbara, rising[10]. She handed it to him. He walked to his wife, put his hand on her arm. 'This is Gillian Teys,' he said, but she turned her face from the photograph he held.

'I don't know, I don't know!' Her voice was high[11] with terror.

'Look at it, darling.' Gently, he turned her face towards it.

'No!' She screamed, tore herself from his grasp[12] and fled into the other room. Another door slammed[13]. A bolt was shot home.[14]

Wonderful, Barbara thought. She pushed past[15] the young man and went to the bathroom door.

1. qui s'étendait à
2. un kilt
3. des chaussettes montantes
4. se figea
5. chercha à tâtons la poignée de porte
6. Elle porta la main à sa gorge.
7. calmement
8. Elle recula contre la porte
9. Ne vous approchez pas de moi !
10. en se levant
11. montait dans les aigues
12. s'arracha à son étreinte
13. claqua
14. Un verrou se referma.
15. bouscula

1. secoua la poignée

2. à part déclarer qu'elle avait assassiné

3. un sanglot étouffé

4. Un cri d'angoisse

5. robinet

6. fut ouvert à fond

There was silence within. She rattled the handle[1]. *Be tough, be aggressive.* 'Mrs Clarence, come out of there.' No reply. 'Mrs Clarence, you need to listen to me. Your sister Roberta is charged with this murder. She's in Barnstingham Mental Asylum. She hasn't said a word in three weeks other than to claim to having murdered[2] your father. Decapitated your father, Mrs Clarence.' Barbara rattled the handle again. '*Decapitated*, Mrs Clarence. Did you hear me?'

There was a choked whimper[3] from behind the door, the sound of a terrified, wounded animal. An anguished cry[4] followed. 'I left it for you, Bobby! Oh God, did you lose it?'

Then every tap[5] in the bathroom was turned on full force[6].

14

Clean. *Clean!* Have to do it. Have to get it. Fast, fast, *fast*! It will happen *now* if I don't get clean. Shouting, pounding[1], shouting, pounding. Ceaseless, endless.[2] Shouting, pounding. But they'll both go away – God, they *must* go away – once I'm clean, clean, clean.

Water hot.[3] Very hot. Steam gushing forth in clouds.[4] Feel it on my face. Breathe it deeply[5] to be clean.

'Nell!'

No, no, no!

Cupboard handles slippery[6]. Get it open. Pull it open. Get the shaking hands to find them, hidden safely under towels. Stiff, hard brushes.[7] Wooden backs, metal bristles[8]. Good brushes, strong brushes. Brushes make me clean.[9]

'Mrs Clarence!'

No, no, no!

Ugly[10] breathing, tortured breathing. Fills the room, pounds[11] in ears. Stop it, stop it! Hands at head can't stop the echo, fists on face can't kill the sound.

'Nellie, please. Open the door!'

No, no, no! No doors open now. No escape can come that way. Only one way to escape it. And that's clean, clean, clean. Shoes off first. Kick

1. Des cris, des coups
2. Sans arrêt, sans fin.
3. De l'eau, chaude.
4. Des nuages de vapeur qui jaillissent.
5. Respire-la profondément
6. qui glissent
7. Des brosses à poils raides.
8. des poils métalliques
9. Avec les brosses, je serai propre.
10. horrible
11. résonne

them off.[1] Shove them[2] quickly out of sight. Socks come next.[3] Hands don't work. Tear it![4] Fast, fast, fast!

'Mrs Clarence, do you hear me? Are you listening to what I'm saying?'

Can't hear, can't see. Won't hear, won't see. Clouds of steam to fill me up[5]. Clouds of steam to burn and sear[6]. Clouds of steam to make me clean!

'Is that what you want to happen, Mrs Clarence? Because that's *exactly* what's going to happen to your sister if she continues not to speak. For life[7], Mrs Clarence. For the rest of her life.'

No! Tell them no! Tell them nothing matters now. Can't think, can't act. Just hurry up, water. Hurry up and make me clean. Feel it on my hands. No, it's still not hot enough! Can't feel, can't see. Never, never be clean.

She called his name[8] Moab, father of Moabites unto this day[9]. She called his name Ben-ammi, father of the children of Ammon unto this day. The smoke of the country went up as the smoke of a furnace[10]. They went up out of[11] Zoar and dwelled[12] in the mountain. For they were afraid.[13]

'How is it locked? Is it a bolt? A key? How?'

'I just …'

'Pull yourself together.[14] We're going to have to break it[15].'

'No!'

Pounding, pounding, loud, relentless. Make them, *make* them go away!

'Nell, Nell!'

Water all over.[16] Can't feel it, can't see it, won't be hot enough to make me clean, clean, clean! Soap and brushes, soap and brushes. Rub hard[17], hard, hard. Slip and slither[18], slip and slither. Make me clean, clean, clean!

1. Enlève-les d'un coup de pied.
2. Fiche-les
3. Et maintenant, les chaussettes.
4. Arrache ça !
5. pour me remplir à ras bord
6. pour brûler et flétrir
7. À vie
8. le nomma
9. jusqu'à ce jour
10. fournaise
11. quittèrent
12. vécurent
13. [Genèse, chap. 19]
14. Ressaisissez-vous !
15. la défoncer
16. L'eau me recouvre entièrement.
17. Frotte dur
18. Glisse

'It's either that or call for help. Is that what you want? The whole bloody police force breaking down the door?'

'Shut up! Look at what you've done to her! Nell!'

Bless me, father.[1] I have sinned.[2] Understand and forgive. Brushes digging[3], brushes digging, brushes *dig* to make me clean.

'You don't have any choice! This is a police matter, not some marital squabble[4], Mr Clarence.'

'What are you doing? Damn you[5], stay away from[6] that phone!'

Pounding, pounding.

'Nell!'

Reader, I married him a quiet wedding we had: he and I, the parson and clerk[7]*, were alone present when we got back from church I went into the kitchen of the manor house where Mary was cooking the dinner and John cleaning the knives and I said Mary I have been married to Mr Rochester this morning.*[8]

'Then, you have exactly two minutes to get her out of there or you're going to have more police than you've ever laid eyes on[9] crawling through this place[10]. Is that clear?'

You *are* some little cat[11]. Not again! Not so soon! God, Gilly, God!

Gilly's dead, Gilly's dead. But Nell is clean, clean, clean. Scrub her hard, dig in deep[12], make her clean, clean, clean!

'I've got to come in, Nell. Do you hear me? I'm going to break the lock. Don't be frightened.'

Come on, Gilly girl. I want *nothing* serious tonight. Let's laugh and be wild and be absolutely mad. We'll have drinks, dance till dawn[13]. We'll find men and go to Whitby. We'll take wine. We'll take food. We'll dance nude[14] on the abbey walls. They can try to catch us, Gilly. We'll be absolutely wild[15].

Pounding louder now. Pounding hard, hard, hard! Bursting ears[16], bursting heart. Rub her skin all clean.

1. Bénissez-moi, mon père.
2. J'ai péché.
3. Brosser pour enlever
4. une dispute conjugale
5. Allez au diable
6. ne touchez pas à
7. le pasteur et l'officier d'état civil
8. [extrait, ponctuation manquante, de Jane Eyre, par Charlotte Brontë]
9. que vous n'en avez jamais vu
10. grouillant partout dans la maison
11. ma petite chatte
12. brosse fort pour enlever
13. on dansera jusqu'à l'aube
14. nues
15. déchaînées
16. Les oreilles qui éclatent

'That's not going to work, Mr Clarence. I'm going to have to—'

'No! Shut up[1], damn you!'

Late at night. I said goodbye. Did you hear me? Did you see me? Did you find it where I left it? Bobby, did you find it? Did you finditfinditfindit?

Shrieking wood, splintering wood.[2] Never safe any more.[3] One last chance before Lot[4] finds me. One last chance to make me clean.

'Oh *God*! Oh my God, Nell.'

'I'm going to phone for an ambulance.'

'No! Just leave us alone!'

Hands gripping.[5] Hands sliding. Water pink and rich with blood[6]. Arms holding. Someone crying. Wrapping warm[7] and holding near[8].

'Nellie. Oh God. *Nell.*'

Pressed against him. Hear him sobbing. Is it over? Am I clean?

'Bring her out here, Mr Clarence.'

'Go away! Leave us alone!'

'I can't do that. She's accessory in a murder[9]. You know that as well as I. If nothing else[10], her reaction to all this should have—'

'She *isn't*! She couldn't be! I was with her!'

'You don't expect me to believe that, do you?'

'Nell! I won't let them. I won't let them!'

Weeping, weeping. Aching tears.[11] Body racked with pain[12] and sorrow. Make it end.[13] Make it end. 'Jonah. ...'

'Yes, darling. What is it?'

'Nell's dead.'

'So he broke down the door,' Havers said.

Lynley rubbed his throbbing forehead. The last three hours had given him an appalling headache[14]. The conversation with Havers was making it worse[15]. 'And?'

There was a pause.

1. Fermez-la
2. Le bois qui grince, le bois qui se fend.
3. Plus jamais en sécurité.
4. Lot ou Loth [pers. biblique qui échappe à la destruction de Sodome]
5. Des mains qui m'agrippent.
6. rougie de sang
7. On m'enveloppe au chaud
8. on me serre dans les bras
9. complice d'un meurtre
10. En tout cas
11. Des larmes qui font mal.
12. secoué de douleur
13. Que ça cesse.
14. un horrible mal de tête
15. le faisait empirer

'Havers?' he demanded. He knew that his voice was abrupt, that it would sound like anger instead of the fatigue that it was. He heard her catch her breath. Was she crying?

'It was … She had …' She cleared her throat. 'It was a bath.'

'She'd taken a *bath*?' He wondered if Havers was aware of the fact that she was making no sense[1]. Good God, what had happened?

'Yes. Except … She'd used brushes on herself.[2] They were metal brushes. She was bleeding[3].'

'God in heaven[4],' he muttered[5]. 'Where is she, Havers? Is she all right?'

'I wanted to phone for an ambulance.'

'Why didn't you, for God's sake?'

'Her husband … he was … It was my fault[6], Inspector. I thought that I should be tough[7] with her. I … It was my fault.' Her voice broke.

'Havers, for God's sake[8]. Pull yourself together.'

'There was blood. She'd used the brushes all over her body. He wrapped her up. He wouldn't let go of her.[9] He was crying. She said she was dead.'

'Christ,' he whispered.

'I went to the phone. He came after me.[10] He—'

'Are you all right? Are you hurt?'

'He pushed me outside. I fell. I'm all right. I … It was my fault. She came out of the bedroom. I remembered everything we'd said about her. It seemed best to be firm with her. I didn't think. I didn't realize she would—'

'Havers, listen to me.'

'But she locked herself in[11]. There was blood in the water. It was so hot. There was steam … How could she have stood the water that hot[12]?'

'Havers!'

'I thought I could do something right[13]. This time. I've destroyed the case[14], haven't I?'

1. qu'elle était incohérente
2. Elle s'était frotté le corps avec des brosses.
3. saignait
4. Dieu du ciel
5. marmonna-t-il
6. C'est de ma faute
7. dure
8. pour l'amour du Ciel
9. Il ne voulait pas la lâcher.
10. Il s'est précipité sur moi.
11. s'est enfermée
12. supporter une eau aussi chaude
13. correctement
14. fichu l'affaire en l'air

'Of course not,' he replied, although he was absolutely unconvinced that she hadn't blown their chances right into oblivion[1]. 'Are they still at their flat?'

'Yes. Shall I get[2] someone from the Yard?'

'No!' He thought rapidly. The situation could not possibly have been any worse. To have found the woman after all these years and then to have this happen was infuriating[3]. He knew quite well that she represented their only hope of reaching the bottom of the case[4]. No matter the reality that insinuated itself from the pages of Shakespeare, only Gillian could give it substance[5].

'Then, what shall I—'

'Go home. Go to bed. I'll handle this.'

'*Please*, sir.' He could hear the despair in her voice. He couldn't help it[6], couldn't stop it, couldn't worry about it now.

'Just do as I say, Havers. Go home. Go to bed. Do *not* ring the Yard, and do *not* return to that flat. Is that clear?'

'Am I—'

'Then get a train back here[7] in the morning.'

'What about Gillian?'

'I'll worry about Gillian,' he said grimly and hung up the telephone.

He gazed down at the book in his lap. He'd spent the last four hours dredging up from his memory[8] every single exposure he'd had to[9] Shakespeare. It was limited. His interest in the Elizabethans had been historical, not literary, and more than once during the evening he had cursed the educational path[10] he had taken[11] all those years ago at Oxford, wishing for expertise in an area[12] that, at the time, had hardly seemed relevant[13] to his interests.

He had found it at last, however, and now he read and reread the lines[14], trying to wring a twentieth-

1. gâché pour de bon toutes leurs chances
2. Dois-je faire venir
3. c'était rageant
4. d'arriver au cœur de l'affaire
5. y apporter de la matière
6. n'y pouvait rien
7. prenez un train pour revenir ici
8. à tenter de se remémorer
9. tout ce qu'il avait étudié de
10. maudit le cursus
11. qu'il avait suivi
12. rêvant d'être expert dans un domaine
13. ne correspondait guère
14. le passage

century meaning[1] from the seventeenth-century verse[2].

> *One sin, I know, another doth provoke[3].*
> *Murder's as near to lust[4] as flame to smoke[5].*

He gives life and death meaning, the priest had said. So what did the words of the Prince of Tyre[6] have to do with an abandoned grave in Keldale? And what did a grave have to do[7] with the death of a farmer?

Absolutely nothing, his intellect insisted. Absolutely everything, his intuition replied.

He snapped the book closed.[8] It was imprisoned in Gillian: the meaning and the truth. He picked up the telephone and dialled[9].

It was after ten[10] when she trudged down[11] the ill-lit[12] street in Acton. Webberly had been surprised to see her, but the surprise had faded[13] when he opened the envelope Lynley had sent. He glanced at the message, turned it over, and picked up the phone. After barking an order for[14] Edwards to come at once, he dismissed her[15] without a question as to why she had suddenly appeared in London without Lynley. It was quite as if she didn't exist for him. And she didn't, did she? Not any longer.

Who gives a shit?[16] she thought. Who bloody cares[17] what happens[18]? It was inevitable. Fat, stupid little pig, snorting around[19] trying to play the detective. Thought you knew everything about Gillian Teys, didn't you? Heard her humming in the next room and even then you weren't smart enough to figure it out[20].

She looked up at the house. The windows were dark. Mrs Gustafson's television blared from next door[21], but not a sign of life glimmered[22] from the interior of the building in front of which she stood. If its inhabitants[23] were disturbed by the neighbour-

1. de trouver une signification, au XXe siècle
2. à ces vers du XVIIe
3. en provoque un autre
4. est aussi proche de la luxure,
5. que la flamme de la fumée
6. [Périclès, prince de Tyr, pièce de Shakespeare]
7. qu'est-ce qu'une tombe avait à voir
8. Il referma le livre d'un coup sec.
9. composa un numéro
10. plus de 22 h
11. parcourut d'un pas lourd
12. mal éclairée
13. s'était envolée
14. avoir ordonné d'un ton rogue à
15. l'avait congédiée
16. Qu'est-ce que ça peut foutre ?
17. Qui se fout
18. de la suite
19. grognant et fouinant,
20. piger
21. beuglait à côté
22. on ne percevait aucun signe de vie
23. occupants

hood noise, there was no indication[1]. There was nothing.

Nothing. That's really it, isn't it? she thought. *There's nothing inside, not a single thing and especially not the one thing that you want to be in there. All these years you've been incubating a chimera*[2]*, Barb. And what a bloody waste it's been*[3].

She steeled herself[4] against the thought, refused to accept it, and unlocked the door. In the quiet house, the smell assailed her[5], a smell of unwashed bodies, of trapped cooking odours[6], of dead air[7], of ponderous[8] despair. It was foul and unhealthy[9], and she welcomed it. She breathed it in deeply, finding it fitting[10], finding it just.

She closed the door behind her and leaned against it, letting her eyes adjust to the darkness[11]. *Here it is, Barb. It all began here. Let it bring you back to life.*

She put her handbag down on the splintered[12] table next to the door and forced herself towards the stairs. But as she reached them her eyes were caught by a flash of light from the sitting-room. She walked to the door curiously to find the room empty, the flash only a brief flicker[13] of a passing car's lights[14] hitting the glass[15] of the picture. His picture. Tony's picture.

She was drawn into the room, and she sat in her father's chair, which, along with her mother's, faced the shrine. Tony's face grinned its impish grin[16] at her; his wiry body twisted with life[17].

She was weary and numb, but she forced herself to keep her eyes on the picture, forced herself back to the deepest reaches[18] of her memory where Tony still lay, wizened[19] and gaunt[20], in a narrow white hospital bed. He was branded[21] into her consciousness as he always would be, tubes and needles sprouting from him everywhere[22], his fingers plucking[23] spasmodically at the covers. His thin neck no

1. rien ne le laissait paraître
2. tu as nourri une chimère
3. quel beau gâchis
4. se cuirassa
5. l'assaillit
6. de relents de cuisine
7. de renfermé
8. pesant
9. vicié et malsain
10. le jugeant adapté
11. s'habituer à l'obscurité
12. fendillée
13. n'étant que l'éclair
14. des phares d'une voiture
15. sur le verre
16. sourire espiègle
17. son corps menu se tordant de vie
18. à fouiller les tréfonds
19. ratatiné
20. émacié
21. gravé
22. bardé de sondes et d'aiguilles
23. agrippant

longer supported[1] a head that appeared by contrast to have grown immense[2]. His eyelids were heavy, crusted[3] and closed. His cracked lips bled.[4]

'Coma,' they had said. 'It's nearly time now[5].'

But it hadn't been. Not yet. Not until he'd opened his eyes, managed a fleeting elf's smile[6], and murmured, 'I'm not scared when you're here, Barbie. You won't leave me, will you?'

He might have actually spoken to her in the sitting-room's darkness, for she felt it all again as she always did: the swelling of grief[7] and then – blasting it away like a breath from hell[8] – the rage. That single reality that was keeping her alive.

'I won't leave you,' she swore[9]. 'I'll *never* forget.'

'Lovey?'

She cried out in surprise, brought back to the shattering present[10].

'Lovey? Is that you?'

Past the pounding of her heart, she forced her voice to sound pleasant. No problem, really, after so many years of practice. 'Yes, Mum. Just having a sit[11].'

'In the dark, lovey? Here, let me turn on the light so—'

'No!' Her voice rasped. She cleared her throat. 'No, Mum. Just leave it off.[12]'

'But I don't like the dark, lovey. It … it frightens me so.'

'Why are you up?'

'I heard the door open. I thought it might be …' She moved into Barbara's line of vision, a ghostly figure[13] in a stained pink dressing-gown. 'Sometimes I think he's come back to us, lovey. But he never will, will he?'

Barbara got to her feet abruptly. 'Go back to bed, Mum.' She heard the roughness[14] of her voice, and she tried unsuccessfully to modulate it[15]. 'How's

1. ne soutenait plus
2. être devenue énorme
3. couvertes de croûtes
4. Ses lèvres gercées saignaient.
5. bientôt la fin
6. un sourire furtif d'elfe
7. le chagrin qui montait
8. le chassant dans une bouffée de l'enfer
9. avait juré
10. ramenée à la terrible réalité
11. assise un instant
12. Laisse-la éteinte.
13. une silhouette fantomatique
14. rudesse
15. en vain de la moduler

Dad?' She took her mother's bony arm and firmly led her from[1] the sitting-room.

'He had a good day today. We thought about Switzerland. You know, the air is so fresh and pure there. We thought Switzerland would be the nicest place next. Of course, back so soon from Greece[2], it doesn't seem quite right to go off again[3], but he thinks it sounds a good idea. Will you like Switzerland, lovey? Because if you don't think you'll like it we can always choose somewhere else. I want you to be happy.'

Happy? *Happy?* 'Switzerland's fine, Mum.'

She felt her mother's bird-claw hand[4] grip her arm tightly. They started up the stairs. 'Good. I thought you'd like it. I think Zurich would be the best place to begin. We'll do a tour this time, with a hired car. I long to see the Alps.[5]'

'Sounds fine, Mum.'

'Dad thought so, lovey. He even went to Empress Tours to get me the brochures.'

Barbara's steps slowed[6]. 'Did he see Mr Patel?'

Her mother's hand fluttered[7] on her arm. 'Oh, I don't know, lovey. He didn't mention Mr Patel. I'm certain he would have said something if he had.'

They reached the top of the stairs. Her mother paused at the door to her bedroom. 'He's such a new man when he goes out for a bit[8] in the afternoon, lovey. *Such* a new man.'

Barbara's stomach turned at the thought of[9] what her mother might mean[10].

Jonah Clarence opened the bedroom door softly, an unnecessary[11] precaution, for she was awake. She turned her head at the sound of his movement and smiled wanly[12] at her husband.

'I've made you some soup,' he said.

'Jo. ...' Her voice was so small, so weak, that he went hurriedly on[13].

1. la conduisit avec fermeté hors
2. si peu de temps après notre retour de Grèce
3. de repartir
4. main crochue
5. J'ai hâte de voir les Alpes.
6. ralentirent
7. voleta
8. un petit moment
9. se souleva en pensant à
10. pouvait bien vouloir dire
11. inutile
12. faiblement
13. se hâta de poursuivre

'It's just the tinned stuff[1] from the pantry[2]. I've some bread and butter here as well.' He placed the tray on the bed and helped her into a sitting position. At the movement, several of the deeper cuts[3] began to bleed again. He took a towel and pressed it firmly against her skin, a movement not only to stem the flow[4] of the blood but also to block out the memory[5] of what had happened to their lives that evening.

'I don't—'

'Not now, darling,' he said. 'You need to eat something first.'

'Will we talk then?'

His eyes moved from her face. Slashes covered her[6] hands, her arms, her breasts, her stomach, her thighs. At the sight, he felt such a burden of anguish[7] that he wasn't sure he could answer her. But she was watching him, her beautiful eyes trusting[8], filled with love, waiting for his reply.

'Yes,' he whispered. 'We'll talk then.'

She smiled tremulously[9], and he felt his heart wrench[10]. He put the tray across her lap, but when she tried to spoon the soup[11] he saw that her weakness[12] had become so pronounced that no effort would make it possible for her[13] to feed herself[14]. Gently, he took the spoon from her and began to help her eat, a slow process[15] in which every bit swallowed[16] seemed an individual act of triumph.

He wouldn't let her talk. He was too afraid of what she might say. Instead he soothed her[17] with whispered words of love and encouragement and wondered who she was and what kind of terrible grief she had brought into his life.

They had been married for less than a year, but it seemed to him that they had always been together, that they had been meant for each other[18] from the moment when his father brought her to Testament House from King's Cross Station – a solemn little

1. le truc en boîte
2. l'office
3. coupures les plus profondes
4. pour juguler le flux
5. bloquer les souvenirs
6. Des entailles lui couvraient les
7. si oppressé par l'angoisse
8. confiants
9. timidement
10. cela lui fendit le cœur
11. prendre une cuillerée de soupe,
12. faiblesse
13. ne lui permettrait
14. de se nourrir toute seule
15. un long processus
16. chaque portion avalée
17. la réconforta
18. faits l'un pour l'autre

waif of a girl[1] who looked twelve years old. She's all eyes[2], he had thought when he saw her. But when she smiled she was sunlight. He knew within the first few weeks that he loved her, but it took nearly ten years to make her his own[3].

During that time, he had been ordained[4], had made his decision to be part of his father's work, had laboured like Jacob in pursuit of a Rachel he[5] could never be certain of winning. Yet that thought had not discouraged him. Like a crusader, he had set out on a quest[6], and Nell was his Grail[7]. No one else would do[8].

Except[9] she's not Nell, he thought. I don't know who she is. And the worst of it is, I'm not certain I want to know.

He had always seen himself as a man of action, one of courage, a man powered by[10] the force of his inner convictions[11], yet still, intimately, a man of peace. All that had died tonight. The sight of her in the bath – mindlessly lacerating her flesh[12], staining the water with her blood – had demolished that carefully constructed façade in two short minutes: the time it had taken to pull her, frail and screaming, from the tub, to try frantically to stop the bleeding, to throw the shouting police officer from their flat.

In two short minutes, he had become not the cheek-turning[13] sincere minister of God[14] that had long been his guise[15], but a maniacal stranger[16] who could have killed, without impunity, anyone seeking to harm[17] his wife. He was shaken to the core[18], even more so when he considered that, in protecting her from enemies, he couldn't think of how he was going to protect Nell from herself.

Except she's not Nell, he thought.

She had finished eating, had been finished, in fact, for several minutes and lay back against the pillows[19]. They were stained with her blood. He got to his feet.

1. une gamine frêle et grave
2. On ne voit que ses yeux
3. la faire sienne
4. ordonné pasteur
5. travaillé de longues années, tel Jacob voulant gagner une Rachel qu'il
6. entrepris une quête
7. son Graal
8. ne lui conviendrait
9. Sauf qu'
10. animé par
11. ses convictions profondes
12. lacérant sa chair machinalement
13. qui présente l'autre joue
14. ministre du culte
15. longtemps été son apparence
16. un fou inconnu
17. voulant faire du mal à
18. profondément ébranlé
19. reposait contre les oreillers

'Jo. ...'

'I'm going to get something for the cuts. I'll just be a moment.[1]'

He tried not to see the gruesome condition[2] of the bathroom as he rooted[3] in the cupboard. The tub[4] looked and smelt as if they had been butchering livestock in it[5]. Blood was everywhere, in every crevice and crack[6]. His hands weakened as he grabbed[7] the bottle of hydrogen peroxide[8]. He felt faint[9].

'Jonah?'

He took several deep breaths and went back to the bedroom. 'Delayed reaction.[10]' He tried to smile, clutched[11] the bottle so tightly[12] he thought it might break in his hands, and sat on the edge of the bed. 'Mostly surface cuts[13],' he said conversationally[14]. 'We'll see what it looks like in the morning. If they're bad, we'll go to hospital then. How does that sound?[15]'

He didn't wait for a response. Rather, he washed the abrasions[16] with the chemical[17] and continued speaking determinedly. 'I thought we might go to Penzance this weekend, darling. It would be good to get away for a few days, don't you think so? I was talking to one of the kids about a hotel down there that she'd stayed at as a child. If it's still there, it should be wonderful. A view of St Michael's Mount[18]. I thought we'd take the train down and hire a car when we got there. Or bicycles. Would you like to hire bicycles, Nell?'

He felt her hand on his cheek. At the touch, his heart swelled[19], and he knew he was horribly close to tears[20]. 'Jo,' she whispered. 'Nell's dead.'

'Don't say that!' he returned fiercely[21].

'I've done terrible things. I can't bear for you to know.[22] I thought I was safe from them, that I'd run from them right into forever[23].'

1. Je n'en ai pas pour longtemps.
2. l'état épouvantable
3. tandis qu'il fouillait
4. baignoire
5. on y avait abattu du bétail
6. fissure, chaque lézarde
7. prenait
8. eau oxygénée
9. faillit s'évanouir
10. Le contrecoup.
11. serra
12. si fort
13. des coupures superficielles
14. sur le ton de la conversation
15. Qu'en dis-tu ?
16. nettoya les éraflures
17. la solution
18. [Mont-Saint-Michel anglais, en Cornouailles]
19. son cœur se gonfla
20. au bord des larmes
21. avec véhémence
22. Je ne supporte pas que tu le saches.
23. à tout jamais

'No!' He continued mindlessly, passionately to see to[1] her wounds.

'I love you, Jonah.'

That stopped him. His face sank into his hands.[2] 'What do I call you?' he whispered. 'I don't even know who you are!'

'Jo, Jonah, my love, my only love. ...'

Her voice was a torment he could barely endure[3], and when she reached out for him[4], he was broken and ran from the room, slamming the door firmly, and irrevocably, behind him.

He stumbled to a chair, hearing his own breathing tear at the air[5], feeling wedges[6] of panic drive themselves into his stomach and groin[7]. He sat, staring unseeing at the material objects that comprised[8] their home, and desperately pushed away from him the one piece of information[9] that was at the core of[10] his terror.

Three weeks ago, the police sergeant had said. He had lied to her, an immediate response rising from[11] the horror of her incomprehensible allegation. He had not been in London with his wife at that time but, rather, at a four-day[12] conference in Exeter, followed by two additional days of fund-raisers[13] for Testament House. Nell was supposed to have gone with him but at the last moment had begged off with flu[14]. So she said. Had she been ill? Or had she seen it as an opportunity[15] to travel to Yorkshire?

'No!' The word came out involuntarily, from between his teeth. Despising himself for even considering the question[16] for a moment, Jonah willed his breathing to calm, willed his muscles to relax.

He reached for his guitar, not to play it but to reaffirm its reality and to re-establish the meaning it had in his life, for he had been sitting on the back stairs of Testament House, in the semi-darkness, playing strains of the music he loved when she first spoke to him.

1. à s'occuper de
2. Il s'enfouit le visage dans les mains.
3. qu'il pouvait à peine endurer
4. tendit la main vers lui
5. sonner rauque
6. des pointes
7. lui piquer le ventre et l'aine
8. qui composaient
9. l'unique information
10. au centre de
11. en réaction immédiate à
12. de quatre jours
13. levée de fonds
14. ayant la grippe, avait demandé à être dispensée
15. vu là une occasion
16. de s'être juste posé la question

'That's so nice. D'you think anyone could learn?' She came to crouch[1] next to him on the step, her eyes on his fingers as they moved expertly among the strings[2], and she smiled, a child's smile, lit with[3] pleasure.

It had been simple to teach her to play, for she was a natural mimic[4]: something seen or heard was never forgotten. Now she played as often to him as he did to her, not with his assurance or passion but with a melancholy sweetness[5] that long ago should have told him what he didn't want to face now.

He stood abruptly. To assure himself, he opened book after book and saw the name, *Nell Graham*, written in each volume in her neat script[6]. To show ownership[7], he wondered, or to convince herself?

'No!'

He picked up a photograph album from the bottom shelf and hugged it to his chest[8]. It was a document of Nell, a verification[9] of the fact that she was real, that she had no other life but the one[10] she shared with him. He didn't even need to open the album to know what lay within its pages: a pictorial[11] history of the love they shared, of the memories that were an integral part of the tapestry of their lives being woven together[12]. In a park, on a trail[13], dreaming quietly at dawn, laughing at the antics of birds[14] on the beach. All of these bore testimony[15], were illustrations of Nell's life and the things she loved.

His eyes drifted, for more assurance, to her plants in the window. The African violets had always reminded him the most of her. The beautiful flowers poised themselves delicately[16], precariously, at the tips of their stalks[17]. The heavy green leaves protected and surrounded them. They were plants that looked as if they could never survive in the rigours of the London weather[18], but in spite of their ap-

1. s'accroupir
2. sur les cordes
3. rayonnant de
4. une imitatrice née
5. une douceur mélancolique
6. de son écriture soignée
7. Pour montrer que c'était à elle
8. le tint serré contre sa poitrine
9. confirmation
10. que celle
11. en images
12. de la vie qu'ensemble ils avaient tissée
13. sur un sentier
14. des cabrioles des oiseaux
15. étaient un témoignage
16. se tenaient avec délicatesse
17. au bout de leurs tiges
18. climat

pearance they were deceptive[1] plants really, plants of remarkable strength.

Looking at them, he knew at last and fought fruitlessly to deny it[2]. Tears, long in coming, broke the surface and a sob[3] escaped him. He made his way back to the chair, fell into it, and wept inconsolably.

It was then that he heard the knocking at the door.

'Go away!' he sobbed.

The knocking persisted.

'Go away!'

There was no other sound. The knocking continued. Like the voice of his conscience. It would never end.

'Damn you, go away!' he screamed and threw himself at the door. He flung it open.

A woman stood there. She wore a neat black suit and a white silk blouse with a froth of lace[4] at her throat. She carried a black shoulder-bag[5] and a leather-bound[6] book. But it was her face that riveted his attention[7]. It was calm, clear-eyed[8], and masked by tenderness. She might have been a missionary. She might have been a vision. But she extended her hand and made it clear[9] that she was real.

'My name is Helen Clyde,' she said quietly.

Lynley chose a corner. Candles flickered[10] some distance away, but where he was darkness shrouded[11] the church. The building smelt vaguely of incense, but more strongly of age, of guttering[12] candles, of the burnt ends of matches[13], of dust. It was utterly peaceful. Even the doves, who had been stirred into momentary rustling upon his approach[14], had fallen back into stillness[15], and no night wind made tree branches creak and scratch against the windows.

He was alone. His only companions were the youths and maidens[16], entwined Grecian-urn-like[17] in a soundless eternal[18] dance of truth and beau-

1. trompeuses
2. dut se résoudre à l'admettre
3. sanglot
4. un nuage de dentelle
5. sac à bandoulière
6. relié en cuir
7. le captiva
8. le regard limpide
9. montra clairement
10. Des bougies vacillaient
11. enveloppait
12. qui se consumaient
13. de bouts d'allumettes brûlés
14. que son arrivée avait lancées dans un froufrou d'ailes
15. recouvré leur immobilité
16. les jeunes gens et jeunes filles
17. enlacés comme le long d'un vase grec
18. perpétuelle et silencieuse

ty on the doors of the Elizabethan confessionals nearby.

His heart felt heavy and sore[1]. It was an old story, a Roman legend from the fifth century, but as real at this moment as it had been to Shakespeare when he used it as the foundation for his drama. The Prince of Tyre went to Antioch, pursuing a riddle[2] and marriage to a princess. But he came away[3] with nothing, fleeing for[4] his life.

Lynley knelt. He thought about prayer, but nothing came.

He knew he was near the body of the hydra, but the knowledge gave him neither triumph nor satisfaction. Instead, he wanted to flee from the final confrontation with the monster, knowing now that, although the heads were destroyed and the trunk well seared[5], he could not hope to emerge unscathed[6] from the encounter.

' "Fret not thyself because of evil-doers."[7]' It was an insubstantial, disembodied, wavering[8] voice. It came out of nowhere, tremulous[9] and uncertain, and it hovered mistily[10] in the frigid[11] air. It was some moments before Lynley located its black-robed source[12].

Father Hart knelt at the foot of the altar. He was bent over double[13], his forehead pressed to the floor. ' "Neither be thou envious against[14] the workers of iniquity[15]. For they shall be cut down[16] like the grass, and wither[17] as the green herb. Trust in the Lord and do good; so shalt thou dwell in the land[18], and verily thou shall be fed[19]. Delight thyself also in the Lord: and he shall give thee the desires of thine heart. Commit thy way unto the Lord[20]; Trust also in him, and he shall bring it to pass[21]. Evil-doers shall be cut off[22]; But those that wait upon the Lord[23], they shall inherit the earth. For yet a little while and the wicked shall not be."[24] '

1. lourd et douloureux
2. attiré par une énigme
3. en repartit
4. fuyant pour sauver
5. le tronc bien entamé
6. sortir indemne
7. « Ne t'irrite pas contre les méchants. »
8. désincarnée, tremblante
9. frémissante
10. nébuleuse, elle flotta
11. glacé
12. en détecte l'origine, en soutane noire
13. courbé en deux
14. N'envie pas
15. ceux qui font le mal
16. fauchés
17. se flétriront
18. et tu demeureras en sécurité
19. en vérité tu seras nourri
20. Remets-t'en au Seigneur
21. Il agira
22. seront retranchés
23. espèrent en l'Éternel
24. le méchant ne sera plus. » [Psaume 37]

Lynley listened to the words, anguished, and tried to deny their meaning. As a hush swept over[1] the darkened church once more – broken only by the priest's stertorous[2] breathing – he sorted through himself[3], trying to find the detachment he needed to carry him, disinterested[4], to the end of the case.

'Have you come to confess?'

He started[5] at the voice. Unseen to him[6], the priest had materialized from the dark. Lynley stood. 'No, I'm not a Catholic,' he replied. 'I was just gathering my thoughts.'

'Churches are good places for that, aren't they?' Father Hart smiled. 'I always stop for a prayer before locking up for the night. I always check first, as well, to make sure no one is still inside. It wouldn't do[7] to be locked up in St Catherine's in this kind of cold[8], would it?'

'No,' Lynley agreed.' It wouldn't do at all.' He followed the little priest to the end of the aisle and out into the night. Clouds obscured moon and stars. The other man was merely a shadow[9], without form or feature. 'How well do you know *Pericles*, Father Hart?'

The priest didn't answer at first as he fumbled with his keys[10] and locked the church door. '*Pericles*?' he repeated musingly[11]. He moved past the other man, out into the graveyard. 'It's Shakespeare, isn't it?'

' "As flame to smoke." Yes, it's Shakespeare.'

'I … well, I suppose I know it fairly well[12].'

'Well enough to know why Pericles fled from Antiochus[13]? Why Antiochus wanted to have him killed?'

'I …' The priest groped[14] in his pockets. 'I don't think I quite remember all the details of the play.'

'You remember enough, I dare say[15]. Good night, Father Hart,' Lynley replied and left the graveyard.

1. le silence se faisait dans
2. ronflante
3. fit un travail sur lui-même
4. pour l'amener, indifférent
5. sursauta
6. Sans qu'il l'ait vu
7. Il ne faudrait pas
8. par ce froid
9. n'était qu'une ombre
10. tandis qu'il maniait ses clefs
11. d'un air songeur
12. plutôt bien
13. a fui le roi d'Antioche
14. fourragea
15. à mon avis

He descended the hillock[1] by the gravel path, his footsteps sounding unnaturally loud in the night-time peace. On the bridge, he paused to gather his thoughts, and he leaned against its stone side[2], surveying the village. To his right, Olivia Odell's house was dark, and woman and child slept in innocent safety[3] within. Across the street, organ music floated eerily from[4] Nigel Parrish's cottage on the edge of the common. To his left the lodge awaited his entry[5], and beyond that the high street curved[6] in the direction of the pub. From where he stood, he couldn't see St Chad's Lane with its council houses. But he could imagine them. Not wanting to do that[7], he returned to the lodge.

He'd been gone less than an hour, but he knew as soon as he walked in the door that, during his absence, Stepha had returned. The building held its breath[8], waiting for him to discover and know. His feet felt like lead[9].

He wasn't entirely sure where Stepha's rooms would be, but his instinct told him that they were somewhere on the ground floor[10] of the old building, past the reception desk, in the direction of the kitchen. He went through the door.

As he did so, he had his answers, palpably alive[11] in the atmosphere that surrounded him. He could smell the cigarette smoke. He could almost taste the liquor[12] in the air. He could hear the laughter, the whispered passion[13], the delight. He could feel the hands drawing him relentlessly forward[14]. All that was left was to see the truth.

He knocked on the door. There was immediate quiet[15].

'Stepha?'

Movement within, hurried and suppressed[16]. Stepha's soft laugh hung[17] in the air. At the last moment, he nearly stopped himself, but then he turned the knob[18], to enter and to know.

1. la butte
2. le rebord en pierre
3. du sommeil des innocents
4. provenaient, étranges, de
5. l'attendait
6. tournait
7. Comme il ne le souhaitait pas
8. retenait sa respiration
9. étaient lourds comme du plomb
10. au rez-de-chaussée
11. palpables
12. l'alcool
13. le murmure de passion
14. l'attirer sans relâche
15. le silence
16. empressés et étouffés
17. flottait encore
18. tourna la poignée

1. un alibi qui tienne la route
2. une claque possessive
3. sa cuisse nue

'Perhaps now *you* can give me an alibi that sticks[1],' laughed Richard Gibson, giving the woman a proprietary slap[2] on her naked thigh[3]. 'I don't think the inspector believed my little Madeline for a moment.'

15

Lady Helen saw him as they made their way[1] over the crowded pedestrian walkway[2] from the arrivals platform[3]. It had been a harrowing enough[4] two hours on the train, one moment afraid that Gillian might go all to pieces[5] in any one of a dozen ways; the next moment desperately trying to rouse[6] Sergeant Havers from whatever black pit of humour[7] she had decided to inhabit[8]. The entire experience had filled Lady Helen with such anxiety that the very sight[9] of Lynley, brushing his blond hair back off his forehead against the breeze[10] of a departing train[11], made her nearly weak with relief[12]. People in the crowded station bustled and pushed[13] round him. But still he looked as if he were quite alone. He raised his head. Their eyes met and her steps slowed momentarily.

Even at this distance, she could see the difference in him. The smoky darkness[14] under his eyes. The tension in the set of his head and shoulders[15], the deepening lines[16] round nose and mouth. He was Tommy still, but somehow not quite Tommy at all. There could be only one reason for it: Deborah.

He'd seen her in Keldale. His face told Lady Helen as much. And for some reason – in spite of the year that had passed since he'd broken his engagement to Deborah, in spite of the hours that she'd

1. se frayaient un chemin
2. par la passerelle piétonne bondée
3. quai des arrivées
4. assez pénibles
5. s'effondre totalement
6. sortir
7. puits d'idées noires où
8. de rester
9. la seule vue
10. à cause du courant d'air
11. d'un train en partance
12. défaillir de soulagement
13. s'affairaient et se bousculaient
14. Les cernes gris
15. visible de son port de tête
16. les lignes qui se creusaient

spent with him since then – Lady Helen found that she couldn't bear the thought of him talking about seeing her[1]. She desperately wanted to avoid giving him an opportunity to do so. It was craven[2]. She despised herself for it.[3] And she didn't at that moment care to reflect upon[4] why it had suddenly become so crucial that Tommy never speak to her of Deborah again.

He appeared to have been reading her thoughts – how typical of him, really – for he gave her that brief, quirky smile of his[5] and walked to meet them at the foot of the stairs.

'How absolutely wonderful to see you, Tommy,' she said. 'I spent half the journey[6] – when I wasn't frantically eating every pastry that wandered by[7] – terrified that you'd be stuck[8] in Keldale and we'd have to hire a car and drive wildly about the moors[9] in best Earnshaw fashion[10], trying to find you. Well, it's all ended for the best[11], hasn't it, and I needn't have given in to my craving for[12] week-old[13] *pain au chocolat* in order to dull[14] my anxiety. The food is absolutely dreadful on the train, isn't it?' She tightened her arm round Gillian protectively. It was an instinctive gesture, for, although she knew the young woman had nothing to fear from Lynley, the last twelve hours had bonded Gillian to her[15] and now she found herself reluctant to hand the young woman over[16]. 'Gillian, this is Inspector Lynley,' she murmured.

A tentative smile touched[17] Gillian's lips. Then she dropped her eyes. Lynley began to extend his hand to her, but Lady Helen shook her head in warning[18]. At that, his glance slid[19] to the young woman's hands. The angry red scoring[20] that covered them was ugly but not as deep or serious as the abrasions[21] that covered her neck, breasts, and thighs, hidden by the dress that Lady Helen had carefully selected for her to wear.

1. qu'il lui dise l'avoir vue
2. lâche
3. Elle s'en jugeait méprisable.
4. n'avait nulle envie pour l'instant de se demander
5. son petit sourire bizarre
6. la moitié du voyage
7. à portée de la main
8. bloqué
9. foncer dans la lande
10. comme un Earnshaw [des Hauts de Hurlevent]
11. tout est bien qui finit bien
12. céder à mon envie de
13. vieux d'une semaine
14. pour tromper
15. créé un lien entre elle et Gillian
16. remettre la jeune femme à quelqu'un
17. effleura
18. pour le mettre en garde
19. Alors, son regard obliqua
20. marques rouge vif
21. écorchures

'I've the car just outside,' he said.

'Thank God,' Lady Helen declared. 'Lead me to it this moment[1] before my feet suffer irreparable damage from these ghastly[2] shoes. They *are* fetching[3], aren't they? But the agony I endure[4] hobbling about in them[5] simply beggars belief[6]. I keep asking myself why I'm such a slave to fashion.' She airily dismissed the[7] question as unanswerable[8]. 'I'm even willing to put up with[9] five minutes of the most melancholy Tchaikovsky in your collection just to get off my feet[10].'

He smiled. 'I'll remember that, old duck.'

'Darling, I haven't the slightest doubt of it.' She turned to Sergeant Havers, who had plodded wordlessly[11] behind them since they had disembarked. 'Sergeant, I need to pop into the ladies'[12] and undo the damage[13] I did to my make-up by burying my face in that last pastry just before that nasty[14] tunnel. Will you take Gillian out to the car?'

Havers looked from Lady Helen to Lynley. 'Of course,' she replied impassively.

Lady Helen watched the pair walk off before she spoke again. 'I'm really not sure which one of them is the worse for wear[15], Tommy.'

'Thank you for last night,' he said in answer. 'Was it awful for you?'

She took her eyes off the departing women. 'Awful?' The terrible desolation in Jonah Clarence's face; the sight of Gillian lying vacant-eyed[16], scarcely covered by a bloodied sheet[17], her wounds still seeping slow crimson[18] where the self-inflicted damage was most severe[19]; the blood on the floor and the walls of the bathroom and deep in the grout[20] where it would never come clean; the smashed[21] door and the brushes with bits of flesh[22] still adhering to their horrifying metal bristles.

'I'm sorry for putting you through it[23],' Lynley said. 'But you were the only one I could trust to

1. immédiatement
2. épouvantables
3. ravissantes
4. le martyre que je vis
5. à clopiner avec ça aux pieds
6. dépasse l'entendement
7. éluda joyeusement cette
8. qui n'appelait aucune réponse
9. prête à endurer
10. ne plus être debout
11. marchait d'un pas lourd et sans mot dire
12. faire un saut aux toilettes
13. pour réparer les dégâts
14. méchant
15. en plus mauvais état
16. étendue, le regard vide
17. d'un drap ensanglanté
18. des gouttes écarlates perlant encore de ses blessures,
19. aux endroits les plus violemment atteints
20. imprégnant les joints [du carrelage]
21. défoncée
22. des bouts de chair
23. de t'avoir infligé ça

manage it. I don't know what I would have done had you not been at home[1] when I phoned.'

'I'd only just got in. I have to admit that Jeffrey wasn't at all pleased at the manner in which our evening ended.'

Lynley's reaction played at the corners[2] of his mouth and eyes, equal parts amusement and surprise. 'Jeffrey Cusick? I thought you threw him over[3].'

She laughed lightly and took his arm. 'I tried, darling Tommy. I *did* try. But Jeffrey is quite determined to prove that, whether I realize it or not, he and I *are* on the path to true love. So he was working on advancing us a bit further[4] towards the journey's end[5] last night. It *was* romantic. Dinner in Windsor on the bank[6] of the Thames. Champagne cocktails in the garden of the Old House. You would have been proud of me. I even remembered that Wren[7] built it, so all these years of your seeing to[8] my education haven't been in vain.'

'But I hardly thought you'd be throwing it away on[9] Jeffrey Cusick.'

'Not throwing it away at all. He's a lovely man. Really. Besides, he was only too helpful in assisting me[10] with my dressing.'

'I've no doubt of that,' Lynley remarked drily.

She laughed at his grim expression. 'Not that way. Jeffrey would never take advantage. He's far too … too …'

'Fish-like?[11]'

'Spoken like the most petulant[12] Oxonian[13], Tommy,' she declared. 'But, to be *perfectly* honest, he is the teeniest bit like a cod[14]. Well, what can one expect? I've never in my life known a Cambridge man to get caught in the throes of passion.'

'Was he wearing his Harrovian tie[15] when I phoned?' Lynley asked. 'For that matter, was he wearing *anything*?'

1. si tu n'avais pas été chez toi
2. perça aux coins
3. que tu t'en étais débarrassée
4. essayait de nous faire progresser
5. vers la fin du parcours
6. sur les berges
7. [Christopher Wren, architecte notamm. de la cathédrale St Paul]
8. passées à t'occuper de
9. que tu la gâcherais auprès de
10. m'a aidée très volontiers
11. Ressemblant à un poisson ?
12. mal léché
13. étudiant d'Oxford
14. a un vague air de morue
15. cravate aux couleurs de [l'école de] Harrow

'Tommy, how vicious! But let me think.' She tapped her cheek thoughtfully. Her eyes twinkled up at him[1] as she pretended to consider[2] his question at some length[3]. 'No, I'm afraid we were both fully clothed[4] when you phoned. And after that, well, there simply wasn't time. We rushed[5] desperately to my wardrobe and began looking for something that would do. What do you think? Is it a success?'

Lynley eyed[6] the beautifully tailored black suit and matching[7] accessories. 'You look like a Quaker on the path to hell[8],' he said soberly. 'Good Lord, Helen, is that really a *Bible*?

She laughed. 'Doesn't it just *do*?[9]' She examined the leather volume in her hand. 'Actually, it's a collection[10] of John Donne[11], given to me by darling grandfather on my seventeenth birthday. I may actually open it some day.'

'What would you have done if she had asked you to read a few verses[12] to her to get her through the night?'

'I can sound positively biblical[13] when I want to, Tommy. A few *thees* and *thous*[14], a few *lays* and *begets*[15] and ... What is it?' He had stiffened[16] at her words. She felt the sudden rigidity in his arm.

Lynley was looking at his car parked outside the station doors. 'Where's her husband?'

She regarded him curiously. 'I don't know. He's vanished.[17] I went directly in to see Gillian, and later, when I came out of the bedroom, he'd gone. I spent the night there, of course, and he never returned.'

'How did Gillian react to that?'

'I'm ...' Lady Helen considered how best to answer the question. 'Tommy, I'm not even certain that she's aware[18] that he's gone. This sounds a little strange, I'm sure, but I think he's ceased to exist for her. She hasn't mentioned his name to me.'

'Has she said anything?'

1. Elle lui jeta un regard pétillant
2. faisait mine de réfléchir à
3. longuement
4. complètement habillés
5. On s'est précipités
6. étudia
7. assortis
8. en route vers l'enfer
9. N'est-ce pas pile ce qu'il faut ?
10. recueil
11. [Prédicateur et grand poète du XVIIe s. anglais]
12. quelques psaumes
13. sortir une prose très biblique
14. exemples de tutoiement caractéristique
15. connut et engendra
16. s'était raidi
17. Il s'est envolé.
18. qu'elle soit consciente

'Only that she left something for Bobby.'

'The message in the newspaper, no doubt.'

Lady Helen shook her head. 'No. I have the distinct impression that it was something at the house.'

Lynley nodded pensively and asked a final question. 'How did you talk her into coming[1], Helen?'

'I didn't. She'd already made up her mind[2], and I credit that to[3] Sergeant Havers, Tommy, although from the way she's been acting[4] I think she believes that I performed some sort of loaves and fishes[5] in the Clarence flat. *Do* speak to her, won't you? She's been positively monosyllabic[6] since I rang her this morning, and I think she's blaming herself for[7] everything that's happened.'

He sighed. 'That sounds just like Havers. Christ, what I don't need is one more thing to have to deal with in this *bloody* case.'

Lady Helen's eyes widened fractionally. Rarely, if ever, did he give vent to anger.[8] 'Tommy,' she said hesitantly, 'while you were in Keldale, did you happen to ... Is it ...?' She didn't want to speak of it. She *wouldn't* speak of it.[9]

He flashed her his crooked[10] smile. 'Sorry, old duck.' He dropped his arm round her shoulders and squeezed affectionately. 'Did I mention how damnably good it is[11] to have you here?'

He hadn't said anything to her. He hadn't so much as acknowledged her beyond a cursory nod[12]. But, then, why should he? Now that her little ladyship[13] was there to save the day[14] – just as she'd managed to do last night – there was no reason for them to communicate at all.

She might have known that Lynley would use one of his mistresses rather than someone from the Yard. Wasn't that typical of him? An ego so enormous that he had to make certain his London women would jump to his bidding[15] in spite of his

1. l'as-tu persuadée de venir
2. l'avait déjà décidé
3. à mon avis, c'est grâce au
4. vu son attitude,
5. miracle [de multiplication des pains et des poissons]
6. ne parle que par monosyllabes
7. se reproche
8. Il s'énervait rarement, voire jamais.
9. Non, elle n'en parlerait pas.
10. en coin
11. le bien fou que ça me fait
12. un bref hochement de tête
13. sa petite lady
14. pour sauver la mise
15. accourraient à son appel

catting about[1] in the country. Wonder if her ladyship will still jump through hoops[2] when she finds out about Stepha, Barbara thought. And just look at her with her perfect skin, perfect posture, perfect breeding[3] – as if her ancestors spent the last two hundred years throwing out the rejects[4], leaving them on hillsides like unacceptable Spartan babies[5] in order to arrive at the eugenic masterpiece[6] that was Lady Helen Clyde. *But not quite good enough to keep his lordship faithful, are we, sweetheart?* Barbara smiled inwardly.

She observed Lynley from the rear seat. *Had another big night with little Stepha, I'll bet.* Of course he had. Since he hadn't had to worry about how much the woman howled, he probably banged happily away at her[7] for hours on end. And now here was her precious ladyship to be serviced tonight[8]. Well, he could handle it. He could rise to the challenge[9]. Then he could move right on to give Gillian a treat[10]. No doubt that anaemic[11] little husband of hers would be only too happy to give the reins over[12] to a *real* man.

And weren't they both handling the little bitch[13] with kid gloves[14]! One couldn't really blame her ladyship for that approach. She didn't have all the facts on Gillian Teys. But what was Lynley's excuse? Since when did the accessory to murder get the red-carpet treatment[15] from CID?

'You're going to find Roberta very much changed, Gillian,' he was saying.

Barbara listened to the words with incredulity. What was he doing? What was he talking about? Was he actually preparing her to see her sister when[16] both of them knew damn well[17] she'd seen her only three weeks ago when they'd killed William Teys?

'I understand,' Gillian responded in a very small, nearly inaudible voice.

1. bien qu'il ait couru le guilledou
2. se laisser mener par le bout du nez
3. son éducation parfaite
4. à se débarrasser des ratés
5. les bébés rejetés [à la naissance, par le conseil des Anciens] à Sparte
6. ce chef-d'œuvre d'eugénisme
7. a pu la baiser tout son saoul
8. à honorer ce soir
9. saurait relever le défi
10. pour faire une gâterie à Gillian
11. anémié
12. de passer les rênes
13. à traiter cette petite garce
14. avec égards
15. avait droit au tapis rouge
16. alors que
17. savaient pertinemment

'She's been placed in the asylum as a temporary measure,' Lynley continued gently. 'It's a question of mental competence[1] arising out of her admission to the crime[2] and her unwillingness[3] to speak.'

'How did she ...? Who ...?' Gillian hesitated, then gave up the effort. She seemed to shrink into her seat[4].

'Your cousin Richard Gibson had her committed[5].'

'Richard?' Her voice grew even smaller[6].

'Yes.'

'I see.'

No one spoke. Barbara waited impatiently for Lynley to begin questioning the woman, and she couldn't understand his obvious reluctance[7] to do so. *What* was he doing? He was making the kind of solicitous conversation that one generally made with the victim of a crime, not with its perpetrator!

Furtively, Barbara examined Gillian. Good God, she was manipulative, right to the bitter end[8]. A few minutes in the bathroom last night and she had the whole lot of them right where she wanted. How long had she been trotting out[9] *that* little routine[10]?

Her eyes moved back to Lynley. Why had he brought her back on the case today? There could be only one reason, really: to put her in her place[11] once and for all, to humiliate her with the knowledge[12] that even an amateur like her sweet ladyship[13] had more expertise than Havers the pig. And then to condemn her, forever, to the street.

Well, the message was received, Inspector. Now all she longed for was a return to London and to uniform, leaving Lynley and his lady to sweep up the shards[14] of the mess she had made[15].

She'd worn her hair[16] in two long, blonde plaits[17]. That's why she looked so young that first night in Testament House. She spoke to no one, instead taking a quiet measure of[18] the group, deciding whether

1. responsabilité mentale,
2. du fait qu'elle ait avoué le crime
3. qu'elle refuse
4. se recroqueviller sur son siège
5. l'a fait interner
6. se fit encore plus ténue
7. son évidente réticence
8. jusqu'à la toute fin
9. Depuis combien de temps répétait-elle
10. manège
11. la remettre à sa place
12. en lui faisant savoir
13. madame
14. balayer les débris
15. de ce qu'elle avait foiré
16. avait coiffé ses cheveux
17. nattes blondes
18. évaluant silencieusement

they were worthy of her trust[1]. The decision once made[2], she said only her name: Helen Graham, Nell Graham.

But hadn't he known from the first that it wasn't really her name? Perhaps the slight hesitation before her response when someone addressed her had betrayed her. Perhaps it was the wistful look in her eyes[3] when she said it herself. Perhaps it was her tears when he first entered her body[4] and whispered *Nell* in the darkness. At any rate, hadn't he always known – somewhere in his heart – that it wasn't her name?

What had drawn him to her? At first, it was the child-like[5] innocence with which she embraced the life[6] at Testament House. She was so eager to learn[7], and then so passionately involved in[8] the purpose of the community[9]. After that it was her purity he so admired, the purity which allowed her to lead a new life, unaffected by personal animosities[10] in a world where she had simply decided that such ugliness would never exist. Then it was her devotion to God – not the breast-beating, ostentatious piety[11] of the religious reborn[12] but a calm acceptance of a power greater than her own – that touched him. And, last, it was her steadfast faith[13] in his ability to do anything, her words of encouragement when he felt despair, her abiding love[14] when he needed it most.

As I do now, Jonah Clarence thought.

In the last twelve hours he had looked deeply, unforgivingly, at[15] his own behaviour and had come to see it for what it was: unremitting cowardice[16]. He had left wife and home, running to an unknown destination, fleeing so that he wouldn't have to face what he was afraid to know. Yet what was there to fear when Nell – whoever she was – could be nothing more or less than the lovely creature[17] who stood by his side, who listened, rapt[18], to his words,

1. s'ils méritaient sa confiance
2. Une fois sa décision prise
3. son regard mélancolique
4. la première fois qu'il l'avait pénétrée
5. enfantine
6. avait adopté la vie
7. si avide d'apprendre
8. investie dans
9. l'action de la communauté
10. détachée de tout ressentiment personnel
11. la piété ostentatoire et autoflagellante
12. de ceux qui reviennent à la religion
13. sa foi inébranlable
14. son amour irréductible
15. sondé sans merci
16. d'une lâcheté absolue
17. cet être adorable
18. captivée

who held him in her arms at night? There could be no dark monster in her past for him to dread[1]. There could be only what she was and always had been.

This was the truth. He knew it. He could feel it. He believed it. And when the door to the mental hospital opened, he stood up quickly and strode across[2] the central hall to meet his wife[3].

Lynley felt, rather than saw, the hesitation in Gillian's footsteps as they entered the hospital. At first he attributed it to her understandable trepidation[4] about seeing her sister after so many years. But then he saw that her gaze was fixed on a young man who came across the lobby in their direction. Curious, Lynley turned to Gillian to speak, only to see[5] on her face an expression of unmitigated dread[6].

'Jonah,' she gasped[7], taking a step backwards.

'I'm sorry.' Jonah Clarence reached out as if to touch her but stopped. 'Forgive me. I'm sorry, Nell.' His eyes were burnt out[8], as if he hadn't slept in days.

'You *mustn't* call me that. Not any longer.'

He ignored her words. 'I spent the night sitting on a bench at King's Cross, trying to sort it all out[9], trying to decide if you could love a man who was too much of a coward[10] to stay with his wife when she needed him most.'

She reached out, touched his arm. 'Oh, Jonah,' she said. 'Please. Go back to London.'

'Don't ask that of me. It would be too easy.'

'*Please*. I beg you.[11] For me.'

'Not without you. I won't do that. Whatever you feel you must do here, I'll be here as well.' He looked at Lynley. 'May I stay with my wife?'

'It's up to[12] Gillian,' Lynley replied and noticed the manner in which the young man involuntarily recoiled at the[13] name.

1. qu'il ait à redouter
2. traversa à grands pas
3. pour rejoindre sa femme
4. appréhension
5. et lut alors,
6. pure terreur
7. dit-elle, dans un souffle
8. étaient éteints
9. à essayer d'y voir clair
10. bien trop lâche
11. Je t'en supplie.
12. Ça dépend de
13. frémit à ce

'If you want to stay, Jonah,' she whispered.

He smiled at her, touched her cheek lightly, and looked up from her face only when the sound of voices from the transverse passage signalled Dr Samuels' approach. The man carried a stack of file folders[1] which he handed to a female colleague[2] before swiftly[3] crossing towards them.

He eyed the entire group, unsmiling[4]. If he was grateful for the appearance of Roberta Teys' sister and the possibility of progress that her presence implied[5], he gave no indication[6].

'Inspector,' he said by way of greeting[7], 'is a group this large absolutely necessary?'

'It is,' Lynley responded evenly and hoped the man had the good sense[8] to take a close look at[9] Gillian's condition[10] before he raised a storm of protest[11] and threw them all out.

A pulse beat[12] in the psychiatrist's temple. It was obvious that he was unused to anything short of[13] fawning courtesy[14] and that he was caught between a desire to put Lynley summarily in his place and a wish to carry on with the planned meeting[15] between the two sisters. His concern for Roberta won out[16].

'This is the sister?' Without waiting for an answer, he took Gillian's arm and devoted his attention to her as they started down the passageway towards the locked ward. 'I've told Roberta that you're coming to see her,' he said quietly, his head bent to hers, 'but you must prepare yourself for the fact that she may not respond to you. She probably won't, in fact.'

'Has she …?' Gillian hesitated, seemed unsure how to proceed[17]. 'Has she still said nothing?'

'Nothing at all. But these are the very early stages[18] of therapy, Miss Teys, and—'

'Mrs Clarence,' Jonah interjected firmly.

1. une pile de dossiers
2. à une collègue
3. vivement
4. sans un sourire
5. découlant de sa présence
6. n'en laissa rien voir
7. en guise de salutations
8. aurait le bon sens
9. de bien regarder
10. l'état
11. de pousser les hauts cris
12. Une veine battait
13. ne connaissait qu'
14. une courtoisie servile
15. qu'aient lieu comme prévu les retrouvailles
16. l'emporta
17. ne pas trop savoir comment poursuivre
18. nous n'en sommes qu'au tout début

The psychiatrist stopped, swept his eyes over Jonah Clarence. A spark shot between them[1], suspicion and dislike[2].

'Mrs Clarence,' Samuels corrected himself, his eyes steadily on[3] her husband. 'As I was saying, Mrs Clarence, these are the earliest stages of therapy. We've no reason to doubt that your sister will some day make a full recovery[4].'

The use of the modifier was not lost on Gillian.[5] 'Some day?' Her arm encircled her waist in a gesture very like her mother's.

The psychiatrist appeared to be evaluating her reaction. He answered in a way that indicated that her brief response had communicated far more[6] than she realized.

'Yes, Roberta is very ill.' He put his hand on her elbow and guided her through the door in the panelling.

They walked through the locked ward, the only noise among them the muffled sounds[7] of their footsteps on the carpeting and the occasional cry[8] of a patient from behind the closed doors. Near the end of the corridor, a narrow door was recessed[9] into the wall, and Samuels stopped before it, opening it and switching on the light to reveal a small, cramped[10] room. He motioned them inside.

'You're going to find yourselves crowded[11] in here,' he warned, his tone of voice indicating how little he regretted the fact.

It was a narrow rectangle, no larger than a good-sized broom cupboard[12], which in fact it once had been. One wall was completely covered by a large mirror, two speakers hung[13] at either end[14], and a table and chairs were set up[15] in the middle. It was claustrophobic and pungent with the smell of[16] floor wax[17] and disinfectant.

'This is fine,' Lynley said.

1. Leurs regards jetèrent des étincelles
2. de l'aversion
3. sans quitter du regard
4. se rétablisse totalement un jour
5. Gillian perçut la nuance.
6. en avait dit beaucoup plus
7. le bruit étouffé
8. de temps en temps, le cri
9. encastrée
10. exiguë
11. vous sentir à l'étroit
12. grand placard à balai
13. deux haut-parleurs étaient accrochés
14. aux deux bouts
15. avaient été disposées
16. sentait fortement
17. la cire

Samuels nodded. 'When I fetch[1] Roberta, I shall switch these lights out, and you'll be able to see through the two-way mirror[2] into the next room. The speakers will allow you to hear what's being said. Roberta will see only the mirror, but I've told her that you will be present behind it. We couldn't have her in the room otherwise[3], you understand.'

'Yes, of course.'

'Fine.' He smiled at them grimly as if he sensed their apprehension and was glad to see that they – like himself – were not anticipating[4] that the coming interview would be a diverting lark[5]. 'I'll be in the next room with Gillian and Roberta.'

'Is that necessary?' Gillian asked hesitantly.

'Considering the circumstances, yes, I'm afraid it is.'

'The circumstances?'

'The murder, Mrs Clarence.' Samuels surveyed them all one last time and then buried[6] his hands deeply in the pockets of his trousers. His eyes were on Lynley. 'Shall we deal in legalities?[7]' he asked brusquely.

'That isn't necessary,' Lynley said. 'I'm well aware of them.[8]'

'You know that nothing she says[9]—'

'I know,' Lynley repeated.

He nodded sharply. 'Then, I'll fetch her.' He spun smartly on one heel[10], switched out the lights, and left the room, closing the door behind him.

The lights from the room beyond the mirror gave them some illumination, but their close little cell[11] was alive with shadows[12]. They seated themselves on the unforgiving[13] wooden chairs and waited: Gillian with her legs straight out in front of her, staring passionately down at[14] the scarred tips of her fingers[15]; Jonah with his chair next to hers, cradling its wooden back[16] protectively; Sergeant Havers slumped down[17], brooding[18] in the darkest corner

1. j'irai chercher
2. le miroir sans tain
3. sinon
4. ne s'attendaient pas
5. soit une partie de rigolade
6. enfonça
7. Devons-nous évoquer les aspects légaux ?
8. Je les connais parfaitement.
9. rien de ce qu'elle dira
10. pivota vivement sur un talon
11. petite cellule confinée
12. peuplée d'ombres
13. inconfortables
14. fixant intensément
15. le bout de ses doigts balafrés
16. un bras entourant le dossier de bois
17. affalée
18. broyant du noir

of the room; Lady Helen next to Lynley, observing the unspoken communication[1] between husband and wife; and Lynley himself, lost in deep contemplation from which he was roused by the touch of Lady Helen's hand squeezing his own.

Bless her[2], he thought, returning the pressure[3]. She knew. She always knew. He smiled at her, so glad that she was with him with her clear-eyed sanity[4] in a world that would shortly go mad.

Roberta was very much as she had been[5]. She entered the room between two white-clad nurses[6], dressed as she had been dressed before: in the too-short skirt, the ill-fitting blouse, the flip-flopping slippers[7] that barely sufficed to give her feet protection. She had, however, been bathed[8] in anticipation[9] of the interview, and her thick hair was clean and damp, pulled back and fastened[10] at her neck with a piece of scarlet yarn[11], an incongruous note of colour in the otherwise[12] monochromatic room. The room itself was inoffensive[13] and barren[14], devoid of decoration save for a trio of chairs[15] and a waist-high metal cabinet[16]. Nothing hung on the walls. There was no distraction, no escape[17].

'Oh, Bobby,' Gillian murmured when she saw her sister through the glass.

'There are three chairs here in the room, as you can see, Roberta.' Samuels' voice came to them without distortion[18] over the speakers. 'In a moment I'm going to ask your sister to join us. Do you remember your sister Gillian, Roberta?'

The girl, seated, began to rock[19]. She gave no reply. The two nurses left the room.

'Gillian's come up from London. Before I fetch her, however, I'd like you to look round the room and accustom yourself to it[20]. We've never met in here before, have we?'

1. la communication silencieuse
2. Bénie soit-elle
3. en lui étreignant la main à son tour
4. son esprit rationnel et clairvoyant
5. inchangée
6. infirmières vêtues de blanc
7. les pantoufles [ouvertes]
8. On l'avait cependant lavée
9. prévision
10. en arrière, attachés
11. du fil rouge
12. par ailleurs
13. anodine
14. nue
15. à part un ensemble de trois chaises
16. un placard métallique mi-haut
17. aucune échappatoire
18. leur parvint, sans déformation
19. se balancer
20. afin de vous y habituer

The girl's dull eyes remained where they had been, fixed on a point on the opposite wall. Her arms hung, inanimate[1], at her sides, lifeless, pulpy masses of fat and skin[2]. Samuels, undisturbed by her silence[3], let it continue while he placidly watched the girl. Two interminable minutes dragged by[4] in this way before he got to his feet.

'I shall fetch Gillian now, Roberta. I'm going to be in the room while you meet her. You're quite safe.'

The last declaration seemed entirely unnecessary, for if the hulking girl felt fear[5] – felt anything at all – she gave no sign.

In the observation room, Gillian got to her feet. It was a hesitant movement, unnatural, as if she were being propelled upward and forward[6] by a force other than her own free will[7].

'Darling, you know you don't have to go in there if you're afraid,' her husband said.

She did not reply but, rather, with the back of her hand upon which the heavy scoring[8] from the metal brushes stood out[9] like cutaneous veins[10] on the skin's surface, she stroked his cheek. She might have been saying goodbye to him.

'Ready?' Samuels asked when he opened the door. His sharp glance made a rapid assessment of[11] Gillian, cataloguing[12] her potential weaknesses and strengths[13]. When she nodded, he went on crisply. 'There's nothing to worry about. I'll be in there and several orderlies[14] are within calling distance[15] should she need to be quickly subdued[16].'

'You act as if you believe that Bobby could really hurt someone,' Gillian said and preceded him to the next room without waiting for a response.

The others watched, waiting for a reaction from Roberta when the door opened and her sister entered. There was none. The big square body[17] continued to rock.

1. Ses bras ballants étaient inertes
2. des masses de graisse et de peau bouffies
3. sans être troublé par son silence
4. minutes s'écoulèrent, interminables
5. si la grosse fille ressentait de la peur
6. mue
7. indépendante de sa volonté
8. éraflures
9. ressortaient
10. des veines cutanées
11. évalua rapidement
12. faisant l'inventaire de
13. faiblesses et forces
14. aides-soignants
15. à portée de voix
16. maîtrisée
17. grand corps massif

Gillian hesitated, her hand on the door. 'Bobby,' she said clearly[1]. Her tone was quiet, but matter-of-fact[2], the way a parent might speak to a recalcitrant child. Receiving no response, the young woman took one of the three chairs and placed it in front of her sister, directly in her line of vision[3]. She sat down. Roberta gazed through her to[4] the spot on the wall. Gillian looked towards the psychiatrist, who had pulled his chair to one side, out of Roberta's vision. 'What should I—'

'Talk about yourself. She can hear you.'

Gillian fingered the material[5] of her dress. She dragged her eyes up[6] to her sister's face. 'I've come up from London to see you, Bobby,' she began. Her voice quavered[7], but as she proceeded, it gathered strength[8]. 'That's where I live now. With my husband. I was married last November.' She looked at Samuels, who nodded encouragingly. 'You're going to think it's so funny, but I married a minister[9]. It's hard to believe that a girl with such a strong Catholic background would marry a minister, isn't it? What would Papa ever say if he knew?'

The plain face offered neither acknowledgement[10] nor interest. Gillian might have been speaking to the wall. She licked her dry lips[11] and stumbled on[12]. 'We have a flat in Islington. It's not a very large flat, but you'd like it. Remember how I loved plants? Well, I've lots[13] in the flat because the kitchen window gets just the right kind of sun[14]. Remember how I could never get plants to grow in the farmhouse? It was too dark.'

The rocking continued. The chair on which Roberta sat groaned with her weight[15].

'I have a job, as well. I work at a place called Testament House. You know that place, don't you? It's where runaways[16] go to live sometimes. I do all sorts of work[17] there, but I like counselling the kids

1. d'une voix claire
2. neutre
3. champ de vision
4. Le regard de Roberta fixa à travers elle
5. tripota le tissu
6. leva péniblement les yeux
7. chevrota
8. prit de l'assurance
9. pasteur
10. Le visage ingrat n'eut aucune réaction
11. passa la langue sur ses lèvres sèches
12. poursuivit tant bien que mal
13. j'en ai plein
14. a exactement l'ensoleillement qu'il faut
15. gémissait sous son poids
16. les fugueurs
17. J'accomplis toutes sortes de tâches

the best[1]. They say I'm easy to talk to[2].' She paused. 'Bobby, won't you talk to me[3]?'

The girl's breathing sounded drugged[4], her heavy head hung to one side[5]. She might have been asleep.

'I like London. I never thought I would, but I do. I expect it's because that's where my dreams are. I ... I'd like to have a baby. That's one of my dreams. And I'd ... I think I'd like to write a book. There are all sorts of stories inside me[6], and I want to write them down. Like the Brontës. Remember how we read the Brontës? They had dreams as well, didn't they? I think it's important to have dreams.'

'It's not going to work,' Jonah Clarence said brusquely. The moment[7] his wife had left the room, he had seen the trap[8], had understood that her entry into her sister's presence[9] was a return to a past in which he had played no part, from which he could not save her. 'How long does she have to stay in there?'

'As long as she wants.' Lynley's voice was cool[10]. 'It's in Gillian's hands[11].'

'But anything can happen. Doesn't she understand that?' Jonah wanted to jump up, fling open the door[12], and drag his wife away[13]. It was as if her mere presence[14] in the room – trapped with the horrible, whale-like creature[15] that was her sister – were enough to contaminate and destroy her for ever. '*Nell!*' he said fiercely.

'I want to talk to you about the night I left, Bobby,' Gillian went on, her eyes on her sister's face, waiting for the slightest flicker[16] that would indicate comprehension and recognition, that would allow her words to stop. 'I don't know if you remember it. It was the night after[17] my sixteenth birthday. I ...' It was too much. She couldn't. She fought onward[18]. 'I stole money from Papa. Did he tell you that? I knew where he kept it, the extra money for the house, so I took it. It was wrong, I know that, but I ... I need-

1. ce que je préfère, c'est conseiller les jeunes
2. qu'on peut me parler facilement
3. tu ne veux pas me parler
4. semblait sous l'effet des médicaments
5. était inclinée de côté
6. en moi
7. Dès que
8. décelé le piège
9. l'avoir mise en présence de sa sœur
10. froide
11. Gillian qui décide
12. ouvrir la porte d'un coup
13. entraîner sa femme loin de là
14. sa seule présence
15. créature semblable à une baleine
16. attentive à la plus petite lueur
17. la nuit suivant
18. s'efforça de poursuivre

ed to leave. I needed to go away for a while. You know that, don't you?' And then again, seeking reassurance[1], '*Don't* you?'

Was the rocking faster[2] now, or was it so only in the imagination[3] of the watchers?

'I went to York. It took me all night. I walked and hitchhiked[4]. I just had that rucksack[5], you know the one I used to carry my school books in, so I only had one change of clothes[6] with me. I don't know what I was thinking about, running away like that. It seems crazy now, doesn't it?' Gillian smiled briefly at her sister. She could feel her heart hammering[7]. It was becoming quite difficult to breathe. 'I got to York at dawn. I'll never forget the sight of the morning light hitting[8] the Minster. It was beautiful. I wanted to stay there for ever.' She stopped, put her hands firmly into her lap. The deep scratches showed[9]. It couldn't be helped.[10]' I stayed in York that entire day. I was so frightened, Bobby. I'd never even been away from home for a night by myself[11], and I wasn't sure I wanted to go on to London. I thought it might be easier if I went back to the farm. But I … I couldn't. I just couldn't.'

'What's the point of this?' Jonah Clarence demanded. 'How is all this supposed to help Roberta?'

Wary, Lynley glanced at him, but the man settled himself again[12]. His face was rigid, every muscle tight[13].

'So I caught the train that night. There were so many stops[14], and at every one of them I thought that I would be questioned. I thought that Papa might have sent the police after me[15], or come after me himself. But nothing happened. Until I got to King's Cross.'

'You don't need to tell her about the pimp,' Jonah whispered. 'What's the point?'

'There was a nice man at King's Cross who bought me something to eat. I was so grateful[16] to him. He

1. demandant confirmation
2. Le balancement s'était-il accéléré
3. une illusion
4. j'ai fait du stop
5. sac à dos
6. qu'un jeu de vêtements de rechange
7. son cœur battre la chamade
8. illuminant
9. se voyaient
10. Elle n'y pouvait rien.
11. toute seule
12. se calma à nouveau
13. chaque muscle contracté
14. d'arrêts
15. à ma recherche
16. si reconnaissante

was such a gentleman, I thought. But while I was eating and he was telling me about a house he had where I could live, another man came into the cafeteria. He saw us. He came up and said, "She's coming with me." I thought he was a policeman, that he would make me go home again. I started to cry. I hung on[1] to my friend. But he shook me off[2] and ran out of the station.' She paused, caught in the memory[3] of that night. 'This new man was very different. His clothes were old, a bit shabby[4]. But his voice was kind. He said his name was George Clarence, that he was a minister, and that the other man had wanted to take me to Soho to … to take me to Soho,' she repeated firmly. 'He said he had a house in Euston where I could stay.'

Jonah remembered it all so vividly[5]: the ancient[6] rucksack, the frightened girl, the scuffed[7] shoes and tattered jeans[8] she wore. He remembered his father's arrival and the conversation between his parents. The words 'pimp from Soho … didn't even understand … looks like she hasn't slept at all …' echoed[9] in his mind. He remembered watching her from the breakfast table where he'd been dividing his time[10] between scrambled eggs[11] and cramming for a literature test[12]. She wouldn't look at anyone. Not then.[13]

'Mr Clarence was very good to me, Bobby. I was like part of his family. I … I married his son Jonah. You'd love Jonah. He's so gentle. So good. When I'm with him, I feel as if nothing could ever … nothing ever again[14] …,' she concluded.

It was enough. It was what she had come to do. Gillian looked at the psychiatrist beseechingly[15], waiting for direction from him[16], for his nod of dismissal[17]. He merely watched her from behind the protection of his spectacles. They winked[18] in the light. His face told her nothing, but his eyes were very kind.

1. Je me suis accrochée à
2. m'a repoussée
3. sous l'emprise des souvenirs
4. miteux
5. si nettement
6. vieux
7. éraflées
8. le jean usé
9. résonnèrent
10. où il partageait son temps
11. des œufs brouillés
12. les révisions pour un contrôle de littérature
13. Pas à l'époque.
14. plus jamais
15. d'un air suppliant
16. attendant qu'il la guide
17. qu'il lui fasse signe de partir
18. brillaient

'There. That's it.[1] It's done nothing,' Jonah concluded decisively. 'You've brought her up here[2] to this all for nothing. I'm taking her home.' He began to get to his feet.

'Sit down,' Lynley said, his voice making it clear that the other man had no choice in the matter[3].

'Bobby, talk to me,' Gillian begged. 'They say you killed Papa. But I know that you couldn't have. You didn't look like … There was no *reason*. I know it. Tell me there was no reason. He took us to church, he read to us, he made up games[4] we could play. Bobby, you didn't kill him, did you?'

'It's important to you that I didn't kill him[5], isn't it?' Dr Samuels said quietly. His voice was like a feather floating gently[6] in the air between them.

'Yes,' Gillian responded immediately, although her eyes were on her sister. 'I put the key under your pillow, Bobby. You were awake[7]! I talked to you! I said "Use it tomorrow" and you understood. Don't tell me you didn't understand. I *know* you did.'

'I was too young. I didn't understand,' the doctor said.

'You had to understand![8] I told you I'd put a message in the *Guardian*, that it would say *Nell Graham*, remember? We loved that book, didn't we? She was so brave and strong[9]. It was the way we both wanted to be.'

'But I wasn't strong, was I?' the doctor queried[10].

'You were! You didn't look like … You were supposed to[11] come to Harrogate! The message told you to come to Harrogate, Bobby! You were sixteen. You could have come!'

'I wasn't like you at sixteen, Gillian. How could I have been?' The psychiatrist hadn't moved in his chair. His eyes travelled between the two sisters[12], waiting for a sign, reading the underlying messages in[13] body movements, posture, and tone of voice.

1. Bon, ça suffit comme ça.
2. Vous l'avez fait venir ici
3. n'avait pas le choix
4. inventait des jeux
5. pour toi, que je ne l'aie pas tué
6. une plume voletant doucement
7. ne dormais pas
8. Il fallait que tu comprennes !
9. si forte et courageuse
10. interrogea le docteur
11. censée
12. Son regard passait d'une sœur à l'autre
13. les messages révélés par

'You didn't have to be! You weren't supposed to be! All you had to do was come to Harrogate. Not to London, just to Harrogate. I would have taken you from there. But when you didn't come, I thought – I *believed*[1] – that you were all right. That nothing ... that you were fine[2]. You weren't like Mummy.[3] You were fine.'

'Like Mummy?'

'Yes, like Mummy. I was like her. Just exactly like.[4] I could see it in the pictures. But you weren't. So that made you fine.[5]'

'What did it mean, to be like Mummy?' the doctor asked.

Gillian stiffened. Her mouth formed the single word[6] *no* three times in rapid succession. It was too much to bear. She couldn't go on.

'Was Bobby like Mummy in spite of what you believed?'

No!

'Don't answer him, Nell,' Jonah Clarence muttered. 'You don't have to answer him. You're not the patient here[7].'

Gillian looked at her hands. She felt the burden of guilt heavy[8] upon her shoulders. The sound of her sister's ceaseless rocking[9] filled the air, the sound of tortured breathing, the beating of her own heart. She felt that she couldn't go on. She knew she couldn't turn back[10].

'You know why I left, don't you?' she said hollowly[11]. 'It was because of the present[12] on my birthday, the special present, the one ...' Her hand went to her eyes. It shook. She controlled herself. 'You must tell them the truth! You must tell them what happened! You can't let them lock you away[13] for the rest of your life!'

Silence. She *couldn't*. It was in the past. It had all happened to someone else. Besides, the little eight-year-old[14] who had followed her round the farm,

1. j'ai vraiment cru
2. tout allait bien pour toi
3. Tu ne ressemblais pas à Maman.
4. Trait pour trait.
5. Et donc, ça allait pour toi.
6. un seul mot :
7. sa patiente.
8. le fardeau de la culpabilité peser
9. balancement incessant
10. revenir en arrière
11. d'une voix éteinte
12. cadeau
13. t'enfermer
14. la petite de 8 ans

who had watched her every movement[1] with eyes shining with adoration, was dead. This gross[2], obscene creature before her was not Roberta. There was no need to go further. Roberta was gone.

Gillian lifted her head. Roberta's eyes had shifted.[3] They had moved to her, and in that movement Gillian saw that she had indeed broken through[4] where the psychiatrist had failed these last three weeks. But there was no triumph in that knowledge[5]. There was only condemnation. There was only facing[6], one last time, the immutable past[7].

'I didn't understand,' Gillian said brokenly[8]. 'I was only four or five years old. You weren't even born then. He said it was special. A kind of friendship[9] fathers always had with their daughters[10]. Like Lot[11].'

'Oh, no,' Jonah whispered.

'Did he read the Bible to you, Bobby? He read it to me. He came in at night and sat on my bed and read the Bible to me. And as he read it[12] –'

'No, no, *no*!'

'– his hand would find me underneath the covers[13]. "Do you like that, Gilly?" he would ask me. "Does it make you happy? It makes Papa very happy. It's so nice. So soft. Do you like it, Gilly?" '

Jonah pounded his right fist against his forehead. With his left arm he hugged himself tightly across his chest up to his shoulder. '*Please*,' he moaned[14].

'I didn't know, Bobby. I didn't understand. I was only five years old and then it was dark in the room. "Turn over[15]," he would say, "Papa will rub your back[16]. Do you like that? Where do you like it best? Here, Gilly? Is it special here?" And then he'd take my hand. "Papa likes it there, Gilly. Rub Papa there." '

'Where was Mummy?' the doctor asked.

'Mummy was asleep. Or in her room[17]. Or reading. But it really didn't matter because this was special. This was something fathers share[18] with

1. tous ses mouvements
2. énorme
3. Le regard de Roberta se portait ailleurs.
4. fait une brèche
5. à le savoir
6. Il n'y avait que la confrontation
7. à ce passé immuable
8. la voix brisée
9. Une sorte d'amitié
10. ont toujours eue avec leurs filles
11. [qui, après sa fuite, a engendré deux lignées par des relations incestueuses avec ses filles, restées sans maris]
12. tout en lisant
13. me touchait, sous les couvertures
14. gémit-il
15. Retourne-toi
16. va te frotter le dos
17. chambre
18. que les pères partagent

daughters. Mummy mustn't know. Mummy wouldn't understand. She didn't read the Bible with us so she wouldn't understand. And then she left. I was eight years old.'

'And then you were alone.'

Gillian shook her head numbly[1]. Her eyes were wide, tearless. 'Oh, no,' she said in a small, torn voice[2]. 'I was Mummy then.[3]'

At her words, a cry escaped Jonah Clarence's lips. Lady Helen looked at Lynley immediately and covered his hand with her own. It turned, grasping her fingers tightly[4].

'Papa set up all her pictures[5] in the sitting-room so I could see her every day. "Mummy's gone," he said and made me look at them all so I could see how pretty she was and how much I had sinned[6] in being born in the first place[7] to drive her away[8]. "Mummy knew how much Papa loved you, Gilly, so she left. You must be mummy to me[9] now." I didn't know what he meant. So he showed me. He read the Bible. He prayed. And he showed me. But I was too little to be a proper mummy[10] to him. So he… I did other things. He taught me. And I… was a very good student[11].'

'You wanted to please him. He was your father. He was all you had[12].'

'I wanted him to love me. He said he loved me when I… when we… "Papa loves it[13] in your mouth, Gilly." And afterwards[14] we prayed. We always prayed. I thought God would forgive me for making Mummy run away if I became a good enough mummy to Papa. But God never forgave me. He didn't exist.'

Jonah's head sank[15] to the table, cradled in his arms[16], and he began to weep.

Gillian finally looked at her sister again. Roberta's eyes were on her, although her face remained without expression. The rocking had stopped.

1. secoua la tête, hébétée
2. d'une voix faible, brisée
3. Alors Maman, ce fut moi.
4. lui serrant fort les doigts
5. a installé toutes les photos d'elle
6. comme j'avais péché
7. rien que par ma naissance
8. pour la faire partir
9. faire la maman pour moi
10. une vraie maman
11. élève
12. tout ce que vous aviez
13. adore la mettre
14. après,
15. s'effondra, la tête
16. enfouie dans ses bras

'So I did things, Bobby, things I didn't understand because Mummy was gone and I needed… I wanted my mummy again. And I thought the only way to get Mummy back was to be her myself[1].'

'Is that what you did when you were sixteen?' Dr Samuels asked softly.

'He came to my room. It was late. He said it was time to become Lot's daughter, the real way[2], the way the Bible said, and he took off his clothes.'

'He'd never done that before?'

'Never all his clothes. Not like that. I thought he wanted… what I usually… But he didn't. He… spread my legs[3] and… "You're… I can't breathe[4], Papa. You're too heavy. Please, don't. I'm afraid. Oh, it hurts, it hurts!" '

Her husband swayed to his feet[5], scraping his chair back viciously[6] on the linoleum floor. He staggered to[7] the window. 'It never happened!' he cried against it. 'It couldn't![8] It didn't! You're my *wife*!

'But he put his hand over[9] my mouth. He said, "We can't wake[10] Bobby, darling. Papa loves *you* best.[11] Let Papa show you, Gilly. Let Papa inside.[12] Like Mummy. Like a real mummy. Let Papa inside." And it hurt. And it hurt. And I *hated* him.'

'No!' Jonah screamed. He threw open the door. It crashed against[13] the wall. He ran from the room.

Then Gillian began to cry. 'I was just a shell.[14] I wasn't a person. What did it matter what he did to me? I became what he wanted, what anyone wanted. That's how I lived. Jonah, that's how I *lived*!

'Pleasing everyone?[15]' the doctor asked.

'People love looking into mirrors. So that's what I was. That's what he made me[16]. Oh God, I hated him. I *hated* him!' She buried her face in her hands and wept as the grief overcame her[17], tortured tears held in check for[18] eleven long years. The others sat motionless, listening to her weeping. After long, painful minutes she raised her ravaged face to her

1. c'était de l'incarner
2. pour de vrai
3. a écarté mes jambes
4. Tu m'empêches de respirer
5. bondit sur ses pieds
6. en raclant sa chaise violemment
7. tituba jusqu'à
8. Ce n'est pas possible !
9. sur
10. Il ne faut pas réveiller
11. C'est toi que Papa préfère.
12. Laisse Papa aller en toi.
13. Elle se fracassa contre
14. Je n'étais qu'une coquille vide.
15. En faisant plaisir à tout le monde ?
16. ce qu'il a fait de moi
17. submergée par la souffrance
18. retenues depuis

sister's. 'Don't let him kill you, Bobby. Don't let him do it. For God's sake, tell them the truth!'

There was no response. There was absolutely nothing. Only the unbearable sound[1] of Gillian's personal torment. Roberta was motionless. She might have been deaf.[2]

'Tommy,' Lady Helen whispered. 'I can't bear this. She's done it for[3] *nothing*.'

Lynley stared into the next room. His head was pounding[4], his throat ached[5], his eyes burned. He wanted to find William Teys, find him alive[6], and tear the man savagely limb from limb[7]. He had never known such rage, such sickness[8]. He felt Gillian's anguish overcome him like a disease[9].

But her weeping had lessened[10]. She was getting to her feet. She was walking unevenly[11], numbly, to the door. Her hand reached for the knob. She turned it, pulled it open. Her presence had been useless after all. It was over[12].

'Did he make you have the naked parade[13], Gilly?' Roberta asked.

1. l'insoutenable résonance
2. C'était comme si elle était sourde.
3. a fait tout ça pour
4. le martelait
5. était douloureuse
6. le retrouver vivant
7. l'écharper sauvagement
8. dégoût
9. le submerger comme une maladie
10. diminué
11. à pas irréguliers
12. fini
13. Est-ce qu'il t'a fait parader nue

16

As if under water, Gillian turned slowly from the door at the sound of her sister's husky[1] voice. 'Tell me,' she whispered. She walked back to her chair, moved it closer to[2] the other, and sat down.

Roberta's eyes, heavy-lidded[3] under their protective folds[4] of fat, were fixed but unfocused on her sister[5]. Her lips worked convulsively. The fingers of one hand flexed. 'It was music. Loud. He would take off my clothes.' And then the girl's voice altered. It became honey-toned[6], insinuatingly persuasive, chillingly male[7]. '*Pretty baby. Pretty baby* and *Time to march*[8], *pretty baby. Time to march for Papa.* And he would… it was in his hand… *Watch what Papa does while you march, pretty baby.*'

'I left the key for you, Bobby,' Gillian said brokenly. 'When he fell asleep that night in my bed, I went to his room and I found the key. What happened to it? I *left* it for you.'

Roberta struggled with[9] information buried so long beneath the weight of her childhood terrors[10]. 'I didn't … didn't know. I locked the door. But you never said why. You never said to keep the key[11].'

'Oh God.' Gillian's voice was anguished. 'Are you saying that you locked the door at night but in the day you left the key in the keyhole[12]? Bobby, is that what you mean?'

1. enrouée
2. l'approcha de
3. les paupières lourdes
4. plis
5. fixaient sa sœur sans la voir
6. mielleuse
7. masculine à faire froid dans le dos
8. C'est le moment de parader
9. se débattit pour retrouver
10. sous le poids de ses terreurs d'enfant
11. qu'il fallait garder la clef
12. dans la serrure

Roberta drew her arm across her damp face[1]. It was like a shield[2], and behind its protection she nodded. Her body heaved with a repressed cry[3]. 'I didn't *know*.'

'So he found it and took it away.'

'He put it in his wardrobe. All the keys were there. It was locked. I couldn't get it. *Don't need keys*[4], *pretty baby. Pretty baby march for Papa.*'

'When did you march?'

'Daytime, night-time.[5] *Come here, pretty baby, Papa wants to help you march.*'

'How?'

Roberta's arm dropped. Her face was quickly shuttered[6]. Her fingers picked and pulled at[7] her lower[8] lip.

'Bobby, *tell* me how,' Gillian insisted. 'Tell me what he did.'

'I love Papa. I love Papa.'

'Don't say that!' She reached out, grabbed her sister's arm. 'Tell me what he did to you!'

'Love. *Love* Papa.'

'Don't say that! He was evil[9]!'

Roberta shrank from the word. 'No. *I* was evil.'

'How?'

'What I made him … he couldn't help[10] … he prayed and prayed and couldn't help … you weren't there … *Gilly knew what I wanted. Gilly knew how to do me*[11]. *You're no good*[12], *pretty baby. March for Papa. March on*[13] *Papa.*'

' "March *on* Papa"?' Gillian gasped[14].

'Up and down in one place. Up and down. *That's nice, pretty baby. Papa big between your legs .*'

'Bobby. *Bobby.*' Gillian averted her face[15]. 'How old were you?'

'Eight. *Mmmmm, Papa likes to feel all over*[16]. *Likes to feel and feel and feel.*'

'Didn't you tell anyone? Wasn't there anyone?'

1. sur son visage moite
2. bouclier
3. trembla d'un cri étouffé
4. Pas besoin de clefs
5. Le jour, la nuit.
6. se referma subitement
7. pinçaient et tiraient
8. inférieure
9. méchant
10. il ne pouvait s'en empêcher
11. comment s'y prendre avec moi
12. Tu n'es pas douée
13. Parade sur
14. sursauta
15. détourna le visage
16. toucher partout

'Miss Fitzalan. I told. But she didn't… she couldn't…'

'She didn't *do* anything? She didn't *help*?'

'She didn't understand. I said whiskers… his face when he rubbed me[1]. Didn't understand[2]. *Did you tell, pretty baby? Did you try to tell on[3] Papa?*'

'Oh God, she *told* him?'

'Gilly never told. Gilly never told on Papa. Very bad, pretty baby. Papa needs to punish you.'

'How?'

Roberta gave no answer. Instead, she began to rock, began to return to the place she had inhabited so long.

'You were only eight years old!' Gillian began to cry. 'Bobby, I'm sorry! I didn't know! I didn't think he would. You didn't look like me. You didn't look like Mummy.'

'Hurt Bobby in the bad[4] place. Not like Gilly. Not like Gilly.'

'Not like Gilly?'

'Turn over, pretty baby. Papa has to punish you.'

'Oh my God!' Gillian fell to her knees, took her sister into her arms. She sobbed against her breast, but the girl did not respond. Instead, her arms hung limply[5] at her sides and her body tensed as if the proximity of her sister was frightening or distasteful[6]. 'Why didn't you come to Harrogate? Didn't you see the message? Why didn't you come? I thought you were all right! I thought he left you alone! Why didn't you come?'

'Bobby died. Bobby died.'

'Don't say that! You're alive. Don't let him kill you now!'

Roberta shrank back[7], freeing herself fiercely[8]. 'Papa never kill, Papa never kill, Papa never kill!' Her voice grew high with panic.[9]

1. se frottait contre moi
2. [Elle a cru que Roberta parlait du chien.]
3. dénoncer
4. honteux
5. ses bras pendaient mollement
6. effrayante ou désagréable
7. eut un mouvement de recul
8. se dégageant farouchement
9. La panique fit monter sa voix dans les aigus.

The psychiatrist leaned forward in his chair. 'Kill what, Roberta?' he asked quickly, and pressed the advantage[1]. 'What did Papa never kill?'

'Baby. Papa didn't kill the baby.'

'What did he do?'

'Found me in the barn. Cried and prayed[2] and cried.'

'Is that where you had the baby? In the barn?'

'No one knew.[3] Fat and ugly.[4] No one knew.'

Gillian's eyes were transfixed in horror[5], not on her sister's face, but on the psychiatrist. She rocked on her heels, a hand at her mouth, biting down on her fingers[6] as if to keep from screaming[7]. 'You were pregnant? Bobby! He didn't know you were pregnant?'

'No one knew. Not like Gilly. Fat and ugly. No one knew.'

'What happened to the baby?'

'Bobby died.'

'What happened to the baby?'

'Bobby died.'

'What happened to the baby!' Gillian's voice rose to a scream[8].

'Did you kill the baby, Roberta?' Dr Samuels asked.

Nothing. She began to rock. It was a rapid movement, as if she were hurtling back into madness[9].

Gillian watched her, watched the panic that drove her and the unassailable armour of psychosis[10] that protected her. And she knew. 'Papa killed the baby,' she asserted[11] numbly. 'He found you in the barn, he cried and prayed, read the Bible for guidance, and then he killed the baby.' She touched her sister's hair. 'What did he do with it?[12]'

'Don't know.'

'Did you ever see it?[13]'

'Never saw the baby. Boy or girl. Don't know.'

'Is that why you didn't come to Harrogate? Were you pregnant then[14]?'

1. profita de l'avantage
2. Pleurait et priait
3. Personne n'a su.
4. Grosse et laide.
5. pétrifiés d'horreur
6. se mordant les doigts
7. comme pour s'empêcher de crier
8. devint un hurlement
9. fonçait à nouveau dans la folie
10. cette armure de psychose, imprenable
11. affirma-t-elle
12. Qu'en a-t-il fait ?
13. L'as-tu jamais vu ?
14. à ce moment-là

The rocking slowed to a stop. It was affirmation[1].

'Baby died. Bobby died. It didn't matter. *Papa sorry, pretty baby. Papa never hurt again. Pretty baby march for Papa. Papa never hurt again.*'

'He didn't have intercourse with you again[2], Roberta?' Dr Samuels asked. 'But everything else stayed the same[3]?'

'Pretty baby march for Papa.'

'Did you march for Papa, Roberta?' the doctor continued. 'After the baby, did you march for him?'

'Marched for Papa. Had to march.[4]'

'Why? Why did you have to?'

She looked about[5] furtively, an odd smile of twisted[6] satisfaction dancing on her face. And then began to rock. 'Papa happy.'

'It was important that Papa be happy,' Dr Samuels said reflectively.

'Yes, yes. *Very* happy. Happy Papa won't touch...' She cut the words off[7]. The rocking increased in intensity.

'No, Bobby,' Gillian said. 'Don't you leave.[8] You mustn't leave now. You marched for Papa to keep him happy so that he wouldn't touch someone. Who?'

In the darkened[9] observation room, the terrible realization cut like a sword's swath down Lynley's spine[10]. The knowledge had been there before him[11] all along. A nine-year-old girl being schooled in the Bible[12], being read the Old Testament, learning the lessons of Lot's daughters.

'*Bridie!*' he said savagely and understood everything at last. He could have told the rest of the story himself, but he listened instead to the purgation of a tortured soul[13].

'Papa wanted Gilly not a cow like Roberta.'

'Your father wanted a child, didn't he?' Dr Samuels asked. 'He needed a child's body to arouse him[14]. Like Gillian's. Like your mother's.'

1. oui
2. Il n'a plus eu de relations sexuelles avec toi
3. est resté pareil
4. Il fallait parader.
5. regarda autour d'elle
6. perverse
7. s'interrompit
8. Ne t'en va pas.
9. la pénombre de
10. fendit Lynley en deux
11. sous son nez
12. à qui on fait étudier la Bible
13. une âme torturée se délivrer
14. pour l'exciter

'Found a child.'

'And what happened?'

Roberta pressed her cracked[1] lips together as if to stop herself from speaking. The corners of her mouth were spotted with blood[2]. She gave a ragged cry[3] and a flurry of words escaped[4] as if of their own volition[5]. 'The Pharaoh put a chain on his neck and dressed him in fine linen[6] and he ruled over Egypt and Joseph's brothers came to see him and Joseph said I am supposed to save your lives by a great deliverance[7].'

Gillian spoke through her tears. 'The Bible told you what to do, just as it always told Papa.'

'Dress in linens.[8] Wear a chain.'

'What happened?'

'Got him[9] in the barn.'

'How did you do that?' Dr Samuels' voice was low.

Roberta's face quivered[10]. Her eyes filled with tears. They began to spill down her acne-covered cheeks. 'Tried twice. Didn't work. Then… Whiskers,' she replied.

'You killed Whiskers to get your father to the barn?' the doctor asked.

'Whiskers didn't know. Gave him pills. Papa's pills. He was asleep. Cut… cut his throat. Called for Papa. Papa ran. Knelt by[11] Whiskers.' She began to rock furiously, cradling her bloated[12] body, accompanying the movement with low, tuneless humming[13]. She was in retreat[14].

'And then, Roberta?' the psychiatrist asked. 'You can take the last step[15], can't you? With Gillian here?'

Rocking. Rocking. Savage and furious. Blindly determined. Her eyes on the wall. 'Love Papa. Love Papa. Don't remember. *Don't remember.*'

'Of course you remember.' The psychiatrist's voice was gentle but relentless[16]. 'The Bible told you what to do. If you hadn't done it, your father would have done to that little girl all the things he had done to

1. gercées
2. tachés de sang
3. poussa un cri rauque
4. les mots sortirent en rafale
5. de leur propre gré
6. d'habits de lin fin
7. par une grande délivrance
8. Se vêtir de lin.
9. L'ai fait venir
10. trembla
11. S'est agenouillé près de
12. boursoufflé
13. fredonnement bas et discordant
14. se repliait sur elle-même
15. faire le dernier pas
16. opiniâtre

you and Gillian through the years[1]. He would have molested[2] her. He would have sodomized her. He would have raped[3] her. But you stopped him, Roberta. You saved that child. You dressed in fine linens. You put on the gold chain. You killed the dog. You called your father to the barn. He ran in, didn't he? He knelt down and—'

Roberta jumped off[4] her chair. It flew across[5] the room, striking the cabinet[6], and she went after it[7], moving like the wind[8]. She picked it up, hurled it[9] against the wall, overturned[10] the cabinet, and began to scream.

'I chopped off his head![11] He knelt down. He bent to pick up Whiskers. And I chopped off his head! I don't care that I did it![12] I wanted him to die! I wouldn't let him[13] touch Bridie! He wanted to. He read to her just like he'd done to me. He talked to her just like he'd done to me. He was going to do it! I knew the signs! I killed him! I killed him and I don't care! I'm not sorry! He deserved to die!' Slumping to the floor[14], she wept into her hands, large grey dough-like hands that covered her face, but pinched and brutalized it[15] even as they protected[16]. 'I saw his head on the floor. And I didn't care. And the rat came out of nowhere. And he sniffed at the blood. And he ate at the brains[17] and I didn't *care*!'

With a strangled cry, Sergeant Havers leapt to her feet[18] and staggered from the room.

Barbara crashed into the lavatory, fell blindly into a stall[19], and began to vomit. The room swam[20] round her. She was so ragingly hot that she was sure she would faint[21], but she continued, instead, to vomit. And as she retched[22] – painfully, spasmodically – she knew that what was spewing forth[23] from her body was the turbid mass[24] of her own despair.

1. toutes ces années
2. agressée sexuellement
3. violée
4. bondit de
5. vola à travers
6. heurtant le placard
7. courut après
8. rapide comme l'éclair
9. la lança de toutes ses forces
10. renversa
11. Je lui ai tranché la tête !
12. Je l'ai fait et je m'en fiche
13. ne voulais pas qu'il
14. S'effondrant à terre
15. le pinçaient sans ménagement
16. tout en le protégeant
17. a grignoté la cervelle
18. se leva d'un bond
19. se précipita aveuglément dans l'une des toilettes
20. tanguait
21. qu'elle allait s'évanouir
22. tout en vomissant
23. ce qui jaillissait
24. la masse trouble

She clung to the smooth porcelain bowl[1], fought for breath to redeem her[2], and vomited. It was as if she had never seen life clearly until the last two hours and, suddenly faced with[3] its filth[4], she had to get away from it, had to get it out of her system[5].

In that dark, stifling[6] room the voices had come to her relentlessly[7]. Not just the voices of the sisters who had lived the nightmare[8], but the voices of her own past and of the nightmare that remained. It was too much. She could no longer live with it; she could no longer bear it.

I can't, she sobbed inwardly[9]. Tony, I can't any longer! God forgive me, but I can't!

Footsteps entered the room. She struggled to pull herself together but the illness continued and she knew she would have to endure the further humiliation[10] of being mortally ill[11] in front of the fashionable competence of[12] Lady Helen Clyde.

Water was turned on. More footsteps. The stall door opened and a damp cloth was pressed[13] to the back of her neck[14], folded quickly, and then wiped across her burning cheeks[15].

'Please. No! Go away!' She was sick again[16] and, what was even more despicable[17], she began to cry. 'I can't!' she wept. 'I can't! Please. *Please!* Leave me alone!'

A cool hand pushed her hair off her face and supported her forehead[18]. 'Life's rotten[19], Barb. And the hell of it is that it doesn't get much better,' Lynley's voice said.

Horrified, she spun around[20]. But it was Lynley, and in his eyes the compassion she had seen before: in his treatment of[21] Roberta, in his conversation with Bridie, in his questioning of Tessa. And she suddenly saw what it was that Webberly had known she could learn from Lynley – the source of his strength, the centre of what she knew quite well

1. s'agrippait à la cuvette en porcelaine lisse
2. lutta pour récupérer sa respiration et se calmer
3. confrontée à
4. son côté immonde
5. organisme
6. étouffante
7. lui étaient parvenues sans relâche
8. cauchemar
9. intérieurement
10. en plus subir l'humiliation
11. malade comme un chien
12. si compétente et si chic
13. quelqu'un appliqua un linge humide
14. sur sa nuque
15. le passa sur ses joues brûlantes
16. revomit
17. méprisable
18. lui maintint le front
19. dégueulasse
20. se tourna d'un coup
21. sa façon de traiter

was tremendous personal courage. It was that quiet compassion, nothing else, that finally broke her[1].

'How could he?' she sobbed. 'If it's your child … you're supposed to love, not hurt. Not let him die. Never let him die! And that's what they did!' Her voice spiralled hysterically[2] and all the time Lynley's dark eyes were on her face. 'I hate … I can't … They were supposed to *be* there for him. He was their son! They were supposed to love him and they didn't. He was sick[3] for four years, the last year in hospital. They wouldn't even go[4] to see him! They said they couldn't bear it, that it hurt too much. But I went. I went every day. And he asked for them[5]. He asked why Mum and Dad wouldn't come to see him. And I lied. I went every day and I lied. And when he died, he was all alone[6]. I was in school. I didn't get there in time. He was my little brother! He was only ten years old! And all of us – *all* of us – let him die alone.'

'I'm so sorry,' Lynley said.

'I swore[7] that I would *never* let them forget what they'd done. I asked his teachers for the letters. I framed[8] the death certificate. I made the shrine. I kept them in the house. I closed the doors and the windows. And every *single* day[9] I made sure[10] they had to sit there[11] and stare at Tony. I drove them mad![12] I *wanted* to do it! I destroyed them. I destroyed myself!'

She put her head down on the porcelain and wept. She wept for the hate that had filled her life, for the guilt and the jealousy that had been her companions, for the loneliness that she had brought upon herself[13], for the contempt and disgust that she had directed towards others[14].

At the last, when Lynley wordlessly took her into his arms, she wept against his chest, mourning most of all[15] the death of the friendship that could have lived between them.

1. qui eut raison de son ultime résistance
2. s'envola, hystérique, dans les aigus
3. malade
4. n'allaient même pas
5. demandait après eux
6. tout seul
7. J'ai juré
8. J'ai encadré
9. chaque jour que Dieu fait,
10. j'ai fait en sorte
11. qu'ils soient obligés de s'asseoir là
12. Je les ai rendus fous !
13. la solitude qu'elle s'était infligée
14. manifesté envers les autres
15. pleurant par-dessus tout

Through the transom windows[1] in Dr Samuels' orderly office[2], they could see the rose garden. It was designed in plots and descending terraces, the plants segregated[3] by colour of flower and type. A few bushes still had blooms on[4] them, despite the lateness of the year[5], the cold nights, the rare frost[6] in the mornings. Soon, however, the heavy blossoms would die. Gardeners would cut the bushes back[7] for a dormant winter[8]. But they would renew themselves[9] in the spring, and the circle[10] of life would continue.

They watched the little party[11] wander[12] on the gravel paths[13] among the plants. They were a study in contrasts[14]: Gillian and her sister, Lady Helen and Sergeant Havers, and far behind them the two nurses, their forms[15] hidden beneath the long capes they wore against the wind-blown[16] afternoon.

Lynley turned from the sight and saw Dr Samuels watching him thoughtfully from behind his desk, his intelligent face carefully devoid of expression[17].

'You knew she'd had a baby,' Lynley said. 'From her admission examination[18], I should guess.'

'Yes.'

'Why didn't you tell me?'

'I didn't trust you,' Samuels replied and added, 'then[19]. Whatever fragile bond[20] I could hope to develop with Roberta by keeping that to myself[21] was far more important than sharing the information with you and running the risk of your blurting it out to her[22].' He tempered[23] his words. 'It was, after all, privileged information[24].'

'What's going to happen to them?' Lynley asked.

'They're going to survive.'

'How can you know that?'

'They're beginning to understand that they were his victims. That's the first step.' Samuels took off his spectacles and polished them on the interior of

1. vasistas
2. bureau bien rangé
3. séparées
4. étaient encore fleuris
5. l'arrivée de l'automne
6. les rares gelées
7. tailleraient les buissons
8. le repos hivernal
9. se renouvelleraient
10. cycle
11. groupe
12. se promener
13. dans les allées de gravier
14. formaient une peinture contrastée
15. silhouettes
16. venteux
17. attentif à ne rien montrer
18. Grâce à l'examen d'admission
19. alors
20. Le lien, si ténu soit-il,
21. en gardant ça pour moi
22. que cela vous échappe devant elle
23. nuança
24. une information confidentielle

1. maigre
2. aussi longtemps
3. se sont débrouillées
4. des marques profondes et douloureuses
5. s'étaient formées
6. là où elles appuyaient
7. une façon de se dédoubler
8. d'une part
9. d'autre part
10. qui ne fait que refléter

his jacket. His lean[1] face was tired. He had heard it all before.

'I don't understand how they survived this long[2].'

'They coped[3].'

'How?'

The doctor gave a final glance to his spectacles and put them back on. He adjusted their position carefully. He'd worn them for years, and deep, painful indentations[4] had been created[5] on either side of his nose from their pressure[6]. 'For Gillian it appears to have been what we call dissociation, a way of subdividing the self[7] so that she could pretend to have or be those things which she couldn't really have or couldn't really be.'

'Such as?'

'Normal feelings, for one[8]. Normal relationships, for another[9]. She called it being a mirror, just reflecting[10] the behaviour of those round her. It's a defence. It protected her from feeling anything about what was happening to her.'

'How?'

'She wasn't a "real person", so nothing her father did could really touch or hurt her.'

11. la décrit de manière complètement différente
12. Poussé à l'extrême
13. évité ça
14. vu ce qu'elle a subi
15. un fauteuil capitonné, usé
16. un lieu de repos
17. d'esprits tourmentés

'Everyone in the village describes her in an entirely different way[11].'

'Yes. That's the behaviour. Gillian simply mirrored them. Taking it to its furthest extreme[12], it becomes multiple personalities, but she seems to have prevented that from occurring[13]. In itself, that's remarkable, considering what she went through[14].'

'What about Roberta?'

The psychiatrist frowned. 'She didn't cope as well as Gillian,' he admitted.

Lynley gave a last glance out the window and returned to his seat, a worn upholstered chair[15]: resting place[16], no doubt, for hundreds of tormented psyches[17]. 'Is that why she ate?'

'As a way of escaping? No, I don't think so. I'd say it was more an act of self-destruction.'

'I don't understand.'

'The abused child feels[1] he or she has done something wrong and is being punished for it. Roberta may well have eaten because the abuse led her to despise herself[2] – her "wickedness[3]" – and destroying her body was a scourging[4]. That's one explanation.' The doctor hesitated.

'And the other?'

'Hard to say. It could be that she tried to stop the abuse the only way she knew how. Short of suicide[5], what better way than to destroy her body, to make herself as un-Gilly-like as possible[6]. That way, her father wouldn't want her[7] sexually.'

'But it didn't work.'

'Unfortunately, no. He merely turned to[8] perversions to arouse himself[9], making her part of it. That would feed his need for power.'

'I feel as if I'd like to tear Teys apart[10],' Lynley said.

'I feel that way all the time,' the doctor responded.

'How could anyone ...? I don't understand it.'

'It's a deviant behaviour[11], a sickness. Teys was aroused by children. His marriage to a sixteen-year-old girl – not a voluptuous, womanly[12] sixteen-year-old, but a late-maturing[13] sixteen-year-old – would have been a glaring sign[14] to anyone looking for aberrant behaviour. But he was able to mask it well[15] with his devotion to religion[16] and his persona[17] of the strong, loving father. That's so typical, Inspector Lynley. I can't tell you how typical it is.'

'And no one ever knew? I can't believe it.'

'If you consider the situation, it's easy to believe. Teys projected a very successful image in his community. At the same time, his daughters were tricked into self-blame and secrecy[18]. Gillian believed *she* had been responsible[19] for her mother's

1. L'enfant abusé sexuellement croit
2. l'a conduite à se mépriser
3. vilenie
4. flagellation
5. Hormis le suicide
6. ressembler le moins possible à Gilly
7. ne la désirerait pas
8. a juste eu recours à
9. pour s'exciter
10. Je mettrais bien Teys en pièces
11. un comportement déviant
12. déjà très femme
13. peu précoce
14. un signe évident
15. de bien le masquer
16. sa piété
17. personnage
18. étaient piégées par le secret et la culpabilité
19. que c'était sa faute

desertion of[1] her father and was making reparation for that[2] by, in Teys' words, "being a mummy" to him. Roberta believed that Gillian had pleased her father and that she was supposed to do the same. And both of them, of course, were taught from the Bible – Teys' careful selection of passages and his twisted interpretations[3] of them – that what they were doing was not only right but written by the hand of God[4] as their duty as his daughters.'

'It makes me sick.[5]'

'It *is* sick.[6] He was sick. Consider his sickness: He chose a child to be his bride. That was safe. He was threatened[7] by the adult world and in the person of this sixteen-year-old girl he saw someone who could arouse him with her childlike body and, at the same time, gratify his need[8] for the self-respect[9] that a marriage would give him.'

'Then, why did he turn to[10] his children?'

'When Tessa – this childlike bride of his – produced a baby, Teys had frightening and irrefutable evidence that the creature who had been arousing him and upon whose body he had taken such gratification[11] was not a child at all, but a woman. And he was threatened by women, I should guess, the feminine representation of the entire adult world that he feared.'

'She said he stopped sleeping with her.'

'I've no doubt of that. If he had slept with her and failed to perform[12], imagine his humiliation. Why risk that kind of failure when there in his house was a helpless[13] infant[14] from whom he could get immense pleasure and satisfaction?'

Lynley felt his throat close. '*Infant?*' he asked. 'Do you mean …?'

Dr Samuels took the measure of Lynley's reaction and nodded in sad recognition of[15] an outrage he himself had felt[16] for many years. 'I should think that the abuse of Gillian began in infancy[17]. She re-

1. si sa mère avait quitté
2. se rachetait
3. ses interprétations tordues
4. écrit de la main de Dieu
5. Ça me rend malade.
6. C'est effectivement le fait d'un esprit malade.
7. menacé
8. satisfaire son besoin
9. de respectabilité
10. s'en est-il pris à
11. dont le corps lui avait donné tellement de plaisir
12. avait perdu ses moyens
13. sans défense
14. une enfant en très bas âge
15. acquiesça, reconnaissant avec tristesse
16. l'indignation qui était la sienne
17. pendant la toute petite enfance

members the first incident when she was four or five, but Teys was unlikely to have waited that long[1] unless his religion was providing him with self-control[2] for those years. It's possible.'

His religion. Each piece was falling into place more tidily than the last; but, as each did, Lynley felt an anger that needed free rein[3]. He controlled it with an effort. 'She'll stand trial.[4]'

'Eventually.[5] Roberta's going to recover[6]. She'll be found competent to stand trial[7].' The doctor turned in his chair to watch the group in the garden. 'But you know as well as I, Inspector, that no jury in the world is going to convict her[8] of anything when the truth is told. So perhaps we can believe that there will be a form of justice after all.'

1. aussi longtemps
2. lui a permis de se dominer
3. à laquelle il devait donner libre cours
4. Elle sera jugée.
5. Un jour lointain.
6. va guérir
7. pourra passer en justice
8. la juger coupable

The trees that towered above[9] St Catherine's Church cast long shadows on the exterior of the building so that, even though it was still light outside, the interior was dim[10]. The deep reds and purples[11] from stained-glass windows poured forth[12] bloody pools of light[13] which faded slowly on the cracked tile floor[14], and votive candles flickered[15] under statues which watched his movement in the aisle. The air within the building was heavy and dead, and as Lynley made his way to the Elizabethan confessional he shivered.

He opened the door, went inside the booth[16], knelt, and waited. The darkness was complete, the tranquillity absolute. A suitable ambience[17] for meditating upon one's sins, Lynley thought.

A grille was moved in the darkness. A gentle voice murmured incantations to a nonexistent god. Then, 'Yes, my child?'

At the last moment, he wondered if he would be able to do it. But he found his voice.

'He came to you[18] here,' Lynley said. 'This was the place where he confessed his sins. Did you

9. surplombaient
10. sombre
11. rouges et violets intenses
12. déversaient
13. des nappes de lumière rouge sang
14. sol aux dalles fendues
15. les bougies votives vacillaient
16. entra dans la loge [latérale] du confessionnal
17. L'atmosphère appropriée
18. Il est venu vous voir

absolve him[1], Father? Did you make some sort of mystical configuration[2] in the air that told William Teys he was free of the sin of abusing[3] his children? What did you tell him? Did you give him your blessing[4]? Did you release him[5] from the confessional, his soul purged[6] once more, to go home to his farm and begin it again? Is that how it was?'

In response[7], he only heard breathing, harsh and rapid, that told him a living creature[8] was on the other side of the grille.

'And did Gillian confess? Or was she too frightened? Did you talk to her about what her father did to her? Did you try to help her?'

'I …' The voice sounded as if it were coming from a great distance. 'Understand and forgive.[9]'

'That's what you told her? Understand? Forgive? What about Roberta? Was she supposed to understand and forgive as well? Was a sixteen-year-old girl supposed to learn to accept the fact that her father raped her[10], made her pregnant[11], that he then murdered her child? Or was that *your* idea, Father?'

'I didn't know about the baby. I didn't know! I didn't *know*!' The voice was frantic[12].

'But you knew once you found it in the abbey. You damn well knew.[13] You chose *Pericles*, Father Hart. You damn *well* knew.'

'He … he never confessed to that[14]. Never!'

'And what would you have done if he had? What exactly would his penance[15] have been for the murder of his child? And it *was* murder. You know it was murder.'

'No. No!'

'William Teys carried that baby from Gembler Farm to the abbey. He couldn't wrap it[16] in anything because anything he used might have been traced back to him[17]. So he carried it naked. And it died. You knew when you saw it whose baby it was, how it got to the abbey. You chose *Pericles* for the

1. Lui avez-vous donné l'absolution
2. une espèce de signe cabalistique
3. qu'il était absous du péché d'abus sexuel sur
4. votre bénédiction
5. L'avez-vous laissé partir
6. l'âme purifiée
7. Pour toute réponse
8. qu'un être vivant
9. Comprends et pardonne.
10. l'ait violée
11. l'ait mise enceinte
12. frénétique
13. Vous le saviez très bien !
14. il n'a jamais confessé ça
15. sa pénitence
16. l'envelopper
17. aurait permis de remonter jusqu'à lui

epitaph. *Murder's as near to lust as flame to smoke.* You damn well knew.'

'He said … after that… he swore he was cured[1].'

'*Cured?* A miraculous recovery from sexual deviance[2], nicely engineered[3] by the death of his infant child? Is that what you thought? Is that what you wanted to think? He was recovered all right. His idea of recovery[4] was that he'd stopped raping Roberta. But listen to me, Father, because this is on your conscience and by God you shall hear me, he stopped *nothing* else.'

'No!'

'You know it's the truth. He was addicted.[5] The only problem was that he needed a fresh young fix[6] for his habit[7]. He needed Bridie. And you were going to let it happen[8].'

'He swore to me—'

'He *swore*? On what? The Bible that he used to make Gillian believe she had to give her body to her father? Is that what he swore on?[9]'

'He stopped confessing. I didn't know. I—'

'You knew. From the moment he[10] started on[11] Bridie, you knew. And when you went to the farm and saw what Roberta had done, the real truth came crashing right down[12], didn't it?'

There was a stifled sob[13]. And then growing out of it a keening[14] of grief that rose like the wail of[15] Jacob and broke on the utterance[16] of three nearly incoherent words. '*Mea … mea culpa!*'

'Yes!' Lynley hissed[17]. 'Through[18] *your* fault, Father.'

'I couldn't … it was the silence of the confessional. It's a holy oath.[19]'

'There is no oath more important than life. There is no oath more important than the ruin[20] of a child. You saw that, didn't you, when you went to the farm? You knew that it was finally time to break the silence. So you wiped off[21] the axe, you

1. qu'il était guéri
2. d'une déviance sexuelle
3. bien amenée
4. Sa conception de la guérison
5. C'était une drogue pour lui.
6. une nouvelle gosse comme nouvelle dose
7. nourrir sa dépendance
8. laisser faire
9. C'est sur ça qu'il a juré ?
10. Dès qu'il
11. a commencé avec
12. vous est tombée dessus
13. un sanglot étouffé
14. une mélopée terrible
15. la lamentation de
16. qui cessa à l'énonciation
17. dit Lynley, la voix sifflante
18. Par
19. C'est un serment sacré.
20. que l'anéantissement
21. Alors vous avez essuyé

got rid[1] of the knife, and you came to Scotland Yard. You knew the real truth would come out that way[2], the truth *you* lacked[3] the courage to reveal.'

'Oh God, I … Understand and forgive.' The whisper was broken.

'Not for this. Not for twenty-seven years of physical abuse[4]. For two ruined lives[5]. For the death of their dreams. There is no understanding.[6] There is no forgiveness.[7] By God, not for this.' He shoved open[8] the door of the confessional and left.

Behind him a querulous[9] voice rose in agonizing prayer. ' "Fret not thyself because of evildoers … they shall soon be cut down like the grass … trust in the Lord … he shall give thee the desires of thy heart … evildoers shall be cut off …" [10]'

Scarcely able to breathe[11], Lynley flung open the church door and stepped out into the air.

Lady Helen was leaning against the edge of a lichened sarcophagus[12], watching Gillian, who stood at the small, distant grave[13] under the cypress trees[14], her cropped blonde head[15] bent in contemplation[16] or prayer. She heard Lynley's footsteps but did not stir, not even when he joined her and she felt the sure, steady pressure[17] of his arm against her own.

'I saw Deborah,' he said at last.

'Ah.' Her eyes remained on Gillian's slight form[18]. 'I thought you might see her, Tommy. I hoped you wouldn't but I did think you might.'

'You knew they were here in Keldale. Why didn't you tell me?'

Still she looked away from him, but for a moment she lowered her eyes. 'What was there to say, really? We'd said it already. So many times.' She hesitated, wanting to let it go, to let the subject die[19] between them once and for all. But the backward abysm of time[20] that constituted the many years of

1. vous vous êtes débarrassé
2. éclaterait de cette façon
3. que vous n'avez pas eu
4. de sévices sexuels
5. vies détruites
6. Aucune compréhension n'est possible.
7. Aucun pardon.
8. ouvrit brutalement
9. une voix geignarde
10. [de nouveau le psaume 37]
11. La respiration presque coupée
12. sarcophage couvert de lichen
13. au pied de la petite tombe, au loin
14. les cyprès
15. sa tête blonde aux cheveux courts
16. courbée dans la contemplation
17. la pression ferme
18. la silhouette menue
19. ne plus aborder le sujet
20. l'abîme du passé [altération d'un vers de la Tempête]

their friendship would not allow her to do so. 'Was it dreadful for you?' she made herself ask.

'At first.'

'And then?'

'Then I saw that she loves him. As you did once.[1]'

A regretful smile touched her lips briefly. 'Yes. As I did once.'

'Where did you find the strength to let St James go, Helen? How on earth did you survive it?'

'Oh, I muddled through somehow[2]. Besides, you were always there for me, Tommy. You helped me. You were always my friend.'

'As you've been mine. My very best friend.'

She laughed softly at that. 'Men say that about their dogs, you know. I'm not sure I ought to be flattered by the appellation.'

'But *are* you?' he asked.

'Most decidedly[3],' she replied. She turned to him then and searched his face. The exhaustion was there as it had been before, but the weight of sorrow was lessened[4]. Not gone, that would not happen quickly, but dissolving and leading him out of the past. 'You're beyond the worst of it[5] now, aren't you?'

'I'm beyond the worst. I think, in fact, I'm ready to go on[6].' He touched the fall of her hair[7] and smiled.

The lychgate opened and over Lynley's shoulder Lady Helen saw Sergeant Havers coming into the graveyard. Her steps slowed momentarily when she saw them talking tranquilly together, but she cleared her throat as if in warning of her intrusion and strode towards them quickly, her shoulders squared[8].

'Sir, you've a message from Webberly,' she said to Lynley. 'Stepha had it at the lodge.'

'A message? What sort?'

'His usual cryptogram[9], I'm afraid.' She handed the paper to him. ' "ID positive.[10] London verifies[11].

1. Comme toi, autrefois.
2. j'ai fini par me tirer d'affaire
3. Résolument
4. la souffrance était moins marquée
5. Le pire est derrière toi
6. à aller de l'avant
7. sa chevelure
8. en redressant les épaules
9. Mystérieux, comme à son habitude
10. Identification positive
11. confirme

York informed last p.m.[1],” ’ she recited. ‘Does it make sense to you?’

He read the message over, folded the paper, and looked bleakly[2] off through the graveyard[3] to the hills beyond[4]. ‘Yes,’ he replied, but the words were not coming easily to him, ‘it makes perfect sense[5].’

‘Russell Mowrey?’ Havers asked perceptively[6]. When he nodded, she went on. ‘So he did go to London to turn Tessa in[7] to Scotland Yard. How strange. Why not turn her in to the York police? What could Scotland Yard—?’

‘No. He’d gone to London to see his family, just as Tessa guessed. But he never made it further than[8] King’s Cross Station.’

‘King Cross Station?’ Havers repeated.

‘That’s where the Ripper got him[9], Havers. His picture was on the wall in Webberly’s office.’

He went to the lodge alone. He walked down Church Street and stood for a moment on the bridge as he had done only the night before. The village was hushed[10], but, as he took a final look at Keldale, a door slammed nearby. A little red-haired girl hurtled down the back steps[11] of her house and darted to a shed[12]. She disappeared, emerging moments later, dragging a large sack of feed on the ground.

‘Where’s Dougal?’ he called.

Bridie looked up. Her curly hair trapped the sunlight[13], burning an autumn contrast against[14] the bright green pullover– several sizes too large – that she wore. ‘Inside. He has a stomach ache[15] today.’

Lynley wondered idly how one diagnosed a stomach ache in a mallard and wisely thought better of asking[16]. ‘Why are you feeding him, then?’ he asked.

She pondered[17] the question, scratching her left leg with the top of her right foot. ‘Mummy says I ought to. She’s been keeping him warm[18] all day and she says she thinks he can eat something now.’

1. dernière minute hier soir
2. l’air morne
3. au-delà du cimetière,
4. vers les coteaux lointains
5. c’est tout à fait compréhensible
6. avec perspicacité
7. dénoncer Tessa
8. n’a jamais dépassé
9. là que l’Éventreur l’a eu
10. calme
11. dégringola les marches à l’arrière
12. fila vers une remise
13. captait les rayons du soleil
14. créant un vif contraste automnal avec
15. mal au ventre
16. estima sagement qu’il valait mieux ne pas demander
17. réfléchit à
18. l’a gardé au chaud

'Sounds like a good nurse.'

'She is.' She waved a grubby hand at him[1] and disappeared into the house, a small package of life[2] with her dreams intact.

He walked across the bridge and into the lodge. Behind the reception desk, Stepha stood up, her lips parted to[3] speak.

'It was Ezra Farmington's baby that you had, wasn't it?' he asked her. 'He was part of the wild crazy laughter[4] you wanted after your brother died, wasn't he?'

'Thomas—'

'Wasn't he?'

'Yes.'

'Do you watch when he and Nigel torment each other over you? Are you amused[5] when Nigel drinks himself blind[6] at the Dove and Whistle, hoping to catch you spending time with Ezra at his house across the street? Or do you escape the whole conflict with Richard Gibson's help?'

'That's really unfair[7].'

'Is it? Do you know that Ezra doesn't believe he can paint any longer[8]? Are you interested, Stepha? He's destroyed his work. The only pieces left are his paintings of you.'

'I can't help him.'

'You won't help him.[9]'

'That's not true.'

'You won't help him,' Lynley repeated. 'For some reason[10], he still wants you[11]. He wants the child as well. He wants to know where it is. He wants to know what you did with it[12], who has it. Have you even bothered[13] to tell him if it's a boy or a girl?'

She dropped her eyes.[14] 'She's … she was adopted by a family in Durham. That's the way it had to be.'

'And that's to be his punishment, I take it?'

Her eyes flew up.[15] 'For what? Why would I punish him?'

1. le salua de sa main crasseuse
2. un petit être
3. entrouvertes, s'apprêtant à
4. la bonne partie de rigolade
5. Ça vous amuse
6. boit comme un trou
7. injuste
8. croit qu'il n'est plus capable de peindre
9. Vous ne voulez pas l'aider.
10. Bizarrement
11. il veut toujours de vous
12. tu en as fait
13. As-tu seulement pris la peine
14. Elle baissa les yeux.
15. Elle releva les yeux.

'For stopping the laughter. For insisting on having something more with you. For being willing to take chances.[1] For being all the things you're too afraid to be.'

1. Pour avoir été prêt à prendre des risques.

She didn't reply. There was no need for her to do so when he could read the answer so clearly on her face.

She had not wanted to go to the farm. The scene of so many of her childhood terrors, the farm was a place she wished to bury in the past[2]. All she had wanted to see was the baby's grave. That done, she was ready to leave. The others, this group of kind strangers[3] who had come into her life, did not question her. Rather, they bundled her[4] into the large silver car and drove her out[5] of Keldale.

She had no idea where they were taking her, and she didn't much care[6]. Jonah was gone. Nell was dead. And whoever Gillian was[7] remained to be discovered. She was simply a shell. There was nothing else left.

2. qu'elle souhaitait reléguer au passé
3. gentils inconnus
4. l'embarquèrent
5. la conduisirent hors
6. peu lui importait
7. qui était vraiment Gillian

* * *

Lynley glanced at Gillian in the mirror[8]. He wasn't sure what would happen. He wasn't sure that it was the right thing to do. He was working on[9] instinct, a blind instinct which insisted that something good had to rise[10], like a phoenix triumphant[11], from the ashes[12] of the day.

He knew that he was looking for meaning, that he couldn't accept the senselessness[13] of Russell Mowrey's death in King's Cross Station at the hands[14] of an unknown killer. He raged[15] against it, against its vile brutality, against its diabolical ugliness, against its terrible waste[16].

He *would* give meaning to it all.[17] He would not accept that these fragmented[18] lives could not some-

8. le rétrovuiseur
9. suivait son instinct
10. devait s'élever
11. tel un phœnix triomphant
12. cendres
13. l'absurdité
14. aux mains
15. fulminait
16. gâchis
17. Il allait donner du sens à tout cela.
18. morcelées

how conjoin[1], could not reach across the chasm of nineteen years and find peace at last.

It was a risk. He didn't care. He would take it. It was six o'clock when he pulled up in front of the house in York.

'I'll just be a moment,' he said to the others in the car and reached for his door handle[2].

Sergeant Havers touched his shoulder. 'Let me, sir. Please.'

He hesitated. She watched him.

'Please,' she repeated.

He glanced at the closed front door of the house, knowing that he couldn't possibly face the responsibility[3] of putting the matter[4] into Havers' incapable hands. Not here. Not now. Not with so much at stake[5].

'Havers—'

'I can do it,' she replied. 'Please. Believe me.'

He saw then that she was giving him the final say over[6] her future, that she was allowing him[7] to be the one to decide whether she would stay in CID or return once and for all to the street. It was represented in the matter before them.

'Sir?'

He wanted desperately to refuse her permission, to tell her to stay where she was in the car, to condemn her to the pavements[8] she had walked in uniform. But none of that had been Webberly's plan. He understood that now, and as he looked at her trusting[9], resolute[10] face, he saw that Havers – reading his intention in their destination – had built the funeral pyre[11] herself and was perfectly determined to strike the match[12] that would put to the test[13] the promise of the phoenix.

'All right,' he finally replied.

'Thank you, sir.' She got out of the car and went to the front door. It was opened. She stepped inside the house. And the waiting began.

1. s'unir
2. tendait la main pour ouvrir sa portière
3. assumer la responsabilité
4. confier cette affaire
5. un tel enjeu
6. pouvoir de décider de
7. lui permettait
8. de la cantoner aux trottoirs
9. confiant
10. décidé
11. bûcher funéraire
12. à gratter l'allumette
13. qui mettrait à l'épreuve

He had never thought of himself much as a praying man, but as he sat in the car in the growing darkness[1] and the minutes passed[2], he knew what it was to pray. It was to will[3] goodness out of evil[4], hope out of despair, life out of death. It was to will dreams into existence[5] and spectres into[6] reality. It was to will an end to anguish and a beginning to joy.

Gillian stirred in the back seat. 'Whose house...?' Her voice died[7] as the door flew open and Tessa ran outside, hesitating on the front path, peering[8] towards the car. 'Mummy.' Gillian said it on a breath. She said nothing else. She got out of the car slowly and stared at the woman as if she were an apparition, clinging to the door for support[9]. 'Mummy?'

'Gilly! Oh my God, *Gilly*! Tessa cried and began coming towards her.

It was all Gillian needed.[10] She ran up the slope into her mother's arms, and they entered the house together.

1. la pénombre grandissante
2. s'écoulaient
3. vouloir
4. que le bien naisse du mal
5. que les rêves se réalisent
6. deviennent
7. s'éteignit
8. s'efforçant de voir
9. se raccrochant à la portière
10. Gilly n'eut besoin de rien d'autre.

THE END

Imprimé en Italie par La Tipografica Varese S.p.a
Dépôt légal : mai 2014
314184-01/11026551-mai 2014